D0837057

Chasing Dreams

Chasing Dreams

A Chandler Sisters Novel

Deborah Raney

Kregel
Publications

Chasing Dreams

© 2019 by Deborah Raney

Published by Kregel Publications, a division of Kregel Inc., 2450 Oak Industrial Dr. NE, Grand Rapids, MI 49505.

All rights reserved. No part of this book may be reproduced, stored in a retrieval system, or transmitted in any form or by any means—electronic, mechanical, photocopy, recording, or otherwise—without written permission of the publisher, except for brief quotations in reviews.

Distribution of digital editions of this book in any format via the internet or any other means without the publisher's written permission or by license agreement is a violation of copyright law and is subject to substantial fines and penalties. Thank you for supporting the author's rights by purchasing only authorized editions.

The persons and events portrayed in this work are the creations of the author, and any resemblance to persons living or dead is purely coincidental.

Scripture quotations are from the Holy Bible, New International Version®, NIV®. Copyright © 1973, 1978, 1984, 2011 by Biblica, Inc.™ Used by permission of Zondervan. All rights reserved worldwide. www.zondervan .com. The "NIV" and "New International Version" are trademarks registered in the United States Patent and Trademark Office by Biblica, Inc.™

ISBN 978-0-8254-4640-5

Printed in the United States of America

19 20 21 22 23 24 25 26 27 28 / 5 4 3 2 1

To my sweet sisters,
who were my first friends
and remain my very dearest friends.

Don't be deceived, my dear brothers and sisters. Every good and perfect gift is from above, coming down from the Father of the heavenly lights, who does not change like shifting shadows. He chose to give us birth through the word of truth, that we might be a kind of firstfruits of all he created. . . . Religion that God our Father accepts as pure and faultless is this: to look after orphans . . . in their distress and to keep oneself from being polluted by the world.
James 1:16–18, 27

CHAPTER 1

May

O H, BROTHER . . ." JOANNA CHANDLER SHIFTED the bag of groceries she was carrying and unlooped a pretty little tin can filled with flowers from the front door of the cottage. A May basket—no doubt Quinn Mitchell's doing. The man had it bad for her sister. And if not for the fact that Phylicia was so deliriously happy these days, the two lovebirds would be getting on Jo's last nerve. This romance had been in high gear for a week now, ever since the night Phee and Quinn stayed up till the wee hours "defining the relationship." Though Phee denied it, Quinn claimed *she'd* proposed to *him* that night.

Jo unlocked the door, propped the May basket on the mantel where her older sister would see it, and deposited the groceries on the kitchen table. "Britt? You home?" There was no sign of her younger sister inside.

She went down the short hallway and peeked into Britt's room. Melvin, the spoiled black-and-white tuxedo cat they'd inherited from their mom, looked up from his spot on the bed and yawned. But all was quiet in the house. Did she dare to hope her younger sister was at a job interview?

Jo went back to her car and carried in two more loads of groceries from the trunk. With any luck, one of her sisters would be home in time to help put all this stuff away. Graduation at the local university was less than two weeks away, and not only was the cottage booked for a four-day weekend, but they'd promised breakfast all four days. For five guests.

This was their first official Airbnb rental, and it would take all three of them working overtime to get the place ready for guests. At least they could stay in one of the cabins across the lane this time instead of camping out in the woods like they'd done after a semi-disastrous accidental booking that had led to Phylicia's unofficial engagement.

Jo pulled a jug of coffee creamer from a bag and stuck it in the fridge, begrudgingly grateful that Britt hadn't yet found a job. The bulk of the hostess duties would fall to Britt, since Phee would be working overtime at the flower shop, thanks to the perfect storm that May Day, Mother's Day, and graduations created for the floral industry.

Jo peered out the tiny kitchen window, loving the dappled view of the woods behind the cottage. She'd be lucky to get the weekend off since her boss and his wife had just returned from a ten-day whirlwind tour of Europe. The entire law office was scrambling to get caught up.

Glancing through the archway that led to the combined living and dining room, Jo smiled at Quinn's primitive tin-can bouquet on the mantel. It looked like something a kindergartner had fashioned. He'd used picture wire to form a handle around the tomato can with a pretty label, then filled the can with wildflowers. Jo recognized tickseed, purple prairie clover, and chicory—all flowers that grew wild along Poplar Brook Road.

The back door slammed and Britt blew in, singing something from *Beauty and the Beast* at the top of her lungs.

"Hey, where'd you come from?" Joanna peeked through the doorway off the hall that led to the cottage's two bedrooms and the back door.

The singing stopped abruptly. "Oh. I didn't know you were home." Her cheeks rosy, Britt slipped out of her Crocs and went to the kitchen sink. She scrubbed her hands and tried to blow aside honey-brown bangs that were plastered to her forehead with sweat.

"Where did you think all these groceries came from?" Jo pointed to the grocery bags crowding the kitchen table.

Her sister shrugged. "I didn't notice them. I was working in the garden."

"Um . . . We have a garden?"

Britt shot her a smug grin. "We do now. The start of one at least. In the yard behind the cabin."

"Cool. What did you plant?"

"Flowers. Plants Plus still has flats on sale in Cape, so I figured I'd take advantage. Petunias and coleus and begonias. Oh, and a couple of tomato plants. But mostly begonias." Drying her hands, she tossed her head toward the wooded backyard. "I'll plant a few of them behind the cottage. It's too shady there for anything else."

"Well, good for you." Jo bit her tongue, wondering how much that trip to the nursery had set them back. She and her sisters had bought the property with its three cottages free and clear, thanks to the inheritance their mother had left them. They were living in this cottage, but the funds they'd each contributed to for renovating the two smaller cabins was dwindling at an alarming rate.

And Britt still hadn't found a job. Not that she'd looked that hard.

"There's another load of groceries to carry in."

"I'll get them." Britt started through the living room then paused by the fireplace. "A May basket? Where did that come from?"

"Unless you have a boyfriend I don't know about, I'm guessing they're from Quinn."

"Aww. How adorable."

"Yeah, well, I have a sneaking suspicion that bouquet came straight off our property."

"Oh, so what. I think it's sweet." Britt hugged herself.

"Phee will think so too." Jo shook her head but laughed. She couldn't wait to give her future brother-in-law a hard time about gathering Phee's bouquet from the Chandler sisters' property. Still, she had to give the man credit: a flower-shop bouquet would never have stolen her sister's heart the way these hand-picked wildflowers would.

Jo's smile faded as a twinge of jealousy pricked. She was truly happy for Phylicia. Her older sister would turn thirty in a few weeks, and Jo was glad Phee had found love before that ominous over-thirty stigma descended on her. But now—Jo cringed at the thought—all eyes would be on *her*, waiting to see if the second Chandler sister would find her man before she was "over the hill." Stupid small-town gossip.

Joanna stifled a sigh. She shouldn't care. She wasn't even twenty-seven yet! But soon enough twenty-eight would be nipping at her heels, and *that* felt so far up the proverbial hill, she could almost *touch* the top.

The ominous thoughts settled heavier inside her than she would have liked. She watched storm clouds building across the cove beyond the cabins, and the light inside the house gradually faded, as if someone had turned a dimmer switch. Jo walked through the rooms, turning on lamps and flicking light switches as she went.

She and Britt worked together to put groceries away, growling as they collided in the tiny kitchen. This cottage could feel a bit claustrophobic when all three of them were home, but when Jo was here by herself, she loved the place and secretly hoped she'd end up claiming this one as her own after the two smaller cabins were finished. Of course with Phee getting married sometime soon, she'd probably get dibs on the larger cottage. Unless she and Quinn moved into the house he was building.

But now wasn't the time to think about that. They had less than two weeks to get this place ready for their first official guests, at which time they would all be sleeping on the hardwood floor of an unfinished two-bedroom cabin that still reeked of paint, sawdust, and refinishing fumes.

Her phone trilled from its charger in her bedroom, and she raced down the hall to get it.

Her boss. Trent almost never called her at home, but when he did, it was to ask her to come back in to work. She wanted to pretend she hadn't seen his call, but the truth was, she could use the overtime pay. And tonight, she didn't really have a good excuse anyway. She pressed Accept. "Hi, Trent."

"Hey, Joanna. Sorry to bother you at home, but we've got a bit of an emergency here. Could you come in for a couple of hours?"

She glanced at the clock on her nightstand. "What time were you thinking?"

"Right now, actually. The sooner the better." Something in Trent's voice gave her pause.

"Oh. Okay. Yes. I guess I can come in. Is this—"

The line went dead. Now *that* was the Trenton Pritchert she knew. Never give anyone a chance to argue or even ask questions. At least she hadn't changed out of her work clothes. She blew out a sigh and went to the kitchen to find Britt.

"I've got to go back in to work."

"You just got home."

"Tell me about it." She grabbed her purse and fished her keys out of its depths. "I might be late. Don't worry about me."

"Never do," Britt deadpanned.

"Liar." Her baby sister was a consummate worrywart. Or at least had become one since the onset of their mother's three-year battle with pancreatic cancer. It had been more than five months now since they'd lost Mom—almost half a year—and sometimes it still seemed the grief was as fresh as it had been that dark day last fall.

Pushing away the image of her mom lying in the hospital bed at home, eyes sunken and complexion ashen, she closed the door behind her and climbed into her car. She'd purposefully parked in the shade but now—looking at the windshield—she realized the cooler interior came at the expense of a deluge of bird droppings. *Shoot!* Quinn had warned her not to park under the trees once spring came.

But driving beneath the leafy canopy that rambled out to Poplar Brook Road, she couldn't muster one regret that they'd bought this idyllic property. It had been hard work and brought with it some difficult adjustments, especially where her sisters were concerned. But she loved this place as much as if she'd grown up here. And she had ideas about what their little investment venture could become—even if her sisters didn't quite share her enthusiasm.

She drove through the carwash at the edge of town before heading for the law office where she'd worked the past three years. She'd just started law school at Columbia when Mom was diagnosed. And though her career had been sidelined, she was grateful she'd found a job in the legal field as Trenton Pritchert's administrative assistant. If nothing else, when she finally was able to return to law school, she'd be going in with a more realistic picture of what an attorney did all day.

Pulling into the parking lot of the business complex, Jo was surprised to see Trent's SUV in the front lot. Even more surprising, Cinda, Trent's wife, had parked her ten-year-old—but pristine—Saab beside him. That was odd. They both had reserved covered parking near the back entrance.

Leaving one space between her and the Saab, Jo pressed the lock button on her key fob and hurried into the building. The downstairs lobby echoed with emptiness on this Monday night after business hours.

Clutching the hem of her skirt, she took the stairs two at a time, her footfalls echoing in the concrete space. She reached the third floor out of breath, growing more concerned by the minute. Something felt . . . off.

As she opened the door to Trent's office suite a woman's wailing, an eerie keening, carried down the plush carpeted hallway, sending chills up Joanna's spine.

CHAPTER 2

JOANNA'S STOMACH LURCHED AND SHE stopped, paralyzed. Against her will, painful memories dragged her back to a moment she'd never wanted to revisit. The hopeless wails coming from Trent's office sounded exactly like Britt's cries the day they learned that their mother's cancer was terminal.

Though she knew Britt was safe at home, the desperate sobs, so like her sister's, compelled Jo to move forward. To make sure it wasn't actually Britt in Trent's office. But whoever it was . . . Her heart ached as her imagination took over. And instinct told her that nothing she'd learned in her months of studying law would fix whatever was wrong in that office down the hall.

Trent's door stood open. She tiptoed forward to see him sitting at his desk, eyes wide, one hand clutching his cheek as if he'd been struck, the other pressed hard on the desktop with fingers splayed, as if any moment he might push himself to standing. Cinda sat on the edge of a chair in front of the desk, her arms awkwardly embracing a waif-like woman. It was hard to tell with a curtain of thick black hair shielding the side of the woman's face, but Jo guessed her to be in her late twenties, maybe early thirties.

No one seemed to notice Jo standing in the doorway. The young woman's wailing turned to babbling, the slightest hint of a Spanish accent slipping through. Yet, as garbled and high-pitched as the woman's words were, Jo still understood her.

"What will happen to him then? I can't possibly come up with that much. Not in time." The woman took in a shuddering breath. "I *have* no time. Isn't there *something* you can do? Anything? Luke said you could help me."

Cinda spoke softly, flipping her platinum blond hair over one shoulder. "Maria, I'm sorry. It's not the money. We simply can't take on any more clients right now. With our limited staff, we're barely keeping our heads above water as it is."

"Then tell me where I can go. Who *can* help. Luke promised you could help." Another quivering breath.

Trent pulled his hand away from his cheek and for the first time Joanna noticed he was bleeding from a gash across his right cheek. He opened a desk drawer and extracted a plain notepad. "I . . . I can send you some names. If you'll write down your email address . . ."

Heart pounding, Joanna hurried to the restroom across the hallway and grabbed a handful of paper towels from the decorative basket on the counter.

Returning to the office, she walked to the far side of Trent's desk and, trying to be unobtrusive, slid the stack of folded towels to him.

He flinched as if she'd struck him. Jo didn't think she'd ever seen her boss so ruffled. Trent swabbed at his cheek, then folded a section of the toweling and pressed it to his cheek. Cinda continued speaking quietly to Maria, attempting to calm her.

Trent motioned Jo closer. "I'm going to need you to drive her home. Or to the hospital, if she doesn't settle down."

"What's going on?" Jo mouthed.

"I'll explain later. She's sick," he whispered. "Cancer. She's trying to find a guardian for her kid."

Jo nodded. She recognized the pallor of cancer all too

18

well, and she steadied herself against the desk as memories of Mom's battle flooded in.

"Where is your son now?" Cinda asked, one hand on Maria's shoulder. Jo had never known her boss's wife to be so nurturing—unless it was with her two bichon frise pups.

"My Mateo, he is with his big brother."

"Wait . . . You didn't mention that you have two children. Is your older son still living at home?" Cinda looked puzzled.

And Joanna was growing more perplexed by the minute. Why would Maria have come to Pritchert & Pritchert in the first place? The firm was known for business real estate and estate planning. Joanna couldn't remember them ever taking on a family law case. Not to mention they had a reputation for being one of the more elite—meaning expensive—law firms in Cape Girardeau. Pritchert & Pritchert was *not* who you came to if money was an issue, and judging by this young woman's ranting, that was *the* issue.

"No. You don't understand. Mateo is my only son."

Cinda shook her head. "But you said he was with—"

"No, no . . . I mean the program. Big Brothers and Big Sisters. He's with his Big . . . his mentor." The first hint of a smile came to Maria's face. But it faded just as quickly. "Don't you ever take cases pro bono? Couldn't you make an exception? I am desperate, Mrs. Pritchert."

Jo was afraid she was going to start wailing again.

"Mrs. Castillo . . . Maria." Trent came from behind his desk and scooted a chair beside Maria, opposite Cinda. "As my wife told you, it isn't a matter of payment. And even if we had the staff to take on more work, this simply isn't the kind of legal work we do." He looked up and motioned Joanna over.

"This is my administrative assistant, Joanna Chandler. Jo is going to drive you back home, and we will email you a list of other attorneys who—"

"No. No, that won't work." She pushed away the notepad he'd given her. "I don't have an email address."

"I really think you should be in touch with DFS." Cinda rose and went to shuffle through a rack of pamphlets near the door. "Joanna, could you find me the numbers for the Division of Family Services?"

Jo started toward the bank of mahogany file cabinets opposite the large windows overlooking the Mississippi.

"No!" Maria practically screamed at her.

Jo stopped in her tracks, looking from Trent to Cinda. But they ignored her, their attention on Maria.

The woman wrung her hands and snarled. "Don't you understand? I am not dealing with the State. They took my friend's kids away from her. Connie hasn't seen them since."

"This is different." Cinda's smile looked forced. "DFS can help you work out care for your son. A plan. And you would be the one to have a say in where he . . . is placed."

"Have you not heard one word I've said?" Maria bared her teeth and lashed out, arms flailing.

From where she stood, Jo could only see the woman's profile, but there was rage in her posture. Jo thought she understood the scratches on Trent's cheek now. Involuntarily, she took a step back. Trent wanted her to transport this woman? What if Maria went berserk on *her* while she was driving her home?

Trent rose to his full six feet two inches. "This conversation is over. I am sorry for your misfortune, Mrs. Castillo. I truly am. But we have explained again and again that we aren't able to help you. You come in here and attack us"—he touched his cheek gingerly—"and expect us to offer our services to you free? We would have every right to prosecute you for battery."

Maria's eyes grew round, and she gripped the sides of her chair looking as though she might faint.

"No." Cinda patted Maria's knee as if she were a frightened child. "My husband isn't saying we would *do* that. Just that we would be within our rights if we did. We want you to go home and enjoy whatever time you have left with your son."

20

With a final pat on Maria's back, Cinda rose. Joanna cringed at the dismissive gesture.

But Maria Castillo dug her heels into the carpet and gripped the arms of her chair. "I am not leaving until you promise you will help my son. And no DFS!"

Trent's jaw tensed. "Joanna, please call the police."

Maria turned her glare on Jo. "Go ahead! Call them! What do I care?"

Joanna had never called the police in her life. They employed a security guard, and her boss had threatened a client or two with removal. But never had the police become involved. She looked at her boss, as if he might change his mind.

But Trent waved a hand. "Go. Call them. Tell them to come and remove this woman."

Cinda murmured something Jo couldn't understand, but she didn't wait to see if Cinda could change her husband's mind. She ran from the room and to her own office down the hall. Her hands trembled as she dialed 911. Her voice wavered as she explained to the dispatcher what was going on.

"And will someone be there to let the officers into the building?" The dispatcher's voice was maddeningly dispassionate.

"Yes, I'll let them in. Tell them to come to the back parking lot." She hung up the desk phone and started to go back down the hall to Trent's office, but thinking better of it, she went straight to the staircase. A twinge of guilt nipped at her, knowing that her foremost thought was not to let Trent change his mind about having the woman removed from the building. Because if the police came, Jo wouldn't have to be the one to drive the volatile Mrs. Castillo home.

The more she thought about it, the angrier she became. Had Trent only called her in to play taxi for the woman? He and Cinda had two perfectly good vehicles, both in the parking lot this very moment. Why couldn't *they* take her home? Or get an Uber ride? Carting irate clients—or worse, rejected clients— around town was not in her job description. Not even close.

She reached the bottom of the wide staircase and crossed the lobby to the back outside entrance.

What a night! Wait till she told her sisters. This would one-up her little sister's story of the cops making an after-midnight run when Melvin knocked over a vase and Britt thought someone was breaking in to the house.

She heard tires on the pavement and looked up to see two police cruisers enter the parking lot, emergency lights strobing. Catching her reflection in the plate-glass windows, Jo realized she was smiling at the remembrance of Britt's fiasco. She sobered immediately. It would not be good to have to explain to Cape Girardeau law enforcement what she found so funny about this situation.

It *wasn't* funny. And she was thankful she hadn't been here to witness Maria Castillo's attack on her boss. It was bad enough seeing the young woman's distress.

Three officers emerged from the cruisers and strode toward the building. Joanna met them at the door and held it open.

The oldest of the three stopped long enough to ask her, "Are you the one who called about the Pritchert situation?"

"Yes, sir. Trent and Cinda—the Pritcherts—are both upstairs." She pointed toward the elevators.

"Is anyone in any immediate danger?"

"I don't think so. The woman . . . Maria Castillo . . . wants them to represent her and Trent refused."

The officer repeated the woman's name and wrote something on a notepad.

"She's . . . distraught." Jo told the older officer about the scratches on Trent's face. "I don't know the details. It's just that they can't get her to leave."

"All right, ma'am. We'll take it from here." He asked her about the layout of the building, then caught up with the other two officers waiting by the staircase. He pushed the button to summon the elevator, while the others took the stairs two at a time.

"Do I need to come up with you?"

"No, ma'am. You stay right here. And lock the outside doors until we come back down."

Ten minutes crept by. Joanna paced in front of the windows overlooking the front parking lot. Traffic in the side street slowed as drivers gawked at the strobing cruisers angled in the back lot. Jo strained to hear what was going on upstairs. But only the buzz of a fluorescent light overhead disturbed the silence.

Finally the elevator dinged opened, and the two younger officers emerged with Maria between them, her hands cuffed behind her back. Her long dark hair fell over her forehead, and she looked so thin and pale, Jo worried the poor woman might collapse. Jo supposed the officers had no choice but to remove Maria forcibly, but Jo's heart went out to her.

Trent had said she had cancer. Jo saw other signs now in her hollowed eyes and gaunt frame—the way Mom had looked near the end. How much time did this young woman have? Probably not much, given how desperate she seemed to find help for her son.

The sun was low in the sky now, and Jo watched as they placed Maria in a cruiser, an officer guiding her head beneath the car's frame, then closing the door. Jo turned to go back upstairs, but the elevator door slid open, and Trent and Cinda stepped into the lobby, followed by the older officer.

Trent turned and shook the officer's hand. The policeman left the building and drove off, leaving the parking lot dark and still beyond the plate glass.

Joanna turned to the couple. "Are you guys okay?"

"We're fine." Trent ran a hand over his short, curly hair. "Man, what a night."

"Some welcome home, huh?" Jo felt awkward with them,

not sure what had transpired while she was down here waiting in the lobby. "So, what happens now?"

"I don't know." Cinda took in a deep breath and released it slowly. "And thank goodness, it's not our responsibility. I wasn't sure how this night was going to turn out."

At times, Cinda had seemed genuinely concerned when she spoke with Maria in the office. But it was all an act, and it bothered Jo that she could be so cold and uncaring now. Of course, Cinda had watched the woman attack Trent. Jo supposed her own compassion would have been tempered, too, if she were in Cinda's shoes.

Trent waved a hand toward the parking lot. "You go on home, Jo. I'm sorry you had to get mixed up in this."

"I didn't do any work though. Was there something else you called about?"

Cinda gave a humorless laugh. "No, we just wanted you to take that nutjob home so we could finish up the Wilson Estates paperwork tonight. We did *not* have time for this tonight."

Jo must have looked befuddled because Trent quickly added, "We never would have involved you had we known she was going to go postal on us."

"Trent . . ." Cinda touched his sleeve. "*Postal* might be a little strong."

He swiped a hand over his cheek as if he disagreed.

"Will they tow her car?" Jo scanned the parking lot beyond the windows for an unfamiliar car, but only their three vehicles remained. "Wait . . . How did she get here in the first place?"

Trent came to the window and followed her line of sight to the mostly empty lot. "Didn't she say someone dropped her off?" he asked Cinda.

"I don't remember. And I don't want to. Let's get out of here. We can come in early tomorrow."

Trent jangled his keys, then put an arm around his wife. "You go on home, Jo. We'll lock the door behind you. We may still have to give a statement."

24

"That's ridiculous." Cinda scavenged for something in her purse. "*I'm* going home."

"I hope you guys can get some sleep after all the excitement." Cinda didn't acknowledge her, still digging in her purse.

"Thanks for coming in, Jo." Trent went to open the door. He held it for Jo.

She heard the lock turn behind her as she walked to her car. She unlocked the door and slid behind the wheel. But the minute she turned the key in the ignition, her legs turned to rubber. She drove slowly out of the parking lot so Trent wouldn't worry about her. But her hands were trembling so violently, she turned off on a side street and parked at the curb for a few minutes until she felt safe to drive.

CHAPTER 3

A RE YOU SERIOUS? SHE SCRATCHED his face?" Britt's eyes were as round as the eggs she was frying. "I bet that went over well."

"Well, I didn't actually witness that part. Trent was already bleeding like a stuck pig when I got there." An exaggeration, admittedly, but it wasn't often Joanna had both her sisters' rapt attention the way she did now, and she was going to milk her story for all it was worth.

"Aren't you a little nervous to go back to work?" Phylicia's brow wrinkled.

"A little, I guess. Especially if they let this woman go free."

"Do you think the Pritcherts will press charges?" Britt popped half a bagel in the toaster. "Anybody want the other half?"

Phee declined.

Jo shook her head too. "I've kind of lost my appetite just thinking about last night. I was shaking so hard, I wasn't sure I'd be able to drive home." Her sisters had both been out when she'd returned to the cottage last night, and after calling Ginger, her closest friend and former roommate, to tell her what had happened, she'd collapsed into bed and slept till an hour ago. So, her sisters were only now hearing about her ordeal.

"You should have called me!" Phee scooted Jo aside with one hip and tossed her yogurt cup in the trash can under the sink.

Jo growled good-naturedly. "This kitchen was not made for three women!"

"Hey, it's all yours." Phee held up her hands. "I'm out of here. I'll probably work late tonight. Mary wants to get some stuff up on social media in time for Mother's Day flower orders, and I told her I'd help her set up an Instagram account. Then I'm having dinner with Quinn."

"Oh, big surprise." Jo rolled her eyes, then looked through the dining room to the mantel. "Did you get your May basket?"

Phee glowed. "Wasn't that the sweetest?"

"It was pretty sweet," Jo admitted. She glanced at the clock and gave a little gasp. "I'm already late!"

"What else is new? But hey, you be careful, okay?" Phee gave her a stern look.

"Yes, Mother."

"Well, excuse me for caring about you."

"Just kidding."

"Bye, Britt," they chimed in unison, gathering their jackets and bags.

"I'll be working in the cabin today." Britt trailed after them. "I'm going to wash windows so we can hang curtains this weekend."

"Take Melvin with you." Jo shot her little sister an impish look. "In case . . . you know . . ."

Phee barely held in her laughter. They'd seen a mouse in that cabin the first time they looked at the property, and Britt had freaked out. Well, they all had, much to Quinn's amusement.

"Don't you worry. Melvin's coming with me. But if there's still a mouse in that cabin after all the sawing and hammering and painting that's been going on over there for the last couple of weeks, then he deserves to live out his days right there."

"Wow, you've sure changed your tune." Still laughing, Phee headed out the door for her car.

Jo laughed, too, but Britt was right. The cabin had a new roof, and the interior had been transformed into a clean white slate. They'd even given the ceilings a coat of fresh white paint, making the place look twice as big as it had when they first toured the three houses on the property. The two bedrooms had new carpet, and the floors in the main part of the cabin had been sanded and stained.

They would start on the second cabin once they replenished their renovation fund. Of course, everything had cost more than they expected, but they hadn't gone in debt . . . at least not yet.

Jo had no regrets for buying the property with her sisters. She didn't think Phylicia or Britt regretted it either. And once the cabins were both finished, they'd have better potential income from renting them out through Airbnb. Jo grabbed her keys from the hook near the front door. "I'd better get a move on. See you tonight."

"Seriously, Jo. Be careful. I don't like the sound of that woman."

Jo glanced back to meet her little sister's gaze, touched by her concern. "I don't think she intended to hurt anyone. She was just desperate."

"Well, you know what they say: Desperate people do desperate things."

"I'll be careful." But as Jo drove into town, she couldn't get the phrase out of her head.

The office looked like it did on any normal day. No indication that last night's disturbance had ever happened. Jo put her purse in the desk drawer, smoothed the skirt of her dress, and slipped on her headset, ready to answer the phones and respond to email.

Trent and Cinda were across the hall in his office with some guy. Younger than Pritchert & Pritchert's usual client—and good looking as all get out, at least what she could see of him from the reception room. Dark curly hair like Trent's, a strong jaw that already wore a five o'clock shadow—and wore it well—and broad shoulders beneath a button-down shirt. For a minute she wondered if he might be one of Trent's brothers, but though Jo couldn't make out the conversation, their voices carried the low businesslike tones of a typical client conference. It didn't seem like Trent or Cinda knew the man, and Jo had never seen him in the office before.

She didn't know how long he'd been here, and there was no appointment on the calendar. Her boss sometimes scheduled last minute meetings without adding them to the calendar Jo had access to, but she thought he would have said something last night if he'd known he had an early consultation. Probably just forgot in all the excitement of last night. Or maybe this was *about* last night.

By the time the man emerged from the office twenty minutes later, two other clients were waiting in the reception room. Jo hated when the schedule got backed up this early. It threw the whole day off.

The man caught her eye and gave a polite smile. "I need to make another appointment. Mr. Pritchert said I should talk to Joanna."

"Yes, that's me. How soon do you need to come back in?"

"As soon as possible."

Joanna scrolled through the appointment calendar, frowning. "He could see you two weeks from Friday. May 19. Right after lunch . . . say, one p.m. Will that work?"

The man bit his lower lip. "You don't have anything sooner?"

"I'm sorry, no. I can put you on a waiting list, in case we have a cancellation."

"Yes, please do. It's Lukas Blaine. Lukas with a *k*. Middle initial *P* . . . if that matters." He spelled his surname for her.

Jo took down his information. Blaine. Apparently not Trent's brother. What business did he have with Pritchert & Pritchert? Probably handling paperwork for an aging parent, or more likely grandparent. She guessed him to be about her age, early thirties at most.

"So, were you here for the . . . whole police thing last night?"

She looked up at him, trying not to show her surprise. "How did you . . . know about that?" She probably shouldn't have asked. Trent and Cinda were both extremely cautious about confidentiality and security, and there hadn't been anyone else in the office last night. She was pretty sure even the janitor had left for the night by the time the police arrived.

"I . . . I'm a friend of Maria's. Maria Castillo?"

"Oh. I see. I'm sorry." Was that why he was here? His conversation with Trent and Cinda had seemed too calm to have been about last night.

"Sorry? Why?"

"Oh . . . Just for what happened. That she's ill."

"So, you were here when she came in to talk to Trent?"

"I was, but . . . I'm really not at liberty to discuss it."

That made him smile. "I understand. I'm sorry I said anything. I hope you didn't get . . . hurt."

"Oh, no. Nothing like that."

"Okay. Good." He took a step toward the elevator, then turned back to her desk. "Do you have a card? An appointment card, I mean. I'm afraid I'll forget."

"Sure. Let me get you one." She opened a drawer and pulled a card from the stack. She printed his appointment date on it in careful block letters, then slid it across the desk to him.

"Thank you." He tucked the card in his shirt pocket and

gave her that smile again. "I appreciate it. You'll call me if there's an opening before the nineteenth?"

She tapped the reservation book. "You're on the list. Have a nice day." It was all Jo could do to restrain herself from asking him about Maria. But she wouldn't cross that professional line. Watching him stand with his back to her, waiting for the elevator, she wondered again what his relationship was to Maria Castillo. With his thick, almost black hair, he could have been Latino like Maria. But his complexion was much lighter than Maria's, even given how her illness had grayed her skin. And Jo had noticed that Lukas Blaine's eyes were gray, a paler shade that—under the fluorescent lights of the office—seemed to have gold flecks.

The elevator arrived and he stepped on. When he turned to press the button, Jo was embarrassed to be caught staring at him. She wiped damp palms on the emerald green fabric of her dress.

He gave a little wave across the hall as if he appreciated her appraisal. She nodded briefly and busied herself with the papers on her desk, willing the elevator doors to hurry up and close.

Thankfully, her phone rang from her purse just then. She retrieved it and checked the display. "Hey, Phee. What's up?"

"How would you like to be a wedding planner?"

The elevator door closed and with a sigh of relief, she turned her attention to her sister. "Wedding planner? What do you mean?"

"We just set a date." A little squeal escaped her sister.

"Are you serious? You and Quinn?"

"Of course, me and Quinn. Who else would I mean?"

"So, you really *did* propose to him."

"Cut it out, Jo. It was mutual. But we're doing this. We're really doing this. Quinn doesn't want to wait. And neither do I. Mark June 24 on your calendar."

She opened her mouth, but nothing would come out.

"Jo? Hello? Are you there?"

"June? As in next month June?"

Phee giggled. "That's the one."

"Are you *crazy*? I just saw you an hour ago, Phee. How did you manage to set a wedding date between the time I drove out of the driveway and"—she glanced at the clock above the elevator—"10:17 a.m.?"

"Coffee break." That girlish giggle again. "Quinn stopped by the flower shop while I was on my break and . . . one thing led to another and ta-da!" Phee was a different person since she and Quinn had declared their love.

Jo wasn't sure she liked this giddy version of her older sister. She quickly amended the thought. She was just jealous. Jealous her sister had found what Jo had always dreamed about. And what she'd thought she had with Ben.

Ben. She tried so hard not to let his name enter her thoughts. But rarely was she successful. She and Ben Harven had dated for almost a year before he'd shown his true colors. When Mom started going downhill, Ben couldn't handle losing Jo's undivided attention. And apparently he didn't like being around "sick people."

Jo had been embarrassed and furious and heartbroken. Mostly heartbroken. And yet, she was glad his betrayal had shown her the selfish, petty side of him before things grew any more serious between them.

"Jo? You still there?"

"Phee . . . Sorry. I . . . I'm still trying to wrap my head around this."

"Well, get to wrapping, sister. I already talked to Dad and he's coming back. To walk me down the aisle."

"Oh, Phee. I'm so happy for you."

She wondered how Dad felt about Phee's announcement. Only a few weeks ago, just months after Mom's death, they'd learned that Mom had been married before and that it was quite possible, likely even, that Dad wasn't actually Phylicia's birth father. And to Jo's surprise, Phee and Dad both seemed content not to probe the issue any deeper.

Jo wasn't sure she could have left the unknown alone if it had been her whose paternity was in question. Especially with the health issues Mom had dealt with. Of course, they *knew* Mom's health history—and at her insistence, they'd all had regular checkups with an oncologist.

"Thanks, sis. I'm so happy I'm almost . . . scared to let myself believe this is happening."

"Oh, Phee . . . Nobody deserves this more than you do. And I really *am* happy for you, but . . . *June?* That's only six weeks away."

"Actually, almost seven."

"You do know that wedding invitations are supposed to go out six weeks *minimum* before the event."

"Then we've got our work cut out for us this weekend, don't we?"

"Phee! You are flat-out crazy, woman!"

"Don't worry. We're doing everything simple—and cheap. Just a quiet ceremony and a cake reception. I don't care about a big wedding. Especially without Mom."

"I get that." She'd had that very thought when she imagined her own wedding . . . however far in the future that might be. It wouldn't be the same without Mom to share their joy. And with Dad there alone.

She blew out a sigh, scrambling to fathom how they'd ever pull off a wedding—even a simple one—in six weeks. "I guess you've got the flowers covered."

"Yes. I haven't told Mary yet, but that poor woman has been waiting seven years for me to get married so she can do my flowers. I'm pretty sure she'll say yes."

Joanna gave a humorless laugh. "Okay, so the flowers are taken care of. Have you reserved a church?" Since they'd started hanging out with Quinn, the four of them had gone back and forth between the Chandler family's church in Langhorne and Quinn's community church in Cape Girardeau. A wedding would probably make Phee have to choose a church home.

Not for the first time, Jo worried about how Phee's marriage would affect their plans for the property—the Airbnb enterprise she and her sisters had named The Cottages on Poplar Brook Road and that the three of them had planned to run together.

"Funny you should ask." The mysterious note in Phee's voice made Joanna nervous.

"Funny why?"

"Quinn and I thought maybe we could get married outdoors. Up in the clearing. After all, it's where I proposed." Phee laughed at the running joke that she'd been the one to propose to Quinn. But she sounded absolutely gleeful.

"You can't be serious, Phee. There *is* no clearing. Have you been up there lately? It would take a Bush Hog and a small army with machetes to clear enough space for a wedding *party*, let alone a bunch of guests." She looked at the calendar on the office wall beside her, its squares filled with appointments. And that wasn't even her personal social calendar. *Oh, who are you kidding, Joanna Chandler. You have no social life.*

"Not a bunch of guests." Phee's voice pulled her back. "I told you we want a small wedding. Very simple."

"Well, there would be nothing simple about getting that clearing ready for a wedding."

But even as she spoke the words, Jo knew that no matter what it took, there would, indeed, be a wedding in that clearing. And they had barely six weeks to pull it off.

CHAPTER 4

LUKE STEPPED UNDER THE CRISP white tent, let the duffle bag slide from his shoulder, and scoped out the lay of the land. Twinkle lights crisscrossed from pole to pole overhead, flirting with the yellow glow of tea light candles that flickered on each of the round tables. Somebody had spent some bucks on this wedding reception. Figured. Two doctors' kids.

Luke motioned for Mateo to follow him. "Stick close, okay, buddy?"

The twelve-year-old tugged at the collar of his crisp white shirt as if it were choking him to death. Luke could see the outline of the brown bead necklace under his dress shirt. Mateo had worn that necklace—matching the one Luke wore—for almost five years. Maria said he never took it off, not even to shower.

The DJ table was set up to one side of the dance floor with easy access to an exit. Good. If Mateo got antsy, he could play outside.

Luke gripped the boy's shoulder. "Remember, we're supposed to be invisible."

Mateo jerked out of his grasp. He was still holding a grudge that Luke had made him dress up for the occasion.

"Listen, short-stuff, I *could* have made you wear a tie too." Mateo snarled. "Yeah right. That is not happening."

"Don't forget you're getting wedding cake out of the deal."

"And champagne?" The boy's dark eyebrows rose optimistically.

"Yeah right. *That* is not happening." Luke did an admirable job of parroting Mateo's tone.

Which coaxed a half-grin from the kid. Luke laughed at the tenacity of his "little brother," but hoped he wouldn't regret bringing Mateo on this gig. Or more like he hoped the *bride* wouldn't regret it.

But with Maria so ill, Luke hadn't had much choice but to bring Mateo with him tonight. After the incident in that attorney's office Tuesday, Maria had seemed utterly defeated. Mateo told him on the drive out to the venue that his mom had been in bed most of the week. Luke felt responsible. He'd been the one to suggest Maria contact the law firm. Mostly because it was the only local one he knew much about. The radio station had used the firm's services a few times, but he should have done more research. And he certainly should have known that Maria couldn't afford a big-name firm like Pritchert & Pritchert.

Luke assumed Maria's distant family in California had agreed to take Mateo, though she rarely spoke of extended family and didn't seem to be close to any of them. Luke had assured her that Mateo could stay with him until someone could get to Missouri. Still, she'd insisted that everything be in writing. Legal. She'd been terrified of Mateo going "into the system."

Luke didn't think Mateo knew about what happened at the law office, but he hated that the kid had to see his mother that way. And though Luke hadn't felt it was his place—nor did he have the courage—to bring up the subject with Mateo, surely the boy knew that his mother didn't have long to live.

Had Maria talked to him about where he would go when that happened?

He shuddered, dreading that day already.

Maria had seemed grateful when Luke offered to take Mateo with him tonight. He'd been bugging Luke to show him where he worked. Granted, these DJ gigs weren't exactly what paid the bills, but they were a far cry more interesting than Luke's desk job at the radio station in Langhorne. And after almost five years as Mateo's Big Brother, he trusted the boy enough to know he'd be on his best behavior if Luke let him know how important it was.

"Grab that bag for me, would you? And be careful with it."

Mateo hefted the bulky duffle bag and followed Luke to the other side of the tent.

The night was chilly and Luke wished he'd brought a heavier jacket—and had Maria send warmer clothes with Mateo. But things would warm up once the reception got underway. He didn't know the bride or groom, but the groom's uncle worked with Luke at KQOZ and had arranged a nice discount on the DJ's fees as his wedding gift to the couple. Sounded more like a gift from *him*, Lukas Blaine—or MO-DJ as his little business was called. For a couple he didn't even know. But whatever. He was a pushover. And the truth was, he enjoyed moonlighting as a DJ.

Mateo helped him set up the equipment and check the sound system. Luke meant it when he told him, "Man, I wish I'd thought to bring you with me on these gigs a long time ago."

The boy's brown eyes shone at the compliment, and it struck Luke that Mateo looked more like his mother every day. He'd been a pudgy seven-year-old when the Big Brothers program had first matched him with Luke, but in the past year, playing middle school soccer had thinned him out and put a little swagger in his step. Luke knew Maria worried as Mateo got older that he'd become cocky and self-absorbed.

"Like his father," Maria had said with a grimace that revealed more than she'd likely intended.

"He's just at that age," Luke assured her. "He'll grow out of it."

"Well if he does not, I will count on you to nip it in the butt."

Luke had cracked up, and seeing her curious expression, explained that the saying was "nip it in the *bud*. You know, like nipping off the bud of a flower before it can bloom?"

Maria repeated the phrase as if committing it to memory. "Well, you have my permission to nip Mateo in the *butt* as well, if that's what it takes."

He'd laughed harder, admiring the way she parented her son, firmly but with great love.

Maria's parents had immigrated to the United States from Mexico when she was a young teenager, and she'd worked hard to remove any trace of an accent. But sometimes American idioms still tripped her up. Luke felt bad the first time he corrected her, thinking it might offend. But she claimed she appreciated it and tasked him with alerting her any time she slipped up. He secretly loved it when Mexico lilted into her intonation— usually when she was disciplining Mateo.

Luke did one last sound check and turned to Mateo. "That should do it. Now all we have to do is wait for the wedding party to arrive. You ever been to a wedding before?"

"My dad's cousin got married out in California. I carried the rings on a pillow. Had to wear a tuxedo and everything."

"Ah, the ring bearer."

"I guess. Mama has a picture in her album, but I don't remember it. I was only three or something." His eyes clouded. Probably thinking about his father.

Maria had married Ricardo Castillo only a year after the man came to the United States. Too late, she suspected that he'd married her to gain his citizenship, and he'd left her for another woman and gone back to Mexico when Mateo was only four.

Ricardo had been killed in a motorcycle crash a year later, and Maria confessed to Luke that she was relieved when she heard the news because she'd lived in fear that her ex-husband might try to get custody of Mateo and take him back to Mexico.

Mateo claimed he barely remembered his father, but Luke suspected he had some memories, especially since, at the time Maria signed him up to be a Little Brother, Mateo had been acting out, exhibiting aggression in school and even toward Maria.

Maria always told Luke that he'd played a huge role in helping Mateo get his impulses under control. Luke wasn't sure how true that was, but he knew the relationship—and his friendship with Mateo's mother—had enriched his own life and given him a sense of purpose he hadn't even realized he needed. He would be forever grateful to the campaign the radio station had run for the Big Brothers Big Sisters organization. He fingered the beads that circled his neck and tugged absently at the tarnished silver charm shaped like the BBBS logo—a "big" and "little" with the shadows of their outstretched arms forming a heart. Luke had signed up to be a Big Brother more out of obligation than conviction, never dreaming he would still be involved five years later.

Luke put a hand on Mateo's shoulder. "I should probably warn you that it might get a little mushy out there"—he nodded in the direction of the dance floor—"kissing and stuff like that."

"*Kissing?* Gross! Why didn't you tell me?" Mateo made a gagging sound and pulled a face that made Luke laugh out loud.

"Huh-uh, none of that. And no puking allowed either. You're just going to have to man up and gut it out. You can look away if it gets too bad."

"I'm gonna need some champagne."

He cocked his head. "How do you even know what champagne is?"

"Duh. I've been to a wedding before. And also, we have this thing called a TV."

41

"Well, don't even joke about it. Champagne, I mean. Your mother would kill me."

"No she wouldn't. She likes you."

Luke tensed. It shouldn't have surprised him that Mateo had noticed. After all, *he'd* noticed.

For a while, after Luke realized that Maria Castillo was attracted to him, he'd considered ending the Big Brother relationship with Mateo. But by then, he'd invested so much to foster Mateo's trust he couldn't bring himself to let the boy down, and he really did feel bad for Maria. He put up invisible walls with Maria and was careful to limit their time together. Thankfully, Maria had never once violated the unspoken boundaries.

And then she'd been diagnosed with cancer and that had consumed everything. When he thought of what was now inevitable—that the beautiful young woman would soon take her final breath—Luke was overwhelmed with sadness.

The crunch of tires on gravel made him and Mateo turn and peer beneath the tent's canopy. Half a dozen cars rumbled up the lane to where the tent was pitched, leaving a cloud of dust in their wake.

Half an hour later the tables were full and the room buzzed with laughter and lively conversation as guests waited for the wedding party.

Luke got the signal that the bridal couple was about to make their entrance and he switched into DJ mode, feeling strangely self-conscious with Mateo looking on. This would be a side of him his Little Brother had never seen before.

He double-checked the cheat sheet in his breast pocket. "All right, folks. Let's give a big hand for the beautiful bride and her groom. Presenting . . ."—he nodded for Mateo to cue up the drumroll track the way he'd shown him earlier—"Mr. and Mrs. Jackson Novotny!"

He started the mash-up the couple had chosen for their grand entrance. The guests rose and cheered as the bride and groom ducked under the canopy hand in hand, wearing match-ing thousand-watt smiles.

During the traditional dances, Luke caught a couple of the groomsmen getting a little too cozy with the bar, so when the father-daughter dance ended, he called for the wedding party to take the dance floor. Winking at Mateo—who watched him with a perplexed smile—he slid the fader up, and Andrew Gold's "Thank You for Being a Friend" blasted through the venue.

Once all eyes were on the dance floor, Luke clapped Mateo on the back and raised his voice to be heard over the festive roar. "Hey, good job, buddy. Looks like you're ready to be a DJ's assistant."

"As long as there's no disgusting kissing involved."

Luke chuckled. "I give you two years to change your mind about that."

"No way!" Mateo's shiny black hair swung with every ada-mant shake of his head. "Never gonna happen."

"What do you want to bet?"

"A glass of champagne?"

Luke shot Mateo the stink eye and gave him a good-natured punch in the biceps.

But he couldn't quell the question that hounded him: Where would Mateo be two years from now?

CHAPTER 5

JOANNA'S PHONE TRILLED FROM THE kitchen table. She sighed. She'd just sat down for the first time all evening after a house-cleaning marathon to get the cottage ready for Airbnb guests this weekend.

"Jo?" Phylicia called from her bedroom. "Your phone's ringing."

"I hear it."

"You'd better take the call. It could be about the booking."

Jo huffed and lumbered off the sofa. Why had she let her sisters talk her into using her cell phone for the Airbnb number? She picked up her phone and looked at the caller ID. "Oh! It's about time."

Phylicia came from her room and peered over Jo's shoulder. "Who is it?"

"It's that DJ I've been trying to book. A company called MO-DJ. They had the best reviews online. Pray they'll do it on such short notice." She held up a hand for silence before pressing Accept. "Hello?"

"Yes, this is Luke from MO-DJ. I'm returning a call from Joanna Chandler."

"This is Jo. Thank you for getting back to me."

"I apologize it took so long. I've had someone . . . a friend . . . in the hospital and I've gotten way behind."

"I'm so sorry. And no problem. I'm hoping to book one of your DJs for my sister's wedding."

A chuckle came across the line. "That would be me. I mean, MO-DJ is a one-man show. I'm it."

"Oh. Okay." Her optimism flew out the window. "Well, I know this is really short notice"—she shot Phee a look meant to place all the blame in her sister's court if this fell through—"but the wedding is June 24. Is there any chance you have an opening then? Mid-afternoon until evening?"

He gave a low whistle. "As in *this* June 24?"

She nodded. "That's exactly what I said when my sister— the bride—told me. I know it's short notice. Blame my sister." She frowned at Phee.

He blew a sigh into the phone. "I wish I could help her out, but my first open date *this* year isn't until October."

"I understand. Is there anyone else in the area you could recommend?"

"I guess I could give you a couple of names in Cape Girardeau, but on this short of notice, I'm guessing they're already booked as well. I'm sorry." The man's voice sounded vaguely familiar.

"Well, I knew it was a long shot. Thank you . . . Luke, was it?"

"Yes . . . Sorry. Lukas Blaine. But you can call me Luke. I wish I could help, but I hope you'll try again if you ever need a DJ. I can email you some information or you can find me online." He rattled off a website URL.

But she barely heard, wracking her brain to think why he sounded so familiar and where she'd heard that name. It came to her in a flash. *Lukas.* The man who'd met with Trent after the incident with Maria Castillo. For the sake of confidentiality, she'd best not mention to him that they'd met before. Still, she had a hard time envisioning the man she'd talked to as a wedding DJ. He'd seemed so somber and serious. Of course, he'd been in a stressful situation.

Given the circumstances, Trent had decided not to press charges against the woman who'd "assaulted" him—Cinda's word—and Jo had almost forgotten about the ordeal.

She thanked Lukas and ended the call, then glared up at Phylicia. "I guess you're just not going to have music at your wedding."

Phee gave her an infuriatingly serene smile and shrugged. "Fine by me. One less thing to worry about."

"Phee, you can't *not* have music at your wedding!"

"Settle down, sister. We can set up some speakers and maybe . . . play the wedding march on somebody's phone."

Detecting the trace of humor in her sister's eyes, Jo clapped a hand over her heart. "I cannot believe what my ears are hearing. That would be *so* tacky!"

Phee giggled. "As long as Quinn and I are married by the end of the day, that's all I care about."

Jo had to admit she loved having the carefree version of her older sister back. After Mom's death, Phylicia had become cynical and sullen. Falling in love with Quinn Mitchell had brought the sparkle back to her eyes. And they were all beneficiaries.

Jo grabbed the notebook she'd filled with to-do lists for the wedding. "Where's Britt? We seriously need to sit down and iron out some details or you will *not* be married by the end of that day!"

"She's painting in Near Cottage." They'd been living in the larger cottage on their property and had designated the two smaller cabins "Near Cottage" and "Far Cottage" until they could come up with better names for them. But the names had stuck, and now Phee was even working on nameplates to hang over the doors of the cabins so guests could be sure they were at the right place.

"Britt's there by herself?"

Jo smiled. "I know. Isn't it amazing? I told her I'd help her later this evening. She's worked harder than any of us on this place. Especially since the cabins were ready to decorate."

"It seems like she's really enjoying the work too."

Jo frowned. "Or maybe she just feels guilty she hasn't found a job yet."

"Do you think she's really looking that hard?"

"Maybe not. And really, Phee . . . Why don't we just relieve her of any guilt?"

"What do you mean?"

"Well, as long as there's work to keep her busy, it might as well be her doing the jobs—especially if she enjoys it. If she wasn't doing it, we'd have to hire it done. Especially now that we have a wedding to plan."

"It's fine by me to have Britt do the work. We're paying the bills with no problem, and that's before any income through Airbnb. Speaking of which"—Phee opened her laptop—"have you checked our bookings today?"

"No. Not for a couple of days, actually. Why?"

"No reason. I just thought in case someone had questions or there was a cancellation."

"If you'll check our messages, I'll go get Britt so we can iron out this wedding stuff."

"Deal." Phee opened the browser and started typing.

Jo slipped a sweatshirt from a hook by the door and started down to the cabins. The night air was cool, but the lights blazing from every window of the nearest cabin warmed her. Jo could see her little sister moving about inside the small stone house and she could just hear the twangy chords of Britt's beloved country music.

Only a few months ago, Britt had been afraid to stay by herself in the house in town where they'd grown up. Now she was working away in the cabin by herself after dark.

A black-and-white furball streaked by the window. Melvin.

Britt did have Mom's tuxedo cat to keep her company. And to scare away any mice that might still be in residence.

Jo climbed the steps and gave two short raps on the door before opening it, so as not to alarm Britt. "Hey, sis." The pungent smells of paint, varnish, and new carpet assailed her.

Britt's head jerked up and her eyes went wide. "You scared me half to death."

"Sorry. I knocked."

"I didn't hear you."

"You should have some windows open in here!" Joanna crossed the living room and strained to raise a window that apparently had been painted shut.

"Don't worry. I've got windows open in both bedrooms." Britt went to turn down the music blaring from her phone in the kitchen. Blake Shelton.

Jo rolled her eyes. How three sisters had grown up in the same house yet come away with such different tastes in music, Jo would never understand. Britt had her country music, Jo preferred jazz and fusion. And Phylicia was all about Bach and Mozart and the classics—although Jo had noticed that Quinn actually persuaded Phee to add some country artists to her playlists.

"Sorry." Britt returned, paintbrush in hand. "What's up? Did you come to help me paint?"

"Nice try, but no. Phee's home and we really need to iron out some wedding details. Can you take a break?"

Britt sighed, but put her paintbrush down. "Sure. I could use a break. Give me five minutes and I'll be over."

For the first time, Jo looked around the cabin, seeing what Britt had accomplished. "This is looking good, sis! Painting everything white makes the place look twice as big." From ceiling to walls to woodwork, everything had been painted a crisp white, and Britt was giving the baseboards a second coat—dove white, Jo thought the shade was called. "I was ready to fight you two for the bigger cottage, but this might be even better."

She was halfway kidding, but Britt's expression turned serious. "I think we should offer Phee the cottage, don't you? Phee and Quinn, I mean."

Jo nodded. "I was thinking that too. But I wonder if they'll move out to his place instead? Has she said anything?"

"Not that I've heard."

When the three of them bought the property together, they knew things might change once one of them got married, but they never dreamed that would happen so quickly. "Let's go talk to Phee. She's so gaga for that man, I'm not sure she's thinking straight."

Britt laughed. "You're just jealous."

Jo started to protest, but opted for honesty. "I *am* a little. Mostly, I'm happy to see Phee so happy. I really am."

Britt sighed again. "Me too. I just wish Mom had lived to see it happen. To be at Phee's wedding. And ours."

The thought cast a momentary pall of melancholy. "But at least Mom knew Quinn."

"Yes, and loved him. She would have approved."

That much was true. And the feeling was mutual. They all loved Quinn Mitchell. His presence in their lives had filled some of the empty places left by Mom's death and Dad's move to Florida. Quinn was an anchor for them all.

Dad would be back to walk Phee down the aisle, of course, but it was starting to look like he was settling in to his job—and a church—in Tampa, and Jo had resigned herself to the truth that part of her father's grieving process meant getting away from the place where he and Mom had lived most of their lives.

It hurt a little to have him distance himself from them, but Jo wasn't so sure she wouldn't have done the same in his shoes. A fresh start. In a way, that was what this property—The Cottages on Poplar Brook Road—was for Jo and her sisters.

She and Britt locked up and walked across to the cottage for their "planning meeting." They'd no sooner opened the porch door than Phee handed Jo her phone.

"It's that DJ guy," she whispered. "I answered when I saw it was him."

Jo nodded and took the phone from her. "Hello?"

"Hi, Joanna. This is Luke again, from MO-DJ. You may have found someone already, but in case not, I wanted to let you know that my June 24 wedding just cancelled."

"Cancelled?" Why would someone cancel so close to their wedding date?

"Yep. The slot is yours if you still want it."

"Oh! We do. Yes. It's my sister who's getting married. Phylicia Chandler is her name."

"Yes, I remember. Should I contact her instead?"

"Actually, that's who answered my phone. Hang on just a moment . . ." She tossed Phee a questioning look.

But Phee shook her head and took a step back, motioning for Jo to handle the call.

"I'm serving as Phylicia's wedding planner, so it's fine to keep my name as the contact and—"

"That's great. I just need to get some quick information from you . . . since we're getting a late start. I assume you have a venue reserved for the wedding?"

She hesitated. "I should've mentioned this earlier, I guess. It's going to be an outdoor wedding."

"That's fine. I haven't run into any local venues where that was a problem. I assume you'll have a tent—or at least an indoor alternative site?"

"Yes. We'll have a tent."

Phee looked askance at her. They hadn't talked about any of this yet, but Jo wasn't about to let this DJ go. It was a small miracle he'd had this cancellation.

Jo waved a hand and turned away so the comical faces Phee was pulling wouldn't distract her. "The wedding and reception will be on our property on the edge of Langhorne."

There was a slight pause before he replied. "I assume there's power to the site?"

"Um . . . there *will* be. I should have you talk to the groom about that. He's a contractor, and he assured us we could get power up there, but I don't know what he had in mind."

"Up there?"

"It's a clearing up in the woods on our property. There's an old wooden stairway to get up there. It's not much of a climb, but it's on the rustic side."

"Hmm. You might need to rent a generator to make that all work."

"Let me give you my future brother-in-law's number." She read Quinn's name and number off her phone. "And . . . I probably should mention this—so it's not awkward later—I think you and I have met before."

"Oh?"

"I work as an administrative assistant to Trenton Pritchert. Weren't you in our offices a few days ago? I took your information . . ."

"Oh. Yes, that was me. You were the woman at the reception desk? Long brown hair. Blue eyes? Green dress?"

She couldn't help the smile that came. "That was me." He'd noticed all that in the five minutes they'd talked?

"I thought your voice sounded familiar."

"Yes, I recognized yours too. I thought I should mention it. In case that makes you . . . uncomfortable."

"No. Not unless it's a problem for you."

"How is Mrs. Castillo? Maria?" She probably shouldn't have asked, given that she'd pleaded confidentiality when *he* asked about the incident at the office.

He cleared his throat, hesitating longer before answering. "She's not doing well. I don't know if you are aware . . . Her cancer is terminal."

"I'm so sorry."

"Thank you." He cleared his throat again and became all business. "Well, glad this worked out after all. The DJ date. I'll get in touch with Quinn Mitchell and we'll get everything lined up."

They hung up on a brighter note, but Jo was haunted by the timbre his voice had taken on when he'd thanked her for her offer of sympathy. He'd said earlier that "a friend" had been in the hospital, and his response now to Jo's comment about the woman's illness sounded like the tone of a man who had a personal stake in the outcome.

And though she certainly understood and felt deep compassion for the woman's plight, if she were honest, she was far more worried that something might interfere with MO-DJ being able to do Phee's wedding and reception. He'd said himself he was a one-man show.

It would be a difficult conversation—and maybe she was wrong to assume—but she needed to know for sure that Lukas Blaine could be depended on. Or at least that he had a contingency plan in place should something happen.

CHAPTER 6

I T'S BAD, LUKE. REAL BAD." Mateo's voice wavered. "The nurse said she might not make it until morning."
Luke gripped the phone and glanced at the clock on his computer. He moved a pile of ad invoices from one side of his desk to the other as if that would get them processed and mailed. "They *told* you that?" What were they thinking to give that kind of information to a kid?

"They didn't know I heard." Mateo said it as if *he* had done something wrong.

"Are you at the hospital?" Luke was surprised to find his own voice a little unsteady. He was glad the boy couldn't see his face. It was quiet at the radio station this morning, but nevertheless, he got up and closed the door to his office. "Is someone with you, buddy?"

"We're home now. There's a hospital nurse with Mama. But she's kind of out of it. I rode in the ambulance with her but . . . they made me stay in the waiting room."

"Wait, buddy. Slow down. They took her in an ambulance?"

"Yeah. She was bleeding so bad. It was everywhere . . . the blood. Can you come, Luke? Please?"

"Of course. But you're home now?"

"Yes. A nurse came here. I think they said she was a hospital nurse."

"Oh . . . Hospice?"

"Yeah. Maybe. Can you just come, Luke?"

"I'm on my way. I'll be there in fifteen minutes." He hung up and grabbed his keys. As he passed the reception desk, he told Fran what was going on. "I was already taking off for an appointment this afternoon, so I probably won't be back today. If Rich asks, I'll get those invoices out first thing tomorrow."

"Rich will understand. You go." The receptionist waved him off with a sympathetic smile.

He headed for his car in the KQOZ parking lot. But he wasn't so sure the station manager *would* understand. Luke was already almost a week behind on getting the ad billings out this month, and it wasn't like a radio station their size in a little town like Langhorne had money sitting in the bank. But he couldn't think about that now. Mateo needed him.

Maria needed him.

He'd have to figure out a way to slip away from Maria's this afternoon. If he missed his appointment with the attorney, who knew how long it would take to get in again. There apparently had been no cancellations, and he'd had to wait more than two weeks for this appointment.

After driving too fast across town to Maria's apartment near the university campus, he parked in the lot behind the two-bedroom unit where she and Mateo lived on the second floor. He locked his car and jogged up the stairs to their front door, dreading what he might find inside. If Maria had been dismissed from the ER and hospice had been called, there must not be anything else the doctors could do. Over the past two years, poor Mateo had been in hospitals—and now an ambulance—more times than Luke cared to count.

He raked a hand through hair that was in desperate need of a cut. This news shouldn't chill him the way it did. Surely, deep down, he'd known this day was coming. Sooner rather than later. But he'd let himself pretend otherwise. Pretend that Maria would be the exception to the grim statistics of this cancer. That some miracle would save her, if only because her son needed her so desperately.

His hands shook and his mind reeled. He had decisions to make that a man his age shouldn't have to think about. But then, no child Mateo's age should have to think about losing his mother either.

Luke knocked softly on the front door. Mateo opened it, releasing a gust of stale air into the spring morning. The smell of antiseptic cleaners assailed Luke as he stepped inside. And something worse—the coppery scent of blood.

He gave Mateo a quick one-armed hug, not wanting to make the reason for his visit appear overly grave. Though it obviously was. "Are you hanging in there, buddy?"

Mateo shrugged and looked up at him from beneath a black fringe of bangs.

Luke heard quiet voices coming from the short hallway that led to the bedroom across from Mateo's. "Is your mom conscious? Or . . . awake?"

"She was for a little bit." He tilted his head toward the hallway. "They won't let me go in."

"That's okay. They will soon. They're probably just getting her settled."

"They're cleaning up the blood."

"Oh." Luke's breath hitched that this kid could make such a statement about his mother without emotion. "It'll be okay." He kept his arm tight around the boy this time.

They were still standing side by side when a woman Luke didn't know appeared from the hallway. She carried an armful of wadded up sheets. Seeing Luke, she stopped. "I didn't realize anyone else was here."

He gave a nod. "I'm Lukas Blaine. Mateo is my 'Little'—in the Big Brothers Big Sisters program," he explained.

"Oh, yes. Maria said you'd be coming. Wonderful program, Big Brothers . . . It's so good you could be here." She gave him a knowing look before turning to Mateo. "You can go back and see your mom now. She might sound kind of groggy because of the medicine, but she's awake and asking for you."

Mateo looked up at Luke as though asking permission. Luke nodded. "I'll be right here. Take your time."

Mateo disappeared into Maria's room, closing the door behind him, and Luke met the hospice nurse's eyes. "Is it . . . getting close?"

Her expression answered before her voice did. "I'm afraid so. She's not in any pain, but she suffered a hemorrhage and they decided against another transfusion. At this point, it will just be a matter of keeping her comfortable."

"Mateo knows."

She looked taken aback. "Why do you think that?"

"He told me on the phone—he called when they returned from the hospital . . . He said they didn't know if she'd survive till morning. I think maybe he overheard one of the volunteers talking."

"Oh . . ." She shook her head. "I'm so sorry. They should have been more careful." She repositioned the load of bedding in her arms. "And I should have introduced myself. I'm Megan with hospice. Let me take care of this laundry and I'll be right back."

"You know where the laundry facility is?"

"Oh. No. I thought she had a washing machine in the apartment."

"I can take them. It's downstairs. On the ground floor." He fished some quarters out of his pocket.

"Are you sure? You'll want to . . . use cold water. And maybe some bleach."

"Luke?" Mateo poked his head out from Maria's bedroom door. "Mama wants to talk to you."

"You go on." The nurse nodded toward the hallway. "I'll find the laundry. Be right back."

Luke held out the coins to her, the erratic beat of his heart pounding in his ears.

Mateo held the bedroom door open for him. Luke stepped inside.

He'd only been in this room once, when she'd asked him to help her move a dresser. The nurse had put side rails on her bed. Or, on closer inspection, maybe this was a hospital bed. He couldn't recall what had been in the room before, but the space looked larger than he remembered. And Maria so much smaller.

Her complexion was ghostly pale, as though she were fading away right before his eyes. Her dark hair spread across the white pillowcase, her face turned toward the room's single window. But when Mateo closed the door, she rolled her head toward them.

Her gaze met Luke's before seeking out her son.

"Mutt?" Maria lifted a hand and groped for the bedrail.

It had taken Luke by surprise the first time he heard Maria call Mateo that. *Mutt.* "How do you spell that?" he'd asked.

"M-U-T-T. You know, like a puppy."

"Ahh."

"Some kids on the playground called him Mutt-teo . . ." Maria had giggled in that carefree way she'd had before cancer had stolen her laughter. And the chance to watch her son grow up. "I don't think he understood they were making fun. The boys at school all went by shortened first names, and Mateo just thought they'd given him a nickname too. He liked it, and it stuck, even though the teachers wouldn't let him use that name in class. I know it might sound . . . inappropriate, but I am glad he's the kind of kid who makes lemonade out of lemons."

Luke smiled at the memory. But he'd later learned that Mateo's questionable nickname was what caused Maria to learn to speak almost flawless English. "I don't ever want anyone to pick on my son because I don't speak correctly."

It made him sad to think that she'd ever worried for a minute that Mateo wouldn't be proud of her. He was. And all the more now that his mother had fought this cancer so bravely. She lost her hair during the first round of chemo, grew it back, then lost it again about a year ago. Ironically, now that the cancer had spread to her lungs and liver, her hair had grown back thicker and wavier than before, almost brushing her shoulders now. And she refused to pull it into the chignon she'd often worn before. "I won't ever take hair for granted again."

Mateo rose and hurried to her bedside, squatting down to meet his mother's gaze through the railing.

"Give us a minute, okay, baby? I want to . . . talk to Luke." Each word seemed an effort.

Luke dug in his back pocket for his wallet and handed Mateo a five-dollar bill. "Why don't you go get yourself a candy bar?" The kid was always begging to walk to the Rhodes station across from the nearby college campus. At first, Maria had been a nervous wreck each time until he returned, but she'd agreed he was old enough, and recently, it had been a help to be able to send him on short errands.

Mateo nudged his arm. "You want anything?"

Luke shook his head.

"Mama? You want anything."

"No thanks, baby." She tried to smile, but it came out more like a grimace. She didn't even give her usual warning for him to stay on the sidewalk and look both ways before he crossed the street. "You go on now. I'll see you in a few minutes."

He gave Luke a look that spoke volumes. A look that said he understood something out of the ordinary was going on.

Maria closed her eyes, but the minute the front door slammed, she reached for Luke's hand.

CHAPTER 7

THE ELEVATOR ACROSS THE HALL opened with a ding and Joanna looked up from her desk. Seeing Lukas Blaine step through the doors caused her pulse to skip an odd beat. She'd kept a wary eye on the hallway since returning from lunch, knowing he had an appointment with Trent this afternoon. And the man was as handsome as she remembered, despite the scowl he wore.

When he saw her, he offered a smile that could only be termed *obligatory*. "Is Mr. Pritchert's schedule . . . He's not running behind, is he?" He glanced at the clock on the wall behind the reception desk.

"He just got back from lunch. He's with a client, but you're his second appointment this afternoon, so it shouldn't be long."

"Thank you." His smile turned apologetic. "I really need to . . . be somewhere, so I was hoping I didn't have to wait too long."

"I understand. Please have a seat and I'll let you know the minute he's available." She indicated the grouping of leather chairs in the alcove across from her desk. "Could I get you a cup of coffee or a bottle of water while you wait?"

"I'm fine, thank you."

He walked over to the waiting area, but instead of taking a chair, he paced in front of the windows that overlooked the parking lot.

She stood and leaned over the high desk, hoping to catch his eye. When he didn't look her way, she cleared her throat. "I wanted to say again how thankful I am that you're able to DJ my sister's wedding after all."

"Oh?" He looked up as if not realizing she'd been talking to him. Then recognition dawned in his expression. "Oh, yes. Of course. I . . . I'm glad to. I talked to the groom about the power and he said the electric wasn't hooked up yet, but they were working on it."

"Oh, good. I'm glad you got hold of him. I know this was awfully late notice. But I hope it won't—" The buzzer on her desk rang and she held up a hand. She answered Trent's call, glad he wasn't making Lukas wait.

When she hung up, Lukas was watching her, a question on his face.

"You may go back now. You remember which office?"

"Yes. Thank you." Without another word, he strode down the hallway.

Jo felt oddly disappointed. And yet, she didn't think the man's aloof manner had been directed at her. He'd seemed . . . distressed about something, and in a hurry. But she had to admit that Trent's clients rarely aroused her curiosity the way this man had. No doubt it had more to do with his good looks than with his reasons for needing Trent's services. But she did wonder about how he'd come to be a DJ—and about his relationship with Maria Castillo.

The phone rang, shaking her from her daydreaming. But twenty minutes later when she heard Trent's office door open, she looked up to see an agitated Lukas rushing down the hall, his phone at his ear. She couldn't help but overhear his end of the conversation.

"I'm less than ten minutes away. It'll be okay."

He stopped and listened for a moment, then slipped into the alcove outside the restrooms, lowering his voice. "I know. I'm sorry. I should have been there."

Joanna tried not to listen, but the anguish in his tone compelled her. Was he talking to Maria Castillo?

"Shh . . . Shh . . . Listen to me. Stop! Listen." He lowered his voice. "Just wait until I get there, okay, buddy?"

Silence for another minute while he apparently listened. Then speaking as he walked. "Just stay there. I'm on my way right now. You stay right there, buddy. It's going to be okay." Not even looking in Jo's direction, he pushed the elevator button.

It opened almost immediately. He stepped in and jabbed at the panel on the wall, still speaking in a consoling tone. But now Joanna imagined it was a child he was speaking to. Maybe the son Maria Castillo had been so concerned about that day she'd caused such a stir? But as the doors closed, Jo stole another glance. And she could have sworn the poor man was weeping.

The elevator dinged and the phone on Joanna's desk rang simultaneously. Her breath caught.

For some reason, she felt paralyzed, almost the way she had that day with Maria.

Composing herself, she answered the call and transferred it to Cinda's office, operating on auto-pilot. She wasn't sure why she felt so invested in whatever was happening in this Lukas Blaine's life. But the way he'd spoken to the person on the other end of the phone had instantly endeared him to her.

She'd never wanted so badly to ask Trent about a client's circumstances. But she couldn't explain to herself, let alone to her boss, why she was so mesmerized by this man.

An elderly couple stepped off the elevator and shuffled toward the desk. She recognized them from previous visits, but had forgotten their names. She scrolled through the appointment calendar on her desktop before greeting the couple. "Good afternoon, Mr. and Mrs. Beaumont. Mr. Pritchert will be with you in just a moment. May I offer you some coffee or a glass of water?"

They waved off her offer and the gentleman proceeded to engage her in a long story . . . something about his brother and the farm their father had owned. She listened half-heartedly, nodding and smiling in what she hoped were appropriate places. But she couldn't stop thinking about Lukas. Or Luke, as he'd introduced himself on the phone last week.

She found herself praying that everything was okay with him. And suddenly it wasn't only because she needed him for Phee's wedding. Her heart went out to him. Having so recently lost her mother, she thought she'd recognized the pain of grief on his face. And whoever he'd been talking to on the phone, he loved deeply.

Once the elderly couple took their seats to wait for Trent, Joanna opened the browser on her computer and, on impulse, entered Luke's name. The website for MO-DJ where she'd first found his information popped up first in the search along with a website for a radio station in Langhorne, which listed him as a contact for advertising. There were several people with his name on Facebook, but none of them were him. The fact that he apparently kept a low profile on social media only served to make Jo more curious about him. And mildly cautious.

She started to click on a second page of search results, but stopped herself and closed the browser. "Good grief. Get a life, Joanna Chandler." She whispered the words louder than she intended and quickly checked the waiting room to be sure no one had heard.

But only the older couple was there, and they were engrossed in quiet conversation with each other. Jo watched them, touched by their gentle way with each other. Would she ever have someone who would love her for a lifetime, in sickness and in health, till death parted them?

Trent buzzed her, ready to see the Beaumonts. She walked the sweet couple back to his office, then came back to her desk, determined to keep her mind focused on work. No matter how much her thoughts kept straying to Luke Blaine.

Luke half expected to find an ambulance waiting at Maria's apartment, but everything looked as it had when he'd left. He didn't bother knocking but went straight in the front door.

Mateo flew off the couch and into his arms. "She died, Luke! She died!"

Luke swallowed hard, willing his voice to remain steady. "I know, buddy. I know. I'm so sorry."

The house was deathly silent, and he looked over his shoulder back toward the bedroom, wondering why they'd left Mateo alone. And whether they'd already come to take Maria away . . . take *her body*. He could not make the words be real. And if *he* couldn't, what must Mateo be feeling right now?

He heard muffled movements from the bedroom, and then a shadow fell across the hallway as someone opened the door.

The hospice nurse—Megan—walked down the hallway wearing a soft smile meant, Luke supposed, to convey sympathy. "I'm so sorry. Did Mateo tell you?"

"Yes. When did it happen?"

"Just a few minutes ago," she said softly, then glanced at her watch. "One forty-seven."

Luke closed his eyes and tightened his grip on Mateo. If only he'd canceled the appointment and stayed just a while longer. Not even an hour. Over Mateo's head, he mouthed to the nurse, "Was he with her?"

She nodded. "It was very peaceful. She just . . . fell asleep. Mateo was so brave. He was right there with her, praying her home."

The thought of Mateo praying for his mother as she left this earth was almost more than Luke could bear. As was recalling what Maria had said to him in their last few moments together, just the two of them. Swallowing hard, he moved his hands to the boy's shoulders and knelt to meet those dark, now-glassy eyes. "I'm so proud of you, buddy. I know your mama was proud too."

He shook his head and scrunched his face up, weeping silently.

"I'm so sorry I wasn't here with you."

The nurse's phone vibrated and she read a message, then gave Luke a knowing look. "You two might want to go for a drive for a little while."

Almost panicked, not wanting Mateo to see them take his mother's body out, Luke told the nurse, "We'll hang out at my place for a while. I'll give you a call later."

"Do you want me to stay with Mateo for a minute? So you can go back and . . . see her?" She motioned over her shoulder to the room where Maria lay.

But Luke had no desire to see her cold and lifeless. "I think we'll just go. Mateo's going to stay with me tonight. We'll come back and get some clothes and things later."

He wished he'd thought to have Mateo pack an overnight bag before he left for the attorney's office. He dreaded coming back here later. But he hadn't expected Maria to *die* while he was gone. Not yet. It still seemed unbelievable.

But even more unbelievable, he was now officially Mateo's guardian. Maria had asked him when she first got sick. And he agreed, never dreaming that her illness might be terminal. Never thinking he'd actually bear the sole responsibility for this boy who was at least six years from being grown and on his own.

But this morning, although she'd never made anything legal, she had begged Luke—made him promise he wouldn't let Mateo go into foster care. The scrap of paper in his pocket weighed heavily. Maria had written it in her own trembling hand, signing in front of the hospice nurse. It had ostensibly been made legal in the attorney's office not even an hour ago.

A simple sheaf of paper that might bind him to this boy for the rest of Mateo's childhood.

And he did love Mateo. He knew nothing about being a father, knew nothing of that kind of love, except what he'd received from his own father. But being on the receiving end of his father's love had been sufficient to make his heart well with emotion for this twelve-year-old who reminded him so much of himself at the same age.

Luke had loved Maria too. As a friend. As Mateo's mother. Judging by the weight of his heart right now, those things had bonded him to Maria more than he'd acknowledged. And while this thing he'd committed to in the presence of a witness seemed unfathomable, neither could he imagine letting Mateo be taken away by strangers. Especially when the boy had lost the only person in his world who loved him enough to comfort him.

Luke shook his head. He couldn't think about tomorrow. How would he ever keep the promises he'd made? He sighed and tightened his grip on Mateo's shoulders. They would figure things out. *Somehow.*

But tonight was for mourning.

CHAPTER 8

JO PLOPPED CROSS-LEGGED ON THE sofa and opened her laptop. "If I don't have a reply from that DJ, I am going to forget him and start looking for somebody else."

"Be nice, Jo. It's not even June yet." Phee carried the vase of flowers she'd just arranged over to the fireplace and set it on the mantel, moving some of the other knickknacks on the shelf.

Jo gave a little growl. "When you wake up tomorrow morning, Phylicia Chandler, it *will* be June and you will be twenty-four days away from becoming Phylicia Mitchell. It's just ridiculous that he hasn't gotten back to me yet."

She scrolled through her inbox, somehow not surprised that MO-DJ was absent from the list of new messages. "Okay. That does it. I'm calling."

She found the number in her previous calls and dialed. As it had the last time she tried to call a week ago, it went straight to voice mail. But a few seconds in, she realized the greeting message had changed. It was Lukas Blaine's voice, but this message lacked the chipper friendliness of the one that had played last time she'd called this number.

"Straight to voice mail again," she told Phee.

"Can you leave a message?"

"Another one, you mean?" She lifted a hand, listening, but only catching the greeting midway. ". . . apologize if you've been unable to get hold of us. We will be away from the office for a few days due to a death in the family. Please be assured we have not canceled any booked events and if you've left a message, I will get back to you as soon as possible."

She hung up, mildly shaken. "It said he'd had a death in the family."

"Oh no. Did he say who?"

"No. It was just a recording. But don't worry, he said he's not canceling any bookings and he'll get back to us as soon as possible."

"That's a relief. But how sad he had a death. I wonder who it was. Do you know anything about him? Is he married? Kids?"

"I don't think so." She told her sister about the connection between Lukas and the woman who'd had a breakdown in Trent's office that night. "I wonder if it was her. I think he referred to her as a friend. At least I didn't think they were related, but maybe I'm mistaken."

She should have been relieved at the reassurance they weren't canceling any bookings. And she was, but she couldn't get past the "death in the family" phrase. She quickly typed the Castillo woman's name into a Google search, adding "obituary" after the name.

The obituary section of the *Southeast Missourian* was the first link to pop up. She skimmed half a dozen obits looking for the name. "Oh. Here it is. Maria Castillo." She scrolled, skimming the text. "That woman died."

"Really? Does it say how?"

"Trent said she had cancer. She looked like death warmed over that night at the office." She wondered if Trent had heard that the woman died. Her boss hadn't talked about the incident since that night, but then Jo was only an administrative assistant and Trent and Cinda were both sticklers for confidentiality.

70

"So, how was she related to the DJ?"

"I'm looking . . ." She scanned the three short para-graphs, feeling bad for being angry that Luke hadn't returned her call. But there was no mention of Lukas in the obit. "It says she's survived by a son. Remember that's what she was ranting about? The son can't be very old though. She was only twenty-nine."

"Really? About my age?" Phee looked stricken. "Wow. That's young."

"I know. So sad." Melvin jumped up on the sofa and started the distinctive purr that said he wanted some atten-tion. Jo stroked him from head to tail, blowing the feather-light black-and-white hairs from her hands with each pass.

Phee frowned. "You're going to vacuum, I assume."

"Settle down. We don't have anyone coming until the weekend, right?"

"Yes, but I just vacuumed last night. I wasn't planning on doing it again before they come."

"Fine. I'll vacuum before they get here. Is it just one night?"

"Yes, and then we only have one booking before the wedding."

"That's because I blocked off the calendar."

"That early?" Phee's brow knit. "That's a long time to go without any income from the rentals."

"I don't care. We're doing okay money-wise, and we have too much to do to get you married off. Have you guys decided where you're going to live yet?"

Phee's smile was enigmatic. "I was going to talk to you about that. But let's wait for Britt. I don't want to have to explain everything twice."

"Can you at least give me a hint?"

"No. Britt should be home any time."

"Where is she anyway?"

"Book club."

"Oh, that's right. It's Wednesday night." She closed the

lid on her laptop. "So, how are the rest of the wedding plans coming?"

Phee shrugged. "Good, I think. There's not that much to do." She lifted her left hand and turned her wrist to and fro, admiring the dainty diamond engagement ring she'd gotten for her birthday two weeks ago.

"Not that much to do?"

"Well, it'll be crazy the week before the wedding. Baking cakes and getting everything ready to haul up to the clearing. But it's not like there's a lot we can do until then."

"You could clean up the clearing so people can get up there."

"Don't worry, Jo. We've got it all under control. Quinn has a crew coming up this weekend to take care of that. And they won't even let us pay them. They're saying it's their wedding gift to us."

Jo felt a measure of relief at that news. "Remember, Dad suggested we use Mom's memorial money to fix up the clearing. I think it's a great idea, especially since Britt and I might want to get married there too."

Dad had bent over backward to prove to Phee that he loved her equally whether she was his biological daughter or not. It made Joanna love and admire her father more deeply than ever, even if it made her just a bit jealous of the special attention Dad had showered on Phee since the discovery that he might not be her birth father.

Phee frowned. "That's really sweet of Dad to suggest that. But cleanup is the tip of the iceberg. We'll need lights and seating—and probably some work on the stairs. Aren't you a little afraid people will think it's kind of selfish to use the money to set up the venue? I mean, it might look like we're just using it to fund our own weddings. Or *my* wedding."

"I can't imagine anyone would dream *you* could have a selfish bone in your body, Phee. And that money was given freely to remember Mom however we see fit. No one is going to judge how we choose to spend it. I think Mom would have loved that it went toward our weddings. Besides, who knows, we may end up with an actual wedding venue in that clearing and it would benefit a lot more young brides."

"I thought about that, but wow . . . that would be a *lot* of work, Jo. We'll see what Britt thinks. I guess I'd feel better if you were both engaged, too, and we could tell people we're all getting married there."

"Well, don't hold your breath waiting on me." Jo scoffed. "And it's nobody's business, Phee. Don't even worry about what *people* will think."

Phee shrugged. "I suppose you're right. But it's easier said than done."

The sound of tires on gravel made them both turn toward the front door.

"That'll be Britt." Jo was curious about Phee's news and glad her sister hadn't been late getting home.

Britt blew in, her face flushed. "You guys should be glad I'm not in jail."

"What are you talking about?" Jo went to take the bags of groceries from her drama queen sister.

"I came this close to killing a couple people at book club tonight."

"Britt! You did not." Jo used her mother-hen tone but couldn't help laughing. She didn't know why Britt stayed in her book club when it got her so riled up every time they gathered.

"Some of those people are so dense! They wouldn't know irony if it hit them over the head." Britt tossed her purse on the kitchen table and came back to join Jo on the sofa. She looked from Jo to Phee and frowned. "So, what's up? You two look like something's going on."

"I'm just waiting for the big reveal."

"Reveal?" Britt looked between them.

"Phee's going to tell us about her and Quinn's plans."

Phee moved to the easy chair by the fireplace. "I guess I'm not really telling you, I'm asking you."

"Us?"

"Quinn and I have been talking and we'd like to build a house on the other side of the cabins."

Britt's eyes went big and her mouth hung open.

Jo laughed because she knew her own expression must look the same. "Seriously? Oh, Phee! That would be so awesome!"

"We thought we could let the new house be one of the main Airbnb offerings for The Cottages on Poplar Brook Road. We'd be able to charge a lot more for it since it'll be new, and it will have a waterfront view too." Phee winced. "Well, at least until the next drought. Anyway, Quinn and I can stay in one of the cottages any time our house is booked."

Jo eyed Phee, trying to gauge whether she was really okay with that. Her perky nod said she was wholly in agreement.

But then, Jo suspected her sister would live in a tent pitched in the lane as long as Quinn was there.

"That would be totally amazing, Phee!" Britt bounced on her heels, her hair bobbing.

"Perfect!" Jo said. "I was already hating the thought of you leaving us. But what about Quinn's house?"

"We'll live there while our house is being built out here. I'll help him get everything finished in his house and get it ready to list, and then we'll move out here. That way you guys can each have your own place and we'll always have one place free to rent."

"This is just perfect, Phee!" Britt beamed.

"Well, you know how much Quinn loves this property. I was hoping you guys would be willing to let us stay here."

"Are you kidding? I couldn't be happier." Her burden lifted. She hadn't realized how much she was going to miss having her sister on the property. "I figured you guys would just live in his house."

"I would have been okay with that. I really would have.

74

But since Quinn started out building it with an old girlfriend in mind, he wanted us to have something that was just for us."

"How sweet. He's a keeper, that guy." Jo sighed and those troublesome twinges of jealousy came again. *Your turn will come, Joanna Chandler.* Maybe if she told herself that often enough, it would eventually take. She only hoped she could find someone half as thoughtful and kind as her sister's fiancé.

Phee wrapped her arms around herself and echoed Jo's sigh. "He is *such* a keeper. And I'm so glad you guys are okay with us building here. I can't wait to tell Quinn."

"Phee . . ." Britt beamed. "Was there ever any doubt?"

Phylicia looked sheepish. "I was *pretty* sure you guys would be happy about it. But the looks on your faces said more than any words ever could."

"I'm so excited!" Britt clapped her hands. "That means we'll get to live next door to any *little* Mitchells that might come along."

"Well, Lord willing, we won't make you wait too long. We're not exactly spring chickens."

"Oh, cut it out, sis," Jo huffed. "Thirty isn't exactly ready-for-the-nursing-home either."

"Well, *I'm* not, but Quinn is getting up there in years." Phee giggled, but quickly turned serious. "I'm so happy it scares me, you guys."

"Scares you? Why?" Jo went to sit on the edge of her sister's chair. "Is everything okay?"

Tears welled in Phee's eyes. "Everything is amazing. More amazing than I could have ever dreamed just a few months ago. I miss Mom. I wish she could be here to share this time, of course, but I've started to feel a real peace about . . . everything that happened."

Britt nodded and Jo knew what they meant. This wasn't the life they would have asked for . . . losing their mother at such a young age, Dad moving away and not being as big a part of their lives as he had been. But God was good, and

He had provided this beautiful spot for them to live. They'd become closer than ever since Mom's death, and now, with Quinn and Phee moving out here to the property, they'd get to stay together—at least until the next one of them got engaged.

Jo's heart overflowed. But even as it did, she couldn't help thinking of Lukas—and that desperate woman who'd died so young, leaving behind a motherless child. She still wondered what Luke's connection was to them—but it must be significant if he'd taken time off from work on their account. Jo wasn't sure why those people—practically strangers—had captured her heart so, but she whispered a prayer for the families involved, that God would see them through this tragic season, even as He had seen her family through.

CHAPTER 9

June

JO STARED AT THE PAGE on the wall calendar behind her desk and panic rose in her throat. *June*. Already. The month her sister was getting married. Twenty-four days from now to be exact. Phee seemed calm as the proverbial cucumber, which was wonderful. *For Phee!* Jo sucked in a deep, calming breath—that didn't quite work. Why had she agreed to be her sister's unofficial wedding planner? The thought of letting something important fall through the cracks almost paralyzed her.

Thankfully, work hadn't been as busy as usual, and Trent had given her permission to work on wedding tasks in her downtime. It was past noon and she still hadn't heard back from Luke about DJing the wedding. Quinn said he hadn't been contacted either, not since he'd first talked to Luke about the electric.

Luke's voice mail message had given her confidence that he intended to fulfill his commitments despite the death in the family. She hesitated to call him too soon given his circumstances, but she couldn't wait long. She had questions that needed answering before she could move forward with *her* plans. Not to mention if he *did* bail on them, they would need time to make other arrangements.

She checked Trent's appointment calendar and saw she had a few minutes before his next client arrived. She slipped off her headset, grabbed her phone, and pulled up the phone number for MO-DJ.

She didn't even have time to be nervous. He answered on the second ring. "Joanna. I am so sorry I haven't gotten back to you. I truly was planning to give you a call this afternoon."

"No problem. I just had a few minutes and thought I'd call while I was thinking of it. And I know the past few days must have been busy—and hard—for you. I was so sorry to hear about Maria . . . Mrs. Castillo's death."

His sigh filled a momentary silence. "Thank you. It's been . . . very difficult."

Now it was her turn and as the silence stretched, she reached for what to say next, wondering if she dared ask the question foremost on her mind. "Forgive me if I'm prying, but I didn't realize she was related. Or . . . maybe I misunderstood?"

"No . . . Maria wasn't related exactly. Her son is my Little— in the Big Brothers Big Sisters program."

"I see." Jo nodded to herself, the picture beginning to make more sense. "And again, I'm so sorry. How old is her son?"

"Mateo is twelve. She was the only close relative he had. She was only twenty-nine. A year younger than I am." His voice faded as if he were talking to himself.

"Oh, that's so tragic. My oldest sister is the same age as you. What . . . what will happen with him?" If he went into foster care, that might affect whether Luke got to see the boy or not.

"We don't know yet. For now . . . he's staying with me."

"Really?" She hadn't meant to sound so . . . incredulous. But she was. That a thirty-year-old single guy would take on the care of an almost-teenager when their only connection was a program like Big Brothers? That was rare. And it made her wonder again what Luke's relationship with Maria Castillo had been.

"There weren't many options. Now, about your sister's wedding . . ."

"Yes, of course." Jo felt rebuked, and deservedly so, but she sensed it would only make things worse if she apologized. "Are you still going to be able to DJ the reception?"

"I'm definitely planning on it. Unless you've decided to go with someone else."

"Oh no. We're counting on you, if you can still do it."

"Great. What I'd like to do is meet you at the venue some-day next week for a walk-through. Just so I can see where you want me to set up, double-check that the electrical meets our needs, and go over the music the bride has selected. If the bride and groom can be there, that's preferable."

"I'll talk to them and get back to you about a time that works for all of us. What is your schedule like? Can you do after-work hours?"

He gave a little laugh. "Sadly, after-work hours is all I *can* do. I still have to keep a day job to support my DJ habit."

"That should work great for us then. Do you have some-thing maybe next Thursday or Friday? A week from today?"

A pause. She pictured him leafing through a calendar smudged with coffee rings and potato-chip grease.

"Looks like either of those dates would work. Why don't you just text me at this number once you've talked to the couple, and I'll get you on my calendar for the walk-through."

"Perfect. Is . . . is there an extra charge for that? The walk-through?"

"Oh no . . . it's all included in the package you selected."

"That's great. Thanks so much. I'll text you when I have a date."

"I'll watch for it. Um . . ." He paused. "Would you mind if I bring Mateo—Maria's son—with me to the walk-through?

He's old enough to stay home for a short time, but I haven't wanted to leave him alone so soon after his mother's death."

"Oh, of course. That's not a problem."

"I can ask your sister, if you'd rather. He's very well-behaved and won't be any trouble."

"I'm sure Phylicia will be fine with that. Just count on bringing him."

"Thank you for understanding. That means a lot."

She could have sworn the man's voice broke. This whole thing had to be beyond stressful for him. And Jo truly didn't mind the boy coming for the walk-through, but she hoped Luke wouldn't bring him to the wedding. She'd seen too many weddings upstaged by unruly kids. Some people had a pretty broad definition of "well-behaved." Ah well, they'd cross that bridge when they came to it. At least the DJ was set. One huge thing to cross off her to-do list for the wedding.

"Mateo?" Luke poked his head in the door of the room they'd designated as Mateo's bedroom—a small room that had been Luke's den, but they'd fit his bunk bed from the apartment at one end and a small desk and chair at the other. "Hey, buddy, I told you to put your phone down. It's lights-out time."

Without looking up, the boy scooched down on the pile of pillows in the lower bunk where he reclined. "I just have to finish this level." His thumbs danced across the smartphone's screen.

"No. You've had time to finish ten levels." Luke waited, his patience waning. "Hey. Look at me."

"Wait! Just one more minute. I'm about to get another coin."

"Mateo." His voice came out sharper than he'd intended.

Tears welled in the large brown eyes, but just as quickly

Mateo's face turned red with rage. He slammed the phone down on the bed. "It's your fault!"

Luke stilled, not sure if Mateo was talking about the video game . . . or his mother's death. It had been a rough couple of weeks, and Luke had seen behavior in the boy that he hadn't seen since he'd first been matched as Mateo's Big five years ago. He entered the room and scooped up some dirty laundry from the floor. "You can play more tomorrow. Tonight you need to get some sleep. Did you brush your teeth?"

"I told you I did."

"Okay. Just checking. Good night, buddy." He gave the bony knee under the blanket a pat and started to leave the room. But he *couldn't* just leave it at this. He had to acknowledge the boy's feelings, even if they weren't expressed appropriately. "Listen, I know this is hard. And I'm truly sorry. I miss your mom too. You're going to miss her . . . always. But it will get easier. I promise."

"I don't want it to." Mateo glared at him from beneath too-long bangs.

Luke made a mental note to schedule haircuts for both of them. He sat down at the foot of the bed, careful not to hit his head on the upper bunk. "What do you mean?"

"I don't want it to get easier. I don't want to forget her. I don't want—" His face scrunched up and the tears fell in awful silence.

Luke's gut clenched. He'd never been so in-over-his-head. He didn't have a clue how to comfort a grieving child. Or how to help this boy move forward. Mateo said he didn't want to forget, yet he was burying himself in mindless video games. Maybe they needed to find a counselor. *They?* There was no they. He was in this alone.

He clutched Mateo's foot through the blanket. "It hurts to remember. I know that. But that part *will* get easier. And you won't ever forget your mama, bud. Never. She's part of you, part of who you are. We . . . we'll find ways to remember her. Maybe we can start a list tomorrow."

"Wonderful world."

"Huh?"

"That song she liked. The guy with the scratchy voice."

"Oh yeah." Luke smiled, the memory sweet. "Louis Armstrong. Top of the list." He rose and straightened the covers over Mateo's feet. "You be thinking about what else goes on that list. It'll be a long one. We'll write it all down. We can start tomorrow."

That seemed to comfort the boy. Luke wasn't sure where it had come from . . . No, he *did* know. *Thank You, Lord.* He was going to be tight with his heavenly Father in the days ahead. That, he knew.

CHAPTER 10

J O STOOD ON THE FRONT porch of the cottage, watching the lane for Luke's vehicle, her nerves growing more taut with every minute. She didn't know why she was so nervous. This was simply a walk-through.

Phee and Quinn were already up at the clearing waiting for them. Quinn had supervised running electric up to the site and insisted that the sisters all be there when they tested it out last night. They'd taken an old electric boom box Jo had kept from her junior high days up to the clearing. They put a CD in and turned the volume as loud as it would go.

The woodland meadow filled with the majestic strains of Pachelbel's "Canon in D" and they cheered and pranced down the imaginary aisle in the forested area that had recently been cleared by a Bush Hog and some other piece of machinery that had turned the ground under the canopy of trees into a carpet of soft mulch.

Having the clearing transformed in the space of an afternoon had Jo thinking even more seriously about creating a wedding venue on the property. She could already picture the smaller cabin at the base of the stairway serving as a dressing room for the bride. The cabin's stone edifice would be gorgeous in wedding photos. And the fourteen wide board steps that led up to the clearing would create a wonderful grand entrance for any bride. Of course, it would be a major undertaking to get one hundred rented chairs up those same stairs if anyone wanted a larger wedding than Phee's. She'd have to think some more on that.

The sound of a car's engine interrupted the planning "meeting" that was taking place in her head. She laughed nervously at that thought and took a deep breath, not wanting Luke to see how uneasy she was. And not just about wedding details. This man rattled her. In the best possible way. She didn't think it was only his masculine good looks—although there *was* that—but something about his mannerisms and the smooth cadence of his voice attracted her deeply. And that smile. It crinkled the corners of his eyes and lit his whole countenance.

He wore it now as he waved through the windshield.

Jo motioned for him to park beside her car at the far end of the cottage. He got out and a boy with straight black hair and olive skin emerged from the passenger side.

Smiling, Luke strode toward her. "I'm glad this worked out." He put his hands on the boy's shoulders and guided him forward, then reached out a hand to Jo.

She accepted, finding his grip strong and certain.

"Joanna," he continued. "This is Mateo. Mateo, this is Miss Joanna."

Jo shook the boy's sweaty hand. "Hi, Mateo. It's nice to meet you."

"Hi," he mumbled, shuffling his feet and not quite meeting her eyes. Though with the long bangs covering them, Jo wasn't sure how he could see anything.

She wondered if she should offer condolences on his mother, but decided against it, knowing how she would have felt at that age.

Looking past him to Luke, Joanna pointed up to the clearing. "The bride and groom are already up there, so if you're ready, you can follow me."

"Let me grab some equipment." He gave Mateo's shoulders an almost fatherly pat. "Can you help me carry stuff, buddy?"

The boy looked relieved to have something to occupy him. Once they'd unloaded two duffel bags from Luke's car, Jo led the way up the stairs to the clearing. "Is this going to be a problem to have to carry all your stuff up here? Sadly, this is the only way up."

Luke was barely breathing hard, though Mateo had sweat beading at his temples.

"If you have a table already set up for us the day of the wedding, we can probably get everything up in two or three trips. Especially if I have my first-rate assistant here. Or I can bring my own table . . ."

Joanna didn't respond, caught unaware to learn that the boy would likely be coming. He seemed like a nice kid though. And quiet. Luke surely wouldn't be taking him to weddings if he couldn't trust him to behave. Unless Quinn or Phee objected, she would keep her mouth shut.

Quinn must have heard them coming because he met them at the top of the stairs and shook hands with Luke and Mateo in turn. Jo and Phee stood by while Quinn showed Luke where they would set up and helped him plug in the equipment he'd brought. He controlled the system from his phone, and when the heavy beat of a rap song blared from the small speakers Luke had set on the log benches, Jo and Phee jumped a foot in the air, clapping their hands over their ears.

Mateo burst out laughing, then covered his mouth, as though he feared they'd be upset. But when Luke and Quinn broke up, so did Jo and Phee, and soon they were all laughing and jiving to the music.

Luke lowered the volume and turned to Phee. "I'll have better speakers the day of the wedding, obviously—"

"And different songs, I hope?" Phee gave a comical cringe. "I'm more Barry Manilow than Jay-Z."

"Oh dear." Luke's expression turned somber. "I'm afraid I have a very strict no-Barry-Manilow policy."

"Hear, hear!" Quinn cheered. "Please, whatever you do, no 'Mandy.'"

Phee laughed. "Let's say those are the two extremes on the spectrum. Can you give us something in between?"

Luke smiled. "You got it. And actually, I think Joanna sent me your list . . . heavy on classical and soft jazz, am I right?"

"Exactly." Phee threw Jo a grin. "You're one step ahead of me, sis."

Jo jostled her sister's shoulder. "Somebody has to be."

"And more importantly, I have a list of songs *not* to play."

"Jay-Z at the top of that list," Phee teased.

"And Barry Manilow." Luke grinned and nodded to Quinn in male solidarity, then consulted his phone. "Just making sure I have this right. You'd rather not have a lot of banter from me. So, except for the introductions and special dances, you just want the music to play continuously and not too loud?"

"That's right." Jo and Phee spoke simultaneously.

"I want people to be able to visit over the music," Phee said.

"See there." Jo grinned at her. "I know you pretty well."

Quinn pulled a face and nodded at Luke. "It's downright scary is what it is."

Luke laughed. He had a nice laugh and an easy way about him that Jo hadn't seen before today.

He played a sampling of songs, showing them how the transitions and what he called "mash-ups" would sound. He asked Quinn and Phee a few more questions about how they wanted things to go. With nods and smiles, he made Jo feel a part of the conversation too.

Mateo had wandered over to the top of the stairway, and she could just see the top of his head and what appeared to be a makeshift sword that he'd fashioned from a fallen branch. He struck the trunk of a large oak, making Star Wars sounds with his mouth. *Ah . . . correction.* Jo smiled. A light saber, not a sword. Probably a typical kid. But it struck her that she hadn't really been around kids that much in the past few years. Trent and Cinda's daughters were college age now, and she rarely saw them. And she really didn't hang out with anyone who had younger kids.

When Mateo's unintelligible noises got louder, Luke looked up from his phone and hollered. "Hey, buddy. Keep it down a little, would you?"

Mateo didn't acknowledge him but did lower his voice.

"He's cute," Phee whispered.

Jo wondered if Luke detected the sympathy in her sister's voice. He hadn't told her not to say anything about his guardianship of Mateo, but she cringed a little, worrying that Phee might mention what Jo had told her—which was everything. Well, except for how strongly attracted she was to Lukas Blaine.

Mateo's voice rose again and Luke quieted him with a soft "hey." It only took five minutes for the kid's volume to go up again, reminding Jo why she didn't like the idea of kids at weddings.

Still, she felt for Mateo. Watching him play like a typical twelve-year-old, it was strange to realize that he'd so recently suffered a great tragedy. She looked between Luke and Mateo and wondered how much longer Luke would have charge of him. She couldn't imagine such a burden being placed on a man Luke's age. Especially with him being single. She was impressed with how well he seemed to be handling it—and that he managed to keep working. He'd make a great dad someday. Still, it must be overwhelming to tackle it alone and with someone who wasn't a relative.

Dusk was descending by the time they started back down the stairway. Quinn carried the bag Mateo had lugged up the stairs and helped Luke load things back into his car. The four of them stood out in the yard talking while Mateo kicked stones up and down the driveway, looking bored.

Jo considered asking them in for something to drink, but before she could mention it, Luke called Mateo over.

"We'd better get you home, bud. You've got soccer practice in the morning."

"Nice to meet you, Mateo." Jo gave a little wave.

"Yeah. You too." He didn't smile, but at least he met her eyes this time.

She turned to Luke. "Thanks so much for coming out. I feel ten times better about how everything is coming together now."

"Me too," Phee said. "Thank you, Luke. Maybe now my sister will quit nagging me about the music."

He laughed. "I always tell people—not just so they don't faint when they get my bill—that the music is the biggest piece of the pie when it comes to the reception. And you guys are making it easy on me. I don't even have to perform."

"Oh? Do you sing or something?" Confusion clouded Phee's tone.

"Oh, no . . ." Luke shook his head and held his hands up palms out. "Not in public. I just meant—"

"He sings in the shower," Mateo blurted. "I can hear him all the way in my room."

They all laughed and Luke looked embarrassed. He pulled the boy into a playful headlock and gave him a good scalp rub before letting him go. "I just meant the DJ banter I sometimes do. But not always," he added quickly. "A lot of brides are like you and just want their guests to be able to visit and relax. At the risk of shooting myself in the foot, I think those are the best weddings. And wow, with the spot you have for this wedding, you don't need some so-called entertainer distracting from that."

"It really is a pretty spot, isn't it?" Phee glanced up toward the woods. The starry look in her eyes told Jo her sister was dreaming of her wedding day.

"I wish you could have seen it up there a couple of days ago before Quinn got the brush cleared out." Jo was tempted to ask him if he thought they could rent the place out as a wedding venue. But she decided better of it. Phee already thought her idea was a little . . . ambitious. No sense in complicating things tonight. But she made a mental note to ask him next time the opportunity presented itself.

"Well, I had help thinning things out." Quinn described the crew he'd assembled to clean up the jungle that had taken over beneath the canopy of trees, and Luke happened to know some of the men, which started a conversation about acquaintances the two men had in common.

After a few minutes, Mateo tugged at Luke's shirt sleeve. "I thought we were leaving."

Luke gave him a stern look. "In a few minutes. Please don't interrupt."

"But you said—"

"Mateo, you go wait in the car. I'll be there in a minute." The boy didn't budge.

"Mateo. What did I say?"

He gave a low growl, but started moving toward the car. Slowly though. Very slowly.

Luke gave an apologetic shrug. "I'd better get going. It's really nice to be working with you guys. Don't hesitate to give me a call if you have any questions. I'll be in touch a day or two before the wedding just to make sure everything's set."

"Sounds good. But it seems like you have everything under control." Quinn shook Luke's hand, and the three of them stood and watched while he drove away.

When the taillights disappeared around the curve in the lane, Quinn let out a breath and put an arm around Phee. "Man, I don't envy that poor guy. Can you imagine becoming guardian to a twelve-year-old *overnight* like that?"

"He seems like he's handling it really well though." Phee rolled her eyes. "Most guys his age still act like twelve-year-olds themselves."

Jo frowned. "It sounds like Luke plans to have Mateo help him when he does you guys's wedding. Are you comfortable with that?"

"Sure." Phee looked to Quinn. "Are you, babe?"

"I don't see why not."

Jo winced. She'd halfway hoped Phee or Quinn would object. She had no doubt Luke would do a great job deejaying the wedding, but she worried that the kid would somehow mess things up. "I just hope he's not in a surly mood like he was tonight."

"Yeah, he reminded me of *you* when you were twelve." Phee poked Jo's shoulder.

"Yeah, right. You don't even remember that long ago. And I happen to know I was never surly at any age."

"Except maybe the age you are now?" Quinn teased.

Jo feigned a frown. "I know when I'm not wanted. I'm going to bed."

Quinn laughed, but then sobered. "I need to get out of here too. I'm supposed to be at work by six thirty tomorrow."

"Why so early?" Phee asked.

"Because I'm taking off early. I have a hot date."

"It had better be with me."

"Well, duh. I don't know who else it would be."

"Good." Phee gave Quinn a squeeze before extricating herself from his arms. "See you tomorrow night?"

"I'll pick you up around seven." He brushed a strand of hair out of her eyes and leaned to kiss her.

Jo may as well have been invisible, and again, that green-eyed monster reared its head. She was truly happy for them, but that didn't make it any easier to be the fifth wheel. She took a step backward toward the house. "Good night, you two."

"Good night, Jo."

They even spoke in unison. She smiled, but her heart felt oddly heavy and . . . empty . . . as she walked back to the cottage. Maybe she was just missing Mom. And Dad. Or maybe she was just sad that her sister was getting married, and that nothing would ever really be the same after that day.

Who was she kidding? Things had already changed between them. Maybe the ache fanning out in her chest was a stubborn remnant of the pain she'd felt for Ben when they first broke up. Or perhaps her sadness stemmed from the great loss Mateo had experienced. It was hard enough to have lost her own mother at twenty-six. She couldn't begin to fathom what it would have been like to have lost Mom as a preteen. And the burden Luke now bore because of the boy? How had that even come to be?

Still, what she was feeling seemed more . . . *personal*. Maybe she was just good old-fashioned *lonely*. And why not, when it seemed everyone who'd once filled her days was no longer in her life.

CHAPTER 11

JO PACED THE LENGTH OF the kitchen for the third time and peered out the window that looked over the river. It was still too early to tell, but the sky looked awfully dark to the east. *Please, Lord . . . Please don't let it rain!*

They did have a contingency plan to have the wedding at Quinn's church, but in Jo's eyes, that was not at all satisfactory. They'd worked so hard to make everything perfect up at the clearing, and Phee wanted an outdoor wedding. Every evening this week the sisters had worked together to finish yards of flouncy rag garland crafted from paper hearts and little scraps of linen they'd torn from some old curtains Mom had sewn for the bedroom they shared as little girls. Phee had come up with the idea for the garland after she found the old curtains in a box Dad had brought for them to sort through.

Jo had to admit it was the perfect touch. Woven amongst the branches in the clearing along with strings of twinkle lights, the garland fluttered in the breeze like a kaleidoscope of butterflies. Now, to think all the work they'd done to get things ready might go to waste because of a little rain made her queasy.

Of course, they had a large tent set up in the clearing

under the canopy of the woods, but too much rain would make it next to impossible to even get up to the clearing. Not to mention, where would sixty-some guests—as many as fifteen or twenty vehicles—park if the lane was muddy?

"What are you doing up so early?"

Jo whirled at the deep voice, and instantly a smile came. "Good morning, Dad! Did you sleep okay? The paint fumes didn't make you sick?" He'd stayed in the cabin that was still in the process of being "fixer-uppered," as Quinn called it. The other cabin wasn't anywhere close to finished, but it was farther along and was the one they were using as a dressing room for the wedding—assuming it didn't rain.

"I slept fine. I still can't get over my daughters, the land barons. You girls did a great thing when you bought this property."

"I really love it. And I'm so glad Quinn and Phee are going to build here."

"Maybe I'll do the same someday. If you girls would let me."

Joy bubbled up inside her. "Oh, Dad! That'd be the best."

"Well now, don't hold your breath. Someday could be twenty years from now."

She slumped her shoulders. "Way to get a girl's hopes up and then drop her like a rock."

He laughed. "You three are doing just fine without me."

"Maybe, but we'd all be a lot happier if you weren't so far away."

He shrugged. "We'll see."

"Are you ready for coffee?"

"Always. But I can make it. Just show me where everything is."

"Oh, no . . . I set it up last night. Should start brewing any minute."

"I think my coffeemaker has that auto setting too. I just haven't taken the time to figure out how to make it work yet. You'll have to show me."

94

How she'd missed him! Dad had flown in from Florida on Thursday, and seeing Phee on his arm as they rehearsed under the tent last night had brought tears to her eyes.

If the wedding went anything like rehearsal, it would be a roaring success, and they'd had so much fun afterward. It was only the small wedding party, Dad, Quinn, Phee's friends who were doing the music for the ceremony, the pastor and his wife, and Quinn's brother and his wife and their darling little girl. Haley wasn't quite old enough to handle flower girl duties, but she'd kept them all entertained, swaying and prancing to the music and sharing cookies with anyone who would eat "just one mo'." She did worry a little about Quinn's brother. Phee had intimated that Markus might have a problem with alcohol, and Jo suspected he'd been drinking last night even though no liquor had been served at the rehearsal. She shook the thought away. She had plenty to worry about without adding Quinn's brother to the list.

"Hey, you. That frown is ruining your pretty face. What are you worrying about now?"

Jo shook away the worrisome thoughts and forced a smile. "Oh, just . . . *everything*."

Dad laughed, hovering by the coffeemaker, empty cup in hand. "So, what do you need me to do? I'm at your service."

"I need you to pray it doesn't rain."

He put an arm around her shoulder. "If it rains, everything will still be fine. Not a thing you can do about it, so no sense worrying."

"Easier said than done, Padre."

"I get that." He gave her a squeeze, then let out a little cheer when the coffeemaker sputtered to life. He patted the machine. "Here . . . This'll help."

She laughed and went for her own mug.

"I'm surprised Phee isn't up yet."

"I'm up!" Phylicia sashayed into the kitchen, hair in a towel. Melvin traipsed behind her, batting at the loose belt of her robe. "You didn't think I'd sleep in on my wedding day, did you?"

Dad greeted Phee with a hug, then stooped to scratch behind Melvin's ears.

Jo gave an inward sigh. Everything was like it had been before Dad moved to Florida to be with that woman—Karleen. It was a rash thing he had done, starting a relationship with one of Mom's hospice nurses so soon after Mom's death. He'd apologized to them all and assured them it was over between him and Karleen—that his actions had been a result of grief and loneliness.

But Phee had told Jo and Britt about Karleen coming into the flower shop where Phee worked to order flowers for the family of a hospice patient. It worried Jo to learn that the woman was still here in Cape Girardeau. She couldn't let herself think about what might happen if Dad ran into her while he was here. Still, he was more like his old self again, and it seemed like he was truly happy with his life in Florida. She tossed up a little prayer of thanks. For Phee's sake especially.

"Are you nervous, sis?"

"Not one tiny bit." Phee beamed, then tilted her head, eyeing Jo. "Are you?"

"If it doesn't rain, I'll be fine."

"And you'll be fine if it does rain. Not a thing we can do about it, so no use worrying."

Dad and Jo exchanged a look and burst out laughing.

"What?" Phee looked from one to the other, her brow furrowed. "What did I say?"

"Just word-for-word what Dad said five minutes ago when I mentioned rain."

Phee looked up at Dad, her face brimming with love for him. "I am my father's daughter."

The look he gave her in return said, *that settles it.*

And in that moment, Jo decided that even if it did rain, she wasn't going to waste another minute worrying about it. The first Chandler sister was getting married today and wherever it happened, and under whatever skies God ordained, that was just fine with her.

"Do you, Phylicia, take this man to be your wedded husband, to have and to hold, from this day forward, for better or for worse, for richer or for poorer, in sickness and in health, until death parts you?"

Jo stood close behind her sister, holding her bridesmaid's nosegay in one hand and in the other, Phee's huge bridal bouquet that had been a gift from her boss at the flower shop. The rain had held off and, although the skies were gray, Phee's smile made up for any lack of sunshine.

Her sister was radiant with her hair in an old-fashioned French braid and a crown of baby's breath in lieu of a veil.

Tears had flowed down Dad's cheeks as he gave Phee away, and Jo knew that everyone under this tent had noticed the gaping hole when his answer to "Who gives this woman . . ." had been a simple "I do," rather than the traditional "her mother and I" that so many took for granted.

There was a candle burning on the makeshift altar in honor of Mom, and the rag garland fluttering overhead had Mom's fingerprints all over it. Jo hoped Phee felt their mother's presence as much as she did. Like Dad said, Mom lived on in her three daughters. As Quinn and Phee pledged to love and honor each other, Jo determined to make Mom proud and to be as much like the woman who'd raised her as she could possibly be. Though in this moment, that seemed an impossible task.

Phee had carefully planned the timing of the ceremony so that Pastor Franklin would pronounce Quinn and Phylicia man and wife just as the sun began to set. But she couldn't possibly have planned what actually happened. A little gasp went up from the guests as the sun broke through the haze just in time to sink slowly behind the hills in a blaze of sherbet colors. Pink and orange light bathed the tent as Quinn kissed his bride.

Seconds later, tiny lights began to twinkle like starlight in a wave that swept from the back of the tent forward. Jo cheered under her breath, and she knew Phee and Britt were doing the same. She and her sisters and Quinn had practiced the effect with a timer at least a dozen times in secret, and as they'd hoped, it was magical. *More* than magical coming on the tail of the sunset God provided.

The string quartet lifted their instruments and the recessional began. And just like that, Phylicia was no longer technically a Chandler. She was a Mitchell now. And that was a lovely thing. Still, Jo fought tears that weren't entirely happy ones.

Pasting on a smile, she handed Phee her bouquet, knelt to straighten the hem of her sister's simple bridal gown, and cheered with the rest of the loved ones beneath the tent. She took the arm of Quinn's brother, the best man, and followed the bride and groom to the rear of the tent.

They'd taken pictures earlier, so now, while guests mingled at the edges of the clearing, the plan was for the sisters to meet back in the cabin that had served as their dressing room and wait while the caterers brought in the dessert table and Quinn's friends set up the small makeshift dance floor they'd built. Then they'd make their grand entrance. Jo had asked them to put the flooring in storage after tonight because she still had hopes of renting out the clearing as a wedding and reception venue.

As they descended the steps built into the side of the hill—lit tonight with myriad twinkle lights—she caught a glimpse of Luke's truck with the MO-DJ logo parked down by the cottage. Good. He'd have plenty of time to get everything set up while guests were entertained by the wedding musicians. After that, Phee's special night would continue to be filled with music, thanks to MO-DJ. Jo had talked to two other summer brides this past week who'd told her how lucky she was to find Luke on such short notice.

With that thought, she relaxed a little for the first time since Phee had announced her wedding date. Everything was going beautifully, and tomorrow it would all be only a memory— a beautiful one—as Phee and Quinn winged their way to Hawaii for their honeymoon. Only she, Britt, and their dad knew that the honeymooners were staying at Quinn's house tonight. And only she and Britt knew about the flowers, champagne and chocolates, and other special little gifts that would be waiting for them there.

Quinn had agreed to sleep in the guest room at his own house this past week while Jo and Britt sneaked behind their sister's back, replacing the masculine decor in Quinn's master bedroom with pretty new curtains, bed linens, and plush towels for the master bath. It was a gift from the sisters that could be moved to the new home they would build here on Poplar Brook Road.

It had all turned out to be such a perfectly happy ending for Phylicia. *No, not an ending at all,* Jo thought. It was only the beginning for Quinn and Phee.

Tonight she would celebrate that new beginning for her sister. But picking her way down the spongy steps in the hillside lit only by flickering twinkle lights, Jo sighed and whispered a prayer that somehow, someday, she could have her own happily ever after.

CHAPTER 12

LUKE SLID UP THE VOLUME on a new set of dance tunes and straddled the bar stool behind his table. He'd gotten through the parts that required the most of him—announcing the father-daughter dance and the other special dances the couple had requested. From here on out he just needed to keep the music flowing and change things up every few songs. "Something for everyone" was his motto. Well, except the Barry Manilow fans. They were out of luck. He smiled to himself, remembering his conversation with Joanna Chandler and the bride and groom during the walk-through.

He thought that Joanna was happy with the way things were going. He could almost see her pride in having pulled off this simple but delightful wedding for her sister. He'd been watching her all night, somehow unable to keep his eyes off her, much as he tried. She was simply radiant tonight. And the . . . was it *longing*? . . . in her expression while the bride and groom danced to Matthew West's "When I Say I Do" put a lump in his throat. Of course that song got to him anyway. This *was* a crazy life and Luke had always hoped to have a wife by his side to share it with. And if that woman turned out to be as beautiful as Joanna Chandler, he certainly wouldn't complain.

If he'd known Joanna better, he would have left his duties and asked her to dance. But he didn't, and besides, it was almost more fun to watch her work the room. She never stole the spotlight from the bride, but made everyone feel welcome.

Still, every time a different man asked her to dance, Luke watched carefully to be sure sparks weren't flying. But Joanna wasn't a flirt, and instead treated every man more like an older brother or a beloved uncle.

Joanna thanked an elderly man for a dance and, still smiling, headed toward the DJ table. Winking at Luke, she approached Mateo, who stood off to one side of the table. "Would you like to dance, young man?"

There was such confidence in her question. Luke could tell it hadn't crossed her mind that he might turn her down. He shot up a prayer that the boy wouldn't be rude to her.

Mateo shuffled his feet and twisted the brown beads at his throat.

Come on, buddy. Just say yes. You can do it. Luke would have traded places with him in a heartbeat.

But as Luke expected, Mateo dropped his head and mumbled something that could only be interpreted as a refusal.

"Oh. Okay." She smiled, but it wasn't the genuine smile of a few seconds ago. "Did you get something to eat yet? There's plenty for seconds if you want."

Mateo gave a curt nod and turned away, pretending to be interested in something on the ground. Luke made a mental note to work on manners. He debated whether to apologize to Joanna on the boy's behalf.

She turned and caught his eye, making up his mind for him.

"Sorry," he mouthed, pointing at Mateo and frowning.

Her smile brightened and she came up to his table. He quickly cued a set that would give him a good ten minutes to talk with her.

He came around to the front of his table so he wouldn't need to shout and apologized for Mateo again. "We need to work on manners, I guess."

She waved him off. "Don't worry about it. I wasn't Miss Manners at that age either. And I'm guessing a wedding is about the last place on earth a twelve-year-old boy wants to be on a Saturday night."

He laughed. "That's probably about right. Although you'd think the food would balance things out."

"Oh! Speaking of food, did you get a plate?"

"Oh, no." He held up a hand. "I'm working."

"You can't work and eat? I'd be happy to bring you a plate."

"Well, I must admit I caught a glimpse of that angel food cake and . . . I might have drooled a little bit." He feigned wiping his mouth on the cuff of his shirt.

That earned him a smile. "Stay right here. I'll get you a piece. What else do you like? There are still some finger sandwiches left and maybe something bacon-wrapped."

"I would not turn down any item you just named."

She looked pleased. "I'll be right back. Can I bring a plate for Mateo?" She looked over her shoulder toward where he'd been standing earlier.

Luke followed her line of sight, but didn't see Mateo anywhere. "That's probably where he is right now. He had some cake earlier, so I think he can fend for himself. Especially if he won't even dance with you."

She winced, then tried to conceal it. "It's okay. Really."

"Well, I didn't hear the whole exchange, but if he was rude, I do apologize."

"He wasn't rude exactly." Luke had put her on the spot. She didn't want to be a tattletale, but the way Mateo had spoken to her was anything but polite. "Don't worry about it. How . . . how are you both holding up?"

Luke didn't mean the sigh to come out as loud as it did.

"That bad, huh?"

"Mateo is great. He really is. It's just *weird* having responsibility for another human being. Twenty-four seven."

"So, how much longer do you have him for?"

He shrugged. "We're just kind of taking one day at a time right now." He knew it sounded like an evasion, but the truth was, he didn't know the answer to her question. He'd made promises he wasn't sure he could keep.

"Well, I think you're doing a wonderful thing. Letting him stay with you while things get worked out."

"No. I'm just hanging on for dear life." He spotted Mateo headed their way with a plate of food. He gave a little nod to let Joanna know the object of their conversation was approaching.

She understood immediately. "Listen, let me go get that angel food cake I promised. Back in a minute." With a smile, she ducked away before Mateo reached the table.

"How many plates *is* that? You're not being a pig, are you?"

"This is only three." He spoke over a huge wad of something chocolate.

Luke laughed. "That better be the last plate, okay, bud?" He might have to give the Chandlers a discount on his services. Especially if the kid threw up on the dance floor.

"Awww . . ."

"I'm serious, Mateo." He made his tone stern. "Lay off the champagne, too, will ya?"

Mateo laughed so hard Luke was afraid the kid *would* throw up.

"It wasn't *that* funny." But Mateo's laughter *was* and Luke couldn't help but laugh too. Thankfully Brooks & Dunn's "Boot Scootin' Boogie" had the crowd wound up, and nobody seemed to notice the two of them in stitches behind the DJ's table.

When Mateo finally quieted down, Luke put a hand on his shoulder. "Hey, be nice to Miss Joanna, would you?"

He drew up to his full four-foot eleven, shaking his head, in defense mode. "I wasn't mean to her."

"I never said you were. But if you didn't want to dance

with her, the correct response is, 'No thank you, ma'am, but thanks for asking.'"

Mateo made a gagging sound.

Just then, the song ended and Joanna appeared from the edge of the dance floor, her cheeks flushed.

"*Shh*, here she comes. Now you be nice."

"I'm *being* nice," he hissed.

Luke angled his face away from Joanna and threw Mateo a stern look.

"Here you go."

He turned and she thrust an oversized plate at him. It overflowed with delectable cakes and appetizers.

"That ought to keep you fueled for another hour or two."

"I guess!" He took the plate from her. "Thank you. That's so thoughtful of you."

"Well, we can't have our DJ fainting from hunger before the dance is over, can we?"

"Definitely not. And speaking of which, this set is about over. I'd better get back to work."

"Of course. Let me know if you need anything else."

He lifted the plate with one hand. "I'll never need anything else ever again."

Laughing, she went back on the dance floor, weaving her way through the crowd, speaking to people as she went, the quintessential hostess. He watched as her dad caught her and twirled her into a dance. Luke scrolled through his list and chose a couple of audience favorite tearjerkers.

"Are you gonna stare at her all night?"

Luke jumped and turned to find Mateo looking at him with a disgusted expression. "I just might. What's it to you?" he teased. But it struck him that his showing interest in a woman might not sit right with Mateo. He'd better cool it. At least in front of the boy.

"How much longer?" Mateo whined.

"At least another hour, buddy. That's the way weddings

are. If you're getting tired, you can go sleep in the truck. You brought your sleeping bag, right?"

"Yeah, but how am I supposed to find the truck with all those cars parked down there?"

Luke took the boy's shoulders and steered him to the edge of the tent. "Look down there. I can see the truck from here."

"Where?"

He pointed. "Follow my finger. See?"

"Oh. Yeah. Okay, maybe I'll go later or—" A giant yawn cut off his words.

Luke laughed. "Tell you what, I need a bathroom break. Let me cue up some music and I'll walk down with you. But we'll have to make it snappy."

Mateo cocked his head, listening. "Wait."

"For what?"

"That song."

Luke listened. The intro to Louis Armstrong's "Wonderful World" had just started playing. Maria's favorite song. Filed under "sappy tunes" in his playlists. Shoot! He hadn't been thinking. But he couldn't stop the music now. Guests were responding to the song, older couples getting up to dance for the first time. "Wonderful World" was a lot of people's favorite song.

"Do you want to stay and listen? Or go on down to the truck?"

"Stay." But already his chin was quivering.

Luke put an arm around Mateo and ushered him into the shadows behind the DJ table. He could feel the boy's shoulders heaving beneath his arm. Luke kind of wanted to cry too. He didn't know what to say that would bring comfort, so he didn't say anything. Just stood there with his arm around the weeping boy.

The song faded and segued into another. Mateo looked up at him, brown eyes red-rimmed. "It's a lie, isn't it?"

"What's a lie, bud?"

"Wonderful world."

"Mateo." *Oh, God. Give me the words.* "It's not a lie. It *is* a wonderful world most of the time. I know it doesn't feel that way for you right now. But your mom would want you to look for the wonderful stuff, don't you think? I know she did. And I guarantee you it's out there. You'll see."

A new song started, but it was the last one in the queue. He loosened his hold on Mateo, but that only made the kid hang on tighter. Luke gave him another minute, then squeezed his shoulder. "Hey, buddy. I need to go take care of the music. Hang on just a sec, and then I'll walk you down to the truck."

Without waiting for an answer, he went to cue the next set. Looking out over the dance floor, he noticed Joanna watching Mateo still huddled at the edge of the tent. Her expression looked more peeved than sympathetic. But of course, she didn't know the significance of the song that had just played. And Mateo *had* been rather rude to her.

Luke looked away before she could catch him staring again, but it was all he could do to not go and make excuses for the boy.

Why did it matter what she thought? *Well, duh.* He knew the answer to that.

He set up another ten minutes of music and went to tell Joanna where he was going so she wouldn't think he'd ditched his post.

CHAPTER 13

USCLES ACHING, JOANNA STRETCHED HER arms over her head before going to fold up another row of chairs. The cars that had lined the lane only an hour ago were mostly gone now. The guests had sent Quinn and Phee off in a hail of birdseed minutes before midnight. Now only a skeleton crew remained to clean up the worst of the mess. The rental place would come to pick up the chairs and tables and take the tent down tomorrow.

Dad and Britt had hauled the leftover food down to the cottage, and Quinn's brother and the other groomsmen were folding chairs and tables, doing the bulk of the heavy lifting. Jo leaned another two chairs against the stack, recalling Dad's encouragement for her to come back with them and to let the crew clean up. But she had ulterior motives.

She looked over near the edge of the tent where Luke was packing his gear. Mateo must still be sleeping down in the truck. He might be a little rude and surly, but she was grateful he hadn't misbehaved. She was trying to give him the benefit of the doubt since he'd so recently lost his mother. She knew what that was like. And after all, he *was* a preteen—a breed not exactly known for being docile and cooperative on the best of days. Still, she didn't have much patience for someone who couldn't even look a person in the eye when spoken to.

"Looks like you lost your helper, huh?"

Luke looked over his shoulder at her from where he was crouched over the larger of his two duffel bags. "Like you said, weddings aren't exactly a favorite of twelve-year-old boys. He's still sacked out in the truck."

"That's what I figured. Do you need help carrying things down?"

"Thanks, but I can get it. That's what you're paying me the big bucks for."

That winsome smile of his was going to be the death of her. "Well, we *are* paying you pretty big bucks, but you did a great job." She meant what she said. By any calculation, the wedding had been a huge success. Phee had seemed especially pleased with how the night turned out. And Luke had played a big part. He must have a sixth sense for what people enjoyed because every time Jo had thought things might lag a little, Luke spun the perfect song.

"I hope so. I thought people looked pretty happy. You must be exhausted though. I think you managed to dance with *every* single guest." He winced. "Well, except Mateo."

And you. But she didn't dare give voice to that regret. Instead, she waved off his comment. "It was fun. I haven't danced like that in years. I mean like . . . probably since high school."

"Seriously? You looked like an old pro out there."

"Thanks. I think." She looked askance at him. "Old?"

He laughed. "That didn't come out quite right."

"I see where Mateo learned his manners." After the words were out, she was afraid she might have hit below the belt.

But Luke grinned again and beat a fist to his chest. "Ooh, ouch."

"I'm just giving you a hard time. He's cute."

"He has his moments." He rose and reached behind Joanna for a cable lying on the table where his equipment had been set up.

She tried not to stare, but even with his tie loosened and his shirtsleeves rolled up, the man did a white shirt and tie justice.

He coiled the cable into a neat circle and tucked it in the duffel bag. "He's taking things pretty hard."

"Understandably. Poor kid."

"Speaking of which, I'd probably better get down to the truck and check on him. He was still zonked when I took the speakers down a little while ago, but I'd hate for him to wake up and not remember where he is."

She reached for his duffel. "Here. Let me carry something. I'm headed down too."

"You sure?"

"Positive."

"Hang on. Let me fold up this table and I'll be ready."

"Hey!" Quinn's brother, Markus, yelled across the length of the tent. "You need some help there, little lady?" He headed in their direction but veered off course, stumbling and barely righting himself before he reached her. She'd seen his wife and their little girl head down to where the cars were parked earlier in the evening. She hoped they were safely back at their hotel.

She gave a nervous chuckle. "Thanks, but I think we've got it."

"You did a fine job today, sunshine." Markus's words slurred as he sidled up to Jo, standing uncomfortably close. His breath reeked of alcohol. He reached for the duffel bag on her shoulder. "Here, here, lemme get that for ya."

She took a couple of steps backward, clutching the bag tightly in front of her, erecting a wall between them.

But Markus matched her step-for-step, gripping her arm. "Quinn didn't tell me his wife had such pretty sisters. In fact, I'd say he let the cream of the crop get away."

Panic rocketed through her. But just as quickly, Luke was at her side. She was grateful for his possessive hand around her shoulder.

Markus must have gotten the message because he took an unsteady stride backward.

"Thanks for offering," Luke said. "But I think we've got it under control here." Moving with finesse, he put himself between Jo and Quinn's brother, effectively dismissing the man. "I'll walk down with you in just a minute, Jo."

He spoke loud enough for Markus to hear, and Jo mouthed a relieved *thank you*.

He brushed off her thanks, finished folding the table, then handed her a light tote bag. "You have room to carry this?"

"Sure." Still a little shaken, she lifted the bag, adjusted the duffel bag strap on her shoulder, and led the way to the stairway, but not until she'd located Markus safely on the other side of the tent.

They picked their way down the stairs in silence. For the sake of Phylicia's wedding dress and the guests' shoes, Dad had layered sand on the spongy top of each step a few days ago, hoping to keep the stairway dry even if it rained. The sand was packed down now, but the hillside alongside the stairway was littered with stray paper cups, discarded birdseed bags, and wedding programs.

Despite the burden of the two heavy bags he shouldered, Luke stooped to pick up a clear plastic champagne flute off the path.

"Oh, don't worry about that. If it's nice tomorrow, my sister and I will come up and do litter patrol. You would think people could respect personal property." It was something she hadn't really thought about in regards to running a wedding venue. She wondered how many other things she hadn't considered.

"You'd think," Luke echoed, looking disgusted. He scooped up a wadded-up napkin and a crushed Coke can.

"Seriously, don't worry about it."

"Well, it wouldn't shock me to learn that Mateo was guilty of at least a couple of these."

Smiling, she motioned to the collection of trash in his hand. "Probably not the champagne flute."

He looked dubious. "That better not have been his. Although he did tell me if things got too mushy he might need some champagne."

She gave a little gasp. "I hope he wasn't serious."

That got a laugh. "He seemed clean and sober when I walked him down to the truck."

"That's more than I can say for Quinn's brother. Thank you for coming to my rescue."

Luke blew out a disgusted huff. "I hope I didn't interfere too much. I know you can probably take care of yourself, but I didn't like where things were headed."

She shook her head. "You don't know how thankful I am you were there."

He changed the subject. "I am sorry about the trash. Hopefully the wind won't come up tonight."

"Next time, we'll put trash cans at the top and bottom of the stairs. I should have thought of that."

"Next time? You planning on getting married soon, are you?"

Her cheeks heated. "Not me. I've just—It might be a pipe dream, but I thought maybe we could turn the clearing into a wedding venue. Make a little extra money that way."

"Not a pipe dream at all. It makes a great venue, that's for sure. You could tell everybody had a great time. And not because they were hammered either. Like too many of the weddings I do."

"Do you think maybe Quinn's brother had his own bottle somewhere? I didn't think you could get snockered on champagne, but Markus seemed pretty tipsy."

Luke grunted. "That's an understatement. But FYI, I think

you *can* get snockered on champagne. I'm pretty sure Mateo didn't want it for its delicious flavor."

He pulled a sour face that made her laugh.

"Well, Phee and Quinn had fun," she said. "I guess that's all that really matters."

"Exactly. It was a really nice wedding. You did a good job, little sister."

His compliment warmed her. "Thanks. I think I'm going to sleep really well tonight."

"I just hope Mateo didn't sleep so hard in the truck that he's up all night."

"Wow, I never considered the fact you have to worry about a twelve-year-old sleeping through the night."

Luke rolled his eyes. "It's usually the opposite. I've never seen a kid who could sleep away so many hours. I know it's an age when they have a growth spurt and hormones and all that, but I worry a little bit that it might be more about grief."

"Oh. I hadn't thought of that."

"There's a lot I hadn't thought of. Most days I fear I'm in way over my head. And then the kid will turn around and do something that makes me laugh or makes me proud—" He groaned. "You probably think I'll be whipping out the baby brag book next."

She smiled. "My Grandma Clayton actually had one of those."

"With you in it?"

"Probably."

"I bet you were a cutie."

She warmed at his comment, but chose to ignore it. "I don't actually remember the photos in it. I just remember Mom got it for her, but later, she told my dad she was afraid she'd created a monster."

"Well, I don't own a brag book. I promise."

She feigned a stern look. "I'll take you at your word."

They came to the bottom of the hill and followed the

lane to where his truck was parked. Across the driveway, the lights were out in the cottage, but a lamp still glowed in the unfinished cabin where Dad was staying.

"Do you want me to walk you to your cabin?"

"No. I'm fine, really. It's right there." She pointed, giggling. "I'm pretty sure I could outrun him if I had to."

"Well, be careful." Luke set the bags on the ground, then rummaged through his pockets until he produced his keys. He pressed a button and the horn tweeted and the doors unlocked. He tossed a sheepish look over his shoulder. "If that doesn't wake him up, nothing will.

"Here . . . Let me get that." He took the duffel bag from her and started to open the back driver's side door. But instead he turned to face her, scuffing the toe of his dress shoe in the grass. "Hey . . . you wouldn't want to go out to dinner Friday night, would you?"

She tilted her head, but hesitated, not wanting to appear too eager.

"With me," he said. "In case you were confused."

Why was this droll sarcasm annoying when it came from Mateo, and utterly charming coming from the boy's guardian? "I'd love that, Luke."

"Great." He sounded a little surprised, though she doubted he had much experience with women turning him down for a date. "I'll call you Thursday about what time and everything. Does that work?"

"Perfect. I look forward to it."

"Me too."

"Thanks again for everything. It was a good night."

Nodding, he opened the truck door slowly, putting a finger to his lips. "Talk to you soon," he whispered.

She gave a little wave and started across the lane to the cottage. But she stopped short of the front door and stood in the shadow of the ancient oak tree that towered over the roof, watching until his taillights disappeared around the curve.

She slipped off her shoes on the porch and entered the cottage quietly, thankful Britt was already in bed and no one was waiting up for her. Because she couldn't seem to stop smiling.

CHAPTER 14

HOLDING A BOUQUET OF FRESHLY clipped wildflowers from the woods in one hand, Joanna opened the back door to the cottage with her free hand and slipped off her muddy shoes before stepping inside. Her cell phone was vibrating on the washing machine in the back hallway where she'd left it.

Luke! Finally! Seeing his name on the screen sent a crazy rush of relief and excitement through her. She'd determined not to sit around waiting for his call after work every day. So she'd cleaned every cupboard in the cottage and had almost resorted to cleaning the bathtub when she'd spotted a patch of wildflowers in bloom up in the woods behind the cottage.

She laid the bouquet on the washing machine and quickly wiped her hands on her shorts, absently checking her reflection in the mirror. Good thing he couldn't see her right now. She was what Britt would have declared a hot mess.

She sucked in a breath, picked up the phone, and tapped Talk. "Hello?"

"Hi. Joanna?"

"Yes."

"Oh good. I wasn't sure if this was your cell or a landline and I can't tell you sisters' voices apart."

"It's me. This is my cell number. How are you?"

"I'm good. Just checking to make sure tomorrow night still works for you?"

"I'm planning on it. What time? Do you want me to just meet you in Cape?"

"No, I'll pick you up. I'm . . . a little old-fashioned that way."

She smiled into the phone. "That's fine with me." Actually it was more than fine.

"Why don't we say six o'clock? That work?"

"I'll be ready. Do I need to dress up?"

"Oh. No. Casual. And comfortable shoes for walking . . . if that's okay?"

"Sure. Sounds nice." She slipped off her flip-flops in the back hallway, tucked the phone onto her shoulder, and retrieved the bouquet from the washer.

"So, did you have to bring in a dumpster for all the wedding trash?" Luke's voice held a smile.

Laughing, she rummaged in the cupboards for a vase. "A large leaf bag did the trick. It's spotless up there now."

"Good. I was feeling bad for you and Britt."

"Oh, don't. My dad helped us clean up."

"That's good. Is he still there? I don't mean to keep you from time with him . . ."

"No, Dad went back Tuesday. But that's sweet of you to ask. It's been pretty quiet around here, especially with Phee and Quinn gone." She trimmed the stems of the bouquet and tucked them into the vase.

"Oh? The honeymooners aren't home yet?"

"Not until Sunday. But Phee's been sending us pictures and texts. It looks like they're having a blast."

"I forget where they were going. Or maybe they aren't telling?"

"Oh, they're telling now. They're in Hawaii. On Maui as of yesterday. Phee says it's beautiful."

"I've never been, but it sounds like a nice place to go. Maria—Mateo's mom—always wanted to go there before she . . ." An overlong pause. "Well, she never made it."

"I'm so sorry. That's so sad." After the words were out, she worried it sounded too . . . personal. But he was the one who'd brought up the subject of Maria.

"Yeah, well, it's probably pretty nice where she is now. She and Jesus were pretty tight. Especially there at the end."

Again, Jo could hear the smile in his tone.

"Oh, that's good to hear. I'm glad." She wasn't sure if his comment made her feel better or just made her wonder more about what, exactly, Luke's relationship with Maria had been. She determined to find out before she got too . . . *attached* to the man. Then again . . .

Too late, Chandler.

"Right this way." The hostess turned to lead the way through the darkened dining room of Bella Italia.

Jo started to follow, but Luke raised his voice. "Excuse me . . . Miss?"

The server turned, eyebrows raised.

"Is the patio open tonight?" He turned to Jo, a question in his expression. "Is it okay with you if we eat outside?"

"Sure. It's a gorgeous evening. I'd hate to waste it being inside." Yet another reason to like this man. He understood the charm of an *al fresco* meal.

The young woman consulted the seating chart at the host stand. "Yes, I can seat you on the patio. Follow me."

A few minutes later, they were sipping sweet tea on the covered patio in front of the restaurant. Red-and-white checked tablecloths fluttered in the breeze and though traffic passed slowly on North Spanish Street in front of them, the everyday noises in this lively section of the city near the Mississippi River provided a rather pleasant cacophony for dinner music. And they caught whiffs of tangy red sauce and fresh-grated parmesan every time their server opened the door from the inside.

Luke perused the menu. "Have you tried their lasagna?"

Jo shook her head. "I've only eaten here one other time. I don't remember what I had, but it wasn't lasagna."

Luke shot her an incredulous glance. "You've lived here all your life and you've only eaten at Bella Italia once? The lasagna is my favorite. But order whatever you like."

"Sure, I'll try it. I've never met a lasagna I didn't like." She didn't tell him that she made a pretty mean lasagna herself—one reason the Chandlers rarely chose Italian when they ate out.

While they waited for their entrees, Luke tore off hunks of yeasty warm-from-the-oven bread from a round loaf and handed one to her. They dipped the bread in the plate of olive oil and herbs the server brought. They spoke easily of the weather, of Phee and Quinn's wedding, and about the sights passing by their little window on the world of Cape Girardeau, Missouri.

"So, where is Mateo this evening?" She felt guilty for not wanting to bring up the subject of Mateo, but it was only polite to inquire.

She was sorry she'd asked when a deep V of worry furrowed the spot between Luke's dark eyebrows. "He's with a guy I work with and his wife."

"Oh? Are they foster parents?"

"No. Just good friends. They offered to take him for a few hours this evening. So he wouldn't have to be alone."

"Oh, I see." Her own disappointment surprised her a little and she realized she still held out hope that Mateo would be going to a foster family. "Well . . . it's nice you have someone to watch him for an evening."

"It is. I want to make sure he's handling everything okay

. . . with Maria's death . . . before I leave him for too long. Especially at night. It seems like things are always worse after dark."

She nodded, remembering that had been true for her and her sisters when Mom was so sick.

"It's just hard to know how he's doing. He's usually a pretty easygoing kid. And quiet. So I can't tell if he's *more* quiet than usual or if it's something I should be worried about."

She wouldn't have labeled the kid *quiet* from what she'd seen. But maybe he was, in comparison to other kids his age. "Is Mateo seeing someone . . . for counseling?"

"He's had a couple of sessions, but he doesn't say much afterward. And I don't want to pry. His mom always said to just wait. That he'd get around to telling her whatever was eating him when he was ready. I wasn't really around him enough to know if that was true or not."

"Wow . . . That's got to be hard."

"It's sure not easy. Mateo's confided in me about some things . . . issues at school, that kind of thing. But I'm sure there's a lot going on inside his head that he's not saying." He took a sip of iced tea. "Now that he's lost his mom, I mean."

Taking a deep breath, Jo decided to just go for it. Get it out in the open. "So, were you and Maria . . . dating?"

He hesitated for half a second too long before shaking his head. "No. No, we were just . . . friends." Another crucial hesitation.

She stared at him across the table. There was definitely something he wasn't telling her. The thought that came next made her take in a sharp breath. Was Luke Mateo's *father*? That would explain why he'd been saddled with raising a child whose only relationship to him was as Big and Little. Otherwise, it just didn't make sense. Surely the kid had some extended family member who could take him in. And even if not, wouldn't he be better off in a two-parent family?

"Everything okay?" She looked up to see Luke staring at her with a quizzical glint in his eyes.

She tilted her head. "What?"

"Did you forget something?"

"What do you mean?"

"You just . . . almost *gasped* there a second ago."

"Oh. Sorry. I . . . didn't mean to." She dared to meet his gaze. "I admit though . . . I'm curious. May I ask you something?"

"Sure."

"I don't mean to pry, but it seems like there's maybe more to the story—with Mateo—than I . . . understand. You don't have to tell me if you don't want—obviously—but I just wondered."

"More than the Big Brothers thing, you mean?"

She nodded, her stomach muscles tensing.

"I don't know that there's *more*. I think I told you we were matched through the program five years ago. I got involved in Big Brothers through a campaign the radio station was doing for the organization. To be honest, I figured it'd just be a short-term thing." He gave a low laugh and fidgeted with the string of brown beads at his neck. She'd noticed he always wore those beads. "I *sure* never thought it would end like this."

Jo nodded, her silent question still not answered. "I bet. So, you just liked it that much? Or . . . you and Mateo just hit it off?"

He shrugged. "A little of both, I guess. I never realized what a difference I could make in a kid's life." He looked down at the table. "That sounded braggy. It just wasn't something I'd ever thought about. I have great parents so I guess I never paid attention to kids who didn't."

"Maria wasn't a good mom?"

"Oh . . . No, that's not what I meant. She *was* a good mom. A great mom. I just meant that Mateo's dad wasn't in the picture. He actually passed away when Mateo was five. Shortly before I became Mateo's Big."

"How sad." Jo didn't know whether to feel relieved or worried. Because if Luke wasn't Mateo's father, then maybe his commitment to the kid had more to do with Maria.

Luke seemed not to notice her disquiet. "Maria really struggled going it alone. She got him involved in the program because he was starting to act out and have issues because of losing his dad."

"Wow. That must have felt like a huge responsibility."

"It probably should have. And the training stressed what a responsibility it is. I'm not sure I took it that seriously the first year or two. But then the little guy grew on me. And after that, he just became part of my life. We're actually not even officially part of the program anymore."

"Really?"

He shrugged. "Once I got to know Maria—and I earned her trust—we kind of turned into friends and interacted that way. I think it was easier for her that way."

"Easier?"

"The organization supervises matches pretty closely—understandably—and when the caseworker who was assigned to our match moved away, we kind of drifted into . . . family-and-friends mode, I guess you'd call it. We'd gotten into a routine over the years, and it seemed easier to keep up what we were doing instead of starting over with a new caseworker."

"I can see that. Either way, it's a really neat thing that you took Mateo under your wing."

He gave a short laugh. "My mom didn't see it that way. She's never been thrilled with the idea."

The server came with steaming plates of lasagna, then grated fresh parmesan over each plate. They ate in silence for a few minutes, enjoying the food with appreciative smiles and moans.

"See? Did I steer you wrong?" Luke looked pleased that she was enjoying the meal so much.

"You did not. It's delicious. Thank you." Then, despite her earlier reluctance to open the topic of Mateo, her curiosity won out. "You were saying, earlier, that your mom wasn't crazy about you being a Big Brother. Why?"

He rolled his eyes, then feigned a falsetto tone. "Oh, Lukas, you don't want to get involved with something like that. Those are rough kids. You could end up getting taken advantage of. Or shot."

She laughed. "I don't even know your mom and I can tell that's a great imitation."

His mouth curved into a charming grin. "I told her I wasn't too worried about getting gunned down by a seven-year-old. But she said, 'That's not what I mean. That seven-year-old will grow up before you know it. And he might blame you for every bad thing that ever happened to him.'"

"Well, I suppose it *has* happened."

He shrugged. "Maybe. But like I told Mom, if that happens, I'll just go into the witness protection program."

Jo laughed again, but stopped when it struck her that he might be serious. Yet his smile said he wasn't. She studied him, that smile of his doing strange things to her insides.

"So . . ." She sopped up the last of the olive oil with a crust of bread. "Have your parents ever met Mateo? Did they meet Maria?" It was a fishing question, but her curiosity didn't care.

He shook his head. "They haven't met either of them. But that's not really their fault. They don't travel much anymore. They're both in their seventies now and my dad's health isn't great. I was their 'oops' kid," he explained with an impish grin. "Came along when Mom was forty-two."

"Wow!" Too late, Joanna realized how horrified she sounded.

Luke laughed. "They'd given up on having kids when nothing happened after their first five years of marriage, and then ten years later, *boom!* Can you imagine?"

She shook her head with a nervous laugh. "Sorry if I sounded . . . *appalled*. But no. I really can't."

"Of course, they thought I was *well* worth the wait."

She laughed again and matched his playful tone. "Oh, I'm sure you were."

"They're cool people though. You'd like them. And my mom has mellowed with the whole Big Brother thing. But um . . . full disclosure: I haven't told my parents that Mateo is living with me full-time now."

"You haven't?"

"I will. As soon as everything gets worked out. But it will only worry them now, and since they're so far away—they live in Phoenix—it really serves no purpose to say anything."

She nodded cautiously. Before Mom passed away, Jo couldn't have imagined not sharing something that significant with her parents. Maybe it was different for guys. And the truth was, now that Dad lived in Florida, there were things—even important things—he didn't know about her life. That she was on a date with Lukas tonight, for instance. It wasn't that she was keeping secrets, but simply because there was no sense troubling Dad about things that might make him worry from afar.

Maybe it was the same for Luke. Especially since his parents were older and didn't live nearby. And his mom was already hesitant about Mateo. "I guess if you're only going to have him for a short time, there's no sense upsetting your parents."

He gave her a look she couldn't interpret. "A short time?"

"Until he gets placed with a family or—"

"Can I interest you folks in some dessert?" The server propped a small dessert menu between them on the table, but they both groaned in response.

The server retrieved their ticket and slipped it into a folder. She placed it on the table in front of Luke, and he pulled several bills from his wallet and tucked them inside the folder. "I don't need change," he told the girl. "Thank you."

Jo took a sip of her sweet tea, then placed her napkin on the table and leaned back in her chair. "I won't need to eat for a week."

"Good stuff though, huh?"

"Delicious." Not as good as what she made, in her humble opinion. But still excellent. "Thank you for dinner."

"It was my pleasure." He pushed back his chair. "I thought we might go for a walk down by the river. Does that sound okay?"

"I wore my comfortable shoes." Smiling, she scooted her own chair back and pointed a toe to show him her shoes—which were comfortable, but also exceptionally cute, according to Britt, who had the fashion sense in the family. "It'll feel good to walk off some of the calories I just consumed."

He patted his flat stomach. "You've got that right." He motioned to the small purse hanging on the back of her chair. "Do you want to put your bag in the truck?"

"That would be good. Thanks."

They walked to his pickup and deposited the purse. Luke locked the vehicle and pointed toward the river. "I've always loved to watch the barges on the river."

She smiled. "Sounds like a guy thing."

He started to say something, but his phone buzzed audibly in his pocket. He gave her an apologetic look. "Sorry, but I'd better check this."

"Of course."

Luke fished his phone out and frowned at the screen. "Uh-oh. It's Don Shubert. Where Mateo is staying. I'm sorry."

She worked to mask her frustration. "It's fine." She did appreciate him asking. Ben never had. In fact, his addiction to his phone had caused more than one argument between them.

It seemed strange to be thinking of Ben after all this time. But the truth was, this was only the third date she'd been on since she and Ben had broken up almost a year and a half ago. It was hard not to make comparisons.

"Hey, Don. Everything okay?" Luke listened, his frown lines deepening. "How long ago was that? Oh, man. I'm sorry about that." More frowning. "No, of course not. I can get there in about twenty minutes."

He clicked off with a deep sigh. "I am so sorry. Apparently Mateo threw up after dinner and he's still not feeling well. I'm going to have to take a rain check on that walk."

"Of course . . ." She had to work to keep the disappointment from her voice. "I understand. I hope it's not something serious."

"Probably just that crud that's going around. Either that or he ate so much he made himself sick. I've seen him do that a time or two."

"Listen, Luke, I can have my sister come and pick me up."

"No. I told Don it'd be twenty minutes or so. I'm happy to take you home."

Happy to take her home? She hoped he didn't mean that literally.

"Hey, buddy . . . You okay?" Luke perched on the edge of the sofa where Mateo was lying, praying the boy didn't puke on his friends' plush carpet—or in his truck on the way home, for that matter. He looked from Don to his wife, Valerie, trying to discern how serious this was.

Mateo was subdued, but he didn't look pale or green around the gills. Luke patted his shoulder, then rose. "I'll gather your stuff up, and we'll get you home and in bed, okay?"

Mateo nodded wordlessly, not meeting Luke's eyes.

Hoping Don would take the hint, he started toward the kitchen. "Are his shoes out here?"

Valerie nodded, trailing behind him. "I'm sure sorry you had to cancel your plans."

"It's okay. I'm glad you called." He winced and lowered his voice. "I hope he didn't ruin anything . . . getting sick."

"No. We were all outside when it happened. He probably needs a shower, but he just wanted to lie down and wait for you."

Don appeared in the doorway between the kitchen and living room. "Mateo's bag is out by the front door. And here are his shoes." He held out the canvas tennis shoes like they were a wet dog. "He may or may not have upchucked on the shoes."

Valerie huffed at her husband and grabbed a rumpled grocery sack and held it out for Don to put the shoes in.

Laughing, Luke took the bag from him. "Sorry about that, man."

Don waved him off. "He's a good kid. Hope he feels better."

"I hope he really did behave for you guys."

"Oh, he was no trouble at all. He's a charmer." Valerie's smile seemed genuine.

But Luke shook his head. Being a charmer wasn't a trait Mateo often got complimented on.

"We'll give you a rain check on the babysitting," Valerie said. "Don't you hesitate to call."

Luke thanked her, but cringed inwardly. Rain checks were piling up on him, and he didn't like to owe or be owed.

Don grinned. "You should have just brought the lovely lady with you."

He shrugged. "I didn't think exposing her to a puking kid was a very good way to make a first impression."

"First impression?" Valerie's brows went up. "Was this a blind date?"

"No. First date though. But I've known Joanna for a while. I DJed her sister's wedding."

"Oh, that's so sweet."

Luke chuckled. "I don't know how sweet it was. It was only a job." He didn't mention that he'd actually first met Joanna at the attorney's office that day.

His conversation with Joanna tonight niggled at him. It was natural she would assume that Mateo was only with him temporarily. That he was awaiting foster care and would be going to another home. But that wasn't the case now, and he needed to come clean with her. But he'd never meant to deceive her. He'd just assumed she knew—because of working at Pritchert & Pritchert—that he was Mateo's legal guardian. He realized now that the law firm probably had hundreds of clients. He'd been ignorant to think that she would be aware of the circumstances of every client. And she was only an administrative assistant, likely not privy to his information.

Carrying the grocery bag, he returned to the front room and slung Mateo's backpack over one shoulder. He lifted the limp form from the sofa. "Man, bud, you weigh a ton."

That brought a wan smile. "Don't forget my shoes."

"I've got them right here." He boosted Mateo up and shifted his weight to the other leg. "Hey, bud . . . Tell Don and Val thank you."

"Thanks." It was barely a whisper. But Luke wasn't going to make a big deal of it tonight. He just wanted to get home. Preferably without getting thrown up on.

CHAPTER 15

July

THE CLOCK ON HER BEDSIDE table seemed like it was hammering out the seconds. Joanna threw back the covers and swung her legs over the side of the mattress. She may as well get up. She'd seen every half hour on the clock since she crawled into bed at eleven last night. Thank goodness it was Saturday and she didn't have to work. Well, not at the office anyway.

Guests would be checking in to the cottage around four, so she and Britt needed to change out the linens on the beds and clean the bathrooms. Britt had already made scones for the guests' breakfast—usually Jo's job—and she hoped there were a few extras so she could have one with her coffee. The cinnamon-scented treats would have tempted her last night if she hadn't been so bummed about the way her date with Luke had ended.

He'd been super apologetic, but somehow Jo didn't think he was as disappointed as she was. Their conversation had gotten a little tense before the server interrupted with the check.

She couldn't even remember now what she'd said, but she'd definitely seen a shift in the expression on his face. Whether it was frustration or disinterest, she couldn't have said.

She went out to the kitchen and flipped on the overhead light only to find Britt bathed in lamplight, sitting in the little reading corner off the kitchen with her Bible and her journal.

Britt looked her way. "You're up early."

Melvin was ensconced in her lap, but the cat lifted his head and eyed Jo as if she might feed him early.

"Couldn't sleep." Jo opened a bag of coffee beans from Red Banner, their favorite roaster in Cape, and poured them into the grinder.

She and her sisters had decided they wanted their little Airbnb venture to support local businesses in Langhorne and Cape Girardeau as much as possible. For that reason, The Cottages on Poplar Brook Road only served locally roasted coffee, their vases would be filled with flowers from Mary's shop in Langhorne, and whenever they didn't have time to bake their own breakfast treats, they'd grab something from Mike Michaels's bakery in Langhorne. Coffee's On was doing a thriving business now that Mike's son was out of prison and working for him. It warmed Jo's heart to see that happy ending.

The thought that came to mind seemed ridiculous by comparison, but she couldn't keep the question from forming: Would she ever get her own happy ending? She knew in her heart that there was no comparison between what her "happy ending" would look like and Mike's son being free after having spent years in prison on drug charges, or a twelve-year-old losing his only parent the way Mateo had. Mike's "happy ending" was nothing short of miraculous. And if Mateo found a good family and made something of his life, that, too, would be a miracle.

But a woman finding a man to marry? That was an everyday occurrence. Except, it didn't feel so "everyday" when you were the woman who *hadn't* found her man yet.

Britt closed her Bible, deposited Melvin on the floor, and

went to get a mug from the cupboard. "So, how was your hot date?"

Jo made a face. "Not so hot."

Britt froze. "Why? What happened?"

"Nothing. That's why it wasn't so hot."

"What do you mean nothing happened? You weren't expecting him to propose on the first date, were you? Or to kiss you?"

She rolled her eyes. "No, you fruitcake." Though she wouldn't have minded the latter.

"Then what happened?"

"Mateo—you remember the kid who's staying with Luke? The one whose mom died? Well, he got sick. Luke had to go pick him up at a friend's. It was like eight thirty when he brought me home."

"Well, that wasn't your fault. And I guarantee he'll ask you out again."

"I'm not so sure."

"Why do you say that? You didn't hit it off?"

"No. I thought we did. At first anyway. We had a lot to talk about and we laughed. Things were going really well before he got the call about Mateo."

"Then he'll ask you out again."

"Maybe. I get the feeling he's kind of focused on Mateo right now."

Britt glared at her. "What a horrible, horrible man. Worrying about a little boy who's lost his mother when he could be dating you instead."

Jo wadded up a dish towel and lobbed it at her. "I never said he was horrible."

"What did you want him to do? Tell the kid, 'Tough cookies, I'm on a hot date and your tummy ache just has to wait?'"

"Okay, okay. You're making *me* sound like the horrible, horrible person."

Britt cleared her throat pointedly. "Hey, if the shoe fits . . ."

"I'm not saying I want Luke to ignore the kid. He's been through a lot. I can't imagine losing Mom when I was his age. And he doesn't even have a dad in the picture. It just seemed like maybe Luke wasn't as disappointed about the whole thing as I was."

"What makes you think that?"

She shrugged. "I don't know. Maybe I'm imagining things. It just seemed like he was a little . . . relieved to have the night end early."

"Why don't you give him the benefit of the doubt, Jo. If he hasn't called you a week or two from now, then you'll know, but you don't need to be all doom and gloom when he had a perfectly legitimate reason for bringing you home early."

Jo poured coffee and blew across the glassy surface trying to cool it down. "If I knew where I really stood with him, I might offer to bring over some chicken soup for Mateo and . . . I don't know . . . watch a movie with them or something."

Britt shrugged. "So, why don't you?"

"Britt, for all I know Luke was having serious second thoughts and he simply used Mateo as an excuse."

Britt studied her. "Or maybe *you're* the one using Mateo as an excuse?"

"No, I'm not. Why would you think that?"

Britt put her hands on her hips. "Did you not learn anything from your breakup with Ben?"

"Meaning?"

"Meaning you sometimes have a tendency to expect the worst of people, and when you do that, they're sure to give you the worst."

"I didn't expect the worst of Ben. He gave it to me without even being asked."

"Jo. I think you know that's not—"

"You know what? I'm not even going there. You didn't see the side of Ben I did . . . after Mom got sick. He just sort of . . . checked out."

She and Ben had been good together. Until Mom got sick.

And even though, technically, she'd been the one to say the words "it's over," he'd pretty much forced her hand because he was struggling with her being so tied down to Mom's care. But she shouldn't have had to choose between him and her dying mother. Never mind that if he'd just hung in there for a year—*one year*—there would have been nothing for him to struggle with.

But Ben had never been a patient man. And of course they hadn't known then whether Mom had a year to live or three. At that time, she'd already beaten all the odds her oncologists had offered.

"I'm sorry, Britt. I'm just taking out my disappointment about last night on you. I really wasn't trying to start an argument."

"I know." Her sister's voice softened. "But I don't want you to give up on a great guy before you even have a chance to see what he's like."

"I'm not giving up on Luke—the *possibility* of Luke. I'm only saying I don't want to push things if *he's* not ready for a relationship."

"He wouldn't have asked you out if he didn't like you. If he wasn't ready for a relationship."

"Maybe. I think maybe I just need to wait until this whole thing with Mateo blows over." She shook her head. "That didn't sound right. I mean until they've found a home for him and Luke is more free to focus on other things."

"Other things like . . . *you?*"

She laughed. "Well, of course."

Britt smiled, but Jo could tell she was a little miffed. "I think it's really amazing what he's doing for that little boy."

"Britt, I do too! I'm not saying anything at all against what he's doing for Mateo. I'm just saying that maybe his focus *should* be somewhere else right now. And I don't want to get in the way of that."

"Whatever." Britt waved a dismissive hand. "I'm going to start a load of bedding. Can you bring me yours?"

"Sure." Jo set her coffee cup down too hard and went down the hall to strip her bed.

She yanked pillowcases and sheets off and wadded them into a ball. She knew her sister was right on some points. And she hadn't fooled Britt for one minute with her self-righteous speech about not wanting to get in the way of Luke's commitment to Mateo.

But she refused to get into a contest for Luke's attention with a twelve-year-old. Or with a dead woman. Because while she couldn't quite put her finger on it, something told her that part of Luke's sense of responsibility for Mateo had some connection with the boy's mother.

No, she'd had enough rejection where men were concerned. She wasn't about to open herself up to more.

CHAPTER 16

THERE'S PHEE!" BRITT POINTED OUT her passenger side window to where travelers loaded down with luggage poured out of the terminal at Lambert International Airport.

Jo leaned forward to peer through the windshield from her place behind the wheel. "Oh, there they are. I see them." Her stomach fluttered with excitement. It felt like Phee and Quinn had been gone for a month. She could hardly wait to hear all about their trip.

She eased the car forward in the pickup lane queue while Britt rolled down the window to flag them down.

When Phee and Quinn spotted them, they waved and hurried toward Jo's car, pulling their bags behind them. Quinn actually wore a crazy Hawaiian shirt with his khakis. But it was Phee Joanna couldn't take her eyes off of. Her older sister positively *glowed*.

Seeing Phee looking so elated, so relaxed and content, did Jo's heart good. But a measure of jealousy stirred inside her at the same time. *Your turn will come, Chandler.* She had to keep reminding herself of that.

She put the car in Park, and she and Britt both jumped out to hug the newlyweds. They hugged Phee in turn, then turned to Quinn, who waited with outstretched arms. "Hey there, sisters! Appreciate the ride."

Jo popped the trunk and helped them stuff their luggage into the small space.

Quinn and Phee cozied up together into the back seat, holding hands. As Jo navigated traffic back to the interstate, they talked a mile a minute and all at the same time, catching up on each other's news.

It was so good to have Phee home. Even if she'd be sleeping at a new address across town for a few months until their house could be built.

"I bet Mabel is going to be glad to see us." Phee tipped her head and kissed the stubble on Quinn's throat. They'd boarded Quinn's dog at a place in Cape while they were gone.

Quinn laughed. "That dog would be glad to see a burglar."

Jo caught Quinn's eye in the rearview mirror. "Do we need to stop and pick her up before I drop you off?"

"And where, exactly, do you propose we put Mabel?" Britt looked pointedly around the full car.

"We could tie her to the luggage rack."

Quinn laughed. "Oh, she'd love that. She'd be wanting to ride that way all the time. But no, I'll go get her later tonight. They said there'd be somebody there to let us in until seven."

"Have you guys eaten?" Jo knew before she even asked what the answer would be.

"We're good," the newlyweds answered as one.

"We're anxious to get home," Phee said. "But don't worry, I'm still planning on coming to help you guys paint tomorrow after work. Oh! How'd it go with the guests this weekend?"

"Never even knew they were there," Britt said. "We left the key for them and they let themselves in and out. Left the place in pretty good shape too."

"You call eating every last scone 'pretty good shape'?"

Quinn laughed at that. "I'm with you, Jo."

Britt grinned. "I may or may not have hidden a couple away in the freezer."

"Dibs!" the sisters all yelled at once.

Quinn groaned and looked at the ceiling of the car. "Dear Lord, what have I gotten myself into?"

The sisters dissolved in giggles and Jo felt her jealousy melt away. At least for now. She wanted to enjoy the fact that her sister was home. Phee had found her happily ever after, and they all had a new brother to dote on . . . and, apparently, to entertain.

With Phee home, Jo found it hard to get up and go to work on Monday. It didn't help that when she got to the office, Trenton and Cinda were both in foul moods and taking it out on anyone who got in their path. She didn't know what they were arguing about, but the tension in the office was thick. Thankfully, tomorrow was the Fourth and the office would be closed for the holiday.

Things were even worse after lunch, and Joanna found Trent's and Cinda's bad moods rubbing off on her. But in truth, the Pritchers weren't entirely to blame. Jo was on pins and needles wondering if Luke would call to apologize for how their date had ended. Did she dare hope he might make good on the rain check he'd promised? After all, wasn't the Fourth of July a great excuse for another date?

But every hour that went by and he *didn't* call caused her hopes to plummet. Despite what she'd told Britt—and tried to convince herself of—she wasn't quite ready to give up on Luke simply because of Mateo. After all, that was a temporary thing. The boy wouldn't always be such a responsibility and distraction for Luke. Of course, if Mateo ended up with a local family, Luke would still be his "Big," but that might be, at most, a twice-a-month commitment. She could live with that. Could even see the three of them spending time together occasionally.

Trenton buzzed for his next appointment and she sent the client back. She organized a desk drawer and filed some paperwork, but she couldn't seem to shake thoughts of Luke. She was glad he was the type of guy to be involved in a program like Big Brothers and Big Sisters, and she was proud of him for being there for Mateo during such a tragic time. She just wished she'd met Luke at a less . . . *distracted* time in his life.

That seemed to be her luck though. She'd met Ben—her first serious boyfriend—just after they'd learned that Mom's cancer was terminal. And she'd met Luke shortly before Maria died.

But really, at her age, was there any man in the world who *wasn't* distracted by the busyness of life? She wasn't a carefree college student anymore either, and life was more than fun and games and romantic searches for Mr. Right. Maybe she just needed to get over herself and realize that there were bound to be complications no matter who she ended up with.

Why did she expect it to be easy? It certainly hadn't been for Quinn and Phylicia. They'd fallen in love while Phee was still grieving over Mom and worse, when Phee had discovered the secrets their parents were hiding about her birth father. But they'd overcome that. And now, they couldn't be happier.

The day dragged on and when she finally turned off of Poplar Brook Road and drove up the lane to the cottage, spotting Phee's car parked near the cabin across the lane pulled her out of her funk.

She hurried in to change clothes and walked over to Near Cottage. Her sisters flanked the large window in the front room, balancing a curtain rod across the span of windows.

"Jo! Just in time!" Britt spoke through a small collection of mounting screws she held between her teeth. "Tell us if that's straight, would you?"

140

Jo walked to the opposite wall and squinted at the rod. "Up a little on your side, Phee."

"There?"

"Right there. Looks straight to me." Her voice echoed in the empty room.

They chattered while they worked, Phee bubbling on about the amazing time she and Quinn had in Hawaii. By the time it got dark, they had all the blinds and curtains in the little cabin hung and had even arranged a grouping of decorative items on a white-painted wall across from the tiny front entry. Nothing expensive or fancy—a 1950s starburst clock, empty frames, and other rustic elements. But the effect was a pleasing cross between mid-century modern and cozy cottage.

With their tools gathered and waiting by the door, the three of them stood on the freshly refinished hardwood floors in the middle of the living room admiring their handiwork.

"It's looking good, ladies!" Phee clapped with glee.

"Now we need to get serious about finding some furniture for this place," Jo said. "Anybody up for shopping some second-hand stores tomorrow?" They'd already furnished one of the bedrooms so Dad would have a place to stay while he was back for the wedding. They'd brought over a couple of chairs and a side table from the cottage for him to use, but Jo had moved those back to the cottage once Dad returned to Florida, so now the dining room and living room were completely empty.

"Do you think the stores will be open on the Fourth?" Britt asked.

"Oh." Jo deflated. "I didn't think about that. You don't have to work, do you, Phee?"

"No. The flower shop will be open, but Mary gave me an extra day so I don't have to go back until Wednesday. I would think most stores will be open."

"Let's at least try. Most people don't start their celebrations until later in the evening anyway."

"I'm in!" Britt and Phee said at the same time.

Phee twirled in the middle of the room, taking it all in. "I can't believe how much bigger this place looks with everything painted white."

"It does, doesn't it?"

"Hey, I have an idea." Britt's eyes lit. "Since Jo and I are going to stay over here whenever we have guests, what if we get both of the bedrooms set up over here? I can move most of my things into this cabin, and Jo and I can each have our own place. Well, except when we have guests. You don't care if I take this cabin, do you? And then tomorrow we can shop for whatever we need to replace at the cottage?"

"Britt . . . Are you sure?" Jo was beyond thrilled at the idea of having the cottage to herself, but since Mom's death, Britt had been genuinely scared to stay by herself at night—in their parents' house in town, and out here at the property too.

"I'm sure. You'll be right across the lane." She looked sheepish. "I think my desire to have a bathroom to myself outweighs my fear of being alone at night."

Jo cheered. "Let's do it."

Laughing, Phee slipped her phone from her pocket and pressed a key. "Let me call Quinn and let him know what we're doing."

"Hey . . ." Jo grinned. "If he should just happen to volunteer to come help us move, say, that mattress, we wouldn't argue with him."

Phee laughed. "I bet I can talk him into it."

"So what's the game plan?" Head tilted, Britt eyed the living room.

Jo knew she was already arranging furniture in her mind. They all were, and Mom would have been right in there with them. "Let's go back to the cottage and see what's there that would work here."

"Good idea," Phee said over her phone. "Guys, Quinn's on speaker phone."

"Hey, ladies." Quinn's voice filled the room. "Quinn is

happy to come and help move furniture, but he would appreciate it if you knew what you were doing by the time he got there."

"Oh, baby," Phee quipped. "As if we *ever* know what we're doing at any given time."

That started them cackling again. Laughing together somehow made Mom feel closer.

"And ladies . . . are you still there?"

Phee held up the phone where Quinn's smiling face appeared. "We're listening, babe . . ."

"I just want to say that I discovered muscles I didn't even know I had in Hawaii. I'd just as soon not get introduced to any additional new ones."

"Snorkeling," Phee mouthed, forming goggles over her eyes with her fingers.

"We promise we'll go easy on you, bro. No swimming involved." Laughing, Jo herded her sisters back to the cottage. With pen and notepad in hand, she made a list of which furniture and paintings would go to Near Cottage, and on a separate page, what they would now need to shop for to replace the cottage furnishings.

"We need to find a table and chairs and something to fill that wall before this weekend." Britt—since she was still unemployed—had become the keeper of the reservation book and monitor of the website. "We have guests coming. And more mid-week. Wednesday and Thursday, I think."

"Then we'll need a bed?" Jo asked. "Maybe we shouldn't risk moving one."

"No, we're fine. If we find one, we'll get it. But the reservations are each for only one couple. So there's no rush if we don't find something."

"What is the budget looking like these days?" Jo was afraid to ask.

"It could be worse," Britt said.

"It could be better," Phee corrected.

"Can I get some solid numbers? So we can get some estimates for what we can afford to spend on each item."

"I assume the checkbook is still in the desk?" Phee started into the room that had been hers here before she married Quinn. She stopped, a strange look on her face.

"What's wrong?" Britt's brow knit.

"It feels strange getting into desks and drawers without asking, now that I don't actually live here."

"Oh, good grief. You don't need permission. Besides, we've been calling your room the library now. So it's a public room."

Phee put a hand over her heart, grinning. "Thank goodness. I feel so much better now."

"Please say you'll still keep our checkbook for us, Phee. I'd hate to guess how much Britt and I could mess things up."

"Don't worry. I'm still all in with this business venture. But Britt, seriously, it might be good if you learned how to manage the checkbook since you're the one who's here most of the time."

Britt frowned.

Phee didn't give her time to argue and changed the subject. "I can hardly wait until our house is finished and I'm living back on the property again."

"Me neither," Jo said, affection for her big sister welling in her. "So . . . what's the damage?"

"Well, don't forget that we'll be able to start bringing in a little more income now that the one cabin is done." Phee opened the top drawer and slid out a savings passbook. "Okay, after paying for new roofs and the improvements to Near Cottage, our balance is"—she ran a finger down the column—"$2,282.67."

"Ouch! Having to replace those roofs killed us." A frisson of worry crawled up Jo's spine. They'd managed to build the fund to more than eleven thousand dollars before paying these latest bills.

"Yes, but it needed doing. And that still leaves quite a bit of money to do the same painting and floors in Far Cottage as we did in the other one. Assuming they keep their price the same."

"Well, you should have some influence over that, Phee." Jo raised her eyebrows. Quinn and a crew from Langhorne Construction had done the work for them.

Phee winked. "I think I can probably swing a deal."

A horn sounded in the lane.

Phee laughed. "Speak of the devil . . ."

It was long after dark when they finished moving furniture, but by the time Phee and Quinn drove away, Near Cottage was furnished and most of Britt's clothes and personal belongings had been moved into the cabin, and Joanna had moved a few of her things into the cabin's second bedroom so she'd be prepared when they had guests in the main cottage.

Britt had gone to bed early, but Jo stood in the middle of the room, admiring their handiwork. And wishing Mom could have seen how the cabin turned out. Jo thought she would have approved of the mixture of textures—woods and basket weaves, linen fabric and nubby pillows, with the subtle addition of rust and peach that read as neutrals, yet gave depth to the overall look.

It amazed her that they could take a shell of a house and in a few hours, have it looking as if they'd always lived there. They'd decided to leave the gallery wall with Mom's paintings and her teal chairs in the cottage living room—at least until Quinn and Phee's house was finished. Phee had expressed a desire to move those things into her new home, and Jo and Britt agreed Mom would have wanted her to have them.

Jo was excited about shopping with her sisters tomorrow and loved that there would be much more shopping together in their future as they decorated the other cabin and then helped Phee decorate her and Quinn's new home. As hard as it was to do all this without their mother's guidance—and the joy Mom had brought to every project—Jo whispered a prayer of thanks that at least Phee would be right here on the property.

She fluffed the cushions on the sofa and straightened a newly hung painting.

If they found a new bed for the cottage on tomorrow's foray to the secondhand stores, they'd be able to accommodate two couples and a single—or a kid or two—in the space. And two more couples in the cabin once the other one was finished enough that they could stay there when the cottage and far cabin were booked.

She and Britt would still probably use the cottage for entertaining friends, and the larger kitchen for cooking. Guests had already expressed how much they loved that the cottage smelled like cinnamon rolls or fresh-baked scones when they arrived. But their little enterprise was growing, and they were on their way to having a viable—

Jo's phone jarred her from her daydreaming. She hurried to the kitchen table where she'd left the phone while they decorated. Glancing at the screen, she couldn't help but laugh. "Wouldn't you know it."

MO-DJ the caller ID announced.

CHAPTER 17

"Joanna?" Luke kept his voice low, not wanting to wake Mateo, who was sleeping in the next room.

"Yes. This is Jo . . ."

"Hi . . . Jo." It felt odd calling her by her nickname. "This is Luke Blaine."

"Hi, Luke."

He waited, expecting her to ask about Mateo—whether he was feeling better—but there was only silence on her end. Finally, he said. "Hey, um . . . I know this is super short notice, but I promised Mateo I'd take him to the park to watch the fireworks. I wondered if maybe you'd want to go with us?"

A moment of hesitation went on too long, but she seemed herself again when she asked, "How *is* Mateo? Is he feeling better?"

"He's fine. I don't know if it was something he ate or if he had that twenty-four-hour crud that's going around. But he's fine now. I promise he won't share the crud with you."

Her laughter seemed forced. "What time were you thinking?"

"I thought maybe we could go eat first. Fireworks won't

start until dark, so we could go as late as seven. If that's not too late for you . . ."

"Yes. That would work. My sisters and I were going to do some shopping. Maybe I could meet you somewhere?"

"That's up to you. I'd be glad to pick you up."

"I'm just not sure what time we'll be done. I may not have time to go back home."

"Okay . . ." It sounded to him like she was creating an escape plan for herself. "Do you like Mexican food?"

"Sure."

"Then why don't you meet us at Muy Caliente at seven. Do you know where that is? On Independence. Not too far from the park."

"I think I know where it is. I'll find it."

"Okay. We'll see you there. Seven . . ."

"Sounds good. Thanks for the invitation."

He clicked off, feeling muddled. *Wow*. She sure didn't sound too enthused about the whole idea. The woman wasn't making this easy. He didn't want to make any judgments until he was sure, but he had a feeling her reserved tone was because of Mateo. Maybe he should have asked if she minded if Mateo came along. He didn't have a clue what the etiquette was for bringing a twelve-year-old along on one's date. But he had promised Mateo about the fireworks and he didn't want to—and wouldn't—back out on that promise.

If Joanna Chandler didn't like the fact that Mateo was part of his life, then that would be that. Because like it or not, Mateo *was* in his life and he'd been there first. If she didn't like that, then she'd have a decision to make. Because they were a package deal.

Luke meant that, heart and soul. But even as the conviction came to his thoughts, it depressed him a little to think that having Mateo in his life might mean he would sacrifice a good woman who wasn't on board with dating a guy with a kid. Not a cute toddler who spent most of the week with his mother. A

148

surly preteen who didn't have a mother. Who was one hundred percent dependent on Luke. That might be a deal breaker for a lot of women.

Sometimes the responsibility overwhelmed him. But he'd promised Maria. No . . . it was more than that. This wasn't simply about keeping a promise. Not anymore. Now, it was about so much more. Because despite himself, he'd grown to love that crazy kid. He couldn't imagine ever loving a son of his own flesh and blood any more than he loved Mateo. The emotion took him by surprise—and made him defensive for Mateo.

He gripped his phone. Maybe he should call Joanna back and tell her to forget it. Lay it on the line and tell her in no uncertain terms, "Like it or not, Mateo is part of my life and any woman I date will have to accept that. If you can't be mature enough to understand why a grieving little boy needs to come first in my life for a while, then maybe you're not ready for a relationship. Maybe you need to grow up and—"

He tossed his phone onto the coffee table with a humorless laugh. Good grief. It was a *date*. Not even really a second date, given how their first attempt had ended. He probably needed to chill a little and not be rehearsing lectures to the poor woman before he even knew if they would hit it off.

But that was just it. He felt like they *had* hit it off. Granted, maybe he was seeing things a little one-sidedly. Simply because a woman flirted with you didn't mean she wanted to marry you. But he was a decent judge of character and he didn't think she was faking it when she laughed at his jokes and seemed interested in his stories, and generally acted like she really liked him.

Okay. He'd give it a shot. He'd wait and see how things went tomorrow night. If she was still blasé about things, that would be the end of it. And—to give her the benefit of the doubt—he would speak with Mateo about his manners and make sure the kid didn't sabotage things before they ever had a chance to test the waters.

Try as she might, Jo couldn't make herself feel laissez-faire about meeting Luke and Mateo for dinner. She'd tried to convince herself she didn't care whether or not things worked out. But the truth was, she did care. Too much.

She got two phone calls about an Airbnb reservation, which made her run late. She was a ball of nerves by the time she arrived at Muy Caliente. Luke and Mateo were waiting outside the restaurant. Jo had always prided herself on being fairly sure of herself, self-confident even. But she felt anything but that walking toward the restaurant from the parking lot.

Still, Luke's disarming smile reminded her of why she liked him so much, and thankfully, Mateo seemed a little less surly than he had the night of Phee's wedding. She was determined not to let the kid get to her.

She pasted on a smile. "Hi there. Hey, Mateo."

"Hi." The boy nodded politely.

"I hope you're not starving." Luke frowned. "There's about a twenty-minute wait." He pointed to Mateo, who held one of the restaurant's pagers in one hand.

"That's okay."

"I should have known we wouldn't be the only ones with this idea."

"It's fine, really. We should still get to the park in plenty of time, right?"

"Sure. Do you want to sit down?"

"I'm okay."

"So . . . How did the shopping go?"

She looked askance at him.

"You said that you and your sisters were doing some shopping?"

"Oh . . . Yes." She'd forgotten she told him that. "We found some great stuff. You should see my car. I was starting to worry I wouldn't be able to get the trunk shut."

He raised his brows in mock concern. "And I suppose that's the sign of a good shopping trip?"

"It is! Phee and Quinn helped us switch a bunch of furniture between the cottage and one of the cabins last night, so we needed to replace some things in the cottage. We found everything we need and then some."

"That's good?"

She flicked an ornery grin at the question in his typical guy response. "If you were Ginger, I'd be dragging you out to my car right now to show you the gorgeous mother-of-pearl trinket box I found." She'd bought the little box at Annie Laurie's, her favorite antique haunt on Broadway. And even though it was a little steep for her budget, she paid thirty-six dollars for the box because she had a feeling it was worth that and more. It would be perfect for the decorative shelf in the bathroom—a place to put aspirin, first-aid items, and a little sewing kit—things guests might need while staying at the cottage.

Luke shook his head, matching her orneriness. "All I can say is thank goodness I am not Ginger—whoever that is."

"Sorry. Friend and former roommate." She loved that he knew when she was teasing and could dish it right back.

"Ah, I see. Well, your enthusiasm is impressive."

"Why thank you. You might think I'm a shopping-crazed maniac. I prefer to think of it as retail therapy."

"Well, of course." He didn't look even remotely convinced.

"We have guests coming this weekend. So we really did need to find that stuff right away."

"Guests? Real company? Or for the Airbnb?"

"Sorry, yes, the Airbnb."

"I've never used Airbnb, but some of the guys at the radio station have stayed in them. How does that work exactly?"

She told him how they'd set up the rental on the Airbnb website and that guests could book a room—or the whole cabin—online. "We're only getting started. But now that we have one of the cabins finished and another one close, we'll be able to rent out the cottage and one cabin for families or larger groups. We'll all stay in the other cabin when both properties are booked." She told him about Quinn and Phylicia's plans to build a house on the property.

"Sounds like business is hopping."

"I don't know if I'd go that far." She tucked a strand of hair behind one ear. "Our rentals have mostly been weekends at this point. And fixing up the cabins is kind of eating our lunch, so we're on a pretty tight budget, but I think it has potential. Especially after Quinn and Phee's place is done and we can rent out three of the four houses at a time. We'll see. At least none of us are paying rent and we don't have a mortgage."

"That's an accomplishment in itself. How did you manage that?" He held up a hand. "Not that it's any of my business. I don't mean to pry."

"No, I know you didn't. You could say it was a gift from my mom. It's how we spent our inheritance from her . . . buying the property. So we can't take any of the credit."

He looked thoughtful. "I think she'd be really proud of what you've done with the place. And I'm guessing any mom would be happy to know that her daughters were such good friends that they wanted to be close."

She flung a wry grin at him. "You haven't seen us fighting over the one bathroom in the cottage."

He laughed. "That sounds more realistic."

"It's one reason we were in such a hurry to move things around last night. We did get Britt moved into the finished cabin so now there are two bathrooms up for grabs. Except the nights we have guests in the cottage—then we'll be back to fighting over one bathroom."

"Apparently that's a big deal for women?" He gave an exaggerated shrug. "I wouldn't know. No sisters. I'm an only child, actually, so I didn't even have to share with—"

"Me too." Mateo piped up. "I'm an only child. Like Luke."

"Yes, you are, buddy." He put his hands on Mateo's shoulders and winked at Jo over the boy's head. "Guess we don't know what we're missing, not having sisters."

She smiled wanly, a little ruffled. She hadn't realized the boy was listening so intently to their conversation. She made a mental note to guard her words more carefully—and hated the resentment that came with the thought. "Count your blessings."

Luke and Mateo both laughed at that. *Was the kid going to horn in on their conversation the rest of the night?* She checked the thought. She *knew* she was being petty and unreasonable where Mateo was concerned. The invitation had been Luke's to make, and he'd made it clear that his Little would be coming with them.

She shouldn't have thought of it as a date in the first place. She simply needed to readjust her expectations. What Luke was doing was admirable and she should be supportive. She knew what it was like to lose her mom. And while she couldn't imagine what that would have been like at twelve, she still didn't want Luke to shunt her to the side because of his Little.

"Hey, speaking of the Airbnb, have you given any more thought to the wedding venue idea?"

She smiled genuinely now, pleased he'd remembered. "A little. I still think it could work. But my sisters seem to think we should make sure we can keep the cottage and cabins rented before we do anything drastic."

"From what I saw at your sister's wedding, it wouldn't take much to recreate the beautiful setting you guys made."

She laughed. "I wish we could take the credit, but God pretty much made everything up there."

"Good point." His smile said he agreed. "I guess it would depend on whether you buy the tent and tables and chairs—all that stuff—or rent them. You could start out with rentals, so you don't have a lot of money tied up in the idea. Of course, if you rent them each time, that cuts into your profits pretty severely."

"Ha! Tell me about it. I haven't even shown Phee the rental invoice yet. She's going to come unglued."

"Well, it would definitely be something to look into and—"

"Hey!" Mateo held the pager aloft, its little red lights chasing each other in a circle. "It's our turn!"

"All right! Let's go."

Inside, Mateo handed the pager to the host, and Luke motioned for Joanna to go ahead of them. Even Mateo held back, as though Luke had coached him that "ladies go first."

The host led them to a booth. Luke waited for Joanna to slide into one side, then he scooted into the other beside Mateo.

Another server brought them jumbo glasses of ice water and left a handful of wrapped straws on the table along with colorful menus.

Jo studied a menu and tried to ignore Mateo as he tore the end of the paper from his straw and blew on it, attempting to launch the remaining paper tube across the table. Not at her, but at the empty spot beside her. When that didn't work and the straw wrapper became a slobbery mess, Mateo grabbed Luke's straw and peeled the end off of it.

Joanna slipped the remaining straws into her lap before they could meet the same fate.

"Hey." Luke spoke sharply to Mateo. "Manners. Remember what we talked about? Now stop messing around." He held out a hand for his straw.

But Mateo yanked it out of reach, his elbow slamming into his glass of water. Before Jo could react, a flood of icy water gushed into her lap.

She gasped as the freezing deluge soaked her white capris clear through. Ice tumbled onto the bench seat around her, even as her temper ignited.

CHAPTER 18

"MATEO!" LUKE SHOT UP OFF the bench, causing other diners to turn and stare. "I told you to quit messing around!"

"I didn't mean to!" Mateo's face scrunched up and turned red.

Luke sucked in a shaky breath. It took everything he had not to lose it and haul the kid out of here by the scruff of his neck. But it had been an accident.

Joanna was the one who needed his attention now. Although he couldn't exactly go help her sop up the flood that had landed in her lap. Not knowing what else to do, he handed her his flimsy paper napkin. "I am *so* sorry, Joanna."

She attempted a smile, but he thought she was as close to tears as Mateo was. Using his forearm as a bulldozer, he cleared the puddle of ice and water that remained on the table, sweeping it onto the floor, then went looking for a busboy.

When he returned with their server, armed with towels, Mateo was still sitting with his face in his hands, dark eyes peeking over his fingers at the mess he'd made. "It was an accident. I swear," he whispered.

Joanna took one last swipe at her lap with a dripping wad

of paper napkins. She swallowed hard and patted Mateo's arm awkwardly. "I know it was an accident. It's only water. It'll dry."

Luke could have kissed her. And yet, he thought he sensed reservation in her tone. He truly felt for Mateo, who couldn't seem to come out from behind his hands. But it didn't seem fair to forgive the boy too quickly, when he did owe Joanna an apology, not merely the defensive excuse he'd offered up so far.

He spoke Mateo's name. "Hey, buddy. What do you tell Joanna?"

"Sorry." The word was muffled behind his hand.

"Hey. Look up here."

Mateo peeked out. "Sorry," he repeated.

"It's not me you need to tell."

"I said it was an accident. I didn't do it on purpose!" he spat.

Luke looked at Joanna and shook his head. "I'm sorry. Can you give us a minute?"

She started to get up from the table.

"Oh . . . no. I didn't mean you have to leave. We're going to go outside for a little talk."

She nodded, not smiling.

He put a hand under Mateo's arm and lifted him from the bench. "We'll be right back."

She motioned toward the restroom. "I'm going to go stand under the blow dryer in the restroom for a few minutes."

"I'm sorry," he mouthed again.

She'd already turned away, her soaked pants clinging to her thighs as she hurried to the restroom. His spirits plummeted as he realized how embarrassed she must be.

This whole night was turning into a disaster.

But right now, he needed to deal with Mateo. With a firm hand on the boy's shoulder, Luke steered him through the front doors. The patio was crowded with noisy diners, but it was too hot to take Mateo to the car. He eyed a spot of shade around the side of the building. "Let's go over here."

"Am I in trouble?"

"No, buddy. It was an accident. I know that, and Joanna knows that. But it happened because you were goofing off, and you should have told her you were sorry."

"I did!"

"No. You gave her excuses and made it sound like it wasn't your responsibility."

"I said 'sorry,' Luke!"

"Only because I told you to. Are you listening to me? What I'm trying to say is that, whether you meant to or not, you knocked a glass of water over on a very nice lady."

A glint came to the brown eyes. "So, you're saying if she wasn't a nice lady, it would be okay to dump water on her."

It was everything Luke could do to curb a smile. But he made his voice firm. "No, that's not what I'm saying. And please don't be a smart aleck. This is not the time."

Mateo smirked, but seeing Luke's glare, he quickly turned somber. "I'm sorry."

"Thank you. I appreciate that. Now, you need to tell Joanna that same thing. And not just one word. How should you say it? To her?"

Mateo scraped his flip-flop on the asphalt, eyes downcast. "I'm sorry."

"Not too bad, but you can do better. You need to look her in the eye. Now, what will you say to her when you see her inside in a few minutes? Pretend I'm her."

"You're not nearly as pretty as she is."

"Very true. But Mateo, I'm not joking about this, and I don't think you're taking me very seriously. Now what are you going to say to her?"

Mateo met his eye. "Miss Joanna, I am very sorry I spilled my water on you."

Luke chose to ignore the hint of defiance in his tone. "That's more like it."

"Wait. I wasn't done."

Luke reared back. "Oh . . . Sorry. Go ahead."

"I am very sorry I spilled my water on you. I shouldn't have been messing around, and it won't happen again."

Smiling big, Luke raised his right hand for a high five. Mateo gave it begrudgingly and Luke pulled him into a quick side hug, proud of him for going the extra mile.

Now if the kid could just pull it off when he actually apologized to Joanna.

Jo took one last glance at the full-length mirror by the restroom door. Not quite dry, but she couldn't hide out in here all night. This would have to do. She hiked her purse over one shoulder, inhaled deeply, and opened the door.

Mateo was back in their booth, which looked as if it had been wiped off and reset with new silverware and napkins. And little bowls of salsa and a basket brimming with chips. Luke was speaking to the server, pointing at a menu.

Jo was suddenly ravenous. She approached the table with a smile she wasn't quite feeling, but she was determined not to let this ruin the evening. Looking at Mateo, she stretched out her arms. "See? You can barely tell I went for a swim in my clothes."

Luke laughed and nudged Mateo with a stern look.

"Miss Joanna, I'm very sorry I spilled water on you." He sucked in air and recited, his words gaining speed and volume as he went. "I shouldn't have been messing around and I promise I will never let it happen again, and you have every right to be mad at me and I don't blame you if you can't forgive what I did to—"

Luke cleared his throat loudly. "That's probably good, bud." He clapped Mateo's shoulder.

Joanna flicked a wink at Luke before turning back to Mateo. "Hey, I forgive you. I know it was an accident. No harm done."

"Thanks." The boy looked at his lap, suddenly shy again. And obviously relieved when the server appeared at their table again.

"Everybody here now? Are you ready to order?"

Luke looked at Jo with a question.

"I know what I'm getting. Whenever you're ready."

"We're ready. You go ahead."

She told the server what she wanted and watched Luke with Mateo as they placed their orders. If she'd been a casual observer, she would have thought they were father and son. Mateo even looked a little like Luke with the same dark complexion and almost black hair, the same athletic build. Only Luke's gold-flecked gray eyes set his appearance apart from the boy's.

While they waited for their order Mateo quizzed Luke from a list of riddles and questions printed on the kids' menu. Luke played along and laughed at the corny jokes. A few times he stopped and tried to draw her into the "game," but she felt awkward and very much a fifth wheel. She scarfed chips and salsa in silence and pretended to enjoy their playful interaction.

When their food came, Mateo shoveled his tacos down in five minutes flat, then turned the extra silverware into fighting machines. Luke made him quiet down, so she and Luke were finally able to visit—albeit with Mateo *vroom-vrooming* under his breath in the background.

She was in the middle of telling Luke about the plans for decorating the last cottage when Mateo's noises got noticeably louder. Luke lifted a hand, looking apologetic.

He bent and whispered something in Mateo's ear. The kid grinned, but he quieted down.

Somehow, the way the two of them interacted made Luke seem older, mature beyond his years. He would be a good father someday. *Someday.* Right now, she simply wanted to enjoy getting to know the man without any distractions. She had to admit she'd be glad when Mateo was finally placed with a family and Luke was free of the responsibility. She hoped there was a good family waiting for him, one who would be everything a boy like Mateo needed.

CHAPTER 19

OOOH! AAAH!" LUKE'S FEIGNED APPRECIATION of the fireworks made Joanna and Mateo both laugh and echo his *oohs* and *aahs*.

Jo leaned back on her elbows on the denim quilt Luke had brought for them to sit on. The darkness of the crowded park afforded her a chance to admire him without worrying he might catch her staring. Even though she *was* staring. Hard. Physically, the man was her ideal—a glorious cross between Milo Ventimiglia and Zac Efron.

Between flashes of light, she memorized Luke's silhouette, the firm line of his jaw and the way his hair curled around his temple. With his guard down, relaxed on the blanket—Mateo plopped between them—Luke was even more handsome than she'd judged him to be that day she first saw him talking to Trent at the office.

Not that she was hung up on physical appearances. That had never really been important to her in a man. Ben was nice-looking, but it had been his personality that attracted her initially. His quick wit and friendliness. And the more she'd gotten to know him, the better looking he'd become in her eyes. Of course, that was before she discovered that he had a fatal flaw: When the going got tough, he ran.

Luke was different. But sometimes, she almost couldn't appreciate his personality because he was so *stinkin'* good looking. The thought made her smile. And wish her sisters were here so she could whisper with them, find out if they thought he was as handsome as she did.

Despite the waterworks at the restaurant, and Mateo's admittedly disruptive presence, she was enjoying herself, and was beginning to wish she hadn't insisted on meeting Luke at the restaurant. Because once the fireworks show was over, they would walk back to their cars and that would be it.

Luke scooted back on the blanket, and noticeably closer to Joanna, leaving Mateo in front of them.

Jo gave him her best smile. "It's been a perfect night . . . weather-wise, I mean. For the fireworks." *Good grief. Shut up, Chandler. While you're still ahead.*

Luke laughed. "I was gonna say . . . If you consider getting doused in ice water part of a perfect night, you might want to reevaluate your standards. Or have your head examined."

She gave a sidewise glance at Mateo, who had made some kind of weapon with a branch he'd picked up and was back to making noises and didn't seem to be paying attention to them. "It's really okay. Although I *am* very grateful it wasn't a cherry limeade."

He winked. "That would have been a sticky situation, for sure."

She laughed, relaxing a little more. Another volley of fireworks lit the night sky and they tipped their heads to watch. But Joanna went back to studying Luke long before the colored lights fizzled into embers.

He turned, too, and caught her eye. "I'm glad you came."

She nodded. "Me too."

He glanced at Mateo and lowered his voice. "I'd like to see you again. If that's okay."

Her heart raced. She couldn't remember the last time she'd felt that little thrill. "I'd like that."

"I'll call you."

She flashed a grin. "Oh, sure. That's what they all say."

"I *will* call you."

"If you don't, I might have to call *you*." She said it teasingly, but she meant every word. She liked this man. A lot. And she was willing to wait for Luke. Even if it was a few months until Mateo was settled in his forever home.

She supposed it could be longer than a few months. Things in the foster care system sometimes moved like molasses.

She laughed to herself. She could already hear her sisters chiding her for falling so hard for a man she'd now officially had exactly one-point-five dates with.

Driving home, Luke found himself wishing it was Joanna Chandler buckled in the passenger seat beside him instead of a sleeping twelve-year-old boy. The thought brought with it a twinge of guilt—only because it also brought a thought of Maria. Luke wouldn't have wanted her to think Mateo was a burden. That was too strong a word, but it *was* a pain in the butt to have an adolescent along on a date—especially when you really liked the woman. Really, really liked her.

Mateo was almost asleep, his head lolling against the window when Luke pulled into his garage. "Hey, buddy. Wake up. We're home."

"No." Mateo moaned and played possum. "Leave me right here. I'll come in later."

"No. Come in now. Come on . . ." He gave Mateo's knee a few sharp pats. "Come on."

"You're mean!"

"You're right. I am. Now come on. Unbuckle and go brush your teeth."

It was an uphill battle, but after twenty minutes Mateo was in bed with teeth brushed and prayers said. Luke sat on the side of his bed as had become Mateo's bedtime ritual. He tucked the blankets around the narrow shoulders. "Sleep tight, okay?"

"Uh-huh. You too."

Luke reached up and turned off the lamp on the nightstand, the one he'd brought from Mateo's bedroom in Maria's apartment. "See you in the morning."

He rose and started to leave the room, feeling his way the short distance in the dim light from the hallway. But as he pulled the door halfway closed, Mateo's voice made him halt. "How come you talk to that girl—Miss Joanna—the same way you talked to Mama?"

Luke stopped short and returned to Mateo's bedside, grateful for the darkness. "What do you mean, buddy?" But he was only buying time. He knew very well what Mateo meant.

He and Maria had joked around and teased each other. Some might have called it flirting. Whenever their interactions veered in that direction, it had usually been him who put the skids on things. Especially if Mateo was in on the conversation—which he invariably was.

That last day of her life, Maria had made him promise to take care of Mateo, to raise him as a son. But she'd also made a confession that, even now, he wasn't sure how to process.

Luke had always been very conscious of the expectations Big Brothers and Big Sisters had of their volunteers, and since the radio station was involved in supporting and promoting BBBS—and he was their employee—he felt a double obligation not to do anything that might call the ethics of either entity into question.

And by the time Mateo's social worker had moved away and his Big/Little relationship with Mateo continued without benefit of the organization's oversight, he'd felt even more obligated to keep things the way they had been.

But that last day, sitting by her bedside, with Maria clutching his hand through the rails of the hospital bed that hospice had moved to her apartment, she told him, "I love you, Lukas. I think I've always loved you."

The words were threaded, with great effort, through parched lips, but there was no question Maria knew what she was saying. She wasn't speaking under the influence of drugs or out of desperation. It was a simple declaration of her love.

For one desperate moment, he wondered if she expected him to echo her words. Would he regret it if he disappointed her . . . broke her heart, even by not exchanging declarations? What harm would it do to let her go to her grave believing he felt the same?

And he did love her. But it wasn't the same kind of love she'd declared for him.

Maria took the decision out of his hands a few seconds later. She looked up at him with love in her rheumy eyes. "You don't have to say anything, Lukas," she whispered. "You . . . you've loved me in the best way I could ever hope for. By loving my son."

"Is it? Is it, Luke?" Mateo's words made Luke's breath catch.

"Sorry, buddy. Is it what?" He'd been so mired in thought he hadn't realized Mateo had been trying to get his attention.

"Is it because you love her?"

"Whoa . . . What are we talking about, buddy? I must have missed something."

"Is that why you talk to Miss Joanna like you do? You know . . . All *goo-goo-ga-ga*? Because you love her?"

Luke laughed at the kid's facial gymnastics when he said *goo-goo-ga-ga*, but behind the laughter, he was scrambling to figure out how to answer that question in a way that didn't incriminate him. "Mateo, I haven't even known Joanna—Miss Joanna—long enough to know if I like her, let alone mention *love*." His own words sounded very convincing, but he'd never fallen for a woman as hard—or as fast—as he'd fallen for Joanna

Chandler. Which seemed ridiculous given that she was making it very clear that she wasn't a fan of Mateo. And Mateo wasn't going anywhere. It was a problem he didn't know how to get around.

Jo had barely been home an hour and had just settled on the sofa with a cup of decaf when her phone buzzed. Probably one of her sisters. Britt had been staying in the cabin alone, but Jo noticed she usually found some excuse to call as soon as it got dark.

But when she picked up her phone, it was Luke's name on the screen, or more accurately MO-DJ. She hadn't really expected him to call her *tonight*. But she wasn't exactly surprised either. She *was* pleased, and her "hello" must have communicated that.

"Hey, you." There was a smile in his voice. "I hope I'm not calling too late."

"No. Of course not. I'm still up. Sipping a cup of decaf, in fact."

"Ah. So, are you one of those flavored coffee lovers or a purist?"

She laughed. "I can tell which you are by that snarky 'one of those' comment."

"And I can tell you're 'one of those' by your snarky comeback."

She gave a little huff. "Glad we got that settled. Note to self: Do not serve Luke amaretto vanilla caramel pumpkin coffee."

"*Please* tell me there's not really such a thing."

"I can tell you that all night, but there is. You might even like it."

"I doubt it. But I'll tell you what I *did* like."

"Oh?" She cradled the phone to her ear, not wanting to miss one word.

"The evening with you. Except it ended too soon. For me anyway."

Laughing softly, she curled her feet beneath her on the sofa, burrowing into the corner. "I agree. It did."

"Mateo was mad that I didn't ask you to go for ice cream after the fireworks."

"What? You went for ice cream without me?"

"Don't worry, I told him no."

"Ah, so he wasn't mad on my account as much as his own."

Luke laughed. "Well, maybe. But he did use you as the reason he thought we should have gone."

She was pleased—and, frankly, surprised—that Mateo had actually mentioned her. "I was afraid he'd be mad at me. About the spill. It shocked me so much I . . . hope I wasn't rude to him."

"Are you kidding? If anybody should be mad at anybody, it's you. At me."

"I'm not mad. And why you? You're not the one who spilled all over me."

"Well, me by proxy."

"No. I know it was an accident."

His heavy sigh held shades of relief. "I'll be honest, for a minute there, I was afraid that would be the end of the date."

"I didn't say anything rude, did I?" She held her breath. What if she *had*? "I honestly don't even remember *what* I said. It happened so fast . . ."

"Well, if you ignore the part where you cussed a blue streak, then no, you didn't say anything rude."

She could imagine the ornery smirk accompanying his laughter.

"Just so you know, sir, I do not cuss. But I'll tell you what, that water was *cold*!"

They laughed together.

"Mostly what I remember, Miss Chandler, was a lot of gasping and sputtering."

"Well, hey, Mr. Blaine, let me dump a huge glass of ice water in *your* lap and see if you might gasp and sputter a little bit too."

"Nah . . . I'd probably just cuss a blue streak."

Oh . . . this man. Smiling, Jo stretched out on the sofa, wishing he were here with her now, and knowing that no matter how cautious she was attempting to be, her heart was not listening. At all.

CHAPTER 20

JO HAD A HARD TIME concentrating at work the next day, replaying her conversation with Luke over and over. They'd talked on the phone until almost midnight, when he finally apologized for keeping her up on a work night, and then hung up . . . but reluctantly, she thought. She *hoped*.

And he *had* asked her out for another date. He implied that this time it would be just the two of them. Without Mateo. After their fun phone conversation, she was excited about the prospect of another date, and even though it was only two days away, the hours would drag until Friday finally came.

She'd already started praying that the kid would stay healthy, wouldn't get in trouble at school, wouldn't talk Luke into letting him tag along, and every other contingency she could think of. She felt a little guilty about that.

And more than a little petty. But was it wrong to want a man's full attention when they were on a date? How was she supposed to get to know—let alone fall in love with—someone who was so busy cleaning up messes and teaching manners and giving hugs and high fives that he could hardly pay attention to her? And someone who got interrupted every time it finally started to feel like they were finally having a decent conversation and learning to know each other a little?

She was jealous, plain and simple. Of a twelve-year-old orphan. How pathetic was that?

When she went home for lunch, Britt was washing out paintbrushes in front of the unfinished cabin where she'd been working for the past week.

"How's it going?" Jo called across the driveway.

Britt sighed. "Slow. And hot." She headed Jo's way, shaking a wet paintbrush as she walked. The droplets of water sparkled in the midday sun.

"It's not even eighty degrees yet. Do you have all the fans set up?" The two smaller cabins didn't have central air, although Quinn had put a window unit in Britt's cabin. Thankfully, here by the river with the houses all deep in the shade, it rarely got hot enough to run the AC.

"It's not so much hot as it is humid. I'm sweating like a dog."

"You're working like a dog too." Jo reached up and tried unsuccessfully to brush flecks of dried paint from her sister's hair. "Why don't you quit for the afternoon? I can help you when I get off work tonight."

"No, it's okay. I'm on a roll. I'll eat later." She propped the paintbrush on the ledge of the porch to dry and opened the door to the cottage's enclosed porch. "I made some chicken salad if you want a sandwich. I can go get it."

"That's okay. It's carrot sticks for me. I'm saving the calories for Friday night."

"What's Friday night?"

Jo grinned. "I have a date. Dexter Bar-B-Que."

"You have a date with Dexter Bar-B-Que?"

"Haha. Very funny."

"With Luke?" Britt's brow knit. "This is starting to sound serious. Well, except for the Dexter's part. Not exactly your top date-night restaurant."

"For your information, it was my choice. And I wouldn't exactly call three dates serious."

"So, do you like him?"

"I do." Avoiding her sister's gaze, she went to the fridge and rummaged for something to go with her carrots. "I like him a lot. I have some . . . reservations, but—"

"What do you mean reservations?" She could feel Britt's eyes burning a hole through her back.

"Mateo." She grabbed a cup of yogurt and closed the refrigerator door. "Oh. You want some yogurt? I have plenty."

Britt waved off her offer. "I'll have some chicken salad later. So, how much longer will Luke have Mateo?"

"I'm not sure. But I'm starting to wonder if it's a sort of semipermanent thing."

"Semipermanent? You mean Luke's going to raise him?"

"I don't know. We haven't really talked about it. Or at least every time I try to bring it up, it feels like he changes the subject." It had happened again on the phone last night, which was making her more than suspicious. "I really do like Luke, but I don't know that I want some kid tagging along everywhere we go."

"Why? Is he coming on your Dexter Bar-B-Que date?"

"He's not supposed to. Luke said it'll just be the two of us. But Luke *did* bring him last night for the fireworks." Between bites of yogurt, she told Britt about Mateo spilling water in her lap.

Britt's laughter faded. "You don't think he did it on purpose, do you?"

Jo paused, spoon suspended midair. "I hadn't thought about that possibility. But . . . no, I think it was an honest accident. Luke made him apologize. It wasn't that big of a deal. But kind of embarrassing."

"Wow. Well, if I were you, I'd sure find out what the deal is. I mean, what if things got serious, Jo? You'd be the mom of a teenager!"

"Good grief, we haven't even been on our third date and you have us married already? And anyway, *that* is not happening." She couldn't fathom living in a house with a teenager, let alone being a mother figure to one. Most days, she still felt like a teen herself. Although her friend Ginger's sister was Jo's age and she had a ten-year-old daughter. Of course, she'd gotten married right out of high school with a baby on the way. Still . . . She gave a little shudder.

"I like Luke, too, but really, Jo . . . what if you fall in love with him? Then what are you going to do?"

"Do?"

"About the Mateo situation?"

"It's crazy to even think that far ahead. We've had two dates."

"Going on three. Remember what Mom always said?"

"Which thing? Mom said a lot of good things."

"Never go on even one date with someone you already know you wouldn't marry." Britt quoted the advice in a tone so like their mother's that it took Jo's breath away.

An ache—raw and physical—washed over her, and she realized it had been a while—maybe weeks—since she'd felt that soul-deep homesickness for Mom. She would have given anything in that moment to talk to her mom, tell her about Luke, and ask her advice about Mateo. She supposed she could call Dad, but it wasn't the same. He wouldn't understand like Mom would've. And he'd only try to fix her "problem" and then be disappointed if she didn't take his advice.

"It's not that I wouldn't marry Luke," she started. "He's a great guy. I really do like him. But we're just getting to know each other."

"Okay, I get that. But let's say"—she held up a hand—"hypothetically, that you date him for six months and everything about him turns out to be perfect. He's the man of your dreams. Smart, good looking, kind, brave . . . everything you could want in a man. Except! He has a teenage son."

"Mateo's only twelve."

"I bet in six months he'll be thirteen. So, would that be nonnegotiable for you? A teenage son?"

"Britt! Cut it out. I can't even think about that."

"Well, there's your answer. And maybe you *should* think about it. I'm just saying."

But the truth was, she *had* thought about it. More than she dared to admit. If she and Luke got serious, would Mateo think she was trying to fill his mother's shoes, and resent her for it? What if they got married, but Mateo always came first in Luke's eyes? Would their own children be neglected or feel like they came in second? What if, after her own babies came along, Mateo harmed them?

Maybe she was being dramatic. But you heard about these things in the news all the time. She just didn't see how any of this would work.

She tossed her spoon in the sink and threw the empty yogurt cup into the trash can under the sink. "Wow. Sure glad I came home for lunch so you could cheer me up."

Britt giggled, but Jo wasn't exactly teasing.

"Sorry, sis. Didn't mean to rain on your parade."

"Yes, you did." Jo offered a weak smile.

Britt shrugged and started out of the kitchen. "I'm going to go eat something and get back to work. See you at five?"

"Make it five thirty. I need to stop at the post office on my way home."

"Okay." Britt left and the cottage suddenly seemed deathly quiet.

Joanna went to touch up her makeup in the bathroom mirror, but her sister's words haunted her. If Mateo *was* a deal breaker for her, then what was she doing leading Luke on?

No. She shook her head at her reflection in the mirror. She didn't even know the details yet. For all she knew plans were in the works for finding Mateo a home. She wasn't going to cancel their date and then find out that Luke would be free a month or two from now.

But she *would* ask him, and not let him evade her question this time. It was a touchy subject because, like she'd told Britt, they weren't serious yet. And she didn't want Luke to think she was reading more into their casual dating than she actually was. But neither did she want to wait until they *were* serious before she found out exactly what Mateo's place in Luke's life was.

Of course, if she revealed why the question was so important to her—that she wasn't sure she'd want a relationship with Luke if Mateo was part of the "package"—that might be the end of their friendship anyway.

And it did make her appear petty and lacking compassion to feel like she did about Mateo. She truly did care about what happened to him. And even felt a sort of kinship with him, having lost her own mom. But that was part of the reason she didn't want her dreams derailed—or rather what was left of her dreams. Her longing to someday place her babies in her mother's arms, to see Mom as a grandma, had died. She couldn't let the dream of a cozy home with a husband and a baby—just the three of them—die too. Besides, Mateo deserved to have a mom who was more than just a few years older than him and actually knew what to do with a teen.

She washed her hands and went through the house turning out lights. She locked the cottage and texted Britt to let her know she was leaving. Her sister appeared on the stoop and waved goodbye, smiling, as if she hadn't just built a cloud over Jo's week with her piercing questions.

CHAPTER 21

"OKAY, BUDDY, YOU'VE GOT YOUR PJs laid out?" Luke stuck his head in Mateo's room, making sure his instructions had been followed.

"Yep."

Spying a stray sock at the foot of the bed that he'd missed when gathering up laundry earlier, he went to retrieve it. "And you won't forget to brush your teeth."

"Never do."

Luke punched Mateo in the shoulder and the kid fell back on the mattress feigning injury. But his smile matched Luke's.

"You scamp!" He tousled the kid's dark hair and pulled him into a headlock. "You'd forget to brush every single stinkin' day if I didn't remind you—and you know it."

Mateo squirmed, trying to escape, grinning the whole time.

"You be good for Sarah, you hear me? She has my permission to send you to bed early if she needs to."

"Why can't I just go with you?"

"We already went over that. This is a date. I don't think Joanna would appreciate me bringing a big lunkhead like you along."

"You brought a big lunkhead on your Fourth of July date."

The kid had a point. "That wasn't exactly a date. That was Joanna tagging along with you and me."

"So? Why can't I tag along with you and her?"

"Because I said so."

"Oh, man." Mateo rolled his eyes. "That's what Mama always used to say when she didn't have a good answer."

"Hey! That *is* a good answer. And don't you forget it."

Mateo plopped back on the bed, lacing his fingers behind his head. Luke saw the too-familiar faraway look come to his eyes. The one that came whenever they talked about Maria.

But Mateo came back to the present long enough to pout. "I don't see why I have to have a babysitter. I'm old enough to stay by myself."

"You soon will be. But not quite yet. Besides, you like Sarah." He'd hired a college girl from church to watch Mateo tonight.

"How could I like her? I don't even know her."

"Yes, you do. From the worship team."

"Whatever."

"You be nice to her." Luke matched his expression to the firmness of his voice. "I'm not kidding."

"I heard you the first twenty-seven times."

"Mateo." Luke struggled with knowing where to draw the line with the kid's sass. He knew a certain amount of it was just the age. Heaven knew he'd had a mouth on him when he was twelve. And some of Mateo's issues were no doubt a reflection of his grief—and the major life adjustments he'd been forced to make over the last few months. "Watch the mouth, okay?"

Mateo hung his head. "Okay . . . Sorry."

"How about we go for donuts tomorrow morning?"

Mateo perked up. "Can we come back and eat them while we watch cartoons?"

"Sure. For a couple of hours maybe, but we're not going

to veg out in front of the TV all day. Maybe we can go to the batting cages tomorrow afternoon."

"Promise?"

Luke nodded. "If it doesn't rain."

"Awesome!"

"But remember, Saturday is housecleaning day too."

Mateo groaned.

"The batting cages will be our reward. I bet you can—"

His cell phone jangled. He fished it out of his pocket. Sarah. The babysitter. *Uh-oh.*

He answered. "Hey, Sarah. Do you need a ride?"

"Uh, Luke . . ."

He didn't like her tone. *Please, Lord, don't let her be calling to cancel.*

"Gosh, Luke, I really hate to do this, but I'm going to need to cancel tonight. See, my grandparents drove up from Chicago and surprised me. They're only going to be here tonight and tomorrow, so this weekend is the only chance I'll have to spend time with them. I . . . I haven't seen them since Christmas, so I really couldn't tell them no and—"

"No . . . Of course. I understand." He stifled a sigh. "You have a great time. I'll take a rain check on the babysitting."

"I'm not a baby!" Mateo hissed in a stage whisper.

Luke shushed him with a look.

"Thanks for understanding, Luke. I won't let you down again, I promise. But I just couldn't say no to my grand—"

"You go and have fun, Sarah. Talk to you later." He tapped End and blew out the sigh he'd been holding in. Now what?

A hopeful gleam filled Mateo's eyes. "So now I get to go with you to Dexter's?"

Luke couldn't help but laugh at the kid's expression. But he wasn't sure he'd be laughing at Joanna's reaction when he broke the news to her. He got the distinct impression she thought Mateo was a "temporary" situation in his life.

He'd tried—more than once—to tell her the truth of the matter. Well, sort of anyway. He'd just have to try harder.

"Let me call Joanna and see what we can work out. You go comb your hair and put on a clean shirt."

Joanna clamped a hank of hair in the flatiron and wound it slowly before releasing a perfect spiral curl. Melvin perched on the edge of the sink, his head tilted, waiting for her to turn on the tap for him.

"Melvin, why can't you drink out of your water bowl like a normal cat?" But she turned on the water for him, smiling as the cat's pink tongue *lap lap lapped* at the thin stream of water.

She picked up the flatiron again and started another curl. Her phone buzzed on the bathroom counter, making Melvin jump.

She laughed, and still gripping the flatiron with one hand, she turned her phone over to see Luke's name—his smiling face where MO-DJ had once appeared.

She'd added the photo from his Facebook profile to her phone. It might have been a little premature, given that tonight might very well be her last date with him, but she did enjoy seeing his handsome face pop up on her phone.

Except . . . it was never good when a guy called twenty minutes before he was supposed to pick you up for a date.

"Hello?"

"Joanna, it's Luke. You are going to hate me, but . . . there's been a little hitch in the plans for tonight?"

"Oh?" She tried to keep the trepidation from her voice.

"The girl who was going to babysit Mateo had to cancel."

"Oh . . ." She stared at her reflection in the mirror, hair half-curled, the other half hanging limp. Like her spirits. She was glad Luke couldn't see her glum expression. "Well . . ." She wasn't sure what he wanted her to say.

"If you want to cancel, I'll understand, but let me suggest a couple of options first," he added quickly. "If you don't mind Mateo tagging along, we can still go eat at Dexter's. It's his favorite place to eat, actually. Oh, and I cross my heart and hope to die he will not spill water on you."

She laughed, but it came out forced and weak. She could have pointed out that Luke had no control over whether the kid did or didn't spill on her. But she said nothing, waiting to hear his other option.

"If you're okay with that, we could come back to my place and sit out on the back patio. Mateo goes to bed early so once he's down, we can make a fire and sit outside, maybe have some ice cream . . . Would you be okay with that?"

"Sure. That'd be all right." She was careful not to sound too enthused because if she was going to continue seeing Luke, she didn't want this to become a habit—Mateo "tagging along."

"Okay, great." He didn't seem to notice her hesitance. "Oh, one thing. Would you mind too much meeting us at Dexter's? I won't be able to leave Mateo alone to take you home. I'm so sorry."

"No, it's okay. I'll meet you there. The one in Jackson, right? Seven?"

"Yes. We'll be waiting."

Jo tapped End and released a sigh. Melvin looked up from his drinking fountain as if to inquire what was wrong. She stroked his silky fur and wiped a drip of water from his chin. "This isn't what I signed up for, Melvin. You know?"

He replied with a squeaky *yip* that made him sound more like a dog than a cat.

But the truth was she hadn't "signed up" for anything. As much as she liked Luke, they hadn't made any commitments to each other, hadn't even really declared their feelings for each other. They were in that awkward phase between friendship and love—*possible* love—and she had no right to dictate how he chose to live his life or the decisions he made regarding

Mateo. If she didn't want to date a man with a kid—because that's what this seemed to amount to—then it was time to break off the relationship.

But I like him, Lord. So much.

Enough to wait until Luke was free? She should be thankful there wasn't an ex-wife or even a beloved late wife to contend with. But at least with an ex-wife, Luke wouldn't be wholly responsible for Mateo. They'd have a break from him and time for just each other once in a while.

She wound another hank of hair into the flatiron and by the time she her hair was styled, she'd decided that no matter what, tonight was the night she'd talk to Luke about the "Mateo problem." It wasn't fair to Luke—or Mateo—for her to let them believe that she was on board with this. Better to break it off now than let herself fall in love with Luke when she would only be setting herself up for heartbreak.

She was twenty-six. Almost twenty-seven. No, it wasn't ancient, but most of her friends were married. Most with children. In fact, Ginger was the only friend she could think of from high school or college who was still single. And that was by choice. As much as Jo hated making marriage sound like a business arrangement, could she *afford* to wait for the perfect man in the perfect set of circumstances?

What if she ended things with Luke and there *was* no one else? Still, she wasn't desperate enough to compromise on something this important. Not yet anyway.

CHAPTER 22

LUKE PULLED THE DOOR TO Mateo's room closed and went across the hall to the bathroom. He flipped on the light over the sink and ran a hand through his hair. He made sure he didn't have something stuck in his teeth, then swished some mouthwash and spat in the sink.

He turned off the light and started to leave, then glanced out the window that overlooked the patio where Joanna sat waiting. He felt a little guilty "spying" on her like this, but he had to admit he liked the looks of her curled up on the wicker chaise lounge. Waiting for him.

It had taken longer than he intended to get Mateo settled in bed—and he still wasn't sure the crazy kid was asleep yet. But at long last he was in bed with strict instructions not to get out unless there was fire or a zombie apocalypse.

The meal at Dexter's had gone okay. At least nobody had spilled anything on anybody. But it was a mixed blessing that Mateo had warmed up to Joanna, because now the kid apparently felt comfortable enough around her to hog the conversation and generally make a pest of himself. Luke sensed Joanna had been a little annoyed. And he didn't really blame her.

Preteens took "pesky" to a new level. But her coolness toward Mateo made him defensive for the boy. *His* boy.

Still, he liked Joanna enough that he'd made up his mind to talk to her about Mateo. It might be the nail in the coffin, but it was only fair she know where things stood with Mateo. And he needed to know whether or not she could accept that Mateo was a part of his life. Here to stay. Well, at least for the foreseeable future.

Luke continued down the hallway, eager to have Joanna to himself, yet dreading the conversation he knew they needed to have.

He'd been thinking a lot lately about his commitment to Mateo. Once Maria had asked him to take the boy in upon her death, Luke had never wavered in his commitment to give Mateo a safe home. But lately, it seemed like God might be calling him to make that commitment deeper.

He and Mateo had called each other "brother" almost from the beginning. Since neither of them had a brother by birth, it seemed natural to "adopt" each other as brothers. But as Mateo grew older, Luke suspected he would need more than a big brother. Perhaps they'd been calling each other "brother" too long to make the adjustment to father and son. And Luke was barely old enough to actually *be* Mateo's father, but he wanted to provide the security and sense of belonging that Maria would have provided.

He'd been reading and researching, and he was beginning to wonder if legally adopting Mateo was not only the right thing to do, but something God might be asking him to commit to.

But it was the next question that sobered him most. What if God were also asking him to give up the hope of marriage?

Because Joanna was as kind and sweet as they came, and if *she* was adverse toward the idea of Mateo being part of a relationship with him, then he didn't know any woman who would be open to it. Not that any other woman mattered. Already, he had a strong sense that Joanna Chandler was everything he wanted. And more.

It seemed a strange thought, given they'd only known each other for a few weeks. But every time he was with her, the feeling grew stronger: she was everything he'd ever desired in a woman.

Except for the small detail of her feelings toward Mateo. But Mateo had become part of Luke's life as naturally and surely as if he were his own flesh and blood. And if raising Mateo for the next six years meant holding off on having his own family—or giving up the idea of ever having a family at all—that was a sacrifice he would make. His heart simply gave him no choice.

He went to check on Mateo once more before heading for the patio. The boy stirred, but soon his even breathing resumed, and Luke gave a sigh of relief.

Downstairs, he opened the sliding French doors and poked his head out. "Do you need a refill?" He'd sent Jo out with a Diet Coke twenty minutes ago.

"No thanks. I'm good." She put down the cell phone she'd been looking at and turned her full attention to him.

"Did you think I'd forgotten you were out here? Sorry, but I think he's down for the count. Are you ready for ice cream?"

She gave a little groan and patted her stomach. "I'm still stuffed from dinner. But you go ahead."

"No, I'll wait. Sorry that took so long." He grinned, pulling the sliding door shut behind him. The sky was a dusky navy, with only a faint glow outlining the tree branches.

"I can't imagine a prettier place to kill time." She waited for him to settle across from her in a cushioned lawn chair. "You never told me you were a master gardener. This is absolutely beautiful, Luke. And it smells divine!" She swept her gaze around the patio and the woods beyond as if she were seeing it for the first time.

The strings of twinkle lights he'd woven through the

pergola made the masses of white annuals planted in flower beds glow, and he'd lit lanterns at each corner of the patio to illumine the colorful pots. A small fountain opposite where they were seated splashed musically and a sweet scent wafted on the night air.

"That's the sweet peas you're smelling, I think." He stretched to pluck a pink bloom from the flower bed and handed it to her. "I planted them for Mateo. They were Maria's favorite."

He immediately regretted mentioning Maria. Mateo's mother had only been in the garden once, a few years ago when she'd picked up Mateo from Luke's house. It was before she'd gotten sick. She'd followed him through the house to the backyard where he and Mateo had been playing catch. Their conversation had definitely bordered on flirtation that night, though they'd never acknowledged it.

But Joanna seemed not to notice his mention of Maria. She rubbed the petals of the flower between her fingers, then lifted them to her nose. "Mmm . . . That's it. That's what I was smelling. It's lovely."

"You make me glad I decided against a fire. You wouldn't have been able to smell the sweet peas for the smoke."

"I love the smell of a fire, too, but I prefer flowers any day. Besides, it's plenty warm." She stretched her arms overhead and resettled into the chaise. "It's gorgeous out here, Luke!"

"Well, I can't really take any credit for all this. I did plant the annuals myself, but the flower beds were already here when I bought the house six years ago. And I just bought planters that the nursery put together. They're a little pricey, but they look good nine months out of the year—well, as long as I remember to water them anyway—and I like having an outdoor space to hang out in."

"I can see why. You make me want to start our landscaping at the cottage. Unfortunately, getting the cabins livable—*rentable*—has been the priority right now. Maybe next spring.

I'll have to pick your brain then about what to plant. Sweet peas for sure."

"How's the wedding venue project going?"

She gave a humorless laugh. "It's not. But the second cabin is almost finished—except for furnishing it—so I'm hoping to get back to the wedding venue idea by the end of the summer."

"I still think it'd do great."

"I don't remember if I told you Quinn and Phee plan to build a house on the property. On the other side of the cabin we used for a dressing room . . . you remember?"

He nodded. "That will be nice—to have your sister close by. Well, I assume it will. You three seem to get along really great." His brow furrowed, turning it into a question.

She laughed. "Britt and I couldn't be happier about it. We have the usual sisterly spats, but I was sad to think of Phee moving away, so yes, we're thrilled. Plus, it will give us one more place to rent for The Cottages. Phee and Quinn haven't seen the final plans yet, but the house they're planning has a walkout basement that will be a full studio apartment—at least until they fill the house up with kids."

He saw his opportunity. "Speaking of kids . . . Joanna, I wanted to talk to you . . . about Mateo."

She stretched out her legs and leaned forward. "I've wanted to talk to you about that too."

"You have?"

"Yes, but . . . you first."

"No. I'm curious what you wanted to say."

She tilted her head slightly. "I'd prefer you go first, because what I was going to say might be a moot point."

"Oh?" That majorly upped his curiosity, but he'd been the one to bring it up first. He took in a shallow breath. "I just wanted . . ." He leaned forward, planting his elbows on his knees and pressing his hands together, steepling his fingers. "I feel like I should let you—"

This was proving more awkward than it had seemed when

he rehearsed his end of the conversation in his mind. He started again. "This might seem premature. I know it's not like we're"— he gestured between them—"a couple or anything. But I've sensed you're a little cool toward Mateo . . ." He paused, hoping she would dispute that observation.

She didn't.

Disappointed, he continued. "I guess what I'm trying to say . . ." Pausing, he glanced up toward the bathroom window, the same one he'd peered out a few minutes ago. He lowered his voice, suddenly fearful that Mateo might be watching them. And listening. "Mateo is part of my life and he always will be. Maria—his mother—asked me to take him in, and I agreed."

"Do you mean you agreed to raise him? Until he's . . . grown. On his own?"

He looked her in the eye. Wanting there to be no doubt. "Yes. Look, Joanna, if I'm honest, I'm not sure I counted the cost before I agreed to such a . . . profound responsibility. But it was . . . kind of a desperate situation. And Mateo has been in my life for five years. There's no way I could let him go into the system. I love that kid like he *is* my brother. Or . . . my son." Should he tell her what he'd been thinking? How he thought God might be leading? He hadn't told anyone. Not even his parents. And yet, he felt he could trust Joanna.

Still, this wasn't exactly the kind of thing you sprang on a woman you'd barely started dating.

Her expression became . . . pained. She leaned forward. "Luke, I . . . I think it's wonderful what you've done. It's really an incredibly noble thing and I'm so glad Mateo has—"

"But?" He cocked his head, waiting.

"I don't understand." Her brows knit.

"I sense a 'but' coming . . . to follow that you're-so-wonderful speech."

She smiled, but an unmistakable sadness slipped into her eyes. "It feels funny saying this when we've barely started dating, but I'm not sure I'm cut out to . . . to be part of Mateo's life. You're talking about being a father to him. But are you even old enough to be his father?"

He gave a rueful nod. "Barely. But I'm old enough to be *a* father. I mean . . . does age really matter when a kid needs a home?"

"No. Of course not. And I didn't mean to question the rightness of what you're doing. It's just . . ." She curled her legs back underneath her and hugged a pillow from the chaise. "I really like you Luke, and if things continue between us, then suddenly *I'm* involved in Mateo's life whether I wanted to be or not."

He winced at the stab of disappointment her words brought. "So I take it you don't want to be?"

"That's not what I meant . . . exactly. But I'm even younger than you are. I just can't see myself as . . . a *mom* to a kid Mateo's age. I don't even feel . . . qualified."

He worked to keep his expression neutral, but his spirits sagged. "So, is this the big breakup speech? Is that what you wanted to talk to me about?"

"Kind of." She bowed her head for a brief moment. "I guess. I don't know. If you had a kid from a former marriage or something . . ." She shrugged. "I'm just . . . I'm not sure this is what I want for my life, Luke. Like my sister said, Mateo would be a teenager by the time we . . . well, you know." A sheepish look veiled her face.

"You mean by the time we got married."

She gave a low groan. "This is the most awkward conversation in the history of the world."

He laughed. "Maybe not the *world*."

She tossed him a fleeting smile. "You know what I mean. And maybe I'm way off base, Luke, and you don't even see our relationship going anywhere. But I don't want to wait too long and . . . have to break up with you when it would be really painful for everyone involved."

"And you don't think *this* is painful? For me?" He was baiting her, but she'd started it.

"I hope it isn't."

He exhaled, the breath taking his hopes with it. Staring out into the darkness, he wondered again if this was a cost God was asking him to pay. Then it occurred to him. He looked back at her, his hope struggling to regain its footing. "So, you've talked to your sisters about me?"

She met his steady appraisal, an "uh-oh-I've-been-found-out" look shading her own. "A little. Especially about Mateo."

He leaned in. "Joanna, it's not like I can make a choice between you and Mateo. He's in my life. I believe God put him there. And as much as I like you—and I do—I'm *not* going to get rid of him."

"I'm not asking you to get rid of him!" Insult tinged her tone.

But he was merely stating the truth.

"No, Joanna, you're not. What you're saying"—he tried to gentle his tone—"is that you don't want anything to do with me *unless* Mateo's out of the picture."

She sat silent, her attention glued to her lap.

"I'm right, then?" He felt his defenses rising, even while he did understand her reluctance to commit to Mateo.

"When you put it that way, it makes me sound like a terrible person."

"No. That's not my intention at all. But if you don't like me enough to take me with all the . . . *baggage* I come with, then I understand. And it's probably best—for Mateo's sake—that we end things now. Before he gets too attached."

"That's just it! He's *not* attached to me. At all. In fact, I get the feeling he doesn't like me very much."

"It's not that, Joanna. He's still reeling from his mom's death. I'm pretty much all he has, so maybe he views you as a threat. Someone that takes my attention away from him."

"Well, welcome to my world." She hugged the pillow tighter to her midsection.

Luke stared, fierce love for Mateo rising in him. "Are you really going to get in a competition with a twelve-year-old about this? That's a little childish, if you ask me."

Tears welled in her eyes and glistened in the glow from the string lights, and Luke immediately regretted his words.

"I'm sorry, Joanna. That wasn't fair."

"No. I probably *am* being childish. And a selfish jerk. This simply . . . isn't what I've always dreamed about. And that's not your fault, Luke. Maybe I should be willing to put aside those dreams. But it seems—"

"What is it you've always dreamed about?"

She tilted her head.

"I want to know. Really." He scooted his chair closer, leaning in.

"Luke . . . This feels weird. For all I know you don't see us having a future together at all."

Her words surprised him. "Why would I ask you out—three times—if I didn't think there was something there? I wouldn't, Joanna. First of all, I'm too old to waste time dating someone I don't like—a lot. And I'm not the kind of guy who sees women as toys. Something to entertain them until the next one comes along."

"No. I know that. I could tell that about you from the first time we met. Why do you think I said 'yes' to *you*—three times—even after your kid tried to baptize me in ice water on our second date?"

He laughed. "Okay. So we've established we like each other. And maybe you even think I could be the man of your dreams—if only I didn't come with a built-in kid."

"It's not only that. It's . . . I've always looked forward to the newlywed phase. Being just a couple. Getting to know each other and really . . . bonding, I guess. *Before* babies come along. But even then, I've always dreamed of my husband and me and the baby we've made, all cozy together in the house we've created. I know that probably sounds stupid to you, but all those

189

romantic firsts that a couple should share . . . just the two of us . . . them," she corrected quickly. "It doesn't seem like there should be an almost-teenager tagging along. And please don't think I'm planning a wedding yet or anything"—she shot him an ornery grin—"although I do have the venue picked out."

Maybe he should have taken advantage of her attempt to lighten the mood. But this was no light subject. Bottom line, if Joanna couldn't accept that he was raising Mateo—whether as a brother or a son—then he had no business continuing to see her. For both his and Mateo's sake.

And right now, staring into those crystal blue eyes of hers, he sensed her final answer, and felt certain a door was closing between them.

CHAPTER 23

JOANNA WATCHED LUKE IN THE dim glow of the twinkle
lights, waiting for his laughter that usually came so easily.
But it never came. Instead, he sighed deeply and rose to
pace behind the chair where he'd been sitting. Finally he sat
back down and looked her in the eye. "I don't really know what
to say, Joanna. Except that I'm really disappointed. In you. In
. . . everything."

In you. Those two words hurt more than she'd expected
them to. And yet, she'd anticipated them. Even though she
didn't think it was wrong to hold out for what she'd dreamed
of for marriage, the fact that Luke was sacrificing so much for a
boy he wasn't even related to made her feel like her own wishes
were petty and self-centered. Were they?

A lump lodged in her throat and tears threatened. Humil-
iation washed through her. Not Luke's intention, she knew. But
that was exactly the emotion filling her now. She bent her head,
struggling to compose herself.

"I'm sorry if I've disappointed you. But Luke . . ." She
fought back tears. "Is it so wrong to want the things I've always
dreamed about?"

"No. It's not. And honestly, if you're not willing to give up those dreams for what I have to offer, then I'm glad to know it now." He scraped the toe of his shoe on the flagstone. "I guess I just wonder what happened to 'I think you're doing a wonderful thing'?"

She looked askance at him.

"That's what you said to me the night of your sister's wedding. About Mateo. I guess I hoped you'd be willing to . . . adjust your dreams a little if the guy was right. But obviously, I'm not Mr. Right."

"It's not you, Luke. It truly isn't. If—" She stopped. She'd been about to say "if it wasn't for Mateo." But that wasn't right. The boy was like a brother to Luke, and she knew her claws would be out if Luke dared criticize one of her sisters. "If things were different, I'd be . . . pursuing you. Hard." She smiled, even as sadness overwhelmed her.

He didn't return her smile. "I didn't really need to hear that. And I sure don't know how I'm supposed to respond to it."

She felt chastened, deservedly so, perhaps, but she wanted to help him understand. "I only meant that someone else, someone who hasn't held out all their lives for . . . certain things, will be able to accept things for what they are." Even as she spoke the words, she felt a stone in her gut thinking of Luke with someone else. "I'm sorry. I'm not making sense, am I?"

He frowned. "Oh, you're making perfect sense. I'm sorry I wasted your time."

"Luke, I never said it was a waste of my time. And what you're doing for Mateo *is* a wonderful thing. But I didn't even know for sure what the situation with him *was* until tonight! You can't blame me for that."

He held up both hands to her, palms out. "I'm sorry. That wasn't fair. I should have been more clear. But you said yourself that it was a little awkward when we didn't even know what this"—he motioned between them—"would become." He shrugged. "Apparently it won't become anything."

She bit the inside of her cheek. He wasn't making this easy. "I'm sorry, Luke. I wish I could change the way I feel. I wish I could adjust. But . . . I've tried. And I can't seem to let that dream go." Had she really tried? Oh, she'd thought about it constantly. She had raised the subject with her sisters and with Ginger. But had she prayed about it? More than a half-hearted prayer tossed up before she gripped the dream tightly again?

Standing behind the chair where he'd been sitting, Luke scooted it to the side as if opening a gate. "Then you'd best go."

She stared at him, realizing her jaw must be hanging. Her cheeks heating, she moved her mouth to ask if he meant *now*. But the tight cords in his neck and the tension in his jaw left no doubt. If she'd felt humiliated earlier, this *dismissal* was a dozen times worse.

Refusing to meet his eyes, she grabbed her phone from the side table and rose from the chaise. Thankfully, her car was parked outside and she wouldn't have to endure him taking her home. She trudged toward the side of the house that was most brightly lit.

But Luke called after her. "Joanna? Wait. It's muddy over there. Let me walk you through the house. Did you have a purse . . . or a jacket?" He sounded contrite, even tender.

"No. I left them in my car." Suddenly she wanted nothing more than to stay here with him. But they were at an impasse. And he'd all but kicked her out.

She preceded him through the house, feeling his stare as she walked to the front door. With one hand on the doorknob, she turned. "Thank you for dinner. I'm truly sorry, Luke."

"I am too. I wish things could have been different."

She nodded, too close to tears to speak. She exited, closing the door behind her. Halfway to the car, she reached for her purse on her shoulder, but grasped only air. *Oh, no!* Her purse was in the car. She reached for the handle, dread filling her.

Her keys were locked inside.

Luke flipped off light switches and gathered the pillows from the patio since there was rain in the forecast. As he "tucked in" the patio for the night, his thoughts were dark. He couldn't say he was surprised by the way the evening had ended, but he'd certainly hoped for a different outcome.

He stopped and stood still for a moment, thinking he heard something. It came again. The doorbell. Tossing all the pillows onto the chaise, he went through the house to the front door.

Joanna stood there, looking meek. "I am so sorry. I locked my keys in the car."

"Oh no. Do you have another set?"

"Yes. I called Britt and she's going to bring them, but she's on her way home from St. Louis with friends, so it might be a few minutes." She motioned toward the car. "I just didn't want you wondering why my car was still out here."

"I'm sorry." He opened the door wider. "Come on in."

Joanna hung her head. "No. Britt was only about twenty minutes away. I'll just wait outside."

"Don't be ridiculous. Come in. We can go back out to the patio and wait. Do you want something to drink while you wait?"

For a minute, he thought she was going to refuse again, but instead she sniffled and stepped through the front door. "Thank you. But I can wait by myself. You probably have things to do."

"Joanna—" He risked putting a hand on her forearm. "I'm sorry if I was rude. I didn't—"

"No. I understand . . ." She took a half step back, but didn't move her arm. "You had every right to end the evening early."

He shrugged. "It just didn't seem to serve any purpose for you to stay . . . since you've made up your mind and I don't have the option to change mine. But that doesn't excuse my rudeness."

"You weren't rude, Luke. But . . . it hurt. I wish things were different."

"They could be."

She tilted her head. "I don't know what you mean."

"If you'd just open your heart to something different than you've always imagined."

"I'm . . . I'm going to have to think about it. And pray about it. I don't know if a person can simply change their mind by force of will when they've dreamed about things being a certain way for all their lives."

Maybe she was right. He didn't think it should be as difficult as she was making it. But he couldn't change her mind for her. And she was right about one thing: She needed to pray about it.

But then, he did too. "Let's go sit outside while we wait for Britt to get here. It's too nice out to waste the evening. Hang on and I'll get us some waters."

He slipped into the kitchen and returned with two icy cold bottles of water from his fridge. He handed her one, then cleared all but one of the throw pillows from the chaise.

They settled in the way they'd been before, talking about the garden and their jobs, the meal they'd eaten at Dexter's earlier. Their conversation came easily and seemed to be a "reset" of sorts. Luke found himself praying Britt wouldn't get there too soon.

After thirty minutes, Joanna checked her phone. "I'm sorry. It's already nine o'clock. Britt must have been farther away than she thought. I can go wait out front . . ."

"No. I'm enjoying this. I don't turn into a pumpkin until eleven or so."

She smiled. "I'm up by five on weekdays, so I'm usually in bed by ten. Don't you work an early shift at the radio?" She uncapped her water bottle and drank deeply.

"I used to. I've been going in a little later since Mateo moved in. They've been really good to let me come in after I drop him off at school." He cringed inwardly, not wanting the subject of Mateo to change the pleasant mood they'd somehow managed to recapture. But since he'd already broached it—and knowing that Britt would likely be here any minute—he took a risk. "Listen, Joanna. I want to apologize again for how this evening went. I'm afraid my life is going to be one big everything-is-subject-to-change for a few years, but"—he braced himself for a rejection—"assuming my babysitter can come and stay with Mateo, would you want to go for ice cream some night next week?"

She eyed him as if he were playing a trick on her.

"No reason we can't just be friends, is there?" He smiled, even as he wished he hadn't implied a promise of mere friendship. That's not what he wanted with her. Not at all.

Still, her demeanor indicated that his words brought relief. The smile that bloomed on her face said the same. "I'd like that. And . . . if you need to bring Mateo, that's okay too."

"No. I'll work something out. He could even stay by himself for a couple of hours if we go before dark. I do realize he kind of hogs the attention—my attention—and I'd like to have an uninterrupted conversation with you. This has been nice." He waved a hand over the patio to clarify that he meant these last few minutes they'd shared.

Her phone pinged and she glanced at it. "Britt will be here in a couple of minutes." She rose and tucked the pillow into one corner of the chaise. "Thank you for letting me wait here. I . . . I like this ending to the night better than before."

"Me too. Bet you never thought you'd be glad you locked your keys in the car."

She laughed. "That's for sure."

"I'll call you. Unless you already know a night that would be best. Mateo has a baseball game Monday night, but the rest of the week is free."

"Would Thursday work? I can usually get off a little early then."

"What if I picked you up from work and we can go to Andy's from there? We could grab some supper, too, and maybe go for a walk if the weather's nice?" For a minute he was afraid he'd pushed too far, turning ice cream into dinner and a walk.

But her smile was back. "That'd be perfect."

It did his heart good. The funk that had come over him the first time she'd walked out his front door tonight had taken him by surprise—and not in a good way.

"It's a deal then. And my treat."

She started to answer him, but her phone pinged again. She glanced at it. "Britt just pulled up."

He thought she looked as disappointed as he felt. But he consoled himself with the fact that they'd see each other again in a few days.

He led the way through the house to the front door. "I'll pick you up Thursday. Do you want me to come in to your office, or . . ."

"If you come around to the back parking lot, I'll come down and meet you there."

"Sounds good."

Britt flashed her lights at the curb in front of the house. Luke laughed. "Looks like your sister is in a hurry."

"She's just letting me know she's here. Thank you for dinner, Luke. I'll see you Thursday."

She walked across the lawn, stooped beside the car to speak with her sister, then walked to her own car without a backward glance. But Luke went back through the house to sit on the patio and replay every word of their conversation. He liked this woman. More than he could admit to her. Because, despite the fact that they'd found their way back to the easy, friendly way they'd first known with each other, nothing had really changed.

He still came with Mateo. They were a package deal— one that Joanna saw as "baggage." And that was a problem. One that divided his heart and made him feel disloyal to the boy he'd committed to care for and support as long as Mateo needed him.

CHAPTER 24

JOANNA EXITED THE ELEVATOR AND peered through the plate-glass windows, surprised at the relief that came in seeing Luke's car waiting outside in the back parking lot. He wasn't the type to stand someone up, and yet, if he'd been thinking things through the way she had these past few days, he'd surely come to the same conclusion: things couldn't possibly work out for them. Their life situations, their dreams and goals, were on a collision course with each other.

Worse, feeling as she did about Luke, how could she agree to being merely friends? Her attraction to him went far beyond friendship. And thinking about him meeting someone who was willing to embrace both him *and* Mateo made her feel a little sick to her stomach. But envy was not an emotion that had a place in a platonic friendship. Besides, she didn't believe in having such a close friendship with a man who belonged to another woman. But if she was willing to let Luke go as a boyfriend, she knew it was only a matter of time before another woman snatched him up. Joanna wouldn't—couldn't—stand in the way.

She opened the door to a rush of hot air. Summer was here in full force.

Luke waved through the windshield, sporting that drop-dead smile of his. He hopped out of the car and came around to open the passenger door for her. Ben had rarely done that. And frankly, it hadn't bothered her in the least—until now.

"Hi there." Luke waited until she was buckled in before closing her door, then jogged in front of the car and climbed back behind the wheel. Once he was buckled in, he turned to her. "The weather sure cooperated with our plans, didn't it?"

She must have looked confused because he laughed. "Perfect ice cream weather," he said.

"Oh . . . Yes. That's going to hit the spot for sure." She held up a hand. "Do you mind if I make a quick phone call? We have guests checking in tonight and I need to make sure Britt left the keys where they can find them."

"No problem."

He drove through town while she called her sister. When she hung up, she adjusted the air conditioner vent on her side, aiming the stream of air at her face. "I'm not sure I even want dinner at all. I might go straight to ice cream." After the words were out, she hoped he didn't think she was trying to cut their time together short. The truth was, she was thrilled to be with him again.

"No reason we can't have dessert first. Andy's still okay with you?"

"Is there any other place when it comes to ice cream? I might even have a triple dip. Or a Concrete—the biggest one they make."

He laughed. "I've always liked a woman who wasn't afraid to pig out."

"Now hold on . . . I don't think it's considered pigging out if you're eating ice cream *instead* of dinner."

"Duly noted." He spoke the phrase so formally that for a minute she wondered if he was making fun of her lawyerly aspirations. Then again, his comment seemed innocent enough. As far as she knew, he wasn't aware she was a law school dropout.

A few minutes later, she spotted the distinctive giant ice cream cone towering over the frozen custard store with its turquoise-and-white checkerboard tile border. Luke turned into the parking lot and slid into a spot across from the walk-up window where a group of college students congregated.

He started to turn the key in the ignition, but angling his chin at the rowdy crowd, he turned to her. "Mind if we do the drive-through instead? We can take our ice cream to the park where it's quieter."

"Good idea."

He backed out of the parking spot and pulled up to the lighted menu board. After studying the list of choices for a minute, Joanna ordered a mint chocolate chip Concrete and Luke ordered the signature Jackhammer with butterscotch in the center.

They dug their spoons into the treats before they were even back on the street and ate in comfortable silence. Luke steered with his forearm and spooned frozen custard into his mouth. They made identical appreciative noises, then laughed at themselves.

Joanna knew she should ask about Mateo, but it was so nice to have Luke's undivided attention, she opted not to broach that subject just yet.

They drove slowly to one of the city's parks and Luke pulled his car beneath the shade of a stand of poplars. He cut the engine and rolled his window down. Joanna did likewise, letting a slight breeze through the car.

"Would you rather get out?" he asked over a bite of frozen custard. "We could go sit under the picnic shelter." He pointed up a hill to the shelter in the distance.

"This is fine with me. The ice cream cooled me down."

He nodded and unbuckled his seatbelt, turning in his seat as if he was settling in for an easy conversation.

Joanna did likewise and relaxed, happy at the prospect of having him all to herself.

They talked until they finished their ice cream and Luke took her cup and nested it inside his in the cup holder. "Do you want to walk for a while? It feels like it's cooled down a little." He put a hand outside his window as if testing the temperature.

"Sure. It'd be good to walk off some of those calories."

"Those don't count. They were supper calories. And besides, you don't need to worry about calories."

She was flattered, if a little disconcerted by his observation. "Sadly, I *do* have to worry about calories. And while I like your theory about ice-cream-for-supper calories, I'd enjoy a walk."

"Sure." He climbed from the car and almost before she could open her door, he was there, holding it for her.

He locked the doors with the key fob and they set out on the trail that meandered through the park. Conversation came easily. They talked about their experiences growing up in Missouri and about the families they'd grown up in. Joanna was surprised to learn that he'd grown up here in Cape Girardeau. He'd told her his parents lived in Phoenix and she assumed that's where he'd lived and that it was the university that brought him to Cape.

"No." Luke shook his head. "I went to college here because I had a scholarship. Once I graduated, Mom talked Dad into moving someplace that didn't have winters. She grew up in Minnesota, so you'd have thought she'd consider Cape's winters to be nothing."

"Especially last year. We almost didn't have a winter."

"Not according to my mom. The first time it dipped into the thirties, she tried to get me to fly to Phoenix for a few weeks until 'the worst of it was over.'" He chalked quotation marks in the air. "I'm not sure where she got the idea that I could just up and take off from my job."

Joanna laughed. "It would be nice if it worked that way, but I'm lucky to get my week's vacation all at once. Of course, I took a lot of time off when my mom was so sick."

"How long has it been now . . . since she passed away."

"November. Last year." She sighed. "Like some people have said, it's kind of a blessing we got that first Thanksgiving and Christmas without her over with right away."

He nodded, then frowned. "I've also heard the second year is sometimes harder than the first." He shook his head. "Sorry. I didn't mean to be discouraging. I've been reading a lot about grief. The stages of grief, timelines. All that. Because of Mateo."

"How is he handling everything? It's still early in the process for him. And I'm sure it's worse for a little kid." They'd covered a lot of territory before the topic came back to Mateo. But here they were. And it was only natural.

"Yes. It worries me a little how well he *is* handling it. Maybe because he's known for quite a while that he was going to lose her. Maria was very honest with him from the time she got the terminal diagnosis."

"I don't pretend to know how it really is for kids," she admitted, "but my sisters and I—and Dad too—definitely did a lot of our grieving before Mom actually died."

"That may be the only good thing about cancer. That chance to say everything you need to say."

She nodded, feeling afresh the weight of having lost Mom. And feeling guiltily grateful that she'd had her mom all through her twenties. Unlike Mateo. "We've all been so thankful we had Mom as long as we did. She outlived so many prognoses . . . We had her a good three years longer than they first said."

"Good for her. I wish I could have known her."

The conviction in his voice made her smile. But at the same time, it made her sad that Mom had never known Luke. She remembered Phee saying how thankful she was that Mom had known and loved Quinn long before he and Phylicia even started seeing each other as potential sweethearts. But Phee gained great comfort from knowing that Mom would have approved of her choice.

"I wish you could have known her too," she told Luke now. "I'm biased, but she was an amazing woman—one of a kind."

"I don't doubt that. Because her daughter is pretty amazing too—and one of a kind."

Joanna demurred. "Well, I don't know about that. But . . . thank you." It struck her that even though Mom knew Ben, her mother never gave Joanna the same "seal of approval" for Ben that she'd given Quinn. Of course, she'd never told Mom the reason Ben gave for breaking up with her, but Mom was always perceptive—and interestingly, more so after she became ill—so maybe she guessed the reason for their breakup.

Not that Mom ever tried to dissuade her about Ben. Or about any of the other guys she'd dated. But Ben was the only one she'd ever gone with for any length of time.

They circled back around to the picnic shelter and Joanna looked across the park, shocked to realize that the sun was already setting. "You probably need to get back to Mateo?"

"Yes." He sounded as disappointed as she felt. "I should. Even though Maria let him stay alone after school, it still makes me nervous any time I leave him alone. I think you feel even more responsible for kids who aren't your own."

"I can see how you would." She wasn't sure she really could. The truth was, while she knew she did want kids eventually, it wasn't something she spent a lot of time thinking about the way some of her friends did. First, she wanted a deep friendship with the man who would become her husband. She'd always figured that the desire for children with the man she loved would spring naturally from their love.

But of course, she couldn't tell Luke that. Not when he'd all but said they could only be friends.

A commotion from the other end of the path made them both turn. Two men and a woman headed their way, deep in conversation. When they drew closer, Joanna realized with a start that the taller man was Ben. The other guy was a friend of Ben's she'd met once, though she couldn't remember his name. Leon or Leo? She didn't know the woman, but she appeared to be with Ben's friend, judging by the guy's arm possessively around her.

Joanna envied their obvious affection. Then came the misplaced thought that she was glad the woman wasn't with Ben.

Luke greeted them with a brief wave as they all moved to single file to pass on the narrow walking path. It was nearly dark, and Joanna didn't think Ben recognized her, but after they'd passed by, he called her name.

"Jo?"

"Oh . . . Ben! Hi." She felt disingenuous pretending she hadn't recognized him before, but she didn't want him to think she'd purposely snubbed him either.

Luke turned back with her and she felt obligated to introduce them. "Luke, this is my . . . friend . . . Ben Harven. Ben, Lukas Blaine." She turned to the other man. "I think we've met but I'm sorry, I don't—"

"Leland."

"Of course."

Leland drew the woman close. "And this is Rachel. Rachel, Joanna Chandler."

"Oh, you're Britt's sister?"

"I am. How do you know Britt?"

"I'm in a book club with her."

"Ah. Well, nice to meet you. I'll have to tell Britt we met."

They all stood in a loose circle now, but an awkward silence fell over them.

"Nice evening for a walk." Luke put a hand at the small of Joanna's back.

She relished the warmth of his touch, even as the possessiveness of his gesture confused her. She'd never mentioned her relationship with Ben to Luke, yet he seemed to sense that there'd been something between them once upon a time.

"So how's it going, Joanna?" Ben ignored Luke's comment and stepped closer to her. "I heard you and your sisters opened a bed and breakfast?"

"It's an Airbnb, actually." She explained briefly how that worked. "We're just getting started."

"Well, I have no doubt you'll make a success of it. You Chandler sisters always were the creative ones." Ben turned to Luke. "You should have seen the seven-course dinner they put together a couple of Christmases ago."

Joanna didn't think it was her imagination that Ben was vying for "possession" too—or at least for her attention.

"I can imagine." Luke winked at her before turning back to Ben. "The wedding they put on for Phee was one of the prettiest I've ever seen."

Joanna curbed a grin. She didn't think Luke had ever referred to Phylicia by her nickname. But suddenly he and Ben were in an all-out who-knows-the-Chandler-sisters-best competition.

She'd be lying if she said she didn't like the way it felt to be "fought over" by two handsome men. And while Ben couldn't compete with Luke's dark, gray-eyed good looks, he was handsome in his own way, especially now, with a summer tan setting off his blond hair. She thought he'd put on a little weight—and it looked good on him.

"How is Phee doing? Are she and her husband living here?"

"They're actually building on our property. They're hoping to break ground sometime this month."

Luke increased the pressure on her back ever so slightly. "We probably should get going." His whisper was just loud enough for Ben to hear.

"Yes. Of course." She turned to Leland and Rachel. "It was nice to see you. And to meet you, Rachel."

"Yes," Luke said. "Nice to meet you all."

The trio walked on, but Ben looked back and threw Joanna a smile that could only be described as "knowing."

She and Luke walked on to the car in silence, but once inside the stifling interior, Luke turned to her with a questioning smile. "So, how is it you know . . . Ben, is it?"

"Yes. Ben Harven. We dated. Once upon a time."

"I gathered that."

"Oh? How?"

"He was sending messages."

"Messages?"

"He just . . . he was making it clear that he was here first."

"*Here?* What's that supposed to mean?"

Luke shrugged. "It's a guy thing."

She hesitated, then decided to plunge in. "It kind of seemed like you might have been sending your own messages. What was that all about?"

"What do you mean?" He was suddenly intent on the steering wheel.

"I'm not sure how I'm supposed to feel having two guys who, by the way, have no claims on me, getting into a 'guy thing' match over my affections."

He put a hand over his heart, looking sheepish. "I deserved that."

She smiled. "Just so you own it."

He backed out of the parking lot and started onto the street, but then braked and turned to her, twisting the brown beads at his throat. "So, just how serious *were* things with you and this Ben character?"

CHAPTER 25

LUKE WATCHED JOANNA'S FACE, SEARCHING for telltale clues, but finding none. He had no right to even ask her the question, let alone entertain the jealousy clawing at him. But knowing that didn't change the intensity of his emotions. Ben had seemed like a nice enough person, but Luke didn't like the . . . *familiar* way he looked at Joanna. The way he called her *Jo*.

He smirked to himself. Who was he to judge? He'd flung out a *Phee*, as if he knew Joanna's sister well enough to refer to her by a nickname he'd never used himself. But hey, like he told Joanna, it was a guy thing.

And he didn't blame Joanna for disliking being the pawn in their masculine one-upmanship. Especially when he had no claims on her whatsoever. But that was just it. He *wanted* claims on her. Maybe even more, now that he saw the competition. "You don't have to answer that. Your relationship with this Ben guy is none of my business." He immediately regretted giving her an out because he really wanted—needed—the answer.

"We dated for a year. Almost a year."

"That sounds pretty serious."

"It was. I guess . . ."

"Was? How recently *was*?"

She looked askance at him. "We broke up more than a year ago. I wouldn't be here with you if there was still anything between Ben and me."

The simple declaration—*I wouldn't be here with you*—planted a seed of hope. "So, why'd you break up?"

She tucked the corner of her bottom lip between her teeth. "Basically, he didn't like me spending so much time with my mom. When she was sick."

"Seriously?" *Shut up, Blaine.* He'd said it as if Ben was a jerk. And it sounded like he was, but Luke knew better than to make a woman defend her choice of boyfriend. Even a former boyfriend. And besides, that had to have been hurtful.

"He was a little immature," Joanna said, sounding as defensive as he'd expected. "He's a nice guy though. I'm sure he's grown up since then."

Exactly. And with Joanna's mom gone and Ben's supposed reason for their breakup no longer an issue, the guy posed a genuine threat. *And he didn't have a kid.* At least not that Luke knew of. "So, you still like him?"

"Not *that* way . . . if that's what you mean."

"I guess I just want to know where I stand."

"Where you stand? Luke, I thought this was about just being friends."

His face heated. "I said that, didn't I?"

"Unless you have a doppelgänger." Her smile was more like a smirk.

"True confession: I said that because it seemed like the only way to keep you in my life."

"In your life?"

"Joanna, if Mateo is something—someone—you absolutely can't see in your life, then maybe . . . it's not fair to either of us to try to—" He was bungling this big-time. "What I'm trying to say is, I don't think I can just be friends with you. I will always wonder . . . wish there was more. And quite honestly, after meeting your Ben, I don't think I'll handle it very well when—"

"He's not *my* Ben. I told you we haven't been together for a year and a half."

"Yes, but he still likes you."

She put a hand on her hip. "And you know this, how? And don't tell me it's a guy thing."

"Even if it is? Come on, Joanna . . . Surely you saw how he was acting with you."

"Acting?"

"Behaving. Conducting himself. Posturing."

"Thank you, Mr. Dictionary."

"Mr. Thesaurus, actually." He grinned, hoping she saw the humor.

"And he wasn't posturing. Not really. That's . . . just Ben."

"Fine. But I still contend that he likes you."

"I doubt he would have dated me for almost a year if he didn't."

"I thought you said a year and a half."

"No, I said we haven't *been together* for almost a year and a half. It's actually been a year and six and three-quarter months now, if you want to get technical about it."

"And the fact that you know down to the quarter month surely says something."

"It's a girl thing."

He smiled, not feeling it. "Okay, I had that coming."

The smile she returned didn't quite reach her eyes. "There's nothing between me and Ben. This is only the second time I've seen him since we broke up. And, for the record, there's nothing between you and me either, right? We're just friends?"

"Only because it seems like that's the only way you'll have it. Because of Mateo."

She nodded. "And speaking of Mateo, he's probably worried about you."

He checked the time on his phone, mildly alarmed at how late it was. But Mateo would have called if he was worried. He nodded. "I should probably get back. But . . . this discussion is to be continued, okay?"

She pondered his question a few seconds too long. "Can you give me some time?"

"How much time?"

"I'm not sure, Luke. Maybe a week or two. I need to think about it, pray about it, okay?"

"That's a long time." He shrugged. "But I can't exactly argue with that—the praying part, I mean."

She smiled, as if she'd just won a bet.

And maybe she had.

Joanna lifted a hand over the steering wheel in a half-hearted wave as Luke drove from the parking lot of Pritchert & Pritchert. He'd insisted on waiting until she was behind the wheel with her engine running before he drove off.

Why did he have to make it so hard to put him out of her mind?

She drove through town and turned off onto Poplar Brook Road, glad there were guests staying in the cottage tonight so she'd have an excuse to talk things over with Britt. It always helped to talk to one of her sisters. In truth, she would have preferred Phee, who she saw as her older and therefore wiser sister. But Britt had grown up a lot since Mom's death, and Jo had become even closer to her younger sister now that Phee was married.

The cottage was rented all weekend—including Monday night, according to Britt—and the Airbnb rentals were paying the utilities and keeping the renovation fund from drying up. They'd had some of the nicest people stay with them, and the online reviews so far were beyond glowing. Everyone seemed to love the location, and Joanna's scones got high marks from a few reviewers too. Even though their interaction with guests was mostly limited to check-in, Joanna was surprised how much she liked that aspect of the business.

Of course, they'd had a jerk or two rent the cottage, as well, but thankfully even they had left good reviews. Dealing with difficult people was just part of running a business—as Phee often reminded them, having worked in retail for many years. Jo wasn't so sure about the customer always being right, but she did relish seeing other people enjoy the fruit of their labors. And knowing how much their mother would have loved this venture helped keep Mom's memory alive.

Britt was still handling reservations and doing the bulk of the work related to the cottage rentals. They'd finally quit talking about Britt finding a job, since Phee's and Jo's day jobs didn't leave them time to take up the slack if Britt were to take on even a part-time job. Phee and Jo paid Britt a small salary so she'd have spending money, but she still insisted on paying her share of the groceries out of her check.

Even though they'd hired out most of the painting and renovations, it had been hard work getting the cottage and cabins finished. And they still had a ways to go with the third cabin, the one closest to the clearing stairway—the one that would serve as a bride's dressing room if Joanna could convince her sisters to open the clearing as a wedding venue.

Still, driving along the lane to home, Jo was reminded that none of them regretted their decision to buy the property. Since it had been paid for with their inheritance from Mom, it felt like her final gift to the three of them. And sometimes Jo could almost see her mother's smile as she pulled into the place that truly felt like home now.

Rounding the curve, she saw lights in the windows of Britt's cabin. *Every* window. A pretty sight, despite the fact that Jo could almost see the numbers climbing on the electric meter. Behind the cabins, an almost full moon illuminated the rooflines and made a wavering reflection in the slice of the river visible between the two stone buildings.

Inside, Jo discovered Britt on the phone with a friend, deep in conversation about a mutual friend who was apparently in the middle of a messy breakup with a boyfriend. After a quick hello to Joanna, Britt went to her bedroom and closed the door.

So much for talking things over with that sister. Maybe she would call Phee later. But besides the fact that Jo hesitated to bother the newlyweds, it seemed lately all Phylicia wanted to talk about was the plans for the house she and Quinn were building.

Joanna got that. She'd be excited, too, if it were her. And she did enjoy looking at the Pinterest boards and decorating ideas Phee sent her almost daily. But sometimes it seemed like Phee had forgotten that her sisters had lives too.

She changed into yoga pants and a T-shirt, fixed a glass of iced tea, and carried it out to the backyard overlooking the river. The waters had receded considerably since the rains that almost flooded the cabins last winter, but there was still enough water that they could boast river views in their Airbnb listing. Of course, the listing didn't mention the mosquitoes that apparently loved the river views too. She ran back inside for a wand to light the citronella candle.

Britt had planted several terra cotta pots with citronella grass and lavender and placed them at the corners of the tiny flagstone patio they'd uncovered near the back door. The plants were supposed to ward off mosquitoes, but pretty as they were, the pots were the extent of the landscaping out here. Of course, the tree-lined banks of the tributary were free landscaping, but after sitting in Luke's cozy backyard, Joanna looked around the patio with an eye to what they could do to spruce up this space.

Twinkle lights would be a good start. The lights they'd strung in the clearing for Phee's wedding were magical. They'd left them in place, intending to spend more time up in the clearing, but their attention had been focused on getting the cabins ready to list for rental, and they'd only been up there a few times.

A fountain might be nice. She'd loved the one on Luke's patio, but she wouldn't want to compete with the natural sound of the river waters lapping at the banks. The frogs and crickets added their own music, and even now, their lullaby soothed her. She scooted a tattered lawn chair closer to the low stone wall that enclosed the backyard and put her feet up on it.

She'd just begun to relax when her phone shattered the night sounds. She pulled it from her pocket and glanced at the screen. She didn't recognize the number, though it bore a Cape area prefix. No doubt a sales call, but since her cell phone number was a secondary contact for the Airbnb, and with Britt on her phone, she didn't dare ignore the call.

"Good evening. Thanks for calling The Cottages on Poplar Brook Road."

"Joanna?"

"Yes . . . this is Jo."

"Oh, hi. For a minute there, I thought I'd called a wrong number." Ben's deep voice, once so familiar, took her aback.

"No, it's me. We use my number for the Airbnb sometimes. Sorry about that. You must have gotten a new number though. Your name didn't show up on my—"

"Yeah. I was getting too many stupid sales calls with the other one. You can change it to this number in your contacts."

"Okay. Thanks." She hadn't had Ben in her contacts for a year, though she could have rattled off his old number in a flash. But he didn't need to know that.

"No problem." He was silent for a few seconds. "Listen, I . . . It was really good to see you tonight. Man . . . it's been a long time."

"Yes. It has." What on earth was he up to?

"I just wondered how you were."

Jo hesitated a beat. "I'm fine." Hadn't she told him that mere hours ago?

"I wondered . . . I mean, I don't know if there's something between you and this Luke guy, but if not . . . would you want to go out to dinner with me this weekend?"

"This weekend? As in tomorrow?"

"Wait. What day is it? The Fourth holiday has me all messed up. I guess I meant next weekend. Like next Friday night . . . or Saturday if that works better."

"Ben. I don't—"

"Hey, like I said, if you're with someone . . . I'm not trying to horn in or anything. So, *are* you and him . . . together?"

"Not . . . Not exactly." She was tempted to lie and say she and Luke were a couple. Or to tell him the truth—that she didn't have a clue where she stood with Lukas Blaine. "We've had a few dates. That's all."

"I've missed you, Jo."

Seriously? Had he even heard her? "Ben, I don't think it would be a good idea—"

"I'm not saying pick up where we left off or anything. I'd just like to see you. Catch up with you. I really have missed you."

"I missed you too." She purposely used the past tense. Because while it had been true for the first year after he broke her heart, since she'd met Luke, she hadn't given Ben much thought. Except to compare him—unfavorably—with Luke. It was tempting to tell him that truth. To let him see what it felt like. But she wouldn't be cruel.

"Then let's get together. For old time's sake."

"I'm not sure that would be a good idea," she said again.

"Jo, I've thought about you so much. I'm not sure what happened with us, but could we try again? See if there's still something—"

"Ben, I don't—"

"Only as friends. Start slow. See where it takes us. We were good together. You can't deny that."

She couldn't deny it. There'd been a time she thought she and Ben were meant for each other. God's gift to each other

216

even. He was her first love, and he had a lot of qualities she admired in a man. He'd always made her heart beat a little faster—yet in a very different way than Luke did. But that shouldn't be the measure of a man, should it?

She and Ben always had fun together and good conversations. She'd grown as a person with him. And he'd always said she did the same for him. And they'd never fought. Even on the night they broke up.

But tonight, he seemed like the old Ben. Friendly and engaging. And it warmed her heart to know that he'd never stopped thinking about her. That he missed her.

Was it possible this was God's way of redirecting her affections? Had God brought Ben back into her life to rescue her from a situation that had the potential to bring nothing but stress and disappointment? The timing seemed too specific to be a coincidence.

The thought brought a stab of guilt. Luke couldn't help it that he'd been saddled with Mateo. The knife twisted. Luke would never have used that term—*saddled*. He saw his responsibility toward Mateo as a sacred duty. An honor even. It wasn't his fault that he'd committed to Mateo before he'd gotten to know her. And it wasn't her fault that she simply didn't want to take on responsibility for a child.

And now, just when she'd asked Luke for time to consider where their relationship was going, here was Ben, wanting her back. Having had a change of heart, it seemed. Most importantly, Ben was a man without complications. She didn't take that fact lightly. She had to at least explore the possibilities. Especially when the timing seemed almost like divine intervention.

She had to settle things in her own mind, to know if there might still be something between her and the man who'd been her first true love.

"Sure. I guess we could get together. To . . . catch up."

CHAPTER 26

SWEAT DRIPPED INTO JOANNA'S EYES and she leaned back on her haunches, blotting her face with her shirttail, careful to keep her balance lest she fall into the fresh paint on the bathroom floor. "Is that AC even working?"

"Can't you hear it running?" Britt looked up from the stencil she'd meticulously situated at the edge of the tiny bathroom floor.

They'd decided the wood of this cabin's bathroom floor wasn't in good enough shape to refinish, so they were trying a black-and-white painted stencil. It was looking great, but the project had turned out to be a lot more complicated than either of them anticipated.

She struggled to her feet and went to check the thermostat. "It says it's seventy-four in here, but it feels like an oven."

"You just aren't used to working so hard."

"Excuse me? Says the girl who is unemployed?"

"That's not fair."

"I'm only kidding." Joanna immediately felt sorry for her careless comment. "I know you've been working your tail off."

"Phee said you guys were okay with me not looking for

a job . . . at least until both cabins are done." Britt's tone said the barb still stung.

"We are, Britt. I promise, I was kidding. I shouldn't have said that. We truly couldn't keep this place going if it wasn't for you."

Britt didn't respond, but her shoulders seemed to relax a bit, even as she dabbed black paint through the stencil onto the white painted floor.

Joanna had taken off early from work to help Britt, but since there was barely space for both of them in the little bathroom, she'd been relegated to passing Britt the supplies she needed. She felt like a nurse handing instruments to a surgeon. The room was technically a three-quarter bath, since it had only a narrow shower and no tub. Joanna was surprised how many people rejected this rental in favor of Britt's cabin, which had an equally tiny bath, but boasted a clawfoot tub.

"We should paint the floor in your bathroom like this." Joanna aimed to change the subject and find a way to make up for her thoughtlessness.

"I did consider that, but we'd have to paint around the tub. That beast would be almost impossible to move." She repositioned the stencil and dipped her brush into the can, then wiped the brush almost dry before dabbing on the paint.

The effect was like a weathered vintage black-and-white tile. Phylicia had found the pattern on Pinterest and was so enamored with the look that she'd talked about doing a similar treatment in the powder room at the new house. They'd broken ground on Phee and Quinn's house earlier in the week, and a constant stream of workmen and vehicles had clogged the lane ever since.

"So . . . Phee said you have a date tomorrow night. This sounds like it's getting pretty serious."

Joanna frowned. "Serious? What exactly did Phee say?" She'd only mentioned her date in passing when she declined Phylicia's invitation to dinner Friday. She hadn't told her older sister that this date was with Ben.

"Just that you had a date. Why? Was it supposed to be a secret or something?"

"No. It's . . . I'm going out with Ben."

Britt stopped dabbing and turned to look at Joanna. "Ben Harven?"

"No, Benjamin Franklin." Jo smirked and gave her sister a playful shove.

Britt lost her balance and squealed, but she caught herself before she toppled onto the wet paint. "You do not want me to have to start all over on this floor, sister."

"Sorry!"

Britt set her paintbrush on the edge of the can. "You're going out with Ben again? After all this time? How on earth did *that* happen? And what about Luke? I thought you really liked him."

"I do. I like him a lot, but I like Ben too. Maybe even loved him once upon a time."

"Okay. So have you told Luke about his . . . competition?"

"I haven't talked to Luke since the night I saw Ben." She told Britt about running into Ben and his friends in the park and about Ben's subsequent phone call. "Am I terrible that when it comes to Luke, I just can't seem to get past Mateo?"

"Not terrible . . ."

"But? What *aren't* you saying?"

Britt scooted back on the floor and started on another section of the stencil. "I'm not *not* saying anything. Except, you really need to talk to Luke."

"I know. I will. But in my defense, he made it clear that we're just friends."

"He did?"

"We had an argument about Mateo. I told him how I feel . . . that I don't want to start a relationship when a twelve-year-old is part of the deal."

"But Jo . . . what is Luke supposed to do about that? Get rid of the kid? He doesn't really have a choice, does he?"

"No. And I'm not asking him to change anything. Like I told him, I need time to think about it . . . and pray about it."

"And have you? Prayed about it?"

"Yes, Mom."

Her sister gave a guilty smile. "Just checking."

"I know." But *had* she really? Prayed about it? She'd assumed a lot of things were God's direction, but had she really listened for His voice? Had she even taken the time to pray more than a hurried, tossed-up prayer? She had to admit she hadn't spent any time reading the Bible or even seeking wise counsel. Something Mom and Dad had always been big on. She sighed. "I'm about ready to swear off men for the rest of my life."

"Well, I *know* you don't mean that. At least I don't think you do. What happened to going back to law school? Not that you can't go to law school and have a man at the same time."

Joanna shrugged, but the question threw her for a loop. "I don't know. I suppose I will go back eventually. I don't really want to work for Trenton the rest of my life. But after being around the stuff he has to deal with, I'm not sure that's really the direction I want to go anymore."

Did she dare admit, even to her sister, that a career in law had taken a back seat to her desire to open a wedding venue? She would have felt like a failure admitting that to Ginger or any of her other friends. They were all so focused on careers and even after they had a career, on getting advanced degrees. Of course, most of them were already married. And if she was honest with herself, *that* was the desire that most filled Joanna Chandler's heart.

"So what *do* you want? If money were no object and you could do anything you wanted?"

She hesitated. "Promise you won't laugh?"

"Of course I won't. Unless you tell me you want to join the circus or something."

"I'd love to turn the clearing into a wedding venue. Or even an event venue. I don't necessarily want to be a wedding planner or anything, but I think it would be so fun to have events up there. Twinkle lights and tents. The way it looked the night of Phee and Quinn's wedding. Something about that was just magical." She didn't tell Britt that a big part of the magic was the memories she had of Luke from that night—before she knew how . . . *permanent* Mateo was in Luke's life. "I know it probably sounds silly, but—"

"It doesn't sound silly. Just . . . very different from Joanna Chandler, Attorney at Law."

She cringed. "I know. Don't tell anyone."

"I won't. But you should go for it. Why not?"

"Now you sound like Luke."

"What do you mean?" Britt stretched, then scooted back until she was sitting cross-legged in the doorway. "Hand me that masking tape, will you?"

Joanna retrieved the roll of tape and slid down to sit on the floor with her back against the wall. "Luke thinks the wedding venue is a good idea."

"Well, sure he does. It would be job security for him."

"True." But she didn't think that was why he encouraged her. She'd felt his encouragement was because he genuinely believed in her ability to make the dream of a wedding venue come true. She wondered what Ben would think about the idea. But she was pretty sure she knew. He would say she was wasting her intelligence on something frivolous. Something she couldn't begin to make as much money at as she could with a career in law. A lot of people would think the same. People she cared about.

Maybe she'd have Ben come early Friday and give him a tour of the property. Test the waters.

She looked up to see Britt watching her, paintbrush aloft, head tilted.

"Sorry . . . Just thinking. I'm pretty sure Luke doesn't really need the income from DJing. It's kind of an extension of his job at the radio station."

Britt shrugged and went back to painting. "You should just be glad you have two men to choose from."

"Ha! Men! They're nothing but trouble. You can have 'em."

"Thanks anyway. Not my type. But hey, keep sending me your castoffs. Maybe I'll hit the jackpot eventually."

"Castoffs? Please! And what *is* your type?" She'd never really thought of her baby sister as having the same longings she did. To be married. To be settled in life. But Britt was twenty-four, and now that she was mostly stuck out here running the Airbnb rentals, she didn't have as much chance to meet anyone the way she had when she was at college.

"Tall, dark, handsome, talented, kind . . . rich." Britt threw a raised-eyebrow look at Joanna over her shoulder.

"Uh-huh . . . You should have put *rich* first on the list. My spoiled baby sister will need a millionaire husband to keep her in the luxury to which she's accustomed."

"I am *not* spoiled."

"So you say. But if you don't want to be accused of being spoiled, maybe you should cancel that spa appointment I saw on your calendar." She angled her head toward the tidy kitchen where Britt's calendar hung.

"It's not a spa appointment. It's a massage. All this crouching and kneeling is killing my back." She stretched and groaned as if to prove her point.

"A two-hour massage?"

"Snoop! For your information, that includes a manicure. And pedicure." Britt set down the paintbrush on the rim of the paint can and held out her hands. "Look at these claws. That's from sandpaper and paint and paint thinner and—"

"Hey"—Joanna held her own hands out, palms-up—"you don't have to justify anything to me. As long as it doesn't come out of the renovation budget, what you do with your money is your business. I'm just giving you a hard time."

"Yeah, well, cut it out. I don't have time to take a guilt trip."

"Haha." Smiling, Jo struggled to her feet. One silver lining in "losing" their older sister to marriage was that Joanna and Britt had become closer. For the first time in their adult life, Jo had started to see her baby sister as a peer. And one she really liked. Even if there was a little truth to the "spoiled" accusation she'd leveled at Britt. "The floor looks good, sis. Can you finish up without me? I need to go call one of the many men I have lined up wanting to date the likes of me."

"Oh, sure, you go make your call. I'll stay here and work my tail off while you nab the last of the city's eligible bachelors."

"Love you," Jo singsonged as she exited the cabin. She didn't have any clearer insight than she had an hour ago, but the time with her sister had done her heart good.

CHAPTER 27

"SO, YOU'RE A BIG LANDOWNER now. Impressive." Ben stood in the clearing, arms akimbo, surveying the lay of the land.

Joanna watched him, trying to read his expression. He looked good, his hair longer than he used to wear it, and the sleeves of his crisp button-down shirt rolled up to reveal tan forearms.

"This is where Phee and Quinn got married," she told him. "We're—*I'm* thinking about renting this spot out as a wedding venue." She'd gone back and forth about whether to tell him, but now, it came out as naturally as if they were talking about the weather. She'd forgotten how easy Ben was to talk to.

"Do you think you'd make any money at that? It seems like you'd have to charge a lot to make it worthwhile."

"Maybe, but no more than most venues. Of course, it wouldn't work for winter weddings, but I wouldn't want to have to keep it open all year anyway. We bought a lot of supplies for Phee's wedding . . . It seems a shame for them to go to waste."

"You could sell them on Craigslist."

She frowned. But knowing him, he wasn't being negative.

Just practical. "I take it you don't think the wedding venue is a good idea?"

He laughed. "I didn't say that. It just sounds like a lot of work."

"It might be, but I've never been afraid of hard work." Now, she was on the defensive. She didn't like the feeling.

"I'm sure that's true." He turned as if to head back down the stairs to the lane. "Well, it's awfully pretty up here, that's for sure. Nice piece of property."

"We were in the right place at the right time. We bought it with Mom's inheritance . . . from her grandparents. She never spent much of it, so what was left was enough to buy this place and have a little left over to fix up the cabins. We almost couldn't talk Phee into going in with us, but she came around."

"And now Phylicia's building here? What . . . did you make a pact you'd all stick together or something?" She couldn't read his expression, but she thought he was teasing.

"That'll be decided on a case-by-case basis." She tried to match his enigmatic smile. "But Britt and I sure were happy when we found out Phee and Quinn wanted to build out here."

"Do you think you'll want to stay here too?"

She shrugged, then nodded. Because she sensed that was what he expected. "I do like it here. More than I thought I'd like living secluded in the country. But who knows what the future holds."

"True." He took another step toward the stairs. "Shall we go eat? Before it gets crowded?"

"Sure." She was disappointed he didn't seem more interested in touring the rest of the property. She'd personally tidied up the cabins and her cottage was spotless. But he'd barely stuck his head in the door of the cottage and had declined her invitation to see the cabins. She hadn't asked if he wanted to see the clearing, but instead just led the way.

But Ben informed her he'd reserved call-ahead seating

at the Gordonville Grill in the next town over, and he seemed worried they'd lose their spot if they were a few seconds late.

When they reached the lane at the bottom of the steps, he headed for his car.

"I'll be right there. I need to grab my purse from the house."

"I won't leave without you." The charming smile she remembered from the days when she'd been in love with him was back and excitement swelled inside her.

She hurried into the house, stopping only to check her appearance in the mirror. She'd curled her hair and worn a summery dress with sandals. Not so dressy that it made this date look more important than Ben might mean it to be, yet pretty and special in case the evening did turn out to be the beginning of something new.

She had to admit it was going to be nice to not have some chattery kid in the back seat interrupting their conversation at every turn. Ben even opened the door for her and waited until she'd tucked the skirt of her dress safely inside before closing the door.

"You hungry?" he asked when he was buckled behind the wheel.

"I am. I haven't eaten in Gordonville in forever."

"Me neither. But I sometimes dream about their prime rib."

She laughed. "It's the blackberry cobbler for me."

"For dinner?"

"No, but I'll eat light so I have room for cobbler after."

"Sounds like a plan."

He drove slowly down the lane, but once on the highway he sped up. She'd forgotten that Ben liked to drive fast. It hadn't bothered her so much in their early days of dating, but after he'd wrecked his car—thankfully, *after* dropping her off from a date one night—she'd begged him to slow down. Apparently he'd forgotten a hard-learned lesson.

"Hey . . ." She reached and touched his sleeve briefly. "Slow down a little, will you?"

"You sound like my mom."

"I don't want to miss out on that blackberry cobbler."

"Why do you think I'm driving so fast?"

"What I mean is, I'd like to arrive alive."

"So I can drive faster on the way home?"

She frowned. "I wish you wouldn't take such risks."

He leaned back and threw her a look. "Look who's talking, Miss buy a big ol' piece of property and open a hotel."

She laughed. "That's not exactly a life-threatening risk. And it's not a hotel. Airbnb."

"Same difference. You have complete strangers sleeping in your beds." He tapped the brake again. "Doesn't that feel kind of weird?"

"The strangers, you mean? Not really. Maybe it did at first, but we've gotten used to it. People are really nice. Well, most of them anyway."

"And if they're not?"

"We grin and bear it."

"I'll bet."

"No, we really do. I've been blazing mad a couple times, but reviews are huge in this business, so we don't want to tick anybody off."

Ben shook his head. "I don't think I'd survive very long in that business then."

"You'd probably be good at it. You were always good at schmoozing." She laughed. "I mean that in the nicest possible way."

He gave a humorless laugh. "I've gotten grumpy in my old age."

She was inclined to agree with him, but she didn't want to start the evening on a sour note.

They were mostly silent the rest of the twenty-minute drive to Gordonville, but it wasn't an uncomfortable silence. Still, she wondered what they'd talk about all through dinner.

But that turned out not to be a problem. Once they were

seated, the floodgates opened and Ben talked a mile a minute. He caught her up on everything that had been going on with him in the past year and a half, and by the time their food came, they were laughing together like the old friends they were.

"So, you're still working at Pritchert & Pritchert? How's that going? When are you going to start back to school so you can open your own law firm?"

She wiped the corner of her mouth with her napkin. "Funny you should ask. Britt and I were just talking about that the other day. The truth is, I'm not sure I'll go back to school. I'm kind of liking the idea of the wedding venue. And even though Britt is handling most of the Airbnb stuff, she needs help with a lot of it. And I kind of enjoy that too. The hospitality and all."

"But there's no way you'd ever make what you would as an attorney running a bed and breakfast. Is there?"

And there it was. She shook her head. "Probably not. But that's not as important to me as it used to be. Since Mom died . . . my perspective has changed on a lot of things."

He put a hunk of steak in his mouth and took an inordinately long time to chew it. But when he swallowed, compassion filled his eyes. "I'm so sorry about your mom. How is your dad holding up? How are *you* holding up?"

She felt suddenly guarded. "I'm okay. It's been seven months now . . . eight at the end of this month. That doesn't seem possible." The realization startled her and she spoke almost to herself before turning back to Ben. "Dad has really struggled, but I think he's finding his way. You knew he moved to Florida?"

"I think I heard that. Heard he'd sold your house anyway."

"Yes. That was hard. On all of us."

"I bet. You grew up in that house."

She nodded. "Lots of good memories there. But we're making new ones at the new place. Dad stayed with us at the cottage the week before Phee's wedding, and that really made it feel more like home. Now with Phee and Quinn building on the property, it's honestly every bit as much home to me as the house in Langhorne was."

"That's good." He took another bite of prime rib.

"So what about you? You said you left your job at the college? I thought you liked that job."

He shrugged, still chewing. "Maybe slightly better than my job at the med center. Can't say I ever aspired to a career in billing. I'd rather be working outdoors, but the money is pretty good."

"What would you do outdoors?"

He shrugged. "Not sure. Maybe something with the forest service. Or be a golf pro."

She laughed. "Have you taken up golf since we last met?"

"I have, actually."

"Oh." She covered her mouth. "Sorry. I didn't mean to laugh."

"It's okay. Forest service is probably more likely than golf pro. But a guy can dream, right?"

"Of course."

"The truth is, I can barely afford to *play* golf. But it's a guilty pleasure on the weekends."

"Well that's good. Nice you have your weekends off. I like that about my job too." It was becoming one of the only things she liked about her job, but she didn't tell him that.

They ate in silence for a few minutes before Ben laid down his silverware and studied her long enough that she started to feel uncomfortable.

She tipped her head. "What?"

"I didn't think it was possible, but you've gotten more beautiful in the last year."

"Year and a half." She smiled, but his comment warmed her heart, even as it made her a tiny bit suspicious.

"Whatever. Just say thank you for the compliment."

"Thank you, Ben. That's sweet."

"Can I tell you something?" That sultry stare again.

It made her nervous. "I guess . . ."

"I've regretted letting you go almost every day since . . . it happened."

"And you waited a year and a half to tell me this?"

"What can I say? I'm an idiot."

"Well, yes, but . . ." She grinned, feeling as if she had the upper hand and liking the feeling. Even as she worried where he was going with this.

"I'm serious, Jo. I never should have let you get away. We had something good and I blew it. Big time."

"How did you blow it?" She'd waited a long time for an apology she thought she might never get. She wondered if it would be as sweet as it always was in her imagination.

"I was a jerk. You were going through a hard time and I . . . I didn't want to go there. I couldn't stand to see you in such pain."

She bent her head, not sure how to respond. His words were what she needed to hear, but were they genuine? Or was he merely saying what he knew was the right thing to say? And even as the questions plagued her, she hated that she was suspicious of his motives.

"I'm sorry I wasn't there for you. It was a bad time."

"A bad time? For who?"

"Well, for you, of course. But I wasn't in a good place either. I was still trying to figure out what I wanted to do with my life, and I let that get in the way of our relationship. I—I had a lot of growing up to do. I realize that now."

The hurt, the betrayal she'd suffered from Ben—and that she'd had to deal with in the midst of learning that Mom's illness was terminal—came rushing back. "It's . . . in the past. It's okay."

"Still, I'm sorry. About your mom, about us. I *am* sorry."

Joanna sighed. "I know. And I forgive you. I forgave you a long time ago, actually."

"Thank you for that. I don't deserve it."

"None of us ever really deserve forgiveness."

"Well, I've suffered the consequences, if that makes you feel any better."

"What do you mean by that?" She placed her fork across her half-eaten chicken breast and pushed the plate away, her appetite gone.

"I've missed you, Jo. You were always the best thing in my life. I let you go over a petty thing and I've regretted it."

She bristled. "My mother's death was *not* a petty thing."

"No! Of course not." He reached across the table and touched her wrist. "Please . . . That's not what I meant."

She pulled her arm away and folded it across her body, out of his reach.

"Joanna."

She looked up. He'd rarely used her full name, and it had a sobering effect now. "Yes?"

"That's not what I meant. Your mom was the sweetest woman I've ever known—next to you, of course. I almost felt like I'd lost my own mom when I heard that your mom had died. And I am so sorry I bailed on you at the worst possible time."

She swallowed hard. "Ben, you never so much as sent a card after Mom died."

A too-long silence. Then he bowed his head as she'd done a moment ago. "I know. I thought about it. Sending a card. Even calling you. I promise I did. But it seemed like that might be . . . I don't know . . . rubbing it in or something."

"It's never wrong to send a card. Or just to say you're sorry."

"I know. I should have. I should have called you."

"Okay. I didn't mean to . . . belabor the point."

"No. I don't blame you for being upset. I just hope you really mean it. About forgiving me."

She bristled. "I meant what I said. Can we change the subject?"

He pushed his plate away. "Of course. I'm sorry if that upset you, but . . . I just wanted to be sure you knew how sorry I was."

"I know. Thank you, Ben." She flashed him her best smile, relieved to have that out of the way, yet knowing she'd rehash their conversation a million times before she was really satisfied that Ben understood why she'd broken off their friendship.

She knew it wasn't his fault, but the fact that he'd waited until Mom was gone to get in touch again bothered her more than she wanted to admit. Especially when she'd assured him that she'd forgiven him.

"Now what about that blackberry cobbler?"

"Maybe next time. I should take the rest of my chicken home for Melvin though."

"So, ol' Melvin moved out to the country with you?"

"He did. But he's a big disappointment as a mouser." She told him about the mouse they'd seen scurrying across the floor of one of the cabins the first time they looked at the property. "He hasn't brought us even one of the little vermin. And don't tell Britt, but I know there are still mice on the property."

Ben laughed at her story and by the time they'd paid the bill and headed for Ben's car, they seemed to have recaptured the lighthearted mood the evening had begun with.

"Maybe we could go for ice cream. My treat." She thought it a good sign that her appetite had returned.

"Nonsense. This date is on me. You still like Andy's?"

"Is there any other place when it comes to—?" She gave an awkward laugh, realizing she'd said those exact words to Luke when he'd asked about the frozen custard place. Only last week. It seemed a lifetime since she'd seen him.

"What's wrong?" Ben gave her a worried look.

"Nothing. Except . . ." She waved him off. "Except that I'm paying because I want a double dip."

That made him laugh.

And with his laughter, her hopes rose again.

CHAPTER 28

Let's keep it to a single dip tonight, bud, okay?" Luke put his hands on Mateo's shoulders as they studied the menu on the outdoor marquee together. "We need to watch the budget."

These nightly after-supper jaunts to Andy's Frozen Custard were breaking the bank, not to mention the bathroom scales. But in the heat of summer, it had become a fun tradition and something Mateo so looked forward to that Luke didn't have the heart to say no.

"I have money . . ." Mateo dug in the pocket of his athletic shorts and produced a couple of dollar bills.

"No . . . Hang on to that. You can pay once I run out of money."

Mateo's eyes grew round. "*Are* you running out?"

Luke laughed and clapped a hand on the boy's back. "Not anytime soon. But if we keep up the double dips, we'll be skating pretty close to the edge."

Looking relieved, Mateo shoved the bills back into his pocket and ordered a small chocolate cone. Luke ordered vanilla frozen custard in a small cup and paid for the treats.

It was early enough that there wasn't a crowd like there would be later when the movies let out and the baseball games were over. They carried their treats to Luke's car and climbed inside. The sun beat through the window on the driver's side, and he cracked his window, but after eating through half his cup of the cold, creamy frozen custard, the heat started to feel good.

"So how'd things go with Val today?" Mateo had been staying with Valerie Shubert, the wife of Luke's coworker, during the day while Luke was at work. He'd assured Don and Valerie that next summer Mateo would be old enough to stay by himself, but with Maria's death so fresh, Luke hadn't wanted to risk it this year.

Mateo shrugged. "Okay, I guess."

"Just okay?"

"It was fine. Except . . . a little boring."

"Well, you know how to fix that, don't you?"

Mateo eyed him suspiciously. "Don't say chores."

"Actually, I was going to say homework."

"What? I don't have homework. It's summer."

"Oh, don't you worry, homework could be arranged."

Mateo looked up at Luke from under his fringe of black bangs. A wry smile came to his face. "Um, yeah . . . Forget I said anything."

Luke laughed. "That's what I thought."

He finished his ice cream and climbed out of the car to toss the cup and crumpled napkin into the trash receptacle near the building. When he got back behind the wheel, Mateo was still working on his cone.

"I'm going to stop by the post office and check on the mail while you finish your cone."

Mateo gave a noncommittal grunt, and Luke put the car in gear, then crept through the parking lot, careful of the line of cars that had started to form at the drive-through.

There were half a dozen people in line at the outdoor

window. From the corner of his eye, he saw a couple climb from a red Jeep Cherokee and walk up to the window. His breath caught. Joanna.

He couldn't hear what they were saying, but her hands moved animatedly as she talked with the guy, who was cozying up to her a little too familiarly for Luke's taste. The guy turned and Luke recognized him. Ben, the former boyfriend, from the other night. Apparently there was more to their friendship than she'd admitted.

Mateo followed Luke's line of sight. "Hey! That's Joanna!"

Before Luke could stop him, Mateo rolled down the passenger-side window and hollered. "Joanna! Over here!"

"Cut it out, buddy. She's busy. She's . . . with someone else."

"So?" He shook his head and his bangs flopped over one eye. "You're not even gonna say hi to her?"

"It's not polite to interrupt when people are talking—"

"You did it. Just tonight."

Luke squinted, trying to think what the kid was referring to. "Oh, you mean when we ran into Don and Val at Schnucks earlier?"

"Yeah. *They* were talking."

"That's different."

"How?"

"It's—Never mind. Just roll up your window. Please." He pulled slowly around the lot, but too late.

Joanna ducked to look through their windshield and gave a tentative wave.

"They're not talking now." Mateo started to roll his window down again.

"Mateo. Cut it out!" He softened his voice. "Leave the window up."

"Why?"

"Do what I say!" He hadn't meant it to come out so sharply. Feeling like a spy who'd been exposed, he gave a half-hearted wave and kept driving. But the scene in his rearview mirror made him feel mildly nauseated. He patted Mateo's knee. "I'll explain later."

Joanna laughed up into the face of Ben Whatever-his-face-was. The man's hand rested at the small of her back in a much-too-familiar way, and she appeared not to mind in the least.

She'd asked for "a week or two" to pray about things, and Luke had been determined to give her the full two weeks. He huffed. Apparently, she'd gotten an early answer from above.

"What time is it anyway?" As they drove up the lane, the absence of lights in the cottage or in Britt's cabin sent a frisson of alarm up Joanna's spine.

Ben pointed to the clock on the Cherokee's dashboard. "What's wrong? You turn into a pumpkin at the stroke of midnight or something?"

"I can't believe it's so late."

"Time flies when you're having fun?" Ben spoke the familiar adage as a question.

"It *was* a fun night. Thank you, Ben."

"It was my pleasure." He turned off the engine and turned in the seat toward her.

The simple action was so familiar. As if no time had passed since they'd been a couple. In love. Ben seemed to sense her thoughts and reached to brush a strand of hair from her face.

He let his palm linger on her cheek. She covered his hand with her own. But more in defense than affection. She wasn't ready for this. Things were moving too fast.

He leaned across the console and she took a shallow breath, steeling herself for what her body wanted—his kisses, his caresses. But what her heart knew was wrong. It was too soon. She couldn't promise Ben something she was so unsure of.

And even more so after seeing Luke tonight. It had only

been a brief moment. And an awkward one at that. She hadn't realized it was Luke and Mateo until they were almost out of the parking lot. But when her eyes met Luke's, even with a windshield obscuring their vision, she thought something had passed between them. Something that demanded her acknowledgment. Her consideration.

She had promised Luke that she would pray. The implication being that she would let him know the outcome of those prayers. She'd done neither.

Ben had derailed her best intentions. And maybe Ben *was* the answer to her barely spoken prayers. But even so, she owed Luke an answer. It wasn't right or fair to ignore him.

She felt awful that after all her insistence that there was nothing between her and Ben, Luke had seen them together tonight. Guilt tugged at her. She didn't know how much Luke had observed, but despite her attempts to temper things, Ben picked up right where they'd left off a year and a half ago, putting his arm around her, pulling her close, flirting—and even kissing the top of her head while they waited for ice cream.

She'd made motions of pulling away, but then she came right back for more, flirting, encouraging him. The timeless rituals of courtship. But worldly courtship.

She'd known Ben would want to kiss her good night. Or more. They'd remained chaste during the time they dated, though just barely. She'd forgotten how insistent Ben could be, but of course, she shouldered equal blame. She hadn't discouraged his physical affection tonight. Had encouraged it even. Being with Ben tonight—reviving a relationship that had already, in the past, moved through various levels of physical expression—had made her ravenous for physical touch, for the knowledge that someone found her desirable and sexy. She'd placed herself in a dangerous position, and even as she recognized how vulnerable she was, she couldn't deny the physical attraction to this man.

She remembered his kisses, his embrace—remembered

them vividly. And longing overwhelmed her. Yet somehow, she knew it wasn't . . . authentic. Maybe Ben's affection for her was genuine—though by the increasing urgency of his caresses, she doubted it. But hers were purely physical.

"Ben. No . . ." She pressed her hands against his chest and pushed him away. Hugging the passenger side door, she straightened her clothes and smoothed a hand over her hair. "I'm sorry. We can't just . . . pick up where we left off. It's too soon."

He breathed in deeply, then blew out a stream of air. "Jo . . . I know you feel the same as I do."

"I need time, Ben. I don't know what . . . what I want."

"Well, I know what I want." He moved closer, reached for her again. "I want you. It's always been you, Jo."

"No, Ben. It hasn't always been me."

He leaned away, then seeing her face, he scooted back into the driver's seat. "What is that supposed to mean?"

"It wasn't all that long ago when you told me you weren't ready to be tied down."

"I never said—"

"I remember your exact words, Ben. Believe me, I replayed them in my head every day for . . . for too long."

"Okay. Maybe that is what I said."

"Then you understand why I'm a little hesitant to just jump back to where we left off."

"There's a lot of water under the bridge, Jo. Things have changed. *I've* changed."

"In what way? *How* have you changed?"

"How? . . . Lots of ways," he sputtered.

She smiled, feeling triumphant—if a bit guilty. She wanted to hear him say that he'd changed such that now he would never leave her because of something like her mother's illness. "I'd like to know what those ways are."

"Jo . . . I hope we've both done a lot of growing up in the last couple of years."

She nodded. "I hope we have too. We'll talk more, I promise. But right now I . . . I really need to go inside before my sister starts worrying."

Ben looked confused, but he didn't argue.

She opened her door and climbed from the car, bending to wave at him. "Thank you for the evening."

"I'll call you?" It was a question.

But she only nodded in reply, closing the car door.

She turned and picked her way up the uneven walk to Britt's cabin in the dark, overwhelmed by sadness, and feeling more disappointed than she could remember in a very long time. And not just in the way the evening had turned out. Disappointed in herself.

CHAPTER 29

JOANNA WOKE THE NEXT MORNING to the roar of a truck crunching down the lane toward the construction site of Quinn and Phee's new home. She rolled over to look at the flea market clock on the nightstand, which read four o'clock. *That* couldn't be right. It was light outside and she knew she hadn't slept the whole day away.

She threw off the covers and went to retrieve her phone from her purse hanging on the knob of the bedroom door. It was a quarter after seven. They'd had a week of temps in the nineties, and no doubt the construction crew wanted to beat the heat.

Joanna padded out to the kitchen where the windows were still propped open from yesterday to let in the cool night air. The early morning breeze was already humid, but Jo left the windows open, hating to run the noisy window air conditioner yet.

She pulled a package of coffee beans from the cupboard, ground the beans, and started a pot of coffee. Once it was brewing, she went into the bathroom and leaned across the clawfoot tub, trying to look out the high window over the tub.

But all she could see was the tops of the trees swaying in the breeze. Hanging onto the side of the tub, she climbed inside, the porcelain surface cold on the bottoms of her bare feet.

"Do you always take a bath in your pajamas?"

Jo started at Britt's groggy voice and turned to see her sister standing in the doorway, her hair sticking out every which way from a loose ponytail holder.

"Sorry. Did the coffee grinder wake you?"

Britt yawned. "I don't know what it was. But what are you looking at?"

"The construction crew is here already. It looks like they're pouring the foundation today." Still clinging to the side of the tub, she peered out to watch a cement mixer churning beside the gaping hole that was—or soon would be—Quinn and Phee's basement. Quinn stood in front of the crater, directing the driver to its edge, while Mabel, Quinn's dog, pranced at the cusp of the excavation.

Britt climbed over the edge of the tub, elbowing Jo to one side for a spot at the window.

"Hey, I was here first." Jo gave her sister a playful shove.

"Wow, it looks like something serious is going to happen today. I was starting to think there was no way that house could be done by Christmas, but maybe it will be after all."

"Phee thinks it will."

"That would be so awesome to have Quinn and Phee living here by then. Then Dad would have a real place to stay when he comes home for the holidays."

"You don't think the cottage and cabins are *real*?" Jo teased.

"You know what I mean. He'll be with family in a house that's never been rented out."

"Speaking of which, have you heard a peep out of our guests this weekend? I haven't seen them since they checked in Thursday night."

Jo shook her head. "I haven't, but then it was late when I got in last night."

"I didn't even hear you come in." Her sister took in a breath. "Oh, that's right. You went out with Ben. How'd it go?"

"It was . . . okay, I guess."

"Wow. That's not exactly a glowing report."

"No, we had fun. It was nice." That was all true. But something had been missing. Despite the physical attraction she felt for Ben, it hadn't been like she'd hoped between them. Even though they seemed to recapture their easy way with each other, it bothered her that he'd been so ready to jump right into the way things had been before they broke up. Without even talking about what had happened.

And her physical reaction to Ben felt like a betrayal of Luke. Which seemed crazy given that Luke had never even tried to kiss her.

Even though she wanted him to. What was wrong with her? Was she so set on having a man—any man—that she would make herself "love" anyone who showed her the least interest?

"It was nice, but . . . ?" Britt's voice broke through her conflicted thoughts.

But before she could answer, Phylicia appeared in the bathroom doorway. "What was nice? And why are you two standing in the bathtub?"

"Where'd you come from?" Jo climbed out of the tub and sat on the edge of it.

"I rode along with Quinn. They're pouring the foundation today." Phee pointed out the window.

"We saw the trucks." Britt slid down to sit on the opposite edge of the clawfoot tub, her bare feet still resting inside.

"So what did I miss? It sounded like I was missing out on a good conversation."

"Jo had a date with Ben last night."

Jo gave Britt a playful shove. "You little tattletale."

"Ben Harven?" Phee hopped up on the bathroom counter, swinging her sandal-clad feet.

"Yes, Ben Harven. Good grief. Is that such a big deal?"

"Wow. It kind of is, Jo." Her older sister spoke softly, her gaze somber. Phee's expression was so like Mom's it took Jo aback.

And told her clearly what the *real* problem was. What she'd known all along but had done her best to ignore. Why, she wasn't sure. And even now, the reply to her sister was a defensive one. "It was one date, okay? It's not like I'm going to marry him tomorrow or anything."

"I know, but why would you go back into that, Jo?" Britt held her hands and feet out in front of her, inspecting her new mani-pedi from the spa.

"Unless Ben has changed." Phee looked so hopeful, Jo wished she could assure her sister he *had* changed.

"He *has*," she said. "I really think he has." Maybe *she* was the one who was stuck.

"I'm glad then." Phylicia tilted her head. "I always liked Ben. I just didn't like . . . how things ended with him. *Why* it ended with him."

"No. I didn't either. And we talked about that." Until Ben changed the subject.

"Did he apologize?" Britt wasn't backing down.

"He did." But the truth was, he'd given more excuses than apologies.

"Good." Phee nodded, looking thoughtful.

Britt frowned. "His timing sure is funny."

Phee shot a warning look at their younger sister. "Maybe he's just been waiting for a little time to pass . . . you know, since Mom . . . before he let you know he wanted to get back together."

"Maybe," Britt said. "But is he going to drop out of your life every time something hard comes along?"

"Britt. That's not fair," Phee scolded.

Britt gave Phee a look that challenged, then turned to Jo. "Sorry. But how can you be sure he won't?"

Jo held up a hand. "It's okay. It's a fair question."

"But, Jo . . . what happened with Luke? I thought that was getting serious."

"She can't get past the kid . . . Mateo."

"I'm right here, Britt."

"Just filling her in."

Jo rolled her eyes at her younger sister and turned to her older with a sheepish grin. "I can't get past the kid . . . Mateo."

Phylicia laughed, but her smile faded quickly. "Well, maybe this is God's answer then . . . running into Ben."

"I had that thought." But the only thought she was having now was that she needed to *ask* God if Ben was her answer. She'd felt that still, small voice prompting her, and she'd ignored it again and again. But she had gotten into too much trouble in her life assuming things. And this was no small matter.

As if Phee had read her mind, she said, "Hang in there, Jo. There's no rush to get back with Ben. God will show you what to do. Just look at how things worked out with Quinn and me. I didn't think there was any way. But oh, what I would have missed if I hadn't let God do the deciding. He knows what's best for you, Jo. You can trust Him."

Luke picked up his phone for the third time in an hour and stared at Joanna Chandler's image in the circle above her phone number on the screen. So many times today, he'd come so close to hitting Send. But what he would say when—if—she answered, he had no idea.

It wasn't really his place to make the call. The two weeks she'd said she needed—to think and to pray—had come and gone. And he'd heard nothing from her.

Thankfully, the weekend had passed quickly with two DJ gigs, including a wedding last night. Mateo was becoming a big help at these events. Luke got a kick out of seeing him grow more confident, both with helping Luke haul and set up the equipment, and in poise as he interacted with the people attending the events. He was so proud of that kid.

Even though he and Mateo had gone to church *and* Sunday school this morning, the day had dragged. Tonight, part of him just wanted to call Joanna and get the whole thing over with. But what if that was the end of it? Would that be better than the constant wondering and the infernal hope that she might yet come around?

No, the ball was in her court. She was the one who was uncertain. Luke was only uncertain if she couldn't come to terms with the fact that he'd made promises that he was determined to keep. And he refused to feel guilty about that.

He looked down the hall toward Mateo's room. The patch of light that had spilled from the partially open door earlier had disappeared, and all was quiet in the apartment.

Luke laid the phone facedown on the kitchen table so those pretty blue eyes wouldn't cloud his judgment. Joanna had made it crystal clear that Mateo was a deal breaker. Luke didn't have a choice about the boy being in his life, so why was he wasting his time even thinking about her? Even if he'd never promised Maria that he would take care of her son, Luke couldn't imagine loving a child of his own more than he loved that kid. He had no desire to go back on his promise. So why couldn't he let it go at that? Let *Joanna* go?

And yet somehow, he couldn't. Because despite her spelling out the vision she had for her life—a husband, a baby, time alone together with her ideal little family—Luke kept picturing Joanna as part of *his* family. With him and Mateo. It was wishful thinking. It had to be. And yet the images he saw in his mind's eye were as clear as photographs. And in them, Joanna was smiling, laughing, her arm around Mateo's shoulder like a mother with a son.

If he was honest with himself, his feelings for Joanna grew stronger every day. There was just something about her that he couldn't easily brush aside.

He left his phone on the table and walked out to the patio. The flagstones were warm under his bare feet, the air heavy with humidity. Still, his thoughts were always clearer out here beneath the stars.

He turned on the garden hose and filled the fountain, then pulled a few weeds from the edges of a flower bed, remembering the night Joanna had sat in the chaise lounge across from him. Looking up at the night sky through a network of branches and leaves, he whispered a prayer. "Lord, only You know what's best and right. If it's not Joanna, please . . . *please* take away this longing I have for her. Show me what You want me to do, and give me the strength to do it."

He wasn't sure where those last words had come from, but he was afraid the fact that he'd spoken them, almost without thinking, meant he would *need* strength for whatever was ahead.

CHAPTER 30

JOANNA CLIMBED THE STAIRS TO the office early on a Monday morning and found Trent in the waiting room, shirt sleeves rolled up and sans his usual suit jacket, sorting through old magazines from the trio of coffee tables. He'd apparently been at it for a while as a stack of periodicals overflowed the trash can beside her desk.

"Are you trying to put me out of a job?" she teased.

He waved her off. "Don't mind me. This is just my form of pacing."

"Why are you pacing? What's going on?" It wasn't like her boss to pace, and it certainly wasn't like him to bother himself with menial tasks like culling the waiting room magazines. He hadn't mentioned last Friday that anything out of the ordinary was coming up this week. At least she didn't think so. But she'd been so bound up in her own confusion that she wouldn't have sworn to anything.

Even so, it had been a good week and a good weekend. She had finally put everything else aside and taken the time to pray about her situation. She'd prayed while she hung curtains in Far Cottage, and while she painted cabinets in the tiny bathroom there (praying she wouldn't splatter paint on the quaint checkerboard floor Britt had worked so hard on). She'd prayed while she mixed up dough for cinnamon scones and while they baked, filling the whole cottage with their aroma. She'd prayed in church yesterday, and in the shower this morning. And she'd finally remembered to be *still* before God, to simply listen for His voice.

She couldn't say that God had given her any black-and-white answers. But she'd heard His still voice as she read her Bible, and felt His gift of peace. And if she had any direction, it was a compelling sense that she was simply supposed to wait.

Wait. Oh, that had never been an easy thing for her. And yet, it had been in the waiting that she'd found the peace.

She felt mildly guilty because she hadn't called Luke. And when Ben called to ask her for a date, she'd put him off until "next month."

He hadn't seemed too happy about that, but she'd stood her ground. She had her marching orders. And this time, she wouldn't ignore them.

"—are coming in later this morning." Trent's voice cut through her thoughts. "They've gotten themselves in another pickle."

"I'm sorry. Could you say that again?"

"Which part?" Trent squinted and cocked his head at her. "Earth to Joanna . . ."

"I apologize. It's Monday. I was . . . um . . . back in the weekend."

"I was just saying that Cinda's parents are coming in for some . . . financial counseling. Bob's trying to figure out how to drink champagne on a beer budget, and Lillian is trying to figure out how to keep her champagne away from Bob." Her boss rolled his eyes, then studied her with genuine concern. "Is everything okay? You seem a little—"

"Sorry." She gave a nervous laugh. "Everything's fine. And I'm sorry about your in-laws. That can't be easy."

He shrugged. "I've been dealing with it for twenty years. I should be a pro at handling them by now."

She cleared her throat. "I had planned to do lunch with my sisters today. Is that a problem? Or will you need me?"

Trent straightened his tie and propped his hands on his hips. "What? You three don't get enough of each other living together? You've got to have lunch too? If your sisters are anything like Cinda's, you must be a glutton for punishment."

She gave a tentative smile, not sure if he was chiding her or teasing. "We like to get away from the property for planning sessions, but it doesn't have to be today. I can cancel—"

"No, no, not a problem." He tamped down the thin pile of magazines remaining after his purge. "In fact, if you want to take a little longer lunch, I'll probably close the office once they get here . . . in case Cinda's dad gets out of control."

Joanna grimaced. "Out of control? He's not . . . dangerous is he?" She'd never met Cinda's parents, but she'd heard stories about Trent's father-in-law's temper. And she couldn't help but think of the night they'd called her in because Maria Castillo had gone berserk.

"The man is only dangerous to himself. And to their portfolio. He's all blow and no go. But the blow part can get pretty loud."

"Okay . . . if you're sure . . ." She raised an eyebrow. "That sounds like something I wouldn't mind missing."

"Meanwhile, can you please clear my calendar for anything after eleven? I knew better than to schedule anything after their appointment, but given Bob's latest uproar, I think I'd better clear out the waiting room before they get here."

"Sure, I can do that." It was only a couple of appointments, but she dreaded making those calls. People were never happy about having their appointment delayed, and of course, she would be the one they took out their frustration or disappointment on. It seemed like Trent had been canceling more often recently. Ever since the incident with Mateo's mother,

Jo thought Trent seemed a little . . . disillusioned. Or maybe burned out was a better term. But it wasn't her place to say anything. Maybe this thing with Cinda's parents had been brewing for a while and that was what had him stewing.

By ten o'clock, Joanna had the cancellations confirmed and was caught up with her part of the billing and scheduling. She'd be able to go to lunch with her sisters guilt-free.

When she went down to the lobby at ten till noon, Phee and Britt were waiting in the parking lot in Phee's car. Grateful for the extra time Trent had allowed her, she climbed into the back seat only to be blasted with Kenny Chesney's twangy baritone.

"Could you please turn that down?" she shouted. "Phee! How'd you let her talk you into that? In *your* car."

Phee laughed. "We're taking turns. You just have bad timing. Every other song is my choice."

"Well, please put me in the rotation with a little jazz, would you?"

Still laughing, Phee reached for the radio knob and turned it off. "How about we compromise with some nice silence."

Joanna leaned back in the seat with an exaggerated sigh. She'd forgotten how crazy her little sister's country music had made her when they'd lived in the cottage together. Britt had been more thoughtful recently, wearing earbuds whenever Jo stayed with her because the main cottage was rented. But Jo was grateful they'd soon each have their own places to stay when the cottage was in use. Except for the times they rented the two smaller cabins out, and then the tables would be turned—Britt at Jo's mercy, staying in the cottage with her.

Phee pivoted in the driver's seat. "So, where are we going for lunch?"

Jo smirked. "Someplace where they don't play country music."

"Very funny." Without looking behind her, Britt reached back and swatted at Jo.

Phee braked hard at the entrance to the street. "Don't make me stop this car. Now I know why Mom couldn't take you two anywhere in the same car."

"Ha! You have a lot of room to talk, Phylicia Chandler." Britt swatted at her too.

Phee gave an indelicate snort. "Excuse me, that's Phylicia *Mitchell* to you."

"Whatever. You punished us with Beethoven every Sunday on the way to church."

"That was not punishment. That was *education*."

She and Britt both groaned, but even as they did, Jo's heart swelled with love for her sisters. She didn't know how she would have gotten through their ordeal with Mom, and then Dad moving to Florida, without these two. Phee and Britt truly had become her dearest friends, and she was so proud to be their sister. It was fun to go out in public with them, too, because— looking so much alike as they did—they turned heads whenever the three of them went anywhere together. And, according to Ben anyway, that was partly because they were "no slouches." She smiled at the remembrance.

Ben. She still didn't know how she felt about him. If her sisters asked about him today, and if she was honest with them, she'd have to say "indifferent." That wasn't exactly a great endorsement. But maybe it was merely an extension of the peace she'd felt about . . . well, everything . . . since she'd started praying and seeking to discover what *God* wanted for her life instead of relying on her own chaotic desires.

"How about that one coffee shop down toward the river? Do they serve lunch?" Phee flipped her blinker on and merged with traffic on Kingshighway.

"Baristas, you mean?" Jo pulled a lip gloss from her purse and slicked it on then pressed her lips together.

"Ooh, they have hummus!" Britt pointed at the left lane. "Turn here, Phee. Let's go there."

"Fine by me. They have a good salad. And sandwiches

and wraps." Jo zipped her purse and stretched to check her appearance in the rearview mirror.

There was a line at Baristas, but it moved quickly and soon the sisters were seated at a table by the window with salads and hummus to share. They giggled through lunch, but when they'd finished eating, Phylicia pulled out her planner, ready to get down to business. Britt did likewise.

"So, what's the report, Britt?" Phee smoothed a page of her planner and looked expectantly at their youngest sister.

"Nothing really new, but we're still in the black, if that's what you're wondering." Britt caught them up on some issues she'd had with their Airbnb account, and then went over the reservations calendar. "If we can keep the main cottage booked on weekends, that pays the utilities and then some."

Phee frowned. "I just wish we could book one other night during the week so we aren't constantly draining the reno fund."

"What are you thinking? That we need to advertise?" Britt sounded skeptical.

"I don't know. Maybe."

"But where?" Britt's frown matched Phylicia's. "It seems like our listing on Airbnb should be advertisement enough. That's the first place . . . really the *only* place people go looking to book an Airbnb rental."

Jo saw her opening. "What if we brought in income another way?"

"Like what?" Phee looked genuinely interested and Jo took the plunge.

"Like renting out the clearing as a wedding venue. I think we could make some serious money doing that. And I'd love to manage it."

"Oh, Jo . . ." Phee sighed. "I just think there'd be too many hoops to jump through. The insurance alone would probably eat up any profits."

"Trenton would know. Can I just look into it? We've already done one wedding up there, and it was amazing. And all we'd be doing is providing the venue. We wouldn't have to decorate or do the food or flowers unless we wanted to."

"Oh, I'm sure Mary would be happy to do flowers." Phee seemed to be considering her idea. "And that *was* an amazing wedding we put on up there. I can't argue with that."

Britt laughed. "She got you, Phee. Hook, line, and sinker."

"I'll admit it. But seriously, what could it hurt to have Jo check into what it would take? Especially if she's willing to manage the venue."

"Sure, but what do you want to bet that means *I'll* get stuck with even more of the cottage rental duties?"

"Or you could get a job and we could hire it out." Jo smiled, hoping to soften the barb, but it needed to be said. She swore sometimes Britt seemed determined to live up to the spoiled-baby-of-the-family trope.

Britt gave her the stink eye. "Yeah, yeah, fine. I get your point."

"You won't be so swamped once the cabins are finished, honey." Phee patted Britt's hand and spoke in her doting big-sister voice. "I know you've been putting a lot of hours in there painting and stuff, but we're so close to getting the last cabin done. Then things will be easier."

"Except for you," Jo reminded her. "How's the house coming along?"

Phee sighed. "Slow. Everything seems to take twice as long as they say it will. I'm either going to be a very patient woman when this is all over, or—" She laughed. "I don't know what other option I have."

"Well, I'm just glad you guys are going to be living out by us." Britt looked vulnerable and Jo felt sorry about her comment. She knew it was a sore spot for Britt. And they'd already agreed it'd be best if Britt didn't have an outside job.

"Me too." Phee looked from Britt to Jo, pen hovering over her calendar. "Now, shall we get back to our schedule? Jo, do you mind doing breakfasts again next weekend?"

"I don't mind. How many will it be again? It's only the cottage, right? They don't need the—"

Her phone buzzed on the table beside her, and Jo looked down to see Ben's name. "Sorry."

She turned her phone over so her sisters wouldn't see who was calling.

But Phee gave a little wave. "Go ahead, if you need to take that. We're almost done anyway."

She wanted to protest. She wasn't really in the mood to talk to Ben, but her sisters would wonder what was up if she didn't take the call.

Jo tapped Talk and scooted her chair back. "Hello?"

"Hey, Jo. It's Ben."

"Oh . . . Hi." She rose and walked to the entryway of the restaurant, out of her sisters' hearing.

CHAPTER 31

"HOW ARE YOU, JO?" BEN'S deep voice was full of confidence.

"I'm good."

"I hope I'm not interrupting. I was hoping to catch you on your lunch hour."

"You did. But I'm having lunch out with my sisters. Downtown."

"Oh . . . Sorry to interrupt. Well, I'll make this quick. I wondered if you'd like to have dinner this weekend? Saturday night?"

"Ben, I—" She started to turn him down. God had given her peace, but she also knew that things would never be right with her and Ben. But if she told him no now, he'd only call again. And she needed to talk to him face to face. She may as well say yes and get a difficult conversation out of the way. But she'd have to make her intentions clear from the start. Maybe they could be friends now. But that was all.

"Jo? You there?"

"Sorry. I'm here. Just . . . checking my calendar." She did that quickly, so it wouldn't be a lie. But she knew her schedule was free. "Saturday should be fine. Let me meet you somewhere, okay?"

"I don't mind picking you up."

"I know. And I appreciate that. But . . . I'd rather meet you."

"Suit yourself. How about Bella Italia? I know you like that."

She did. But she'd last been there with Luke. She sort of wanted to keep those memories separate. "Would you mind if we went to Port Cape Girardeau?"

"Fine by me." She'd forgotten that peeved tone from their dating days.

"You're sure?"

"Whatever you want, Jo. I'm not picky. You know that."

"Okay. I'll see you there. Six thirty okay? I need to get home at a decent hour. I have to make breakfast the next morning."

A too-long pause. "So now you have to *schedule* time to make breakfast? That sounds like the famous 'Sorry, I have to shampoo my hair that night' excuse."

She laughed. "Breakfast for guests, silly. We have people staying at the Airbnb most weekends now. It's my turn to cook."

"Oh. I forgot about that." His laughter sounded like relief. "How's that going, by the way?"

"Really well. That's why my sisters and I were having lunch. A board meeting of sorts," she explained, hoping he'd take the hint.

"Ahh. Well, tell them hello. I'll see you Saturday. You're sure you don't want me to pick you up?"

"Thanks, but I'm sure. See you at six thirty."

"So six fifty, then?" She could almost see his smirk.

"No . . ." His comment stung a little, but she had it coming. She'd been perpetually late when they'd dated before. "I've reformed my ways. You'll see."

"Okay then. Well . . . Bye."

She hung up feeling bad that she hadn't exactly been kind to Ben. Not that she'd been rude, but certainly not her usual friendly way with him. But maybe her coolness was a good way to preface telling Ben how things needed to be between them. He wouldn't like it, but given how she'd responded to his affection last time, she didn't trust her own feelings. Besides, Ben's moods or attitudes weren't her responsibility, nor were his—

"Hi, Jo."

She looked up from her phone into Luke Blaine's gray eyes. "Luke! Hi."

She felt—unreasonably—like a kid caught with her hand in the cookie jar.

"How are you?" He motioned toward the Marquette Tower building where Baristas was housed on the ground floor. "I'm waiting on Mateo. You here for lunch?"

She nodded. "With my sisters." She pointed through the window where she could see Phee and Britt behind the reflection of North Fountain Street. "We're just finishing up. Were you here for lunch? I . . . didn't see you."

"We ate over in the lobby." He nodded toward the north end of the building where the little restaurant had overflow seating in the elegant lobby. "They have this place looking really nice. I hadn't been here since they were in this building."

"It's great." She caught movement behind the plate-glass windows. Phee and Britt were clearing their table and gathering their things. "Oh . . . here come my sisters now."

"I'm sorry. I hope you were finished eating."

"Oh, long ago. This was actually a lunch meeting." She smiled. "Any excuse to eat out."

It hadn't been even three weeks since she'd seen him last, but she'd already forgotten how his smile lit those gold-flecked eyes of his.

Mateo jogged out from the lobby entrance and Luke bent to whisper in his ear, but loud enough for Jo to hear. "Did you wash your hands?"

The boy opened his mouth to answer, but then his shoulders sagged in resignation. Without another word, he turned to trudge back into the building.

Luke rolled his eyes, looking embarrassed.

But Jo laughed. "At least he told the truth."

"Good point. Score one for the Big."

She started to reply, but just then, Phee and Britt came out of the restaurant entrance onto the sidewalk. She looked over Luke's shoulder at them.

Phee waved a hand at her. "There you are. Everything okay?"

Luke turned to face Phee and Britt and gave a polite nod.

"Well, hi there." Phee greeted him warmly. "Sorry, I didn't mean to interrupt."

"It's okay. We just . . . ran into each other." Jo motioned to Luke. "You remember Luke?"

"Of course! It's good to see you again." Phee put out a hand.

Luke shook it, then Britt's hand in turn. "You too."

"Where's your sidekick?" Phee smiled.

"Oh, he's here with me." He hooked a thumb over his shoulder. "He went inside to wash his hands."

"I hope he's getting along all right." Phee's voice held such compassion. Compassion Jo knew was genuine. "I've thought about him so often. And prayed for him. And you too."

"Thank you." Luke bowed his head briefly, obviously moved. "We're hanging in there."

Joanna's limbs grew heavy with guilt. Had she even once asked Luke how Mateo was doing? Had she prayed for Luke as he tried to take care of a grieving child? Or for the boy as he tried to figure out a world without a mom? A genuine prayer? Not just her selfish wishes that Mateo would somehow be gone from Luke's life.

And yet, even her sister had apparently been praying for them, and was thoughtful enough to tell Luke that.

Jo sighed. She had such a long way to go. She felt even guiltier about her comment—and her unkind thoughts—about Britt just moments ago. *She* was the one who had a lot of growing up to do.

"Well, nice to see you again, Luke." Phee touched Jo's arm and lowered her voice. "We'll meet you in the car. No hurry."

"Yes, you too." Luke gave a little wave.

While Phee and Britt strolled up the street to where they'd parked the car, Luke turned to Jo. "I didn't mean to keep you. You probably need to get back to work."

They stood on the sidewalk in front of Baristas, the awkward silence growing between them exacerbated by the fact that she knew her sisters were waiting for her in the car, no doubt watching her every move.

She was almost relieved when Mateo appeared again, his water-splashed shirt evidence that he'd accomplished the task Luke sent him away for. She tried to think how Phee would have interacted with him. "Hey, Mateo. How's it going?"

He seemed surprised that she'd spoken to him. "Good." He twisted the bead necklace he was never without. The one that matched Luke's. "Did you see us at Andy's that one night? We saw you! But Luke wouldn't let me holler at you."

"I did see you." She smiled woodenly, then looked up at Luke briefly before turning back to Mateo. "I wasn't sure it was you until you guys were almost out of the parking lot."

Luke ruffled Mateo's hair. "Why don't you go unlock the car for me, buddy." He fished in his pocket, then handed the keys to Mateo. "Roll the windows down. I'll be there in just a sec."

Luke watched Mateo stroll to the car, waiting in silence until he heard the abbreviated toots of the horn that indicated Mateo had gotten the car unlocked.

He looked at the sidewalk briefly before meeting her eyes. "I wasn't . . . stalking you. At Andy's. I hope you know that."

"Of course not. I never thought that." She felt bad that he'd worried for a minute that she might think such a thing.

"Listen, if you're . . . seeing someone now, I understand. I didn't mean to put any . . . strings on this." He motioned between them. "You don't owe me any—"

"No, I should have called. I really should have. It's just that . . . I don't really have an answer for you yet, Luke." She felt like a jerk not confessing that she'd just accepted another date with Ben. But if she told Luke that, he'd surely take it as a sign that she was blowing him off.

And she wasn't. Not at all.

"There's no rush on my account."

"I really didn't mean to leave you hanging. I've been praying. A lot. And I . . . haven't forgotten you." She took in a short breath. That hadn't come out quite right. She'd only meant to acknowledge that she remembered her promise to let him know her decision. But she realized too late that the words could mean something quite different to him than she'd intended.

Maybe it was a Freudian slip though, because the truth was, she *hadn't* forgotten him. She thought of him almost constantly. Him and Mateo.

And that was the problem. Luke still came with strings attached. Long strings.

She looked past him to where her sisters waited in the car. "I'd better go. I have to get back to work. But I . . . I would like to talk to you again."

He cocked his head as if trying to figure out what that was supposed to mean. "I'd like that too. You let me know when you're ready. I won't bother you until then."

"You've never *bothered* me, Luke. This isn't about you."

"It's about Mateo?" He looked back to where his car was parked.

Jo could see the boy bouncing around inside the front seat. "No, that's not what I meant. I just mean . . . I'm trying to get my head on straight. Get things right with God before I can figure anything else out."

266

"Well, I can't argue with that."

She smiled. "I'll call you. I will."

"Like I said, no rush. You do what you need to do." He took a couple of steps backward and lifted a hand. "It was good to see you."

"You too. Bye, Luke."

He gave a brief nod, turned on his heel, and walked to the car without looking back.

It was all Jo could do not to run after him. But when he opened the door, Mateo's voice floated on the air like a warning.

Luke and Mateo were a package deal. And there was simply no changing that.

CHAPTER 32

Jo NOTCHED UP THE CRUISE control, determined to arrive on time and prove to Ben that she'd turned over a new leaf. But she'd gotten a late start tonight, thanks to a little midsummer garden project she was working on behind the cottage. Inspired by Luke's backyard, Jo took advantage of the end of summer garden center sales and bought some perennials to plant. She also hadn't been able to resist purchasing a few of the colorful potted arrangements that, sadly, weren't on sale. But they added instant drama to the landscaping. She'd worked outside until dark every evening this week, and tonight that little garden had delayed her leaving the house.

Despite driving a few miles over the speed limit, it was 6:35 when she parked across the side street from Port Cape Girardeau. Late was late, and Ben was the kind of man who considered three minutes late to be as egregious as ten or twenty.

She locked her car, and breathing in the rich aroma of hickory smoked barbecue, she started toward the restaurant's side entrance beneath the historic Coca-Cola mural high up on the brick building. There was a line outside the restaurant, and across the frontage road to the east several couples and young families strolled along the riverwalk, looking at the colorful murals painted all along the concrete floodwalls that held back the waters of the Mississippi.

A few years ago, she'd seen the water at flood stage, but the walls had done their job defending the city against the raging river and disaster was averted. And those walls made for a picturesque view for those waiting to get into the restaurant.

She didn't see Ben in the queue of customers, but spotted a red SUV parked up the street. She didn't know makes and models and couldn't remember for sure what he drove, except that it was red.

It still threw her that after more than two weeks without seeing either Ben or Luke, she'd spoken to both of them within a three-minute span. What were the chances? If she didn't know better, she'd think God was testing her. Though she couldn't for the life of her figure out the right answer to the test. Still, she was determined to take it one day, one step at a time. She'd clung fast to the psalm that reminded her that the Bible was a lamp to her feet and a light to her path. She would pick each step carefully and not run ahead of God as she too often had in the past.

She'd just stepped up onto the curb in front of the side entrance when a horn tooted behind her. She turned to see the red SUV rolling up to the curb beside her. The passenger window rolled down and she bent to see Ben smiling from behind the wheel.

"Hey there. Hop in." He reached across and pushed the passenger door open.

She climbed in beside him. "What's up?"

He angled his head toward the restaurant. "I tried to get us in. It's a forty-five minute wait. Do you have your heart set on barbecue?"

She inhaled. "It does smell good. I don't mind waiting."

"How about if we drive to Dexter's? I like their barbecue better anyway."

"In Jackson, you mean?" He *would* pick the one other restaurant where she and Luke had eaten. And made memories.

"No. Let's do the original . . . the real deal in Dexter." His raised eyebrows made it sound like a great adventure. "Have you ever been?"

"Who hasn't? Mom and Dad always swore the original restaurant was the best." The little town of Dexter, Missouri, home of famous pit-smoked barbecue boasted half a dozen restaurants around the state, including the one in Jackson where she'd eaten with Luke and Mateo that night. She wondered if Ben somehow knew that.

"You game?" Ben tapped the steering wheel and eyed his rearview mirror.

Jo turned in her seat to see a car waiting for them to move. "Sure. But Dexter is almost an hour away, isn't it?"

He inched the car to the stop sign, then made a U-turn. "I can get us there in forty-five. But this way we don't have to wait standing out in the hot sun." As if to prove his point, he cranked up the air conditioner in the car and sped down South Spanish Street winding his way out of Cape via back streets.

He had a point, but it struck her that, intentional or not, Ben had found a way to circumvent her I'll-meet-you-there ploy. At least he'd only be bringing her back to Cape when they were finished. There wouldn't be that awkward time parked in the lane saying good night like the last time they'd gone out.

Within minutes, they were on I-55 heading toward Sikeston. Jo leaned to look at the speedometer. Ben was driving his usual eighty miles an hour, but she kept quiet since traffic was light on the interstate. No sense getting in an argument before they even had dinner.

Ben set the cruise control and leaned back in the driver's seat, resting his right arm on the console. Before, when they'd been dating, she would have taken his hand. But she kept her hands clasped in her lap.

"So, what have you been up to lately?" He threw her a smile before turning his eyes back to the highway.

"Oh, not a lot. Work, of course. And then I've been helping Britt finish up painting and some other projects on the cabin."

"Is business pretty good? I've been hearing a lot about these Airbnb rentals. Seems like it's really taking off."

"We're mostly booking on weekends right now, but once we get the cabins done, we'll probably get more bookings because those will rent for a lot less."

"Do you mind me asking what they go for a night?"

She was a little taken aback by the question, but given that he could easily look it up online, she didn't mind telling him. "The cabins will each go for seventy-five dollars a night. We get quite a bit more for the main cottage—where I live—thanks to Britt."

He shot her a questioning look.

Jo laughed. "When we first opened, Britt accidentally set a price about twice what we'd planned to charge, and we booked it at that! We've actually lowered it a little since then. We aren't looking to gouge anyone."

Ben shook his head. "Hey, I say get what you can. If the market supports it, it's apparently not too high."

"I suppose . . ."

He studied her. "It seems like you really enjoy playing hostess."

"There are parts of it I really enjoy. There's actually not much hostessing to it. A lot of times we don't even meet the people staying with us. We tell them where the key is and they let themselves in. But getting the cottages fixed up has been fun. And you know I like baking."

"Oh, that's right. That's why we have to get you home early tonight." He chuckled. "So, what's going to be for breakfast?"

"Probably scones. That seems to be a favorite. I think it's something people rarely make themselves so it feels like a treat."

"Mmm . . . I remember your scones." He gave her knee a pat. "Maybe you can save me one next time."

She smiled, but tensed at his assumption that there would be a next time. But it wasn't fair to judge him harshly for that. They had a past together, and the fact that she'd been willing to go out with him again made it only natural he would assume she'd thought it through and had at least strongly considered resuming their relationship.

She scrambled to think of something to change the subject. "So . . . are you still going to church at LaCroix?"

He reached and turned the air conditioner up. "It's been a while since I was there, but . . . yeah, I still consider it my home church. What about you?"

"We've been taking turns between our church and Quinn's in Cape." She shrugged. "It's kind of hard to go to Langhorne . . . since Mom died. But I don't want to horn in on Quinn and Phee either."

He laughed. "I doubt they consider it horning in. It is a public place after all."

"True." She didn't feel like trying to explain to him what she meant—that she and Britt had talked about needing to give Quinn and Phee space to live their own life without too much sisterly interference. Especially now that the newlyweds were moving out to the property.

Ben's wishy-washy answer about church concerned her. When they were dating in college, they'd been part of a campus ministry that Ben's home church ran, but since they'd gotten back in touch, he hadn't mentioned anything about church—or God. Her own renewed focus on prayer had made her realize how important it was to her that the man she someday married had a strong faith and a heart for God.

Of course, it wasn't fair to judge Ben when they hadn't really talked about that subject. And even if he was going to church, mere attendance didn't guarantee a man was living his life for God. "You'd be welcome to come to church with us tomorrow. We go to the late service so we can do breakfast for our guests, but we're still usually out by noon."

"Thanks for the invite." Ben gripped the steering wheel tighter and tapped the cruise control up a notch. "I'll . . . think about it. But since I work pretty long hours during the week, weekends are about the only time I can golf."

"Oh." She bit her tongue. And then couldn't any longer. "I really hate to hear that, Ben."

"What?"

"That you're not going to church anymore . . . so you can play golf. That . . . it doesn't sound like the guy I knew."

"Sorry . . . Mom." He tapped the cruise up again.

She winced. "Okay, I had that coming. Sorry. It's just . . . that's really important to me. It always has been. I think you know that."

"It's important to me too. But honestly"—he held up a hand—"and I know this sounds like an excuse, but I feel a lot closer to God out on the golf course surrounded by nature than I ever have in a stuffy church."

"I don't remember LaCroix being stuffy."

"I'm not talking about the church. Just being cooped up indoors half the day."

"Half the day, huh? Their services must be longer than they were back when we were in college."

"Haha. You really *do* sound like my mom." Ben slowed to take the off-ramp onto Highway 60, but the minute they were on the straightaway, he accelerated again.

"Thank you. I always liked your mom." She gripped the door's armrest and gritted her teeth. "Could you please slow down a little?"

He gave her a sidewise glance but tapped the brakes and slowed infinitesimally.

"Ben, the speed limit is sixty-five here." It was an effort to keep her voice even.

"Thank you. I saw the sign."

She pressed her lips together, but didn't say anything. The town of Dexter appeared ahead and she relaxed a little.

But Ben took the exit in silence, and barely slowed down when they entered the city limits.

A traffic light ahead turned yellow, and Jo sucked in a breath, gripping the armrests. From the corner of her vision, she saw a red pickup coming fast—too fast—from the cross street to her right. "Ben!"

He cursed under his breath and hit the gas. "Hang on. We can make it."

CHAPTER 33

"HEY, BUDDY! DID YOU GET that extension cord that was on top of the speakers?" Luke checked the back of his truck, taking a mental inventory to be sure they'd collected everything. He didn't want to have to drive back to Sikeston after some piece of equipment left behind.

"Yeah, I got it. It's in this tub." Mateo nodded, his hair flopping up and down as he jogged toward the truck with the plastic storage tub in his arms.

Sometimes Luke worried that he was taking advantage of Mateo, having him work these weddings with him. The kid was a hard worker, and he always chose coming with Luke over staying at Don and Valerie's. He was glad. Not only that Mateo seemed to like spending time with him, but Luke did not want to wear out his welcome with his friends, who had gone above and beyond in letting Mateo stay with them anytime Luke needed help.

Val had told him she got a kick out of Mateo and saw helping Luke out as a ministry. Luke wasn't sure he liked being seen as a charity case, but he couldn't afford to argue. School would be starting in less than two weeks, and Valerie had offered to provide after-school care again, but Luke talked it over with Mateo and they decided he could stay home alone for a couple of hours until Luke got home from work each evening.

Unfortunately, the occasional late nights weren't the only problem with these DJ gigs. Today he ran up against another issue. One that turned his stomach. This had not been a Christian wedding, and despite it being an afternoon wedding, with the whole thing over by eight, some of the guests were drunk before dinner was even served. Things had gone downhill from there, and got flat-out raunchy as the reception wore on. He'd no doubt have to make some disclaimers and define some embarrassing words for Mateo on the drive home.

They finished loading the truck, and five minutes later, with Mateo buckled in beside him, Luke turned toward home, tired and a little down. Not only about the depressing things he'd witnessed at this wedding, but about the fact that he hadn't heard one word from Joanna.

After running into her at Baristas Monday, he felt hopeful he might get a call from her soon. But five days of silence ensued, and now the weekend was almost over. Maybe he was getting a clearer picture of her faults. Why couldn't he get over someone who clearly didn't want anything to do with Mateo, despite knowing how much he loved the kid? And now it was starting to look like she was the kind of woman who didn't keep her word, didn't call when she said she would . . .

Stopped at an intersection, he flicked his blinker and started to turn onto Highway 60 toward Cape, but before he could make the turn, he spotted the strobe of blue and red lights coming over the hill. He braked and backed up a few feet.

Mateo saw the lights too. He leaned forward in the passenger seat. "Uh-oh! Somebody's gonna get busted."

The police raced by going ninety, Luke estimated. But right behind them, an ambulance and two fire trucks from nearby Sikeston roared by with sirens blaring and lights flashing.

"Wow! Somebody's really in trouble!" Mateo looked positively gleeful.

"No, buddy, there must have been an accident. When you see an ambulance and fire trucks, it's usually more than just somebody speeding."

"Oh." The boy sobered.

The sheer number of vehicles sent a chill up Luke's spine. And as he'd gotten in the habit of doing, he tossed up a prayer for whoever was in trouble and for the emergency teams that would be working the scene of the casualty tonight.

When the parade of emergency vehicles had disappeared in the distance, Luke took a deep breath and tried to gather his thoughts. He'd just as soon ignore everything that had happened at the reception, but he knew little had escaped Mateo's attention. Might as well get this uncomfortable conversation over with. "Listen, Mateo. About the wedding tonight . . . the reception, I mean." He prayed for wisdom. "Some of those guys got a little out of hand, didn't you think?"

Mateo's face reddened. "Now I see why you don't let me drink champagne," he mumbled.

Luke laughed. "Yeah . . . that's one reason. Sadly, I'm afraid some of those guys talk like that, act like that even when they're not drunk."

"Why did they do that? They were gross."

"So you . . . got what they were saying."

The blush on his boyish cheeks deepened. "Some of it."

"I wish you hadn't had to listen to that. But the truth is, you're heading into seventh grade. You're probably going to hear that same kind of talk in school sometimes."

"Not *that* bad."

"Well, I hope not. But if you do, you do the same as you did tonight. Pretend you don't hear it, and walk away if you can. You handled it really well, bud. I'm sorry you had to hear that kind of talk. There's really no excuse for that. But I'm proud of how you dealt with it."

"I kind of wanted to smack that one guy."

Luke nodded. "Yep, I know exactly which guy you mean. I kind of wanted to smack him myself."

"I think the two of us could have taken him, don't you?"

Luke threw back his head and laughed. This kid surprised him at every turn. And he meant what he'd said. Not that he could take any credit, but he was so proud of Mateo he could have busted his buttons. He leaned over the console and lowered his voice. "Between you and me, I think we could have taken him, but that's probably not—"

"I know, I know . . . What Jesus would do?"

"Give me five."

Grinning from ear to ear, Mateo put up a hand and gave him five so hard it hurt.

They rode in silence for fifteen minutes before Mateo broke the silence. "Hey, Luke?"

"Yeah, buddy?"

"Can I get a haircut like that one kid tonight had?"

"Which kid was that?"

"You know . . . business in the front, party in the back."

Chuckling, Luke shook his head. "No, sir. You may not."

"Okay. That's what I thought you'd say."

"And in case you were wondering, you can't get a tattoo like that guy in the band had either."

"Awww, man!"

They laughed together, and Luke couldn't remember when his heart had been so full.

Joanna tried to open her eyes again, but her eyelids felt as if they were made of concrete and she finally gave up, exhausted. A strange whooshing noise went on and on somewhere above her head until she wanted to strike out at it. But she couldn't seem to lift her arms either.

She'd never been claustrophobic, but she felt on the verge of panic now. Where on earth was she? And why couldn't she remember how she got here?

Phee! Britt! She tried to call for her sisters, but no sound came out. Only that infernal *whoosh whoosh whoosh*.

"Joanna? *Joanna?*"

Why were they yelling at her? *I'm here! I'm right here! Stop . . . yelling!* But again, she couldn't get any sound to come out.

It seemed like an eternity passed. And they were still saying her name. They sounded so far away. Was it Phee? Or Britt? She couldn't tell. But it was a woman. And quieter now. With a question in her voice.

Why couldn't she open her eyes?

"She's starting to come to." A man's voice this time. *Dad?*

Come to where? Where was she going? *God help me! Why can't I see?*

"Just keep talking to her. You see how her eyelids are twitching? She's trying to respond."

"Jo?"

She jumped. Or thought she had. That was Phee's voice. Right in her ear.

"Jo? Can you hear me?"

I hear you, Phee! I'm right here! Phee? Dad? Are you there?

"Keep talking to her as if she can hear you, because she probably can. I'll be back in the morning to . . ."

No! Don't leave. Stay here! Please! Stay with me!

"Thank you, Doctor."

Phee again. Wait . . . Doctor? Where was she?

"Jo? Wake up, Jo. Please wake up . . ."

The voice faded into the maddening *whoosh whoosh whoosh*.

"I . . . I'm so sorry, Quinn." Luke held his phone tight to his ear and stared out the windshield. His pulse raced and he slumped against the armrest for support. He was thankful he hadn't picked up Mateo from Don and Val's yet. "When did it happen? Where?"

"Last night. No, Saturday . . . Sorry, time is all running together. It was Saturday. Around eight." Quinn Mitchell sounded absolutely done-in.

"And she still hasn't come to?" That was almost forty-eight hours!

"No. The doctors seem to think she's responding to some stimuli, but she hasn't opened her eyes since they brought her in."

"I'm . . ." He took a breath, trying to regain his composure. "Sorry . . . This is really knocking me for a loop. I just saw her downtown a few days ago. A week ago today, in fact."

"Yes, Phee told me they'd run into you at Baristas."

"Joanna is always so . . . full of life. It's hard to even imagine that precious woman unconscious in a hospital bed." He knew he was tipping his hand, but right now, he didn't care.

"I know." Quinn cleared his throat. "We're all having trouble wrapping our heads around this."

"Was anyone else hurt in the accident?"

"Ben Harven was driving. I don't know if you know him, but he and Jo used to date. Before her mom passed away. Ben was treated for minor injuries and released. We haven't talked to him yet, but he and Jo were supposed to meet in Cape for supper, so we're not sure why they were out there. There are a lot of unanswered questions."

"Quinn, where did it happen?" A vivid image came to his mind: the emergency crews that had gone by Saturday night as he and Mateo were leaving the wedding after his DJ gig.

"Oh, I guess I didn't say. The accident happened out on Highway 60 up by Dexter."

That parade of lights and sirens had to have been for her! And for two days, he'd lived not knowing—as if everything was normal. "I saw all the emergency vehicles go by that night. I . . . had no idea it was for Joanna."

282

"You saw them?" Quinn's tone was incredulous.

"Mateo and I were coming back from doing a wedding south of town. You said it happened about eight o'clock or so?"

"It did. Unbelievable."

"Yes." The word came out in a whisper.

If only he'd known! He would have followed the ambulance. Gone to her. Not that he could have done anything the doctors hadn't already done. But at least he would have been with her.

But . . . she'd been with Ben. That knowledge sat like a rock in his gut.

"I hope we're not being presumptuous to call you, Luke, but Phee thought you'd want to know."

"Yes. Yes, of course. I'm so glad you did. Is there anything I can do?"

"Pray. For her sisters, especially. Phee is worried sick, and she and Britt are still trying to keep the Airbnb afloat in the midst of all this."

"I will. Do they know the extent of her injuries?" He willed Quinn to answer his real question: Will she make it? Will she *live*? But he couldn't bring himself to speak those words.

"Ben's car was T-boned on the passenger side. Frankly, it's a miracle she's alive. She has a concussion. I guess that's what's keeping her from waking up. I'm not really sure."

"So, she hasn't spoken or . . . opened her eyes?"

"No. Not yet. She's pretty bruised up. And her right ankle is broken. Did I say that already? Sorry . . . I've told so many people I've forgotten who I've told what."

"That's okay. And no, you hadn't said that." He tried to breathe and felt like he was ten feet under water.

"They don't seem too concerned about the ankle, but the concussion is apparently pretty serious."

"I'm so sorry. I . . . I'll be praying. For all of you."

"Just pray she wakes up. And soon."

Luke didn't like the level of concern in Quinn Mitchell's voice.

"Of course. I will. And . . . I don't mean to put a burden on you, Quinn, but could you let me know if there's any change?"

"Of course. We'll keep you posted."

Luke hung up and bowed over the steering wheel, scarcely able to catch a breath. "Lord," he whispered. "Be with her. Let her wake up, Father. Please!"

When the words seemed too hard to breathe out, he prayed silently for Jo's sisters and her father. And for Quinn. Such a good family. He couldn't even imagine what it would be like for them if they had to go through another tragedy.

Gathering his wits, he turned the key in the ignition, put the truck in gear, and went to pick up Mateo. Spending time with that kid would be the only way he'd make it through this night. But Mateo would know something was wrong. He was disconcertingly sensitive to Luke's moods. He would have to tell the boy what had happened. And he wasn't sure he could do it without breaking down.

CHAPTER 34

August

TOO BRIGHT. EVERYTHING WAS SO bright it hurt. The darkness had been bad, but this was almost worse. She tried to cover her eyes with her hands, but she couldn't seem to move even her fingers.

"Jo? Joanna! Good morning. Nurse! She's awake. She's opening her eyes!"

It was Phee's voice but Jo could only see a silhouette surrounded by that intense light.

"Jo? You're back. Oh, thank You, God! I'll be right back. I need to get the nurse. And Britt."

"Wait . . . Where is it?"

The silhouette leaned in closer and Phee's features started to come into focus. "Where is *what*, honey?"

"No . . . Where? Am I?"

"Where are *you*?"

Jo tried to nod, then winced at the pain. Why couldn't she make them understand her?

"It's okay. Don't try to move. You're in the hospital. In

Cape—" Her sister's voice broke. "You were in an accident, Jo. But it's going to be okay. Everything is going to be okay."

If everything was going to be okay, why was Phee crying?

She felt a hand on her forehead. That was good, wasn't it? She felt it. She scrunched up her face, opened and closed her eyelids. They were working now. At least she thought they were.

"Jo, I'll be right back. I'm going to get the nurses."

"The button . . ." Why didn't she just push the button? Didn't they still have call buttons in hospitals? "Push the button."

"Oh duh." Phee giggled.

Her sister's voice was music in Jo's ears.

"But I don't see the call button."

The silhouette came closer and she felt jostled in the bed.

"Look! The call button was under your pillow! That couldn't have been very comfortable." More giggling. "Oh. The nurses are here." Phee became a silhouette again, her voice fading into the distance. She was talking to someone else, and then more voices filled the room, surrounding her.

You were in an accident . . . Phee had said that.

Accident. A flash of memory . . . The red truck. She remembered. Ben . . . Oh, Ben. "Is Ben . . . is he . . . ?"

Phee came close again and this time her face was in focus, her expression dark. But her words didn't match her face. "He's fine, Jo. He wasn't hurt badly . . . just a few scratches and bruises."

She tried to reach for Phee's arm. "Is he here?"

"No. He's . . . not here." Phee looked away and when she turned back, her smile was back too. "The nurses are going to check you now, Jo. I'm going to find Britt and Dad. They're going to be so happy you're awake!"

"Dad's here?"

"Of course. He got here as soon as he could."

"Wow . . . that was fast." She felt like she was slurring her words. "Are they . . . at church now?"

"At church?" Phee's brow furrowed and then a look of realization came. "Oh, no. Honey, you've been asleep for a long time. Almost three days. It's Tuesday. Tuesday afternoon."

"Tuesday?" But . . . it was only Saturday when she and Ben . . . *Dexter's*. They'd been on their way to eat barbecue. "What day is it?"

"It's Tuesday, Jo."

"Oh. You already said that."

Phee gave a nervous laugh. "Yes. That's okay."

"Is it . . . July?"

"It's August." Phee patted her arm. "But just barely. Today is August 1."

"School will be starting soon."

Phee's brow knit as if she didn't understand what Jo had said.

Then a new face appeared beside her sister's. "Joanna? My name is Bernice. I'm the ICU nurse. Can you tell me your full name?"

Jo looked to Phee. If she'd been here more than two days, they surely knew her name by now. Dad would have told them. "Joanna Leigh Chandler?"

Phee laughed. "It's not a trick question, sis. They're just trying to make sure you're thinking straight."

Bernice looked from Phee to Jo. "Do you know what day it is?"

"Phee said it was August . . . Tuesday, I mean."

"Do you know who the president is?"

What kind of question was that? But she answered anyway.

The nurse smiled knowingly at Phee, then patted Jo's knee. "Good answers. I'm going to take your vitals, and then your doctor will be in shortly. Are you feeling hungry?"

She had to think about that question. She and Ben never made it to Dexter Bar-B-Que. That meant she hadn't eaten for almost three days. "Yes! Can I please get some barbecue?"

Phee and the nurse dissolved in laughter, but Bernice

shook her head. "I'm afraid you'll have to settle for some nice broth and Jell-O for now."

The door to her hospital room opened slowly, and Jo scooted up in the bed to peek around the partially closed curtain.

Britt appeared on the other side carrying balloons and a vase of flowers and wearing a wide smile.

Phee swept in behind her and pushed the curtain all the way open. "How are you feeling this morning?"

"Sore. But so much better. At least I can move. They took out that stupid cath this morning and I walked to the bathroom without the walker."

"Progress!" Britt handed her a stack of envelopes in pastel colors. "Your mail, madame."

"Those are all for me? Wow, I should get crushed in a car wreck more often."

"Jo! Don't even talk like that!" Phee stopped fluffing the pillows behind Jo's head long enough to swat her leg.

"Ow!"

Phee gasped and covered her mouth with her hands. "I'm so sorry. Are you okay? I wasn't even thinking."

Jo laughed. "Just kidding. Wrong leg."

"You nut!" Phee swatted her again and straightened the bedsheets around her legs. "You must be feeling better."

"I'll feel better when they let me eat some real food."

"What? They haven't let you eat yet?"

"I got oatmeal for breakfast. Apparently if that goes through okay, I can move up to green bean casserole."

"We'll get you some food, Jo." Britt threw her a conspiratorial wink. "Don't you worry."

"I want barbecue. Has Ben been here?" Jo was a little afraid to ask. Her memories were fuzzy from the early hours after she'd come to, but as the meds wore off, she'd started to remember more.

"Not yet." Phee pulled up a chair by Jo's bedside. "But I think there's a card in that stack from him."

"There is. I put it on top." Britt moved the tray table over Jo's lap and placed the stack of cards in front of her. "There's one from Ginger in there too. And the flowers are from your DJ friend."

"Luke? How nice." She wondered how he'd found out about her accident.

"I got to make the bouquet." Phee fiddled with the ribbon on the vase from Luke. "In fact, you've single-handedly kept the flower shop in business these last few days."

"Oh, quit." But the lineup of vases on the windowsill did lend credence to Phee's claim. Jo felt very much loved by all the shows of affection and the prayers she knew were going up on her behalf.

"Did Dad get back okay?" He'd flown in on Sunday night, although Joanna didn't really remember much about her first days. It had about done her in when Dad started crying telling her goodbye last night.

"He's home safe and sound." Britt tidied the water carafe and cup on Jo's bed tray. "He called me from work this morning. Said he'd call you later this evening."

"It was good to see him."

"It was," Phee said, "but I don't recommend your method of getting him to come home."

She threw her sister a wry smile and picked up Ben's card from the stack. She slid a finger under the flap and drew out a fancy get-well card with butterflies and glitter. She skipped over the printed verse to read the brief note in Ben's scrawl.

> *You said it was never wrong to send a card or to say you're sorry. I'm doing both.*
> *Love, Ben.*

She laid the card on the table and blew away a few flecks of glitter that had fallen on the tabletop.

Britt gave her a curious look. "Everything okay?"

Jo pushed the card toward Britt. "You can read it."

Britt read it and handed it to Phee.

Phee read it, then gave a little huff. "What's that all about?"

Jo sighed, a deep sadness welling inside her. "That's just Ben being Ben."

She told her sisters about her conversation with Ben and his quasi-apology for abandoning her when Mom had become so ill.

Phee placed a hand on Jo's knee. "I don't want to upset you, Jo, but do you remember your accident?"

"A little. I remember the light was yellow and . . . there was a truck coming at us. A pickup."

"The police said Ben was going at least eighty miles an hour when he went through that intersection." Anger hardened Britt's voice.

"And witnesses said the light was actually red when he went through."

Jo dropped her head, remembering all too well. "Is Ben . . . in trouble?"

"He's probably looking at some hefty traffic fines. But unless you want to press charges . . ."

"No. Of course not. Is that why he hasn't come? Because he's afraid I'll sue him?"

"I don't know, Jo." Phee frowned. "I called Sunday afternoon to let him know you were still here. But he didn't answer his phone. I had to leave a voice message."

"You're sure he's okay? He wasn't hurt badly?"

"No." Britt shook her head. "The cops who told us about you said he was treated and released that night."

"Do you want me to try to call him again?" Phee didn't sound too crazy about the idea.

"No." Jo felt tears close to the surface. But not for the

reasons her sisters might have thought. "So he doesn't know I . . . woke up?"

Phee shook her head. "Not as far as I know. I'm sorry, Jo."

She sought to relieve the downcast looks on her sisters' faces. "There wasn't anything between me and Ben. Not this time around. I'm sorry he's felt like he can't at least come and see if I'm okay. But . . . I'm afraid that's just the way Ben is. He's not a fan of sickness and death."

"Or integrity, apparently." Britt rolled her eyes, then sighed, her fingers folding into fists at her sides. "But I'm glad there was nothing between you this time."

Jo took Ben's card and slipped it back into the envelope. "Phee, maybe you could text him and let him know I'm doing okay."

Britt gave a little growl. "And be sure and tell him she's not taking visitors at this time."

Jo couldn't help but laugh. "What would I do without my champions? Now let's see who sent these other pretty cards."

CHAPTER 35

J O HOBBLED BACK TO THE hospital bed and climbed up onto the mattress, which at present was cranked up so high it more resembled a big easy chair. It wasn't that the bed wasn't comfortable, but after almost six days in this place, she was so ready to go home. Likely more so after yet another MRI yesterday when her doctor had raised her hopes that she might go home this morning. Then, like an idiot, she admitted to having another headache and a short bout of double vision. Both of which were completely gone now, but of course, being the good doctor he was, he decided to keep her overnight "just to be sure."

Visitors had almost overwhelmed her the first few days after she woke up, but the last two days, the flood had become a trickle. She was going a bit stir-crazy. Her sisters had dropped by this morning—Phee on her way to work, and Britt on her way to get groceries for a house full of Airbnb guests at the cottage. They were pulling all kinds of overtime on her account and she felt terrible about it.

A knock sounded at the partially open door to her room. She tried to check her hair in the mirror across from the bed, but without her contacts she just saw a blur. At least they had let her start wearing her own pajamas once the catheter was removed. Ginger had brought her the cute black-and-blue print set she had on tonight.

"Come in . . ."

The door swung open and Luke took a tentative step toward her. "Do you mind some company?"

"Luke! I'd love some company. Come in." She pointed to the large vinyl-covered chair that Britt had pushed aside earlier. "Pull up that chair."

"I won't stay long."

"Oh, please do. I'm bored out of my gourd. They're making me stay another night."

"That's what your sisters said. I thought I'd come and try to cheer you up."

"Well, it's working. I already feel cheerier." If he only knew!

He laughed. "You look good. I wasn't sure how I'd find you. How are you feeling?"

"A little like I've been run over by a truck." She smiled wryly. "It really could have been so much worse."

"That's what Phylicia said. It sounds like you're lucky to be alive."

"Blessed," she corrected. "Blessed to be alive. I'm trying to be grateful for these aches and pains."

"Of course." He nodded somberly. "They are proof of life."

"I like that," she said. "Proof of life."

She felt more blessed than he could imagine right now, but a lot of it had to do with the fact that he was sitting here in her hospital room.

The emotion of the past week began to catch up with her—and maybe the joy and relief of seeing Luke too—and she suddenly felt near tears. She grasped for something to change the subject. "What's Mateo up to? Is he in the waiting room?"

"No, he's home. We're doing some trial runs with him staying by himself."

"Oh? How's that going?"

Luke chuckled. "Depends on which one of us you ask. He thinks it's the coolest thing ever. I'm pretty much a nervous wreck. But he's handled it really well, actually. Most nights I go home to find the dishes done and his laundry picked up. He's determined to prove that he's old enough to stay alone."

"Well, good for him."

"It will really help once school starts. Which is right around the corner. First day of classes is Tuesday."

"What? Next Tuesday? How can that be?"

"August 10."

"Where did the summer go?"

"Right? And I hear you missed out on a few days of summer altogether."

"I did. It's a really weird feeling to know you literally slept for three days straight."

"Right now that sounds pretty good to me."

"Trust me, it's not."

His expression turned serious. "I didn't mean to make light of what you've been through."

"Of course not. I didn't take it that way."

He cast about the room as if looking for a topic to discuss. His gaze landed on the windowsill. "Looks like you could almost start your own flower shop in here."

She laughed. "You should have seen it yesterday when I was having double vision!"

He laughed his hearty laugh, and the sound of it lifted her spirits like nothing had since she'd landed in this room.

"Your sister said that's why you had to stay. The double vision."

She nodded. "And a whale of a headache. But they're both gone now. I actually feel pretty good. Although I'm not too crazy about this stupid boot I get to wear for the next eight weeks." She stuck her leg out from beneath the sheets to reveal the bulky surgical boot that sported a blue circle.

"Wow. Do you have one to match all your jammies?"

She grinned. "My friend Ginger did actually choose these jammies to color-coordinate with my boot. She will be thrilled that you noticed."

He shrugged. "I'm not usually such a fashion aficionado, but that ensemble did catch my eye. And it matches that eye shadow of yours too. I'm sensing a black-and-blue theme here."

"Oh! I hadn't even thought about that." Laughing, she pulled her hair back and turned the left side of her face toward him.

He winced. "Wow. That *is* quite the shiner you got. Mateo would be impressed."

She told him what she remembered of the accident and by the time she finished—with his compassion and humor applied to every comment—she felt like she'd healed more in twenty minutes than she had the first six days in the hospital. "Well . . . enough about that," she finally said. "I really didn't mean to keep you captive here."

"No. I wanted to come. I would have come sooner, but I wasn't sure . . ." He stared at the floor for a long minute. "I know you were with Ben the night of the accident. I'm not trying to interfere. I just wanted—needed—to see for myself that you're doing okay."

"Luke . . ." She inhaled deeply. "There's nothing between Ben and me. I don't know why I didn't figure that out long ago. But whatever we had is over. Completely over."

His face brightened. "I know I should say I'm sorry. But—"

"It's okay. And maybe I should feel more sorry about things ending—for good—than I do. But I'm good. I'm really okay with it. I know it's the direction God was leading me." She rolled her eyes. "I can be a little hard-headed at times. If you haven't already figured that out."

"I always liked hard-headed women."

"Liar."

He laughed. "So . . . What are the chances you might

296

still—once you're all healed up, of course—give me a call so we can talk things out?"

A look she couldn't quite read crossed his countenance.

He narrowed his eyes. "Or have you already decided?"

"I've decided."

"Okay . . ." He looked at her as if she held his heart in her hands.

"I decided that I really like you, and I think maybe we can figure out a way to . . . make things work. Or at least . . . be friends?"

"I think we already are friends, Joanna." A knowing smile came. "I'd like to get past that and move on to . . . something more."

Her heart soared. "I'd like that too. I'm going to be pretty gimpy for a few weeks, but maybe . . . you and Mateo could come for supper sometime next week?"

"At your place? Are you sure you feel up to it? What if we brought pizza?"

"Let me see how it goes. And I guess I'd better check with Britt to be sure what nights we have guests staying in the cottage. The cabins are a little too cozy for a dinner party."

"You just let me know what works for you. I'd be glad to pick up pizzas."

"Thank you. But I'll cook if I can. I kind of like to show off in the kitchen."

He laughed. "Well, we sure wouldn't want to deny you that opportunity."

A nurse came in to take her vitals.

Luke rose. "I probably should get back to Mateo anyway."

Jo wanted to punt the nurse to the door. Only the promise of seeing him again soon let her treat the woman kindly. "Oh, thank you for the flowers you sent."

He winked. "I bet you don't even know which ones they are."

"Do too!" She pointed to the vase closest to her bed. "That teal vase right there."

He gave an approving nod. "Those *are* pretty. I did good. Well, me and Phee." He winked at her and gave a little wave. "See you soon."

Then, turning on his heel, he strode past the waiting nurse.

The grandmotherly woman turned to watch him go, then came around to the other side of the bed fanning herself. "Now there goes a sight for sore eyes."

Jo giggled. "And *that's* why I'm determined to go home tomorrow."

CHAPTER 36

J O HOBBLED TO THE SOFA in the middle of the room facing the now-empty fireplace. She plopped down in one corner and put her booted ankle up on the ottoman Phee had provided. The cottage was overly warm on this early August afternoon but she'd never been so happy to be home. "How can I be so wiped out? All I've done this past week is sleep."

Speaking the words brought home the fact that one week ago today, she'd been carried by ambulance to the hospital, unconscious. She hadn't realized how profoundly the accident had affected her until the ride home from the hospital.

Every intersection Phee drove through, Jo's heart rate skyrocketed, every yellow light was a reminder, and Phee had gently pointed out that Jo was gripping the armrests as if the car were a roller coaster.

"Just go to bed, Jo. I'll bring in the rest of the bags a little later."

Jo started to protest and then gasped when something— Melvin!—jumped onto her lap.

Phee laughed. "Oh, I forgot to tell you: Britt loaned you her cat for a few days."

"Awww . . . that was sweet of her." Melvin sniffed the walking boot that was starting to look a little worse for the wear. But apparently unfazed, he curled up beside her and went to sleep, tail twitching.

Phee continued to rummage through bags.

"What are you looking for?"

"Oh . . . nothing. I must have left it in the car. And hey, just leave those vases for now. I'll be back over later to combine some of the bouquets and throw out the wilted flowers."

"You don't have to do that."

"I know, but it's my area of expertise. I want to." She gave Jo a cheesy grin. "And I want *you* to go to bed!"

"But if I go to bed now, I won't be able to sleep tonight." She rested an elbow on the back of the sofa and watched her sister sort through bags and totes.

"Suit yourself," Phee said. "But don't you overdo it. You heard what the doctor said. Bed rest for a couple of days, and then gradually work your way back—"

"They have to say that to cover their tails."

"No, Joanna." Phee stopped searching and gave her a firm look that reminded Jo so much of Mom her breath caught. "They say that because they know you won't rest like you're supposed to. Like you *need* to."

"I'll rest. I promise. But I like it out here in the middle of the house. I'll work my way through this mountain of stuff we brought home from the hospital, and when I get tired I'll sleep. Right here." She patted the throw pillows, making Melvin look up briefly.

Phee sighed. "Promise?"

"Cross my heart and hope to die."

Phee looked stricken. "Don't even say that, Jo!"

"Oops. Sorry. Just kidding," she squeaked.

Phee turned away, but not before Jo saw the tears brimming in her eyes.

"Phee . . . I didn't mean anything by it. I'm fine!"

Her sister whirled to face her again, then came to stand behind the sofa, wrapping her arms around Jo from behind. "I can't even let myself think about how close we came to losing you."

"Aww . . . I have the best sisters . . ." She tried to keep her tone light, but she had to swallow the lump in her throat.

Phee let go of her and straightened, her voice steady now. "Okay. I've said all I can say to my bullheaded sister. I'm going to walk up to the house and see if Quinn is still there. I've got my phone. Call me if you need anything. I'll be back in a while to check on you and take care of the flowers."

"I'm fine, Phee. Go." She shooed her away. "And tell that handsome hubby of yours hi."

Phee walked out to the music of the screen door swinging shut, and Jo was left in silence.

She looked around the cottage that had become such a beloved retreat to her, and she imagined Luke—and Mateo— here by the fire, and later gathered around the table eating her lasagna and crusty French bread. The scene in her imagination thrilled her. Maybe she'd call Luke later tonight and set a date for the dinner she'd promised.

But one glance at the sofa littered with bags and clothes and stacks of papers sobered her. She had to get this place cleaned up before she could even think about having company.

She reached for one of the plastic totes the hospital had used to pack her things and started sorting through it.

She placed the greeting cards on the coffee table to go through later and made a trash bag of one of the totes, filling it with brochures and her hospital bracelet and other things she didn't particularly ever want to see again.

She reached for another sack and peered inside. A small stack of books and a receipt. Wait. This wasn't hers. She looked at the outside of the bag. Barnes & Noble. Maybe someone had brought her some books and she'd forgotten. Or never opened them.

She opened the bag wider, peeked inside . . . and froze. There were three books. Two pocket-size books of "best-loved baby names" and a fat tome called *What to Expect When You're Expecting*. What in the world . . . ? Phee!

When she could finally breathe again, Joanna didn't know whether to laugh or cry. This could only mean one thing. Her sister was pregnant! Phee and Quinn were having a baby!

But her stomach churned as she stuffed the books back into the bag. This must have been what Phee was searching for earlier. And now Jo's snooping—accidental though it was—had spoiled her sister's amazing news. Worse, Jo would have to pretend to be surprised when they made the announcement.

A baby! She could hardly picture it. And yet thinking of Quinn and Phee with a baby—and later a toddler—seemed like the most natural thing in the world. Would they be the kind to find out if they were having a boy or girl? Would they tell people what names they'd chosen or keep it a surprise?

She was so excited she thought she might burst!

On a whim, she pulled the smallest book of baby names out of the bag and leafed through it, dreaming on Phee's behalf.

She leafed through the A's and B's, then flipped through quickly to the L section. *Liam . . . Logan . . .* There it was. *Lucas/ Lukas/Luke. Meaning: Bringer of light.*

Interesting. Not that she put much stock in that kind of thing, but the man had certainly been a ray of light in her life. Especially recently.

She kept leafing, mindful that Phee could come back any minute to take care of the vases. She was about to put the book back in the bag when she saw it: *Matthew/Matthias/Mateo. Meaning: God's gift.*

She sat, transfixed, for a full minute. Okay, maybe she didn't put any stock in these things, but it sure did seem like God might be trying to say something to her.

I'm listening, Lord.

Mindful of the other two cooks in the tiny cottage kitchen, Jo hopped from the refrigerator to the stove and back again, getting the vegetables ready to sauté.

Britt laughed at her. "You look like a pirate with a peg leg."

Jo glared. "Aarghh!"

That made her sisters laugh. It seemed like they were all feeling grateful to be together, to be alive. She was excited, but nervous, too, about Luke and Mateo coming for dinner. Her sisters and Quinn would be here too—a "sixsome" to play board games after dinner.

"I don't know what I would have done without you two to help tonight."

Phee frowned. "I'm sorry I couldn't have helped more. Things have been a little crazy with work and especially with the house."

"Not to mention a sister who managed to land herself in the hospital. Sorry about that."

Phee waved off Jo's comment, and Britt looked up from the block of parmesan cheese she was grating. "How's the house coming along, by the way?"

"It seems like all we do is wait." Phee blew out a frustrated sigh. "Wait for the foundation to cure, wait for the contractors to get here, wait on the supplies to come in . . ."

Wait for a baby to be born. Joanna held her breath, certain those would be her sister's next words. But instead, Phee turned to check on the bread. She opened the oven to release the yeasty fragrance that was the whole reason Jo had waited until the last minute to put the two plump loaves in the oven.

A bun in the oven! Phee couldn't pass up *that* opportunity, could she? But her sister moved about the kitchen as if nothing was different. Surely Phee wouldn't keep this secret from her own sisters. Unless . . . *Unless she hadn't even told Quinn yet.*

While the three of them sliced fruit for a salad, Phee

turned to Jo. "You said you wanted to play board games tonight? Which ones?"

Jo wiped her hands and went to the antique pine cupboard that housed a nice collection of games for guests of the Airbnb to use. She held up a box. "Do you think Battle of the Sexes would be too . . . advanced for Mateo?"

Britt made a face that said she was doubtful.

"How about Spoons?"

Phee cringed. "Somebody could get hurt. Seriously."

"True." She put the game box back and closed the cupboard. "Maybe Uno?"

"We don't have Uno, do we?" She opened the cupboard again in case she'd missed it.

"Maybe Luke knows a game Mateo likes," Phee suggested. "You could just ask him. Maybe they could bring something when they come."

"I guess . . ." Joanna tried to concentrate on what Phee was saying, but she couldn't keep her eyes off her older sister. Was it her imagination, or did Phee have a certain glow about her? A new womanly roundness to her body. It was all Jo could do not to drop hints that might make her sister fess up. But if Quinn really didn't know yet, that wouldn't be fair.

"I know! We could play *wooden* spoons." Britt grabbed a wood utensil from the crock on the stove and wielded it like a sword.

Laughing, Jo did likewise—except her pose was rather graceless on account of the boot.

"Are you two going to act like two-year-olds while our company's here?" But Phee laughed at their bantering.

"She started it!" Jo said in her best two-year-old whine.

"It wasn't me," Britt protested, grinning. "It was Jo. And besides, it's her company. If she wants to act like a fool—"

"You two try not to hurt each other," Phee deadpanned. "I'm going to go lie down for a few minutes before everyone gets here."

Yes, sis, you need your rest. Jo smiled to herself, but one look at the clock on the stove and her nerves kicked into high gear. They'd be here in half an hour! How could she be so nervous— and excited—at the same time!

"Britt, will you keep an eye on things in the kitchen? I'm going to go see if I can cover up these stupid bruises with a little makeup."

Britt gave her a knowing look. "He won't care."

"I know." And that was just one more thing she loved about the man.

CHAPTER 37

S O, SCHOOL STARTS TOMORROW, HUH?" Jo was doing her best to make conversation with Mateo, who'd been too busy chowing down—mostly on French bread—to talk.

He threw her a perfunctory nod before turning to Luke. "Can I have another piece of bread?" He looked up at Luke with those dark puppy-dog eyes and Jo fully expected Luke to give in.

But he surprised her. "Miss Joanna asked you a question, Mateo. Tell her about school."

"It starts tomorrow."

Her sisters and Quinn chuckled, and Joanna smiled at Luke over the boy's head before taking another stab at it. "Are you excited about going into seventh grade?"

"I guess." Mateo *almost* looked at her. "I'm happy I get to play basketball."

"Basketball, huh?" Quinn jumped into the conversation. "That was my sport. Not that I was all that good at it."

"Oh, yes you were." Phee nudged him. "Don't be so modest."

"Well, okay, I might have been all-state, all-conference, and an all-around all-star."

"And so modest too," Jo teased.

Luke laughed and Mateo's eyes grew round. "Were you really? All that stuff?"

"No," Quinn said, tongue firmly in cheek. "I just said I *might* have been—if I'd practiced harder."

They all laughed and Luke tried—unsuccessfully—to explain the joke to Mateo.

The boy gave a half-hearted laugh, then looked up at Luke. "Can I have some more bread? Please?"

"I think you've had enough, buddy. Finish the rest of your lasagna and then we'll talk. And what do you tell Miss Joanna about the food. Wasn't that lasagna good?"

Mateo nodded and spoke around a wad of half-chewed bread. "It's good, but not as good as Bella Italia, right Luke?"

Luke stopped chewing, looking like a raccoon caught robbing the corn bin. "Mateo. Manners. That's not really an opinion you needed to share when Joanna has spent all day making this meal for us."

"It's okay." Jo gave a wry smile. "Honesty is a good quality too. So, what do *you* think of my lasagna, Luke? Not quite as good as Bella Italia?" She tilted her head, enjoying watching him squirm.

"I'll tell you what's good," he said, picking up a slice of buttered bread from the edge of his plate. "This bread! I think I could eat a whole loaf on my own."

That broke the ice and they all cracked up.

Jo rolled her eyes, but she was laughing too. "*Nice* save."

Luke at least had the decency to look sheepish.

The rest of dinner went exceptionally well. Quinn and Luke had hit it off that day of the walk-through for the reception, and now they picked up where they'd left off, talking sports and music and housing construction.

Quinn scooted his chair back and stretched. "If you'd like— if everyone's finished—we can take a walk down the lane and I'll show you what's happening at the site. It's beginning to look—"

"Quinn . . ." Phee spoke his name softly, but he turned to her. "I think Jo had some board games she wanted to play."

"Oh, I'm sorry, Jo. Didn't mean to hijack the activities. Board games sound good to me."

"I really don't care. We may as well go outside while it's still light. But"—she frowned at her boot—"I don't think I'll try to hop too far just yet."

"I'll drive you up to the house," Luke volunteered.

"You don't mind?"

He smiled. "I don't think the tenth of a mile up there and back is going to cost too much in gasoline."

"Okay then. I'll take you up on that offer. It's about killing me to be confined to the front porch. My sisters said the clearing is beautiful about now."

Mateo's face lit. "Is that where the wedding was? Can I climb up to there again?"

Jo looked to Luke for permission.

"Fine by me." He touched her wrist briefly. "If you're sure you didn't have your heart set on board games."

"I really don't mind at all. We were having trouble deciding what game to play anyway. And besides, it looks like a perfect evening. Not as hot as they said it would be. Let's go outside."

"Just don't forget there's dessert later," Phee said. "Britt made a cobbler from the cherries on our trees."

"I barely got to them before the birds did. But we have ice cream to make it go further." Britt scraped her chair back.

The rest of them followed suit.

The men helped clear the table and the sisters hurriedly rinsed the dishes and put the food away before they all headed for the front door.

"Can the cat come with us?" Mateo reached to stroke Melvin's tail.

"No, sorry, honey." Jo looked Mateo in the eye. "Melvin is an indoor-only cat. He got lost up in the clearing once and poor Britt was a basket case."

"What's that?"

"A basket case?" Jo laughed. "I guess that sounds kind of funny, doesn't it. It just means she was about to go crazy with worry."

"Oh." His expression said her explanation still didn't make sense, but he trotted toward the front door, looking eager to get outside.

Luke helped her into his car and drove slowly down the lane. As he helped her from the car, she discovered a silver lining in having to wear the stupid boot: She needed someone to hang on to on the uneven terrain, and Luke seemed happy to provide support.

Despite a bright August sun, the breeze off the water kept the air cool, and if they stayed in the shade it was quite pleasant.

Mateo headed straight for the trees that hid the wooden stairway up to the clearing, but Luke pulled him back. "Let's go see the construction site first, and then we can go up there."

Apparently the word *construction* was enough to entice the boy because he happily tagged along. Jo hadn't seen the progress on the house since she'd gotten home from the hospital, and while there wasn't much to see of the house itself, Quinn had been busy with a project behind the house overlooking the tributary.

He'd laid a flagstone patio with a pathway winding down to the water's edge. A wide pergola covered the patio and Jo could just picture it next summer draped in wisteria or trumpet vine.

Quinn was in his element showing off the site. "Of course, until they get everything framed out, we can't do any landscaping too close to where the house will be, but Phee has plans for some flower beds and over here"—he pointed to the far side of the plot where it was sunniest—"maybe some of those raised vegetable gardens."

A look passed between him and Phee, and Jo was positive then that Quinn knew.

Luke seemed enthralled with all the details. "Does the water ever get higher than it is now?"

Quinn laughed. "We wouldn't mind if it did."

"Just not *too* high," Phee added quickly.

"For sure. We had to sandbag the cabins late last winter when we had all that flooding. But this was a dry bed when we bought the place. We're just hoping we can keep it running. Worth a lot more—both for the property and as an Airbnb rental—if it's a waterfront lot."

"I can see why," Luke said. "It's a beautiful spot."

Quinn pointed down to the water. "Of course, we'll fence in the yard a ways back from shore. For safety."

Again that look passed between him and Phee, and Jo felt her heart swell. She could just see a toddler skipping down that flagstone path going to help mommy pick green beans. Maybe someday her own children would play with their cousins in this yard and up in the clearing. Of course, by the time she had babies, Phee's children might be . . . *Mateo's age.*

She let that thought—and all it implied—settle inside her. And for the first time, it felt *comfortable.*

"Oh! Jo, you should show Luke what you've done with your little garden." Phee was playing matchmaker, and Jo didn't care.

She turned to Luke, pointing. "It's behind the cottage. And it's not really anything to brag about yet, but you should come and see it . . . since your backyard was the inspiration."

Mateo tugged at Luke's sleeve. "I thought we were going to go up those stairs."

"We will, buddy. In a little bit."

"We'll take him." Quinn stood behind Mateo and put his hands on the boy's shoulders. "You two go on and see Jo's garden. We'll be down in time for dessert."

Apparently Phee had gotten her husband in on the matchmaking gig.

"Okay. If you're sure." She turned to Luke. "Is that all right with you?"

"Mateo?"

"I'd rather go up in the clear-in with them. If that's okay, Miss Joanna?"

Jo smiled at his pronunciation. And his use of her name. She thought that might be a first.

Britt took a step back. "If you guys don't mind, since I've already seen the clearing and Jo's garden, I think I'm going back to my cabin. I have some bookings I need to respond to."

"I'll save you some dessert," Phee hollered as Britt strode across the lane.

Left alone with Luke, she gave him her best smile. "Shall we go?"

He pointed to his car where he'd parked it along the lane. "Your chariot awaits, Miss Joanna."

CHAPTER 38

THIS IS GOING TO BE wonderful." The genuine admiration in Luke's voice lifted Jo's spirits. "And sweet peas will do nicely here. They should get just enough sun."

"I hope so. I loved how they made your whole backyard smell." Luke's reaction to her little project had been better even than it had played out in her imagination. Somehow, they'd managed to rediscover that same comfortable, yet exciting tone they found that night after the Fourth of July fireworks. Before everything had gotten so difficult and confusing.

Luke looked at her now, as if deciding whether to say something. "It's really been a great evening, Jo. Thank you."

She felt like he had more on his mind, but the sound of lively voices coming from the lane made them both turn. "They must be back from their adventures."

"I think it's time for dessert. I must admit, my mouth is watering just thinking of that cherry cobbler with ice cream."

Jo laughed. "Men! Always thinking with their stomachs."

She was disappointed that their time alone was over, but her mouth was watering too. And besides, getting back inside would give her an excuse to take Luke's arm again.

An hour later, the cherry cobbler pan sat empty on the counter and all five of them worked to clear the dishes from the table. Luke asked for a broom and Jo watched, oddly touched as he showed Mateo how to sweep the floor and whisk the dirt into the dustpan.

Melvin thought it was a game and pounced on the broom, then swatted at the dustpan with one paw. Mateo's giggles over the cat's antics were contagious and laughter filled the cottage.

Melvin eventually lost interest and wandered away. Seeing Mateo's disappointment, Jo opened a drawer and pulled out a package of cat treats that Britt had bought for Melvin. She poured half a dozen into her palm and handed them to Mateo. "If you want Melvin to be your friend forever, just give him one of these every so often."

Jo showed him how to hold a treat flat in his hand and wait for the cat to sniff his hand and then snatch the treat from him. Grinning, Mateo tucked all but one of the treats into the front pocket of his shirt and went to find the cat.

He returned a moment later, Melvin in tow, and the broom game—and the giggling—started again.

Jo surveyed the scene feeling deeply satisfied. The evening had flown by, but it couldn't have gone better. Excitement bubbled inside her for what *could* be—if she could simply find a way to open her heart to something very different than she'd always imagined.

After a while, Luke glanced up at the clock above the fireplace. "Buddy, I hate to break up such a great party, but you've got school tomorrow, and it's going to be a big day."

"Can't we stay a little longer? I can sleep in the car on the way home."

"You'll just have to come out here again soon," Jo told him. "Melvin's going to miss having you to play with."

"Can we get a cat?" The imploring look on Mateo's face made them all laugh.

"Now see what you've done," Luke teased. He nudged the

boy. "You need to go gather up your things so we can let these ladies get to bed."

Mateo frowned. "You mean get *me* to bed."

"Right after you shower and wash that hair."

Mateo groaned and started toward the backpack he'd left by the front door, but then turned back and cupped his hands, standing on tiptoe to whisper in Luke's ear.

"Oh. Good idea." Luke winked at Jo. "Can you direct this young man to the powder room?"

Mateo rolled his eyes, but he followed Jo's directions and headed down the short hallway.

Luke turned to Joanna, but also included her sisters. "Thank you for this evening. We both had a great time, and the food was amazing. Even your lasagna, Joanna."

She laughed. "Yeah, yeah, I know better than that. And don't think I'll ever try to make barbecue for you two either. I know how you feel about Dexter's, and I refuse to compete."

"Maybe we'd best quit eating out altogether then."

Quinn stepped forward to shake Luke's hand, then turned to Jo. "I think we're going to head home if that's okay. Britt said she'd stay and help you finish up."

"There's hardly anything else to do. You guys go on. And thanks."

Quinn held up the foil-wrapped care package Jo had fixed for him. "Thank *you* for the leftovers."

"You're welcome. That ought to keep you fed for a—"

"Why do you have my mom's jewelry box?" Mateo's voice boomed from the hallway, accusing, and made them all turn to stare at him.

He stopped beneath the arched doorway and stood there, feet planted, cradling the mother-of-pearl trinket box in both hands—the box Jo had paid thirty-six dollars for at the antique store that day.

"What's the problem, Mateo?" Luke went to him and bent to eye level with him.

"Did *you* give it to her?" He glared at Luke.

"Hey, slow down, buddy. I'm not sure what you mean."

"Did you give Mama's jewelry box to *her*?" He turned his laser gaze on Jo.

Joanna looked from Luke to her sisters, but they all shrugged and shook their heads.

Quinn pointed toward the front door and mouthed, "I think we'll go."

He and Phee waved tentatively and slipped out silently with Britt close behind.

Jo waited for Luke to sort things out with Mateo, but the boy clutched the box, his jaw set, his face red. "This is Mama's jewelry box."

"Where did you get it, buddy? I've never seen that box before."

Mateo shifted the box to the crook of his left arm and pointed at Joanna. "It was in *her* bathroom! In plain sight."

Still squatted down in front of the boy, Luke glanced over his shoulder and gave Jo a questioning look.

"I—I bought it at an antique store." *Why would Mateo think it belonged to his mother?* "It's the one I told you about that day we ate at Muy Caliente, Luke. Remember? You were teasing me about being a shopaholic?"

He nodded, remembrance coming to his expression. He turned back to Mateo. "Miss Joanna bought this at a store, Mateo. Maybe it's just like the one your mom had?"

"No! This is Mama's. It's exactly like hers." He fiddled with the clasp, growing frustrated when it wouldn't open.

"Mateo." Luke's voice grew stern. "That belongs to Miss Joanna. You don't open it unless you have permission."

"It's okay," Jo said. "You can open it. I just keep supplies in it—aspirin and first aid stuff for our guests."

Mateo looked at her again, as if making sure he had permission.

"It's all right. I don't care if you open it. It's a little tricky."

316

"I know. I *remember*." He worked the clasp and looked inside the box. "Yep, this is hers. The handle turns the same way. And it had this little chunk out right here." He scraped a fingernail over a chipped shell.

Joanna moved closer to see what he was focusing on. There was, indeed, a tiny chip broken from one square of the shell inlay. Was the kid just making this stuff up as he went? If so, he was an Oscar caliber actor.

"There are probably a lot of jewelry boxes like this one around, Mateo." Luke spoke evenly. "They mass market these and sell them in stores."

Joanna cleared her throat. "Actually, I'm pretty sure this one is handmade. There might be others similar to it, but . . . the woman who checked me out at Annie Laurie's thought it was an artisan piece."

Confusion shadowed Luke's expression. "Then how—"

"Annie Laurie's?" Mateo looked up. "Is that the one with umbrellas all over the ceiling? Mama liked that store."

"Yes, that's the one," she whispered.

Without warning, Mateo's face scrunched into a grimace. He clutched the jewelry box to his chest and charged past them toward the front door, almost knocking Luke off balance.

"Mateo!" Luke scrambled to his feet and started after the boy.

Jo trailed him to the door, but when it slammed behind Mateo, followed by the slap of the door to the screened porch beyond, Luke turned and lifted a hand. "Let him go. He needs a few minutes to calm down." He peered through the window.

Jo followed his line of vision and saw Mateo jogging up the lane toward Poplar Brook road. "Luke . . . I'm so sorry. I didn't know it was hers or I never would have—"

"Of course you didn't know. How could you? This isn't your fault, Joanna."

"I feel awful though." The pain on the boy's face had wrenched her heart.

Luke put a hand lightly on her forearm. "It's kind of been two steps forward, one step back for Mateo. The grieving thing. This must have dredged up some memories."

"I get that." Jo shook her head. "It's been the same with Mom. The littlest thing will remind me of her and it's like losing her all over again."

"I'm sorry."

She shook her head, feeling like a selfish jerk. "No. *I'm* sorry. I didn't mean to make it about me."

"You didn't, Joanna. You were just expressing how you *do* understand what Mateo's feeling."

She gave him a wan smile she hoped expressed her gratitude and turned to look out the window again. Mateo had disappeared from sight. "He won't try to walk to town or anything, will he?"

"I think he just needed some space. I'm sorry he took your jewelry box. I don't think he'll damage it or anything. I hope there was nothing too valuable inside."

She waved his words away. "I'm not worried about that. Do you really think it was the actual one his mom had? He seemed pretty sure . . ."

"Yes. I don't think he was making any of that up. Maria must have sold it to the antique store."

She nodded. "That's what I was thinking. I want him to have the box, Luke."

"That's sweet of you, Joanna, but you don't need to do that. It belongs to you now."

"No. I want to. You can see how much it means to him."

He shrugged one shoulder. "If you're sure."

"I'm sure."

"Well, what do you say we wash up the supper dishes while we wait for Mateo to come back?"

"Luke, you don't have to do that."

"Listen, I'm no dummy." That ornery spark came to his

eyes. "You think I'm going to forfeit this chance to spend some extra time with you."

She paused, letting his meaning soak in, her heart lifting as it did. "By all means, then. Push up your sleeves." She did the same and led the way to the sink.

CHAPTER 39

THAT SHOULD DO IT." JOANNA gave the counter one last swipe with the dishrag and turned to survey the tidy kitchen.

Luke had dried dishes while she washed and now everything was put away in the cupboards. "Now see, that wasn't so difficult."

Jo wrapped the dishrag in the damp dish towel Luke had used and headed for the laundry room. "Let me go put these in the laundry. Be right back."

But when she returned a moment later, Luke's brow was furrowed. "Is that clock right?"

"It is." It was after eight o'clock and the light in the house was fading quickly. "Mateo's not back yet?"

"No. He might have just gone to the truck. But I'd better go check."

He didn't protest when Jo followed him to his truck. But Mateo wasn't there. And there was no sign of him as far as they could see in any direction.

"Maybe he did try to walk back to town?" She made it a question.

"I don't think he would do that. But I didn't think he'd be gone this long either."

Jo was thankful Mateo had gone in the direction of the road, and not toward the river. The water wasn't deep, and Mateo could probably swim, but still . . . The mere possibility made her shudder.

Luke cupped his hands around his mouth and hollered for Mateo. They both stood stock still, listening for a reply.

Nothing.

"I'm going to drive up the lane and out on the road a little ways and see if he's there. Do you mind waiting here in case he shows up? I don't want him to think I left without him."

"Of course."

Luke went to the truck and crept up the lane in a zigzag, pointing his headlights into the woods on either side of the lane. His truck disappeared around the curve and Jo stood in the middle of the lane, turning to look in all directions. But dusk blanketed the landscape in gray and it was hard to see anything.

She heard Luke's engine as he turned onto Poplar Brook Road and then it faded into nothingness. But five minutes later, he was back, his worried frown answering her question before he even climbed out of the truck.

As he approached her in the middle of the lane Jo looked up toward the stairway cut in the side of the hill. "Do you think he might have gone back up to the clearing? He seemed to really like it up there."

"Good idea." Despite the darkening sky, he shaded his eyes as if it might help him see up into the wooded edge of the clearing. "I'll go check."

"I'd come with you if it wasn't for this stupid boot."

"No, you stay here. I'm sorry to keep you."

"Don't even think about it, Luke. I'll wait here. Look back down this way when you get to the stairs. If he's down here, you might be able to spot him from there."

"Do you mind if I turn on the lights once I get up there?"

"Not at all. You remember where the switches are, right?"

Luke nodded wordlessly and sprinted to the stairway, taking the wide planked steps two at a time.

A few seconds later, she saw the lights twinkling through the trees like so many fireflies. *Good.* That would help. Luke's voice echoed down the hill, calling Mateo's name over and over.

It was almost dark now and she hobbled into the house for a flashlight. Her ankle throbbed and she knew she'd pay tomorrow for overdoing it. When she came back outside again, Luke was standing in the middle of the lane, hands on hips.

"He didn't show up?" Alarm made his voice thready.

"No. I just ran in for a flashlight." She held it up as if needing to prove she'd spoken the truth.

He blew out a thick breath. "He was up there. At least he has been."

"How do you know?"

He held up a straight strand of beads. The necklace that matched Luke's. "These were lying on the steps. The clasp is broken. But maybe he lost it when he was up there earlier."

"No. I remember he had it on when he was playing with Melvin. I noticed when he put the cat treats in his pocket."

"Okay. So he *has* been up there since he stormed out of your house. I have a feeling he's still there." There was an edge to his voice, but Joanna thought it held more fear than anger. "Just waiting us out maybe. Trying to give us both heart attacks."

"Well, it's working. You don't think he'll come down once it's dark?"

Luke shook his head. "It's pretty dark up there already. I thought about leaving the lights on."

"Do! Please. I don't want him to get hurt up there. Or be scared—if he's still up there." She was scared enough for both of them. If anything happened to Mateo she would never forgive herself.

"I think I will go turn those lights back on and check one more time."

She held out a hand, motioning toward the beads he still held. "Maybe I can fix those."

He dropped the strand into her open hand. "Are there any hiding places up there I should know about?"

"Not adult-size hiding places, but he could probably hide in the underbrush or behind some of the logs Quinn felled up there. Melvin got lost up there this spring. We searched for that stupid cat half the night and—Hey . . ." An idea formed. "Do you think if you took Melvin up there, it might lure Mateo out of hiding? He's pretty crazy about that cat."

Luke cocked his head, but he looked hopeful. "It's worth a try. But I don't want to lose your cat."

"No, Melvin would find his way back down. That's where he ended up the night he got lost—back at the cottage while we all went crazy up there looking for him."

"Okay. Let's give it a try. Will Melvin let me carry him though?"

She nodded. "He's pretty cuddly. But hold him tight so he doesn't think he has the option of getting down."

"Okay."

She went to retrieve the cat, who was purring peacefully on the sofa. She scooped him up and nuzzled his soft fur with her chin. "Melvin, I need you to be cuter and more persuasive than you have ever been in your life. And don't you get lost too. Do you hear me?"

Melvin squeaked out a meow that didn't engender confidence.

"Dear Lord," she whispered, "please help us find Mateo. I don't want him to have to spend the night out there." Not for the first time tonight, she felt a deep compassion for the boy Luke loved like his own.

Luke tucked the flashlight Jo had given him under one arm and gingerly took the monstrous tuxedo cat from her. He was not a cat person, wasn't even sure of the proper way to hold a cat. Melvin twisted and turned, and for a minute Luke thought the animal would escape, but Jo spoke softly and stroked the black-and-white head, while the cat settled into his arms.

"Just go kind of slow," Jo said. "And talk to him. If he struggles like he wants to get down, just let him go. You might not want to yell too loud. That might scare him. Melvin, I mean."

"Okay. What do you say, Melvin?" He looked down at the feline, feeling foolish talking to a dumb cat. "Let's see if we can coax that boy out."

"Is your phone on?"

"Yes. I'll call you if we find him. Wish me luck."

"I'm praying. Hard."

"Even better."

He crossed the lane slowly, but picked up speed when he could tell the cat wasn't going to bolt. At the top of the stairs, he found the light switches again and turned them on. He spoke softly to Melvin, then a bit louder, testing the cat's tolerance. When Melvin seemed calm, Luke called softly. "Mateo? I've got Melvin here. You need to come out. This cat . . . wants to see you."

He walked to the center of the clearing, staying in the dim pools of light the string lights cast. He repeated the whole spiel again, louder, then stopped to listen.

Melvin shifted in the cradle of Luke's arms and pointed his whiskers in various directions, but he stayed put. Luke called once more, louder this time. He thought he heard a twig crack, but the clearing was probably teeming with wildlife. It could be anything. For the first time, he considered that something terrible might actually have happened to Mateo.

He called his name more urgently, yet still trying to strike a balance between urgent and furious—which he was fast becoming.

"Mateo? Are you there? You need to come out, buddy. Let's talk about this. We can work things—"

Melvin struggled in his arms, pushing off with back feet and legs that were surprisingly powerful. "Melvin! Come back here!"

But the cat shot to one side of the clearing, like a soldier on a mission. A rat, no doubt. Or a skunk. *Please no, Lord.*

He started in the direction the cat had gone, but hearing a different sound, he stopped again to listen.

The distinct noise of muffled laughter floated across the clearing.

"Here, kitty, kitty." Mateo called the cat the way Jo had shown him earlier tonight. "Melvin! What are you doing up here, kitty?"

The rush of sheer relief that came over Luke surprised him. Mateo was here. He was fine. Luke tapped out a quick text to Jo: *Found him. Well, Melvin did. All is well. Give us a few minutes.*

He stood motionless, straining to hear what Mateo was saying even though he couldn't see boy or cat in the dim glow of the string lights.

"Hey, Melvin." Mateo's voice pierced the night. "What're you up to? What're you looking for, huh?" Low laughter, and then he spoke just above a whisper. "You crazy cat, how'd you know those were in my pocket? You're a pretty smart one, aren't you?"

Crazy cat was right. Luke smiled and slowly moved closer, straining to hear. Melvin must have smelled the treats Mateo had squirreled away in his pocket. Well, thank the Lord for small miracles. He could hardly wait to tell Jo.

He let Mateo talk to Melvin for a while, the boy's words indistinct but earnest. Probably the best counselor he could have asked for.

Finally, worrying that Jo would wonder what was going on, he spoke Mateo's name again.

A long pause. Then, "I'm over here." Mateo rose from behind a fallen log. But Melvin jumped up on top of the log, stretching his front legs up on Mateo's chest, pawing at his pocket, then licking his chin.

Giggling like a girl, Mateo gathered the cat into his arms. "Sorry, pal, I'm all out."

"Come here, buddy." Luke tried to make his voice gentle and stern at the same time. "And bring Melvin with you. Jo's going to be worried about us."

Mateo started across the clearing, cat in his arms, then caught his breath and turned back. Still clutching Melvin in one arm, Mateo rummaged under the log he'd been hiding behind and retrieved Joanna's jewelry box. Clutching it to his chest like he had back at the house, he started back toward Luke, but kept his eyes to the ground.

When he reached the center of the clearing where Luke was waiting, he finally glanced up and forced his gaze to meet Luke's. "Sorry."

Luke squeezed his shoulder. "We'll talk about it later. I'm just glad you're safe."

CHAPTER 40

THE LIGHTS UP IN THE clearing flickered, then went out. Finally. They were coming down. Jo's knees went weak with relief. She would never admit to Luke the horrific possibilities she'd entertained as she waited, helpless, down here while Luke searched in the dim light of the clearing. But it amplified her relief that Mateo had been found safely.

Standing in the middle of the lane in front of the cottage, she squeezed the coil of brown beads Luke had placed in her hand. While she waited, she'd managed to fix the bent clasp by the light of her phone. She wondered if Mateo had realized yet that he'd lost it. Thank the Lord he *had* lost it, or they might not have persevered in searching the clearing.

The breeze carried the sound of shoes crunching leaves and gravel. A low meow preceded them, and Melvin trotted up the lane to her. She picked him up and hugged him. "Good job, buddy. There will be more treats in store for you tonight."

She hurried back to deposit the cat inside the cottage. By the time she stepped outside again, Luke and a subdued Mateo were waiting. He clung to the mother-of-pearl box, which looked none the worse for the wear.

She forced a smile. "Thank goodness you're okay."

Luke gave the boy a gentle push toward her. "What do you tell Joanna?"

"I'm sorry I took Mama's . . . *your* jewelry box." He held it out to her.

Overwhelmed with sorrow for all this boy had lost, Joanna took a risk and placed a hand on his shoulder. "Mateo . . . I wonder if your mom sold this box to the antique store. To Annie Laurie's. And that's why it was there the day I bought it."

"But she loved that box. Why would she do that?"

Luke moved to stand behind Mateo, catching Jo's eye over the boy's head with a look she read as gratitude. "Maybe she needed the money, buddy. You know things were always kind of tight with her money."

Jo patted Mateo's hand over the box. "I don't know for sure how the box got there, but I want you to have it. I know your mom would have liked that. It would be a pretty cool place to keep baseball cards and stuff like that, don't you think?"

He nodded. And after a long moment, he looked up at her. "I can really have it?"

"Yes. It's yours. If you can get that clasp undone for me, I'll just take my stuff out first. To make room for your treasures. Oh!" She reached into her breast pocket and drew out his beads. "Speaking of clasps, I fixed this one."

Mateo looked down at the beads, then grasped at his bare throat with one hand, obviously unaware he'd lost the necklace. "How'd you get—"

"I found them on the steps," Luke said. "They must have fallen off when you were climbing up to the clearing. It's how we knew you were up there. It was Joanna's idea to bring Melvin up."

"He's pretty smart." Mateo grinned at Jo. "He figured out I still had treats in my pocket."

"He is pretty smart. For a cat." She winked at Luke, then shifted her feet, wincing when she put weight on the booted ankle. But recovering quickly, she stretched the necklace out, gripping opposite ends of the clasp. She held the string up to Mateo's neck. "Turn around and I'll fasten it for you."

He turned his back to her and let her put the beads around his neck. He pivoted to face her, cradling the box to his chest again. "You're sure I can have this?"

"Of course."

He worked the clasp on the box and spilled the contents into Jo's cupped hands.

"What do you say, Mateo?" Luke's eyes, still shiny with gratitude, met Jo's.

"Thank you." The shy smile the boy gave her was worth every penny of that thirty-six dollars.

Luke spread the quilt over Mateo's bed, folding back the corner in the certain way that had become their nightly bedtime ritual. "Okay, hop in here, bud. And no complaining when that alarm goes off in the morning, you hear?"

"I won't."

"So, except for that last hike up to the clearing, did you have fun tonight?" They'd already discussed an appropriate punishment for the trouble Mateo had caused by running away: he was grounded from video games for the foreseeable future. But Luke didn't want to end the night on a sour note. Not with tomorrow being the first day of school.

"It was pretty fun. Up until then." Mateo started to get into bed, then looked at the box on his nightstand. A faraway look came to his eyes. "Luke?"

"What, buddy?"

"Do you think Miss Joanna is mad at me now?"

"Because of the trinket box, you mean?" They'd decided to call it a trinket box since it didn't seem like boys were all that big on owning jewelry boxes.

"Uh-huh. That and me causing all that trouble. Running away."

"I guarantee Miss Joanna is not mad at you."

"But what if she is?"

He'd said a hasty goodbye to Joanna after making Mateo thank her for the box. He'd offer to pay for it next time he saw her.

Luke stifled a sigh. He would make his own apologies to Joanna later. Even though he feared this might be the last straw for her. Still, he'd been beyond encouraged by the way she handled Mateo's outburst—and accusations—tonight. He'd been embarrassed. But that was his problem. Right now, Mateo needed reassuring.

"You know what I think?" Luke slid to the floor and sat cross-legged, leaning against the side of Mateo's bed. He patted the floor beside him. "Park it here for a minute."

Mateo slid down to the floor, his knee touching Luke's thigh.

"If you remember your mama like I do, I think you know that she would think it was pretty stinkin' cool that her jewelry box found its way back to you. And even cooler that the woman who liked it enough to pay for it just happened to be Miss Joanna. Joanna paid a pretty big chunk of change for that, by the way, and she—"

"How much?"

Luke leaned back and gave him the eye. "Doesn't matter. And it's none of your business. But more than you get for allowance in a whole month."

"Seriously?"

"Seriously. And then Joanna handed it right back to you—a gift—as soon as she figured out it had once belonged to your mom. You understand what she did?"

"Yeah." He looked at the floor.

"Joanna didn't do anything wrong, Mateo. Do you understand that? She had no way of knowing that was your mother's jewelry box, and even if she had known, your mama took it to that store exactly so someone could buy it."

"Okay."

"I know you didn't understand how it got there, but I think you owe Miss Joanna an apology."

Mateo's face screwed up and his shoulders heaved. Luke pulled him into a hug and let him cry. When the tears had turned to shuddering breaths, he leaned away from Mateo, still sitting on the floor. "I want to tell you something. And . . . it might not mean much to you right now, but I'll probably tell you this story every once in a while, just to remind you. And I think the older you get, it'll mean more."

Mateo sat like him, except he propped his sun-browned elbow on the floor, making his hand a pedestal for his chin. Luke had his full attention now.

"I want you to think about what happened with that jewelry box . . . *trinket* box."

"What do you mean?"

"Well, it started out with your mama. We don't know where she got it . . . maybe from your dad. Or maybe it belonged to *her* mama. But for some reason, she needed to sell it. And knowing her like I did, knowing that money was sometimes pretty tight, I have a feeling she sold it for you. To feed you, put a roof over your head, or maybe you needed new clothes for church that week. Who knows? But one thing I do know, you were always way more important to your mother than any *thing* could be. So even though she liked that box, she made a sacrifice when she sold it. For you." He tousled Mateo's hair. "You tracking with me so far?"

He nodded.

"So, that jewelry box ends up at your mom's favorite antique store. And then a long time later . . . we'll probably never know exactly how it all went down . . . but along comes Miss Joanna. She sees your mama's jewelry box and it catches her eye. She doesn't have a lot of money either, but for some reason, she feels like this box is worth paying the price they're asking. So she buys it and brings it home to her cottage."

Mateo listened, enrapt, as if he didn't know the ending to the story.

"Now along you come and wind up in that very same cottage where the jewelry box is. But now, if Joanna had put that box in her bedroom, or her dresser drawer, or even given it to one of her sisters as a gift, this story might have a different ending. But no, Joanna puts it in her bathroom, and wouldn't you know it, it just so happens that when you're in that cottage, you have to pee!" He couldn't stop the grin that came at this more earthy juncture in the story.

But Mateo's eyes grew round. "It almost seems like God *made* me have to pee, doesn't it?"

Luke nodded his head solemnly. "That very thought crossed my mind. The Lord works in mysterious ways." He held back laughter at his own joke. "But here's the thing, Mateo. It crossed Miss Joanna's mind too—that maybe God had something to do with this whole thing." He'd spoken with her briefly on the phone while Mateo got ready for bed. Her gracious response to his apology had buoyed him.

"Maybe Mama had something to do with it too."

Luke hesitated. "I'm not sure how that all works, buddy. But who knows? Maybe she did."

"Something for the list, huh?"

"The list?"

"You know. Our list of memories about Mama."

"Ah, of course." A stab of regret came. They hadn't added anything to the list in a long time. "Yep. I think this is definitely something for the list. But not tonight. You've got school tomorrow."

"Awww . . ."

Luke hopped up and pulled Mateo behind him. "Time to hit the sack."

Mateo climbed into his bed. "G'night."

"Good night, buddy. Hey . . ." He pulled the covers up around the boy and squeezed his shoulder, trying for a casual tone. "One more thing. I don't know if you've noticed or not, but Joanna is becoming someone pretty special to me. She told me she wondered if maybe God used that jewelry box—trinket box—to make a connection between *her* and your mama—because of *you*. Do you get what I'm saying?"

"Yeah . . . I think so." Mateo's shoulders relaxed almost imperceptibly beneath Luke's touch.

Luke took in a breath, feeling a little awed by the story he'd unfurled for Mateo. And a lot in awe of the story's heroines. "Well, if you don't, we'll tell the story again soon. I think it'll all come together."

Mateo looked up at him with an embarrassed grin. "Is it 'cause Miss Joanna might end up . . . you know—" He made a smooching sound, then covered his face.

Luke laughed and ruffled the dark head again. "Too soon to tell, buddy. But if I were a gambling man—and I'm not—but if I were, I'd bet a gazillion dollars."

He prayed he wasn't betting on a long shot.

CHAPTER 41

JO HAD BARELY GOTTEN IN the house after work on Wednesday when she heard a car coming up the lane. She hobbled to the window to look. Phee's car pulled up to the cottage. And by the time her older sister rang the doorbell, Britt was right behind her, having walked over from her cottage.

Jo answered the door laughing. "Somehow I knew you'd be over to get the whole scoop."

Phee looked relieved. "I was a little worried about where things were headed. So everything's okay?"

"You worked things out?" Britt's expression matched Phee's.

"I don't remember when you guys left . . ."

"Mateo was accusing you of stealing his mom's jewelry box," Phee prompted. "I didn't want to leave, but Quinn thought we should."

Jo nodded. "It was probably better that you did. He was pretty upset."

"But Luke set him straight?"

"Well . . . turns out the box *was* his mom's. At least I'm pretty sure Mateo was telling the truth."

Britt frowned. "So how'd *you* get it?"

"I bought it at Annie Laurie's. I'm guessing Maria sold it to the shop. Probably needed the money." She shrugged. "I gave it to him."

"To Mateo?" Britt sounded surprised.

"That was really sweet of you, Jo." Phee looked like she might cry.

She shrugged again. "It just seemed like the right thing to do."

"So how are you feeling about the whole Luke-Mateo thing by now?" Phee put a motherly hand on Jo's arm.

"I feel . . . torn, I guess. Not about the Luke half. He called to apologize after they got home."

"Aww . . . I like him so much, Jo." Phee's declaration sounded more like a plea.

"Me too!" Britt crowed. "He's a great guy."

Jo knew her sisters had left unspoken: *I like him so much better than Ben.* She appreciated their discretion, and she agreed. But just because he was "better than Ben" didn't mean he was the right one. There was still Mateo. "Luke *is* a great guy. You'll get no argument from me. But I'm not sure it's fair to Mateo for me to even keep seeing him."

"You're still . . . against him."

Jo almost wanted to laugh at Britt's downhearted expression.

"I'm not *against* Mateo." She was chagrined to realize that she *had* been against him in the beginning. She'd thought only of her own desires. But last night she'd gotten a glimpse of how wounded the poor kid was. And she was ashamed of how she'd behaved toward him. It was a wonder Luke had the patience to put up with her.

"It seems like maybe you're . . . softening toward him a little?" Phee's question was tentative, as if it might upset Jo.

"If I'm honest, I'm still not crazy about the idea of dating a guy with a kid . . . responsibility for a kid. I'm not crazy about the idea of sharing Luke. And I know—at least while we were just dating—that I'd have to come in second in a lot of ways. And it might sometimes feel that way even if we got married."

"That's true. And it would be to Luke's credit. You have to admire him for that, Jo. Even though I know it would be hard."

She sighed. "The thing is, I realized last night that seeing Luke with Mateo is exactly *why* I fell for him. Because of Mateo, I could tell that Luke was someone who would stay through thick and thin, who would sacrifice his own happiness for that of others, and give his very life for what he knows is right."

Her sisters were nodding like a couple of bobbleheads.

She gave a little laugh. "I don't know how I couldn't recognize that before. How I've ever thought I wanted anything other than that? I'm so sorry it took going back to someone like Ben for me to figure it out."

"Have you thought about this, Jo?" Phee's pleading expression was so like their mother's. "In just a few years—what, only five or six?—Mateo will have graduated from high school and likely be living on his own."

"What? That can't be right. Six years?"

"He's twelve now, right . . ." Phee eyed Jo as she did the math.

"Wow. You're right. In some ways that seems like a long time, but I guess . . . If the next six years go by as fast as these past six have. Wow."

"Mom and Dad always said the older you got, the faster the years flew. Boy is that true." Phee shook her head and Jo had to wonder if she was doing her own math. She still hadn't said anything about a baby on the way. Jo was starting to wonder if she'd imagined it all.

But she just nodded, still taken aback by the realization of how short Mateo's time with Luke would be in the whole scheme of things. "I guess, really, it wouldn't be that long before it was back to just me and Luke."

"Well, you'll probably have a baby of your own in the

house by then." Phee's knowing smile gave away more than she likely realized.

"And just think, Jo," Britt piped up, "if Mateo gets married young, you could be a grandma by the time you're forty."

"Britt!" Jo and Phee shouted in unison.

Phee scowled at Britt. "You are no help at all!"

"I'm only kidding!"

"And besides," Jo said. "I don't think we'd call Mateo's kids our grandkids. I think we'd be more like a favorite aunt and uncle."

"I wondered if Luke planned to legally adopt him. No?"

"He has thought about it, but I think he decided not to make it legal. They've had the Big Brother relationship all this time, and it would be hard to change that. And now that he has legal guardianship, he has essentially all the rights of a parent—at least until Mateo turns eighteen."

"That makes sense," Phee said. "Especially since you might have a baby—or two—of your own by the time Mateo is out of high school."

"A baby or *two*. In six years . . ." She looked at Phee, thinking she'd given her sister the perfect opening.

But Phee wasn't biting.

Still, the thought of carrying Luke's babies filled her with joy. And she had to admit, she would get a kick out of seeing Luke as a daddy. Watching the way he was with Mateo, Jo had no doubt Luke would be a wonderful father. And because of watching Luke, Mateo would probably be good with a baby too.

Britt's expression turned serious. "Phee said in six years Mateo would be out of high school, but think about it, Jo . . . Once he *starts* high school, he's not going to want to hang out with you guys much anyway. And *that's* only two years away."

She knew Britt was trying to make up for her "grandma" comment earlier. But the thought of Mateo in high school blew her mind equally. "Wow! I don't know why I hadn't thought of all this. All I could see was . . . right now. And it's been hard."

"I know, but with time, you'll adjust." Phee's smile gave her hope. "There are no guarantees it'll get easier, but I have a feeling you're going to love life with Mateo."

"He *is* kind of growing on me. He's a good kid. He really is."

"Maybe it's not exactly how you pictured your life going, but then, it's not exactly how Luke—or Mateo—pictured theirs going either."

She knew Phee's comment wasn't intended as a reprimand, but it stung nevertheless. And deservedly so. She'd been self-centered and thoughtless, while Luke and Mateo had borne far more difficult things with grace and dignity.

"You three have a lot in common," Britt said. "You can help each other through."

"Oh, you guys. How did you get to be so wise?"

Phee shrugged. "What can I say? It just comes naturally." A funny look came to her face, then a smile bloomed. "And speaking of what just comes naturally—"

Jo pushed herself off the sofa and cheered. *Finally!* "I knew it! I knew it!"

Britt's face was a mask of confusion. "What is going on?"

"Phee is—" She clapped a hand over her mouth. When would she ever learn? This wasn't her news to share. This was Phee's moment. But if her sister didn't hurry up and spill the beans, Jo thought she might explode! "Tell her, Phee!"

"*Wellll* . . ." Phee dragged out the word deliciously while Jo stood there beaming. "Here's the deal, Aunt Britt, Aunt Joanna . . ."

Britt's jaw dropped and her gaze went to Phee's stomach. "No way! Are you serious? You're *pregnant*?"

"Due at the end of March."

"Finally!" It was all Jo could do not to jump up and down like a jack-in-the-box. "It's about time!"

Phee started laughing.

"What's so funny?"

"How can you say 'It's about time'? We practically got pregnant on our honeymoon!"

"Seriously?" Jo hadn't really thought about how soon it was after the wedding when she'd found those books in the Barnes & Noble bag. She'd snuck the bag into Phee's car the next day, and her sister was apparently none the wiser. She hugged her sister again. "I'm just so stinkin' happy for you guys!"

Britt still sat on the sofa with a stunned look on her face. "Did you know, Jo?"

"I guessed."

Phee eyed her. "Seriously? How? I'm not even showing yet."

"You've been looking a little pudgy," she teased.

"Really?" Phee pulled her T-shirt across her flat belly and studied herself in the mirror over the mantel."

"I'm only kidding." Jo's face heated. She was digging herself a hole she might not be able to get out of, and she didn't want to spoil Phee's big moment. Jo had escaped having to pretend to be surprised because Phee's announcement truly had surprised her. Someday she would tell her sister the whole story, but today wasn't the time.

Phee laughed again. "I was going to wait a while to tell you guys because . . . well, it happened so soon, but it's been *killing* me not to be able to share it with you!"

"Well, I think it's wonderful." Jo shuffled across the floor and despite the hated boot, did a little dance.

Phee joined in and after a few minutes they landed, breathless, on the sofa on either side of Britt.

Phee sighed. "Quinn and I said all along that we didn't want to waste any time starting a family. After all, Quinn will be forty-three by the time this baby gets here. But we didn't really plan on a honeymoon baby."

Britt finally found her voice. "That just makes it all the *more* special."

"Have you told Dad?" Jo couldn't seem to stop smiling.

"Not yet. I wanted to tell you two first. We'll probably call Dad tonight."

"Grandpa." Britt laughed. "Can you just picture it?"

Jo sighed. "Oh, Phee, Dad is going to be thrilled!"

They curled up in a row on the sofa, all talking at once, dreaming and planning for the future they would share.

The only thing that could have made this precious moment better was if Mom had been here to share in the glorious news. But if Heaven had a balcony, then no doubt she was peering over that railing, cheering right along with them.

Still, a twinge of sadness crept in. Would Luke—and Mateo—be a part of this future she and her sisters were dreaming of? Could she even be happy if he wasn't?

"Hi, Joanna." Luke stood on the step outside the screened porch, his hand raised in greeting.

"Luke . . ." She opened the door, desperately wishing she'd waited another ten minutes before changing into yesterday's wrinkled gardening clothes after work. "Come on in." She looked past him, wondering if Mateo was waiting in the pickup. But the vehicle appeared to be empty.

He stepped through the door she held for him, but stopped short inside the screened porch. "Mind if we just talk out here? I'll try to . . . keep it short."

"Sure." She frowned, not liking the seriousness of his tone. And the fact that whatever he had to say could be kept short. "Is everything okay?"

He nodded, but not convincingly. "I'm sorry I didn't call first. I hope I'm not interrupting anything."

"No. I was just heading out to the garden." She watched him, equal parts of worry and curiosity growing inside her.

He pointed to the hated boot she still wore on her ankle. "How's your foot?"

"It's okay. A pain in the you-know-what though. I'll be happy to get this stupid thing off."

"I bet." He angled his head toward the new porch swing that hung by heavy silver chains from the pale blue-painted ceiling. "That's new, isn't it?"

"Quinn and a buddy of his hung it just last night." She went to sit on one side of the swing, hugging the armrest. "If you trust these chains, you can help me test it."

At his skeptical look, she quickly reassured him. "Don't worry. It safely held three sisters last night." It was all she could do not to add "including a pregnant sister!" But Phee had asked her and Britt not to tell anyone else yet.

He lowered into the opposite side of the swing, looking up at the massive hooks that held the chains. Tossing a little grin her way, he pushed off with his legs and set them swinging. The swing creaked and groaned, but it held.

"I like a swing." He lifted his feet and let them sway. "Nice addition."

"Yeah. I like it too." The motion of the swing created a breeze that offered relief from the sticky August heat. But she couldn't enjoy it until she knew why he'd come. Especially after everything that had happened with Mateo Tuesday night. She had a feeling that's what this was about.

"I wanted to thank you for dinner the other night. It was delicious."

"You came all the way out here to thank me for dinner? Again? You could have texted, you know." She aimed for a teasing tone, but she feared it didn't come out that way.

He gave her a sidewise glance. "That's not the only reason. We need to talk."

CHAPTER 42

LUKE SWALLOWED HARD. HE WISHED he could just forget the tangled details of their relationship and get back to the playful side that seemed to be what kept drawing them together. But this was far too important to sidestep. And it wasn't fair to either of them to waste any more time together if Joanna couldn't accept him for exactly where he was in life. Mateo and all. It didn't help anyone to pretend they didn't have a pretty significant hurdle to get over before they could move forward. *If* they could move forward. "It's about Mateo," he said finally. "You probably guessed that."

Joanna nodded, an expression of . . . was it *worry* that creased her pretty brow? And why did she have to be so pretty? That wasn't the only thing that attracted him to her, but it sure didn't make things easier.

She folded her hands and slid them between her knees as if she were cold. Never mind it was eighty degrees and muggy as all get out.

He inhaled deeply. "Joanna . . ." *Just get it over with, man.* "I feel like we've gone round and round about this, and I'm at the point . . . We just need to figure this out once and for all."

"I'm listening." She stared straight ahead.

He raked a hand through his hair. It had all sounded so good when he'd rehearsed this little speech in his pickup on the way out here. Now, everything that came to his mind sounded stupid.

He put a foot down to stop the swing and sprang out of it, pacing the short length of the porch. "It's like this, Joanna. I told you on the Fourth of July, that night at Muy Caliente, that I liked you. Well, I still do. I know it's only been five weeks—and you were unconscious for one of them"—he caught her eye and forced a wry grin—"but here's the problem. I like you even more. Maybe even love you. But I can't change my circumstances and if you can't accept me with all the baggage that comes with me, then I need to cut my losses and get out. Because it's driving me crazy not knowing where I stand with you, and every day that I fall harder, I know it's going to be that much worse when you tell me to get lost."

He felt like they were going around in circles saying the same things over and over. But no . . . He'd crossed a line tonight. He'd revealed his love for her. And not in a way that any woman would want to hear that particular declaration.

"Luke, is that what you think? That I'm . . . ultimately going to tell you to get lost?"

He stopped pacing. "I think Mateo is a deal breaker for you . . . that as long as he's in the picture we can't go beyond friends. But if that's the case, then sorry, that's a deal breaker for *me*."

She nodded and closed her eyes briefly.

When she looked up at him, her eyes gleamed with tears, and Luke braced himself for the inevitable. He'd known that pushing her this way might very well be the end of things for them. It was why he waited so long to issue an ultimatum. For a long time, he thought that being friends would be better than not seeing her at all. Instead, it had been torture. Falling in love with her more every time he saw her, all the while knowing that things would eventually crash and burn. And he'd be left without her.

He looked at her, mentally climbing into a suit of armor that he didn't trust to protect his heart. "Go ahead. Get it over with."

"I can't lie, Luke. This isn't how I pictured my life, my *romance*. With a junior high kid in tow. One who doesn't seem to like me very much and—"

"He likes you, Joanna. Don't take his . . . bravado too seriously. He's rough around the edges. He's twelve. He just—"

"Let me finish." She wrinkled her nose. "To be honest, I still have a little trouble wrapping my brain around how things would even work with Mateo. With us. But here's the problem . . ." She mirrored the wry grin he'd given her earlier.

"Luke, *you* are exactly what I pictured. *Exactly*. And . . . if you happen to come with a junior high kid in tow, then . . . I have no choice. I'll adjust."

Hope welled inside him but he pushed it down. He'd half expected this response, but he didn't want her to . . . *settle*. "No. I don't want you to adjust, Jo. I don't want you to settle and then be sorry later. Not when you could have any man you wanted."

She gave a little laugh. "Believe me, Lukas Blaine. I would *not* be settling. In fact . . ." She looked up at him, her expression sheepish. "I probably shouldn't tell you this, but since we're in no-holds-barred mode tonight . . . One of my biggest fears has been that you'd find someone else. Someone who would embrace Mateo and be—" Her voice broke. "Be so much better for him than I am. Than I could ever be."

"But you *could* be. Good for him, I mean. If you'd give him half a chance."

"You're right." She hung her head, feeling shame for the attitudes she'd let fester. "I haven't been good for Mateo. I haven't even tried. But I want to change that. Not because I have to if I want you in my life, but because I finally realized that part of the reason I fell in love with you in the first place is because you have the kind of heart that would be a Big Brother to Mateo. The kind of heart that wouldn't think twice about taking a kid like him into your home, into your life. Even when it came at great sacrifice."

"The only sacrifice I've made was you. Risking not having you in my life."

"I know better than that. You've given up a lot for Mateo."

"No. I'm not saying it's been easy. But the kid already had my heart long before Maria died. There is no way I could let him go into the system."

"And that's why you have *my* heart." The swing creaked as she shifted, curling her good leg underneath her and adjusting the clumsy boot.

He stopped pacing and let the hope rise and expand.

"Earlier, you said I could have any man I wanted? Well, I don't know about that. But here's the thing: *You* are the only man I want. Because I'd rather have you—you exactly where God has you in life . . . Mateo included—than imagine life without you."

"So . . . you're saying—"

She reached a hand out to him and he took it. "I'm saying I'm all in, Luke. If you'll have me, I want to be part of your life. And part of Mateo's. And . . . I'm not perfect. I don't know how to act with junior high boys, but I promise I'll give it my best shot. And I'm sorry I made things so hard for you."

He gave her a wry grin. "You did wreak a little havoc there for a while."

"I'm so sorry, Luke." Tears welled again and she blinked them away.

"Hey . . . hey, it's okay," he whispered. "I was only teasing. I didn't mean to make you cry!" He cupped her face in his hands and smoothed away the tears with his thumbs.

She dipped her head. "Well, I *should* cry. I'm ashamed of the way I acted."

"Joanna. Stop. You were only being honest about your feelings. I get that." He drew her into his arms and rested his chin on her head. "I wouldn't have wanted you to pretend. I'm glad you were honest—with me and with yourself. This way we're both going into things eyes wide open." He drew back and looked into those blue eyes he loved. "Beautiful eyes wide open."

She closed her eyes. "I just wish I'd come around sooner."

"No." He placed a finger under her chin, tipping her face to meet his.

She opened her eyes and met his gaze.

He cupped her face between his warm hands. "Stop wishing for it to be different than it was, Jo. We may never know the reasons everything went down like it did, and that's okay. But we can trust that God knew what He was doing, even when we didn't."

"How'd you get to be so smart?"

"Who knows . . ."

She tilted her chin at him, obviously recognizing the prelude to a joke.

"Maybe if it hadn't happened this way, you would have always wondered if you really should have chosen that Ben guy instead of me."

"Oh, Luke." She snuggled into his chest and shook her head hard against him. "Never. I wish Ben well, I really do, but he has a whole lot of growing up to do before he's ready to make anybody but himself happy." She gave a little gasp.

"What's wrong?" Again, Luke leaned back to study her.

She sighed again. "It's just sad how recently I was saying those very words about myself: 'A lot of growing up to do.' You were probably saying it too."

"You know what? We all have a lot of growing to do. I'm just glad you and I are going to be doing it together."

"With Mateo."

"With Mateo." He hugged her tighter, feeling grateful.

A little stunned, he plopped down on the swing, pulling her down beside him. "This is not how I thought this would go." He turned toward her and folded her small hand between both of his. "I didn't mean to say it so lightly earlier, Joanna, but . . . I love you. I do. I can't seem to help myself."

She bowed her head and leaned into him. "Oh, Luke. I love you too. And I think . . . with time—and patience—I can grow to love Mateo too. The way I need to. The way he needs me to."

Disentangling their fingers, he put his arms around her, drew her head to his chest. "I know you will. And I promise, I'll be patient with you. We'll figure things out. As we go. It'll be fun." He drew back and tipped her chin up, hoping for a smile.

But her expression was pure tenderness. Toward him. For *them*. She reached up and cupped his face between her hands. "I don't deserve you, Lukas Blaine, but I do love you. Oh, how I love you."

He placed his hands over hers and bent to kiss her. Her lips were as soft as they'd always been in his imagination. But the sheer joy he felt at her declaration was more real, more solid than any dream. "Do you have any idea how long I've wanted to do that?"

Joanna laughed softly, her breath warm on his cheek. "Well, it couldn't be too long because you've only known me since May."

He kissed her again, then stroked a finger down the bridge of her nose. "Let me rephrase the question. Do you know how long I want to *keep* doing that?"

"For a very, *very* long time, I hope."

"Only for the rest of your life." The crickets started their afternoon chorus and Luke reveled in their symphony. And kissed her again.

CHAPTER 43

October

G UYS WIN AGAIN!" MATEO HOPPED off his chair, nearly toppling it over, and did a comical victory dance in the middle of the living room.

Jo laughed, in awe of the way Mateo had come out of his shell in the last few weeks. He and Luke had been coming out to the cottage for supper almost every Friday night since school started. It had turned into a routine game night with high guys-against-girls stakes. Losers did the dishes.

"Come on," Britt pleaded. "How about best three out of five? Our team was distracted trying to serve snacks and keep your drinks refilled."

"Oh, right. Try to make us feel guilty." Luke winked at Mateo.

"Don't fall for it, guys." Quinn patted Phee's hand in mock condescension. "These sisters always have some excuse why they couldn't quite pull off a win."

"They aren't excuses." Jo tried to look stern. "They're *reasons.*"

"That's right, reasons." Phee gave her husband the stink eye and pouted. "Not to mention you dealt some lousy cards that last round."

That earned a round of boos from the guys, but nevertheless, Quinn laughed and shuffled the cards. "Tell you what. If you win this hand, we'll go three out of five. But if *we* win, we're the undisputed champs, and you have to do the dishes *without* complaining."

"Yeah!" Mateo slipped back in his chair, rubbing his hands together. "At least Jo can't use her boot as an excuse anymore," he teased.

Quinn and Luke piled on, but her sisters came to Jo's defense. She couldn't deny she'd jokingly milked that broken ankle for sympathy whenever the girls were losing. But she'd been relieved of the boot—and that excuse—at her checkup earlier in the week. She wasn't quite ready to run a marathon yet, but she felt about a hundred pounds lighter having exchanged the boot for a sandal.

And having exchanged a begrudging attitude for one of sheer joy.

She shot playful daggers at Mateo, amazed all over again at the transformations that had taken place. Mateo, yes. He'd come out of his shell and found his place as if he'd always belonged to this little group around the table tonight.

But the transformation that astonished her even more was the one of her own heart. She felt such remorse that she'd been so reluctant to open her mind to Luke and Mateo as a "package deal." She'd told Luke as much so often these past weeks that he'd finally forbidden her to apologize about it again.

And while she hoped Mateo would never learn of her resentment toward him, she'd tried to make it up to him in small ways. As a result, he'd quickly warmed to her. And she to him.

Quinn finished shuffling and dealt another hand. But

twenty minutes later, the sisters had to concede defeat. Grumbling in unison, they slouched off to do the supper dishes.

Quinn went to the front porch, but came back in almost immediately. "Did somebody mean to leave the lights on up in the clearing?"

Britt gave a little intake of breath. "Oh, I bet that was me. I walked up there with my coffee to watch the sunrise this morning, but it was light when I came back down."

"I'll go turn them off." Luke smirked. "Wouldn't want to keep you from those dishes."

"I haven't been up to the clearing in over two months," Jo said wistfully.

"Do you think you could make it now?" Phee looked pointedly at her ankle.

"I don't know. I'd sure like to try."

"You can lean on me," Luke offered.

"Go!" Phee and Britt said in unison.

Britt took the dish towel from her. "We can handle the dishes. I know you've been itching to get up to the clearing."

"Are you sure?"

"Of course. Go." Phee shooed her away.

"Where's Mateo?" Jo looked around the cottage for him. "He'll probably want to come with us."

"No," Quinn said.

A little too quickly, Jo thought. She appreciated her brother-in-law making an excuse for her and Luke to have some time alone.

"Mateo is playing with Melvin in the back bedroom," Quinn explained.

"Okay." Luke cocked his head. "If you're sure you don't mind watching him for a little bit?"

"Of course not," Phee said. "You guys go."

Luke held out a hand to Jo.

"Let me grab a jacket." She ran back to her room and

shrugged into a hoodie. Luke was waiting by the door when she returned. "Ready?"

"We'll see if my ankle thinks I'm ready. You may have to carry me."

He laughed. "Nice try."

She looked up the lane toward the river. The woods all around them were ablaze with crimson and amber and a shade of yellow that glowed like fire in the waning sunlight. "It's so beautiful out here. I love October! But I do hate that it's getting dark so much earlier now."

"Just wait till we turn back the clocks in a couple of weeks."

"Ugh. Don't remind me. But just look at this, Luke! It's so pretty!"

"It sure is."

"I'm sure I've said this half a dozen times since we bought the property, but if Quinn had tried to sell us this place *now*, we wouldn't have hesitated one minute. Not even Phee."

Luke chuckled. "*Especially* not Phee. She got a husband out of the deal. But you're right. You'd have been in a bidding war with a dozen other buyers if the place was on the market now. Except don't forget the reason everything looks so great now is because of all the blood, sweat, and tears you guys have put into it." He took her hand and twined his fingers with hers. "You three have worked your tails off."

"Of course it didn't hurt that God filled up that tributary and gave us a waterfront." She pointed toward the banks behind the cabins where the river trickled musically.

"Good point."

"And Quinn has done probably sixty percent of the work."

"He's definitely a keeper," Luke agreed. "He'll be a big help when you're getting everything set up for your wedding venue too."

She looked up at him, pleased he'd remembered her dream. "You really think that's going to happen?"

He kissed her forehead. "Of course it is. You are a make-it-happen kind of woman."

Her heart swelled at his faith in her. But she sighed and changed the subject. "It's been so long, I can hardly remember what it looks like up there."

They neared the base of the hill the clearing sat upon, and Luke put his arm around her shoulders. She'd grown to love his affectionate ways, even though he was always a bit reluctant when Mateo was around. But she'd noticed he was starting to be a little more demonstrative in front of the boy . . . as if he were gradually getting Mateo used to the idea that she and Luke were a couple.

She knew it was wise on Luke's part, for Mateo's sake, even if she wasn't crazy about having to show restraint. Because the truth was, she was flat-out crazy about Lukas Blaine. And she didn't care who knew it.

When they started up the incline that led to the stairway, Luke looked down at her with a concerned frown. "You doing okay? Do we need to slow down a little?"

But she trudged on. "So far, so good. It hurts a little, but it feels good to get some fresh air." Excitement built as they started toward the stairway. It wasn't quite dark, but she could see the lights twinkling through the trees above. She pointed up at them. "I'm a little surprised Britt didn't notice she'd left them on. But then, I didn't see them either when I came home from work. If electricity was free, I'd leave those things on all the time."

"But then it wouldn't be special when you do turn them on."

She shrugged. "True. I still remember how magical it was when we turned them on the first time before Phee's wedding."

"So, where *are* you on the whole wedding venue plans? And don't think I didn't notice you changing the subject back there."

"Plans? I haven't really done much." She gave him a sheepish look. "Except think about it."

"But you still want to do that, right?"

"Okay . . . true confession, I don't just think about it, I *dream* about it. Kind of obsessively."

"So do it, then. What's stopping you, Jo?"

"Oh, Luke, what if it's a big flop? And besides, I wouldn't even know where to start."

"Of course you would. You planned your sister's whole wedding, didn't you? It was one of the nicest weddings I've ever been to. And I've been to a lot."

"You really think so?" She stopped at the foot of the stairs. "Can we rest a minute? My ankle's aching a little." It was more than a little, but she wasn't about to let him talk her out of making it up to the clearing.

"Here . . ." Without warning, Luke scooped her into his arms. "Come on. Let's get you up there!"

She let out a little squeal, but wrapped her arms around his neck and clung to him, feeling safer than she'd ever felt in her life.

He carried her effortlessly to the near edge of the clearing and without setting her down, he reached high on the pole where the light switches were. "Let's see here, I think this is the one . . ."

He flipped a switch, but instead of the clearing going dark, a myriad of new twinkle lights flickered on. Nearly twice as many strings as they'd put up for Phee's wedding.

Jo tipped her head back and stared. "What . . . ?"

Wearing an enigmatic smile, Luke carried her toward the center of the clearing. As they came over the rise, a grouping of lanterns came into sight, glowing on one of the low log benches. He lowered her to a bench across from the lanterns and knelt in front of her, the smooth planes of his face cast in yellow light.

"Luke?"

"I have . . . some thoughts about that wedding venue idea." His smile held confidence, even though his voice wavered almost imperceptibly.

"You do?" she squeaked. *Was it possible?* Could this be what she desperately hoped it was?

Now that she thought about it, everything had happened quite conveniently to get her and Luke up here to the clearing alone, and she would have bet her last dollar that these lights twinkling overhead hadn't been left on accidentally.

"Exactly what thoughts are you having?" she dared.

"Well, for starters, I think you need to do another test wedding up here."

"You do?" She couldn't hide the smile that came. Or the certainty of what else was to come.

"I do." He brushed a strand of hair from her face and kissed the tip of her nose.

"And who do you propose the guinea pigs would be? For this . . . test wedding?"

His smile faded and his expression turned solemn. Still on his knees, he leaned back and fished in his pocket. He brought out a tiny black box and fumbled with it before holding out a simple diamond ring.

Her breath caught.

But he held up a hand, as if to halt the proceedings. "I know that we haven't known each other all that long and . . . I promise I won't be hurt if you think it's too soon. But I love you, Joanna Chandler"—he reached for her hand—"and if you feel even half as much for me as I do for you, then I don't want to waste another minute that you could be wearing my ring."

"Oh, Luke . . ." The tears came then. "Yes," she managed to whisper over the lump in her throat. "Yes, Luke. Oh, yes! A thousand times, yes."

"That's a yes, then? You're *sure?*" He winked and the gold flecks in his gray eyes seemed to twinkle.

She grasped the hand offering the diamond. "Give me that ring," she teased. She took his face, his precious face, between her hands. Her heart overflowed as he covered her right hand

and slipped the ring onto her finger. "I've never been so sure of anything in my life," she whispered.

"I was kind of hoping you'd say that."

Her laughter was swallowed up in his kisses.

A Note from Deb

Dear reader,

It's finally here! The second book in my Chandler Sisters series! And I'm so pleased with how Joanna's story turned out. Even though I'm an oldest sister (who married an oldest brother), I think I relate more to middle sister Joanna than I do to Phylicia. At least, Joanna's reactions to the dilemma in *Chasing Dreams* is very much like my own might have been. I'm so eager to hear what you think about this second story in the series!

As I write this author's note, my husband and I are surrounded by packing boxes and Bubble Wrap and change-of-address forms, and I'm feeling a bit overwhelmed. But we are excited to be embarking on an exciting new chapter of life. One that will take us closer to our daughters and their families in the beautiful state of Missouri. We're so grateful to have a chance to live closer to five of our nine grandkids and be more a part of their lives than distance has allowed in the past. But our decision to move also means we'll be moving far away from our family and friends here in Kansas. It's especially heartbreaking to be leaving this town where I've been so close to my brother and my sisters—the inspiration for these Chandler Sisters novels.

I'm so very grateful for modern technology that will allow us to keep in touch with family across the miles . . . almost as if we still lived in the same town.

And speaking of technology, I love that social media allows me to keep in touch with you, dear readers! If you don't already follow me on Instagram, Twitter, the blog I write along with several author friends, or my Facebook Readers Page, I'd love to meet you there! You can find links to all those connnection points and more on my website at deborahraney.com.

As I wrap up another novel, my deepest thanks go out to the many people who made this book possible: my agent, Steve Laube, Steve Barclift, and the team at Kregel, especially my editors, Catherine DeVries, Janyre Tromp, and Cheryl Molin.

I owe more than I can express to my beloved critique partner, friend, and favorite author, Tamera Alexander, along with others who read my manuscripts and offer solutions—especially my dear friend Terry Stucky and my sister Vicky Miller.

I'm so grateful for the encouragement and love of my family—in-laws and outlaws alike, as my husband, Ken, likes to say. Perhaps I could still write a book without the support of our four kids and their families, my amazing dad, my wonderful mother-in-law, and so many other friends and family—but I sure wouldn't want to! You all make the journey an absolute delight!

As always, thank you, Ken Raney, for making life such a glorious adventure! Thank you for pushing me to be my best, for encouraging me to step out of my comfort zone, and for your unwavering support over the years.

And most of all, thank you, Lord Jesus Christ, for the immeasurable blessings You have bestowed, along with just enough challenges to produce perseverance, character, and hope.

Deborah Raney
June 20, 2019

Book Club
Discussion Guide

SPOILER ALERT: These discussion questions contain spoilers that may give away elements of the plot.

1. In *Chasing Dreams*, the Chandler sisters are settling into life at their edge-of-town Airbnb and are learning to become business partners as well as sisters. What challenges does owning a business with family members present? What advantages? Have you ever been in business with family members? Share your experiences, both positive and challenging.

2. This novel opens with a dramatic encounter that ultimately changes the direction of Joanna's life and career. Have you ever started down the path toward one career only to have an unexpected change of direction? What caused your change of heart or your decision to go in a different direction? Was it difficult for you to switch gears and change plans? Do you have any regrets for changing course?

3. How do you feel about Joanna's reluctance to accept Mateo as part of Luke's life? Do you identify with her fears and frustrations? Or do you feel she's being selfish or shortsighted? Why do you think she's so resistant to the idea of marrying a man who comes with responsibilities and obligations that will assuredly involve her?

4. Do you think it was wise for Luke to take on the guardianship of Mateo? Were his intentions heroic from the beginning, or did he "fall into" his role as guardian and not know how to extricate himself from a difficult situation?

5. How did Joanna's sisters contribute to her attitude and decisions about Luke and Mateo? How was Phylicia's influence different from Britt's? How, if at all, do you think the sisters' attitudes might have been shaped by their birth order?

6. Why do you think Joanna was so drawn to her exboyfriend? Do you think she was right to forgive Ben and give him a second chance? Do you think she was more influenced by the warm memories of their former relationship and her physical attraction to him, or by her desire to find an "alternative" to Luke and Mateo?

7. Why do you think Joanna found it necessary to have a relationship with "someone, anyone"? Would it have been better for her to remain unattached while she was deciding whether she could accept Mateo as part of Luke's life? Why?

8. How did Mateo change Joanna, both for better and for worse? Why do you think his entrance into her life first brought about negative changes? What do you think was the turning point when Mateo's presence started to be a positive influence on Joanna?

9. Discuss the dynamic that Phylicia's husband, Quinn, brought to the sisters' relationships? How has the entrance of in-laws into your own family affected your relationships with family members? If you are an in-law yourself, how do you think your entrance into a family changed the dynamic? Has that influence fluctuated over time? Does distance make a difference in how in-laws integrate into a family?

10. If you were in Luke's position, do you think you'd be as patient and accepting as he was of Joanna's fears and hesitance about Mateo? Why or why not?

11. How do you think Mateo's presence might change the dynamic of the sisters' relationships? What challenges might his entrance into the family create? What benefits? (Stay tuned for book 3 for the answer!)

FINDING WINGS
COMING IN FALL 2020

Will Britt find the love of her life, following in her sisters' footsteps? Or will she discover that her family is the only love she needs?

Find out in the final volume of The Chandler Sister series!

Trusted, God-honoring storytelling

CHAPTER 1

Tuesday, November 22

BRITT CHANDLER COULDN'T HELP THE smile that came as her car approached the freshly installed, ornate sign near the entrance to their long driveway. *The Cottages at Poplar Brook Road.* Sign? Billboard was more like it. It had cost a small fortune to have it painted and installed along with its smaller counterpart at the highway turnoff. But Britt and her sisters agreed it was worth it, given the rather remote wooded acreage where they lived. More than one of their Airbnb customers had become lost trying to find their way on the curvy Missouri road.

Her phone chirped through the car's speakers. Seeing her brother-in-law's name on caller ID, Britt pressed the button on the steering wheel to answer. "Hey, Quinn, what's up?"

"Not much. Are you home right now?"

"I will be in about two minutes. Why?"

"Would you mind looking in on Phee? At the new house."

"Sure. Is everything okay?" She didn't like the worry that shaded Quinn's tone. "She's working awfully late, isn't she?"

"As usual. And it's probably nothing, but she was feeling kind of puny when I dropped off some lunch around one. I'm at the house here in town, but she's not home yet and she's not answering her phone. She's probably just working outside, but I'm out the door in about five minutes for a meeting at church and I'd feel better if somebody checked on her. Maybe persuade her to go home if you can."

"Ha. You forget this is my stubborn big sister you're talking about."

"I remember. Believe me, I remember."

Britt laughed. "Let me get my groceries put away and I'll run over there. I have something to send home with her for you anyway."

"For me?"

"Well, both of you, but you'll appreciate it more than Phee will."

"That sounds promising. No clues?"

"It's a surprise, but you might want to save room for dessert when you get home from your meeting."

"My mouth is already watering. Thanks, Britt."

"No problem." Britt ended the call, but easing her Ford Escape up the lane, she frowned. Her oldest sister's pregnancy had been pretty routine, but the morning sickness had dragged on for almost five months now—and not just in the mornings. Britt knew Phylicia was weary of it, especially when she had so many things she wanted to accomplish at the house she and Quinn were building on the property.

Britt peered through the windshield and sighed. The glorious autumn colors that had brightened the view only a few weeks ago were all but gone now. The last smattering of leaves clung tenaciously to the poplars and dogwoods lining the lane. Before long, snow would blanket the countryside. Of course, winter had its own beauty here in southeast Missouri, but Britt wasn't ready for that yet. Especially not for how short the days had grown, thanks, in part, to the recent switch to daylight saving time. She glanced at the dashboard. Not even six o'clock and it was already dark!

Still her spirits lifted, as they always did, when the cottages came into sight. Lights gleamed from the cottage windows and even from a distance, Britt could see Joanna moving around inside, no doubt obsessing over the plans for her spring wedding.

Farther up the lane, she spotted Phee's car at the construction site of the two-story home that currently sported a Tyvek wrap—and mud where a front yard would be next spring. Phylicia and Quinn were hoping to move into the house before the baby arrived next March. But since they were doing a lot of the work themselves, Britt had her doubts they'd make that deadline. She would never voice those doubts to her sister though. Phee was nervous enough about being ready for the baby's arrival—a child she and Quinn jokingly declared had been conceived on their honeymoon in Hawaii. For now, they were living a few miles away in another house Quinn had built. Or at least that's where they slept. They spent nearly every waking hour at the new build. Britt loved that they would soon all live here on the same property, but she sometimes worried that her sister overdid it. Half the time Phylicia forgot to eat lunch until Britt or Joanna reminded her, or Quinn brought her a sandwich from town.

Remembering the cookies she'd baked this morning, Britt parked in front of her cabin and pulled her phone from her purse, dialing Phylicia. The phone went to voice mail. "This is Phee. You know what to do."

Britt waited impatiently for the tone. "Hey, you. I'm bringing over some cookies for you to take home. I made Quinn's favorite—oatmeal scotchies."

The sisters all doted on Quinn Mitchell and for good reason. Britt wasn't sure how they would have managed getting their little Airbnb enterprise up and running without him. But things were going surprisingly well, despite some rather major hitches at the beginning. She and her sisters made a good team. In fact, Phylicia had declared just yesterday that they'd built their renovation fund back up to the eleven thousand dollars they'd started with after purchasing the cottages free and clear. If Joanna's idea for opening a wedding venue here at the cottages took off, they could probably breathe easy where money was concerned.

She turned off the ignition, and as she did every time she arrived home, she stopped to admire the tiny cabin she'd claimed for her own. Dim lamplight outlined Melvin's silhouette on the windowsill, tail twitching, anticipating his nightly treat, no doubt. Their mother's tuxedo cat they'd inherited after Mom's death had become decidedly Britt's cat. Her sisters might argue with that claim, but Britt's cabin was where Melvin was fed, where he slept, and, less happily, where his litter box resided. Mom would have loved knowing that Melvin had taken to country life so quickly. In some ways it felt surreal that the first anniversary of her death was approaching, yet in other ways, it seemed an eternity since they'd had Mom in their lives.

Britt unloaded groceries from the back of the Escape and glanced toward Quinn and Phee's house. The lights were on inside and she didn't see Phee anywhere outside. It wasn't like her not to return a call. Of course, she might be on the phone with someone else. Maybe Dad had called from Florida. He'd been keeping in touch with all of them more often now that he was going to be a grandpa.

Opening the front door, she heard the thud of Melvin jumping down from the windowsill, and a second later he appeared in the kitchen. "Hey, buddy. Sorry, but you're going to have to wait a few minutes for your treat tonight."

Britt gave him a quick head-to-tail stroke, then shrugged out of her jacket and put the groceries away before dialing Phee again. Straight to voice mail. *Hmm.* Well, no matter. She'd walk the cookies over and make sure everything was okay. The exercise would do her good after the three warm-from-the-oven

370

cookies—and cookie dough worth three more—she'd snarfed while baking this morning.

She slipped out of her booties, changed into tennis shoes, and donned her jacket again. The night air was cool and the ground soggy from recent rains, but she knew the lane by heart, rain or shine. Picking her way across the makeshift boardwalk Quinn had laid up to the house, she listened to the sounds of the Missouri night. A gentle breeze rustled the branches overhead and a barn owl hooted somewhere above her.

Not that long ago, she would have been terrified to be alone in the night, but something about this beautiful spot of earth she and her sisters owned had cured her of that almost as soon as her name was on the title.

The porch light was on and Britt rang the bell. Muffled chimes sounded from inside. Good. Phee had been pestering Quinn to get the doorbell connected. Britt waited and rang again, knocking on the solid oak door for good measure. When that didn't rouse anyone, she tried the doorknob. Locked.

She knocked again. "Phee? Anybody home?"

Silence. She blew out a breath and stepped off the boardwalk, tiptoeing through the mud to the closest lit window, thankful she'd changed out of her favorite boots. She cupped her hands over her eyes and peered inside.

There was no sign of Phee, but a measuring tape and notepad lay atop a bolt of fabric on the kitchen counter. Britt remembered her sister saying she was going to try to sew all the curtains for this house. Not so much because she could save money that way, but because their mom had made the curtains for their childhood home, and Phee wanted to carry that tradition into the home her own children would grow up in.

Britt knocked on the window and called Phee's name. It was too dark to see a clear path to the next lit window but she trudged blindly, the soft earth giving way beneath her feet. The landscape sloped downward on this side of the house and by the time she reached the window, it was too high for her to look in.

She turned to retrace her steps but stopped, hearing an unfamiliar sound. Like a kitten mewing. Holding perfectly still, she listened. Only this time, she clearly heard her name.

It came again.

"Phee? Where are you?" she shouted. Something was wrong.

She slogged back through the damp sod and knocked on the front door again. Then pounded. She turned the handle and pushed on the door with her shoulder, hoping maybe it was just stuck, but it didn't give.

She stopped to listen again, but only heard the night sounds—water sloshing the riverbanks below the cabins, the breeze, and a distant hoot owl. Maybe she'd just imagined hearing her name. Joanna had accused her more than once of having an overactive imagination.

She dialed Quinn, thinking he might have a key hidden somewhere. But his phone went to voice mail and she hung up without listening to the message.

Feeling more frantic by the moment, she retraced her steps along the side of the house and went on around to the back door. To her relief, it was open.

But once inside the mudroom at the back, she heard it again. Her name.

And this time she was sure it was Phee's voice calling her. Weak and trembling. But unmistakably Phee.

ABOUT THE AUTHOR

DEBORAH RANEY dreamed of writing a book since the summer she read Laura Ingalls Wilder's Little House books and discovered that a Kansas farm girl could, indeed, grow up to be a writer. Her more than thirty books have garnered multiple industry awards including the RITA Award, HOLT Medallion, National Readers' Choice Award, Carol Award, and Silver Angel from Excellence in Media, and have three times been Christy Award finalists.

Her first novel, *A Vow to Cherish*, shed light on the ravages of Alzheimer's disease. The novel inspired the highly acclaimed World Wide Pictures film of the same title and continues to be a tool for Alzheimer's families and caregivers. Deborah is on faculty for several national writers' conferences and serves on the advisory board of the 2,700-member American Christian Fiction Writers organization.

Deb and husband, Ken, recently moved from Kansas to southeast Missouri, the setting of many of Deb's novels. They enjoy spending time with family, searching for treasure at flea markets and garage sales, and exploring the beauty of the United States.

Website: deborahraney.com
Facebook Group: Deborah Raney Readers Page
Instagram: @deborahraney
Twitter: @AuthorDebRaney
Pinterest: @deborahraney

BE SURE TO READ THE START OF THE CHANDLER SISTERS SERIES!

978-1-68370-061-6

Phylicia thought life was passing her by—but maybe this was love's plan all along . . .

GILEAD
PUBLISHING

These no-longer-newlyweds want out
of this road trip–and their marriage.
Too bad they can't find the off-ramp.

978-1-68370-147-7
Available Now

And don't miss *Afraid of the Light*, the next book from
beloved, best-selling author Cynthia Ruchti.

Available June 2020 from Kregel Publications.

Trusted, God–honoring storytelling